TALES OF A RATT

TALES OF A RATT

Bobby Blotzer

with

JIM CLAYTON

Cover photo, courtesy of the one and only rock photographer, Mr. Neil Zlozower.

Blotzer Brothers Publishing

www.blotzer.com

Printed in the United States of America.

First U.S. Edition: March 2010

The text in this publication is registered with the Library of Congress.

ISBN: 978-0-615-36401-8

Dedicated to my proudest achievements...

Michael Robert and Marcus Anthony Blotzer

...the apples of me eye!

I'd like to tip my hat to Robbin, Stephen, Warren and Juan.

In writing this book I was coming from an honest perspective from my memories of life.

Contents

ACT I: THE BIRTH

ACT II: THE DEATH

ACT III: THE RESURRECTION

A QUICK NOTE FROM THE BLOTZ!

My life has been one continuing quest to have fun, and to chase two things...FAME AND FORTUNE!

I've been blessed in many ways. But most of all, by having two great sons, and my on-going great health.

In doing this book, which I've thought about for many years, and listened to many friends tell me, "you need to do a book," I had a lot of fear that it simply would not be interesting enough to the casual reader. I wasn't interested in writing something for those closest to me.

I was finally able to take up the challenge in late 2007 after being introduced to Jim Clayton; the fellow that has assisted me in putting together the pieces of the circus. I don't think I would have had the tenacity to sit and do this solo.

I would also like to just say to anyone that I am friends with or people that know me and of course my family, that in reading this, I pulled back on the reigns and I do hope that no one has any offense to anything I've written in these pages. This is my story, and while I share it with a lot of people, I hold the keys to the memory banks, so it is admittedly one-sided.

I love my family more than anything. I most dedicate this book to them. I'm 51 years of age as of this day of completion, February 28, 2010. But, I will say this, I feel 30, and I plan on staying that way till the eyes close forever, and I'm off to the next level.

One last and most important thing, this book is mainly for my mother who passed away May 7th, 2007. Lois. There will never be a day that I don't think of you Mum and would give it all just to have a simple, "OH, BOBBY!" like you did with glee and excitement when I would call and we talked on phone.

LOVE FOREVER: Michael Blotzer, Marcus Blotzer, Jeni Malara-Blotzer, Carol Blotzer, Michael Schweinberg, Ronnie Blotzer, Jack The River, my dog, and my best friend Leo the Lion - my cat, All the beautiful ex's that I have loved and that have loved me. My nieces and nephews. R.I.P. Pete Schweinberg (1934-2009).

And, a special nod to my Pirates in Crime John Corabi, Carlos Cavazo, Jizzy Pearl, and Kerri Kelli.

And also, a special shout out to: Yamaha, Paiste, Promark, DW, Remo.

So sit back, enjoy the book and know one thing… Blotz loves ya baby!!

ACKNOWLEDGEMENTS

This book would not be possible without the contributions of two great friends Jim Clayton and Mark Lowe. Without the contributions and professional expertise and time, this would have not been possible. Special thanks to Joey Hundall for introducing me to Jim.

Mark Lowe.

Jim Clayton

INTRODUCTION: THE DEBASEMENT OF A ROCK GOD

Cleveland. 1987. It's our third monster tour in as many years, and we are scintillating rock and roll GODS!

The swell of noise from the crowd is testament to that. They have come tonight to worship at the throne of the RATT. And, we have come to receive their sacrifice, in all its various forms.

With my family in the crowd, visiting from Pittsburgh, the arena watches in awe as a monstrous wash of backlight slowly rises. And there, standing on the drum throne with the devil horn's thrown in pride; silhouetted in the coolest rocker machismo possible, is me. Bobby Blotzer, aka.the Blotz. A rock and roll God in person!

The crowd goes ape-shit; yelling and screaming! The sexual energy in the room is flowing like Vesuvius, flooding the people of Pompeii and forever encasing them in it's molten heat.

I prepare for the blast of music already bubbling to the surface in Stephen, Juan, Robbin and Warren. My partners in crime. All they need is my lead. The moment where I'm standing atop of my drum stool, waiting to drop down and start the 4 count into the song.

I'm anticipating the hot sizzle.

All they need is my lead.

CHSHH!! CHSHH!! CHSHH!! CHSHH!! And BOOM!!

The thundering sound of RATT N' Roll motherfucker! Permeating every corner of the building! Creating a frenzy for the masses!

As I jump down from my seat to start, my foot catches the leg of my drum stool.

With my family watching their famous sibling in front of 15,000 screaming fans, I almost kill the tour.

My right foot catches on the leg turning my ankle onto its side, and slamming the side of my foot flat into the floor! The snap penetrating the screaming crowd could be heard by the lead singer, was immediately followed by the most immense pain I've ever experienced...

...and the Blotz is terrified.

The 15,000 adoring worshipers immediately become 15,000 fans that have expectations! Expectations that I can't deliver. The weight and pressures associated with being the band that carries an arena tour come crashing down like a fucking mallet.

My ankle is pulverized. A few seconds, and it's the size of a grapefruit. I'm going to have to cut my shoe off, and my whole lower leg is a white-hot ball of pain. But, I HAVE to play. I don't have a choice! Everyone; the band, the fans, the label and promoters; has expectations of me.

So, I play.

My trusty drum tech feeds me shot after shot of my good friend, Mr. Jack Daniels. This warm and soothing nectar of Tennessee will get me through it. I play the entire show, hardly able to think through the haze of sour mash and broken ankle.

Thus, you have an example of RATT. A band with so much talent and drive, yet so much cannibalistic ego and self-deprecation, so much misfortune, that it can barely hold together through five consecutive multi-platinum records.

RATT. The greatest band ever to almost become rock and roll Gods.

This is my story. Bobby Blotzer. The Blotz. The dubious backbone of the strongest underachievers in heavy metal.

Sit back and enjoy.

I've mentioned Mötley Crüe several times in this book. It's well known that those guys were close to RATT for a long time. They were bros, but also, they serve as a dead on example of what the fuck I'm getting at. Mötley hit the highest of highs, so, as a result, they were destined for the lowest of lows.

They had the furthest to fall.

RATT wasn't as high as those guys. So, when we fell, we didn't make as loud a noise as Mötley did. That's the rules of stardom. It's all about blessings and curses. The good and the bad. The riches and the soullessness.

Fame likes to eat it's young.

RATT has given me some wonderful things. I've experienced so much that I never would have gotten close to otherwise. There's a thousand dudes sitting in their garages, beating the shit out of some off-brand drum kit. Those guys would give one of their balls to have had the run I've had so far.

So, I am a blessed man.

Then, there is the other side of that coin to look at. There's that side that reveals the turmoil and pain involved in this business. It's dealing with the Devil, you know? You're gonna get exactly what he promises your ass, but when you ask for it, you seldom understand the costs. It's never as good as you expect.

When we started out, and hit it huge, I wanted to do this forever. Despite the turmoil that was there from the beginning, I wanted to record with these dudes for the rest of my career. But, shit changes. I've said before, RATT wasn't a family. RATT was a gang. And, while those two things are built on similar standards, they are very different.

I love my brother Ronnie, even though he was a bit of a prick growing up. But, he's family, and family is built on love. When you fight with your family, at the end of it, you'll still be family. That won't change.

But, when you fight with a gang, someone's gonna bleed. RATT has done a lot of bleeding in the past 25 years. I'd never change it, though. Give me my gang. I don't always like them, but I can always trust them to be what they are.

Pi-RATTs.

Our first show was in Denver, Colorado at the Rainbow Theater. That was like, February 15, of 1984. The album had just come out, and we had just shot the video for Round and Round. I.C.M., which is a huge booking agency in LA, was handling all our booking.

That was an amazing feeling to see their roster, and know that we were a part of that. They had everybody. Not just bands, but actors and directors; stars of every kind. They had everybody. That's probably the biggest reason we signed with them.

We had the opportunity to go to Texas and open for ZZ Top.

Ironically, the very first arena I played with RATT was the last arena I played with Vic Vergat. There in San Antonio. It was that old circular dome there in San Antonio. I think it's called the Alamo Dome now.

More about that in a minute.

ZZ Top was very cool; total gentlemen, and really approachable; very different from the metal heads of the day. We played with them again a few years later in England during the Monsters of Rock Tour.

Every step was a huge step, by our standards. Every step felt like a gigantic leap forward. Fame is like that. You fight and fight; you have dozens of setbacks, where you think it's never going to work; and then fame hits! Within a couple of months, you're life becomes a fucking Cheers episode where everybody knows your name.

The "Out of the Cellar" tour lasted close to fifteen months. We weren't quite ready for something like that, but we jumped in with fervor, because we were starved cavemen, out there trying to find food. The longer we were out there, the better life was becoming. The general feeling was "don't ever send us home," even though, by the time that tour finished, we were completely burned out.

Kalamazoo was the first giant gig, and soon to come, it would be small by comparison. We did that show at the ski lodge, and they put the stage at the base of the ski runs. You could look out at the crowd, and just watch this sea of people flow up the side of the mountain. It was a very cool sight. There were a lot of people there that day.

From that show, we went to Wichita Falls, Texas and played some place called the Twilight Zone. So, we went from the biggest gig we had ever played back to the reality of a club tour. The stage in that place was eye to eye with the audience. That stage set-up is the worst in the history of live music. The people in the back of the room can't see shit, and the drummer is buried at the rear of the stage. It's a miserable playing experience.

The headlining bands on those opening tours treated us pretty well. Particularly Mötley Crüe.

We went out with Motley in 1984, while on the Cellar tour. That was...that was...fuck! Oh, my God...

Mötley Crüe is, hands down, the most out of control, decadent, soulless, monstrosity of a band that has ever been. They were also our closest compatriots. T-Bone and I are great friends to this day.

That leg of the tour was nothing but drink, snort, fuck and party day and night.

Complete, out of our mind, debauchery. We Pi-RATTs would invade your port, pillage your town, drink your rum, and fuck your daughters, all while you bought our T-shirts and albums, which we were happy to sign for you ... once we finished with your daughters.

We played this 4000 seat theater in Boston. The place was sold out, and in the dressing rooms, there were windows that looked out on the parking lot. Normally, you don't have windows in the dressing rooms. So, after the show, Tommy and I were getting fucked up, doing shot after shot after shot of Jack Daniels.

Just another day at the office.

We kept looking out the window and seeing all these people hanging out, trying to catch a glimpse of us in the dressing room. They probably thought they'd get a peek at us getting dressed or something. We would keep popping our heads out the window, and the crowd down there was going ape-nuts.

For some weird ass reason, we decided to start throwing them food from the deli tray. Like gasoline on a fire, the whole moment exploded with insanity. They were clamoring and climbing all over each other; tackling one another for these pieces of salami and bologna and cheese!

It looked like "Night of the Living Dead", and they were all cannibalizing a corpse, or something. I'm sure a couple of people actually got hurt in that melee. At the very least, a couple of them were bitten. We laughed our ass off at that crowd. They were so desperate for anything that we did. We couldn't have enough fun with it!

"We love you people!", as David Lee Roth was fond of saying.

The last night of that tour, we played two sold-out shows at the Beacon Theater in New York. Motley decided they were going to fuck with us, which is customary. The headlining band always has some joke or prank that they pull on the opening acts on the last night. Anything to fuck with them.

Mötley Crüe excelled at this.

For us, it was an all night thing. It started off with a dead pigeon on a string. They kept lowering this nasty assed thing down from the roof during the show. It would jump and flop around in the air, this dead bird on a string, right at eye level to the band. The guys at the front of the stage were ducking and dodging, trying not to get hit with this thing.

All right, very funny. The audience loved it.

The pranks continued, and I was a sitting duck for this shit. Behind my drum set, I had absolutely nowhere to go. I was Ground-Fucking-Zero. Unbeknownst to me, directly above my head, they had these huge bags of popped popcorn. Halfway through one of the songs, they promptly dumped this shit all over me. All right, even funnier. Snowing popcorn. Very nice.

That happened pretty early in our set, but I figured the fun was over, and we could get through the rest of the show without too much embarrassment. Popcorn wasn't that big of a problem to deal with. It was just messy.

Then came the coup-de-gras! Towards the end of the show, a giant cloud of white powder cascaded out of the rafters onto the stage! They had dumped huge bags of flour on us. Again, I'm a sitting duck. Nothing I can do about it, but play on.

This shit was everywhere! Clouds of flour went into every nook and cranny on stage. The worst part was my drums. When you dump 50 pounds of flour onto your drum heads, it's like playing with them draped in wet towels. RATT sounded like we were playing from inside a well.

That was pretty hysterical, thought. Really creative.

Cocksuckers!

I guess this joke really worked out for Motley. Because, it turned into a mainstay for their opening acts. They pulled the same trick on Guns N Roses when they toured with them in 1987.

The flour gag immediately made me think of the Vic Vergat tour with Nazareth. All that baby powder.

Karma. What a bitch.

We'll talk about that in just a minute.

Our next big run was with Night Ranger. It lasted about three weeks, and turned out to be the calm before the storm. Night Ranger was a good bunch of guys to work with, and when we left them, all of a sudden, it was on! RATT was huge, with a single roaring toward the top ten.

We got two semis, production, lighting, minor staging with ramps, and Fastway and Lita Ford rolling with us as our opening acts. I had two very good friends playing drums with Lita Ford. One was Eric Singer, and the other was Randy Castillo. Lita was pretty cooperative, despite the fact that she was bumped from our Beverly Theater show the night we were signed. From this point on, the tour really took off.

Twisted Sister joined us, later, as an opening act. Their home turf was New York City and upstate New York. We had three or four shows in those areas, and knew they drew really well up there, so as a favor to Atlantic Records, we went on first for those dates.

In New York City, we played at this place called Pier 18, right on the water in the bowery. Huge. There were 10,000 people in that place, including a very young Jason Bonham, who had just been signed to Atlantic with his band Airrace. Of course, I just wanted to talk about his dad. I mean, one of the main reasons that I play drums it the legendary John Bonham.

These days, Jason and I are still friends. He's got a couple of good gigs. Led Zeppelin and Foreigner. I hope the Zeppelin thing happens for those guys. That will be a monstrous tour. It would set the records for any tour in history. Guaranteed.

I guess it was the middle of June when we really started noticing the changes. Our shows at clubs had been selling out, and after the Kalamazoo show, we were really starting to feel something. By June and July, we were becoming monsters. The next big thing. I remember we did an in-store in Arizona. We were shooting the "Wanted Man" video down there, and we had the film crew with us at the time.

Like all of our in-stores, there were three or four a week, the place was utter chaos! There were so many people packed into that place, it was insane. The film crew actually shot some of that, and the footage appears on a DVD collection of RATT videos, which we released in 2007.

I looked around in this mall, and was like, "Oh, my God." There were cops everywhere, trying to maintain order. It was crazy. But, a lot of our in-stores were becoming like that. Especially after "Round and Round" hit MTV.

…but I'm getting ahead of myself. Let's step back a bit and get a little background.

ACT I: THE BIRTH

1

STEELTOWN NOMADS

"He not busy being born, is busy dying." - Bob Dylan

On October 22, 1958, in Pittsburgh, Pennsylvania, Charles "Chuck" Blotzer, and

his beautiful wife, Lois, welcomed into the world a small, pink bologna loaf with a penchant for making loud noises. They see in their hearts to give this noisemaker the moniker Robert John Blotzer. Bobby, from that point on.

There begins my first day on this rock.

Mum and Dad were good people. Mum was a small-town mother with three kids at a very young age, and Dad, well Dad is a little hard to remember, to be honest. I only have two strong memories of him that I can recall with any clarity.

In one, I'm driving the car while sitting in his lap. It was one of those moments when a kid looks in his dad's face, and knows that he's gone from being his father's "son," to becoming dad's "Little Man." A lot of sons have this memory, and it is one of my earliest.

My second memory of him was on the night I heard he had died. But, I'm getting ahead of myself a little.

They had been married since 1952, and my older brother Ron was six years my senior. I guess you could call him a "wedding present." I also have an older sister, Carol. She is only a little more than a year older than me. Carol was my rock. She was my confidant. She showed me music for the first time, and she let me ogle her friends when we were teens. She gave me music and women. I don't think I've ever thanked her for that. Finally, there's my younger brother Michael, who my first son is named after. Mike was born in 1967.

At the time, we lived in a Pittsburgh suburb called Turtle Creek. "Turtle Crick", to the locals. Picture in your mind a quaint little village like town. Cobblestone streets and buildings. Victorian style houses. The place was so "small town values" that it could have been a Norman Rockwell painting, and no one would have thought a thing of it.

Around this time, which was 1964 or 1965, things were heading south for my Mum and Dad's marriage. It got pretty bad, and before I knew it, Dad was gone, and they were divorced.

It wasn't long after that when it happened.

I remember being in my room, and hearing all hell breaking loose downstairs. Mum was crying. Wailing, really. And, I could hear Ronnie saying stuff. I couldn't make it out, though.

I came down the stairs, as quiet as I could, and stood there watching Ronnie comfort Mum. She was busted up pretty bad. So was Ronnie, for that matter.

They looked at me, called me over, and told me that my father, Charles "Chuck" Blotzer, was dead.

My grandmother had given my dad a car. It was a Pontiac Tempest with a tragic history. One afternoon, she was driving down a quiet residential street, when a 6-year-old kid darted out from between cars. Whether she had the chance to react or not, I have no idea. She hit the kid with the car, and the boy died at the scene.

It destroyed my grandmother. She was consumed with guilt. Then from that point on, she wouldn't drive. Not for any reason. So, she gave the car to my Dad.

Less than a year later, my Dad died in that car. He was driving on an icy road, lost control, and slid into a telephone pole. I guess he broke his neck, or something, because he was dead when they found him.

I don't believe in curses, but that Tempest was born under a bad sign.

My Dad had a brother, my Uncle Ron, who I kept in touch with over the years. Whenever I'd go back to Pittsburgh to visit, I go see him. He's passed away now, as well, but he used to come see the shows and got a big kick out of it. Ron was the only member of my Dad's side of the family that I kept up with. He's got a bunch of kids who are my cousins, and as far as I know, they're all still back in "Turtle Crick."

But, it wasn't long before Mum had found someone new, and Pittsburgh was in the rearview mirror.

Joe Schweinberg, "Pete" to anyone who mattered in his life, was a pretty good guy when he started coming around. He tried to do the right thing with the kids. Treated us good, bribed us with change and dollar bills, or candy, that sort of thing. At least that's how it was in the beginning. Pete married my Mum in 1966.

But, that sweet, innocent and simple life in Turtle Crick wasn't to last for long. Things got tough in the Sixties, and in a snap, Pete had moved us into the projects of East Pittsburgh.

Keep in mind that this was the early 1960's, and what people think of, as "projects" weren't what they are today. It was just families with lower incomes. There wasn't a big crime element, and things weren't divided by race or anything like that. Not that there weren't race issues, but they just weren't that intense. It wasn't anything like it was in other parts of the country. No one had ever heard of crack or drugs or shit like that. It was a fairly respectable place, and people got along.

These days, I go up there to visit, and the place is just a wreck. Run down and dilapidated. Crime is like a cancer in that place, and most of it revolves around the drug scene. It's really sad. But, when we lived there, the place was brand new. It was really like a big apartment complex. Big apartment buildings with mostly white families. The few black families were pretty low key. I never caught on to any racial tension or strife in that place. Certainly nothing like what was going on in the south.

Thinking back on it, there obviously was some division between races. My Mum, for instance, was brought up with the notion that you don't hang out with black people.

It just isn't done. That was something handed down through her family over the generations. Sort of a racially motivated inheritance. I did note that my Mum was much less dogmatic about the subject than her parents were. Personally, I don't give a shit what color you are, so each generation is getting a little weaker in their racial judgments.

I guess there is some hope against that bullshit.

The ironic thing about my Mum and her distrust for black people was that, during her end days, she was befriended by her next-door neighbor, a black woman. This lady really took care of her. She really did right by my Mum. There came a point where Mum couldn't care for herself, and she had to go live in a hospice hospital. She was visited almost daily by a jovial black preacher, who wound up praying her last prayers with her.

Carol and I got a bittersweet kick out of that. She wasn't hating blacks, my Mum. But, her general distrust and ignorance was something given down to her through family, yet, her last days were spent being comforted and cared for by black people. Very cool.

She did pass a few of those stereotypes down to us kids, but nothing to the degree of what she dealt with. I played with Ron Abrams in Firefox, have several black friends, and love Motown music. My distrust of people has nothing to do with their race. There are people of EVERY race that I don't appreciate, like or trust. I'd even go as far as to say hate. We're talking about no good piece of shit people. Their skin tone has nothing to do with it.

I'll just say this. I'm not a racist. I hate everybody equally.

In fact, I can only think of one instance in my tough life, there in the harsh realities of Sixties East Pittsburgh, where anything remotely racist occurred. It ended with me getting my ass kicked... naturally.

I was walking in the woods with a buddy of mine. We were going down into this ravine, just dicking around, you know. There was this big yellow jacket flying all around me. The thing was trying to tag me, so I started running.

Someone had tossed a mattress and box spring out there, and, while trying like hell to get away from that bee, I fell on the old boxspring. My legs were scraped up really bad, as were my knees, hands, and the whole deal. PLUS, the damned yellow jacket stung me right in the corner of the eye.

So, we were taking my bleeding and puffy ass home, and this one kid named Artie Moses, I remember him clearly, started making fun of me.

That just flat pissed me off. I probably called him a nigger, or told him to fuck off, or something. It's hard to remember. Well, Artie came over and promptly finished what the bee and the mattress had started. He "old school projects" beat my ass.

So, I got my butt kicked by a mattress, and my face stung by a bee. Then Artie Moses, who lived two blocks down, took care of business. God bless the fucker, right?

Karen Lozenski. Kindergarten. She was one of the neighborhood girls, as I recall. She was that curious kind of cute that makes pre-pubescent boys go, "Hey, what's that about?" As curiosity would have it, she thought I was "a curious thing", too.

The two of us would sneak off to the lumberyard near where we lived. Then, we'd spend the afternoon "exploring each other." We used to go in there and kiss, take our clothes down, the whole thing.

I look back on that with some moral conflict. Someone just reading those two paragraphs might think, "Dude? What? You were in KINDERGARTEN! What the hell kind of world did you grow up in?" At the time, it was a completely innocent thing. Maybe we had watched a little too much TV, or maybe our older siblings had told us about "that." I've got no idea where our young minds would have gleaned the idea from. Although, I've always been a horn-dog, my whole life, so maybe that has a little to do with it.

Disturbing? Yes, but still funny. I mean ... how? I still can't figure it out. But, it's been that way my whole life.

Karen Lozenski. The woman-child who introduced me to the unmentionable parts of the female world, all at the tender young age of six.

Gotta love forward thinking females.

After Pete and Mum got married, things started to change with him. He was a heavy-handed guy, like a lot of guys at that time, but that wasn't the biggest issue with him. Pete was a nomad. He never seemed comfortable in any one place. Given this base nature of his, we became nomads by association. We were young. We could adapt to it, right? Everyone except Ronnie, that is.

My older brother Ron never got on with Pete. To him, Pete was a gypsy who constantly uprooted the family and bounced us around. In eight years time, we lived in seven different places all over the country. The ground would hardly get warm beneath our feet before Pete had us off on another relocation.

In 1968, Pete moved us to New Jersey. Then, in November of 1971, we were whisked away to Torrance, California when Gino's Hamburgers, who he worked for, transferred him out there. Gino's was a burger place that was supposed to be the next McDonald's. It was owned by a couple of former NFL players. They were expanding the thing all over the country, and offered Pete a position on the other side of the universe, as far as I was concerned.

We stayed almost two months at the Portofino Inn, in Redondo Beach, right on the water before Pete found a house in Torrance. That lasted about 45 minutes, because by 1972, we were back in Jersey. In 1973, it was California again; then to Myrtle Beach, South Carolina in late 1973; and finally, we were back in the Torrance area by 1974.

In seven short years, I had lived in eight different places...and it was getting pretty damned annoying.

Due to my lack of any real structured education, because of the constant relocation and moving around, I was always able to do whatever I wanted whenever I wanted, even from a very young age. We were just always uprooting. Even when I got kicked out of school, they never pushed me or made me go back. That was always very weird to me. Especially now, as a dad, I can look and know I would never allow that of my children.

I guess, for me, things started getting really weird in 1971. I was eleven, and Pete was moving us to California. A whole continent away from home. My whole life was on the east coast. Everything I knew. My memories of my father were there, although the curse of a young mind was taking hold, and his details were fading. Ronnie wasn't coming.

Despite his cruelty and general prickishness, Ronnie was the older brother. There's stability in that for younger siblings. Carol and I unknowingly depended on him.

It didn't matter. I didn't know much about California, except that the hippies loved the place. It was supposed to be this happy Mecca of love and bright colors and experimental drugs. Of course, it wasn't that way at all. Maybe it had been a couple of years earlier, but most of the people there didn't know fuck-all about love and peace. Their whole world was getting dumped on its ass.

The drugs and red wine had worn off and the Woodstock generation had gone their own ways, stopping long enough to cash their reality check.

Pete dropped us down in a world that didn't know itself. The Charles Manson "Trial of the Century" was going on, and Los Angeles wasn't the happy, shiny place that an outgoing eleven year old was hoping for.

Even musically, everything was fucked, and nothing fit. The Beatles had split up the year before, leaving a HUGE, cavernous void. There were some flashes of hope, most of which were going to pay off before long. But in 1971, Aerosmith, Kiss, Black Sabbath, Deep Purple, were just starting. And Hendrix, Joplin and Morrison were dead.

Despite all of this down vibe in LA, I still adapted pretty quickly.

I've always been a self-reliant kid. No one needed to hold my hand and show me the way, because I was going to find it one way or the other. Plus, I've always made fast friends. When you're in your pre-teens, and you're already posting a history of being the perineal new guy in town, these are really great tools to have.

Adapting to LA wasn't hard. At least for me. We spent the first two months living in a hotel. The Portofino Inn in Redondo Beach was right on the water. A great place to just hang out and watch the water slap at the ends of the western world. It made for a mellow transition process for me. East coast steel town steeped in history to west coast Xanadu steeped in self-indulgence.

And, that was that. I had found home.

In short order, I had my first LA drug experience.

When we moved to California, I was twelve years old and I took my first hit of acid. Carol was hanging out with some of her friends, and I was along for fun. There were a few young guys there. I was twelve, so they must have been fifteen or sixteen, which seemed really old. They were a bunch of biker wanna-be's, with the boots and chains, and the teen-angst "I hate my parents" thing going on.

They gave me a hit of Blue Micro-Dot. Acid. Some of you who flew through the Seventies may remember this little joy ride.

We were hanging out at the school. It was New Year's Day, so it was closed, and there wasn't another place we could go where we could drink beer and not get caught. When I took the tab, it hit me like a freight train! I remember being really fucked up and just out of my head.

We lived right across from the Gabel House Bowling Alley on 226th and Hawthorne Blvd., there in Torrance. I remember Carol going, "You can't go home, Bobby. You'll get popped!" So, we went to the bowling alley, instead.

Bad idea. Really bad idea. That place was really freaking me out. It was SO loud and SO chaotic. I just couldn't take it, so I bolted to the house.

When I got home, Carol was sitting at the dining room table with Pete, Mum and Michael, just sitting down to have dinner. The lights above that table were the brightest I think I've ever seen. I wasn't myself. Completely tripped out, and there was no hiding it. Pete made me come over and sit down for dinner.

I started playing in my mashed potatoes. They were moving and swaying. I was hallucinating on my mashed potatoes! I felt like I was eating gobs of ... I don't know what ... glue, or paint, or something like that. All I know is that it didn't have the texture of anything I'd ever eaten before.

Pete looks at me and goes, "What's wrong with your eyes?" He looks at my Mum, and goes, "Look at his pupils!"

I jumped up and ran to the bathroom to look in the mirror. I had eaten some food, and was looking in the mirror, just tripping on my own face. A couple of seconds later, I puked all over the place! We'd been drinking beer that day, too, so it was hideous.

Pete comes in, grabs me, and goes, "What are you on, boy? What did you take?"

I'm like, "Nothing. I didn't take anything. I found an open Reese's cup with one left inside, and I ate it."

"Bullshit. What did you take?"

"Nothing! This guy at the bowling alley had an RC and he gave me a drink off of it." But, Pete wasn't buying it. The interrogation continued until I finally copped to what I had done, which meant that now I would have the biker kids after me.

Pete decided to take me to the police station. So he hauls my ass into the Torrance P.D., with me just blazing on LSD. Lucy in the Sky With Diamond, bro, and she was singing her song loud and clear. This one cop walks up, and I swear, the guy's nose was turned up like a pig's snout, and he was talking in grunts and oinks.

I was like, "Fuck! Look at that!" I wound up embarrassing the hell out of Pete, giggling at the pig-cop. Pete took me outside and roughed me up a little bit, but not as bad as I probably deserved. He took me home, and the Partridge Family was on TV. I was so confused. They looked like a bunch of cartoon people. I looked at my Mum and went, "Are they real?!? They look so funny!"

She got super pissed.

I was tripping out on everything, like the curtains. I watched all these patterns and lines moving around. It was like a kaleidoscope effect. Really fucking bizarre; especially as a pre-teen. In truth, I was scared shitless. So, I kept trying to describe it to my Mum.

Finally, she was like, "Go to your room!"

That was a great call, because I got into my room, killed the light and turned on my blacklight with all of my blacklight posters in the room. I cranked Hendrix and Zeppelin records. Then I understood! Then I got it! I was like, "Oh, yeah. All that other shit's pretty scary, but this makes the whole trip worth it."

With the blacklights and the Hendrix, the whole thing turned out to be really fun.

But, now I had the biker kids after me. Richard Wood and Ron Ellerman. I still remember their names.

LA taught lessons fast, I was to discover. That's fine, because I'm a quick learner; eager, even. The Seventies were all about having a good time at the expense of everything around you. People were too busy getting laid, drunk and stoned; posing in front of their bedroom mirrors with broomstick guitars. They didn't spend time worrying about underlying problems. It's the perfect environment for reckless youth.

It wasn't long before we settled in a little house on 226th street in Torrance. It was the sort of house that blended into the rest of the LA basin. Not spectacular, but not a shit-hole either.

I find it amazing today that our house that sold for $40,000 in 1972 now sells for $750,000.

I went to Sam Levy Elementary on 229th street. Again, it lacked the elements of the spectacular. But, it wasn't long before I had some great friends in that neighborhood.

The best, hands down, was Drew Bombeck. Drew and I were fast compatriots, mutual offenders, and always the usual suspects when something questionable happened around school; that was us. I think it was because the two of us had a general disdain for anything involving structure. Let's just say, we didn't "blend."

First off, we were the only two boys in the school with longhair (and attitudes to match). We had a lot of mutual interests; dirt bikes, chicks (Drew had, hands down, the hottest sister on the planet...alas, I could only love her in my mind...which I did often), but most of all, we bonded over music. Hendrix. The Rolling Stones. And, above all, the Beatles. I don't know if we were just fixated on the music of the Sixties, or if we hadn't found anything better in the Seventies. But, the Beatles WERE music as far as we were concerned.

I'm not getting down on the music of the time. Some of that music was great. But, glitter and glam flooded everything we saw: clothes, music, cars, candy, everything. It was hard to figure the talent from the shit. Some of it was easy; The Sweet, Mott the Hoople, and the absolute genius of David Bowie. That was talent. Some of it wasn't; The New York Dolls, The Sex Pistols, et al. To me, that was shit. It was the whole transvestite thing. I just never got it. Especially when it was used to simply mask a lack of real skill and musical talent. Mind you, Bowie had that look, but he had the brilliant song writing to back up anything he wanted to do.

Punk was experimental, and experimental is fine. Some of it is groundbreaking. But, I wanted to be on the radio. Even back then, I knew what I was going to do with my life. But, to get on the radio, you had to make music that not only spoke to your soul, but spoke to the majority of the other souls in the world, as well. Punk did everything it could to be noticed, but then got pissed off when it did. Okay. If that does it for you. But it doesn't compare to being worshipped by 14,000 people in a stadium, all of who know your music better than you do.

That's how it was with the Beatles. Modern rock and roll, almost without exception, can trace itself to the Beatles. Try to say that for the New York Dolls.

Drew, my bro, got that. We'd hang out for hours at a time, listening to our albums, talking music, talking chicks, and doing everything we could to forget we were only twelve years old. We'd jump on our dirt bikes and destroy anything that remotely resembled a bike trail. It was a free life. And we were indestructible.

Me, Carol, and cousin Chuck.

Me, Carol, Michael with cousins, 1978.

Photo of family above, Jeni, baby Michael, Bobby, niece Heather, Mom, Carol, nephew PJ, nephew Cris, Brother Michael. 1982.

My grandmother on my mother's side Birtha Thorp (bottom row left), and other members of that side of the family.

Me in a dress, don't ask me why.

Uncle Ron Blotzer, my brother's dad.

Me acting kooky Torrance CA, 1972.

Brother, sister Carol and me, 1982.

Aunt Ann and Uncle Ron, after getting into the RATT catering, 1984
Billy Squier RATT Tour.

Real Dad – Charles Blotzer – age 17.

Bar full of Blotzers, imagine that!

Me and nephew Cris – dancing under cover tour, 1987.

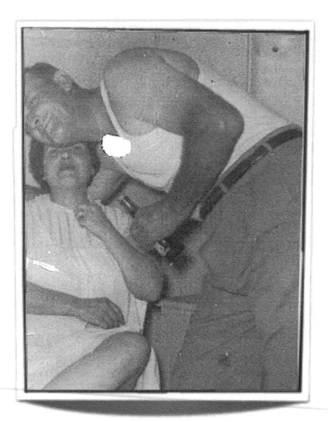

Mom's mom and dad.

Bobby and Carol baby pics.

Ronny, Carol, Bobby, 1964.

The first guy I played music with, Harold Hawthorne. We lived in same apartment
building, 1974.

Harold and Me in 2003.

Me, Jeni, and Pete, 1985.

Stepdad Pete and Mom Lois 2003.

Loved playing arcade games – Asteroids was my favorite.

2

THE VIRTUES OF CINNAMON TOAST

AND BLACK SABBATH

Another of my good friends during this time of turmoil and self-expression was

Tom Farnsworth. I met Tom in the 6th grade, at the aforementioned Sam Levy Elementary.

Tom was a good cat. Likeable. He wasn't Drew, but I enjoyed hanging out with him. He gave me another excuse to be out of the house, especially since Pete had taken to punishing me by cutting my hair. My hair was very important to me. It was my look. So, when he would get piss drunk and take it out on me, my hair was always a casualty. The more I could stay out of the house, the less chance I had of looking like a cancer patient.

So, Tom was a good alternative. But, it was Tom's brother, Lee, who had a much more influential impact on my life. Especially for my tendency to self-medicate.

Lee sold weed. Actually, that doesn't do it justice. Lee sold a shitload of weed.

One of the first times I saw Lee, he had an entire pound brick of pot laid out and ready to cut up. He was a generous guy, and introduced his brother's thirteen-year-old friend to the truly lofty feelings enjoyed by inhaling the smoke from a burning Cannabis Sativa plant!

I don't remember much about that day. Lee got Tom and I soooooo stoned. All I remember was just lying under the bed, out of my mind. When I came out of it, I was as hungry as I've ever been in my life. I biked home as quickly as I could, put on Black Sabbath's Paranoid album, and ate twelve pieces of cinnamon toast.

That was my first introduction to weed. Black Sabbath and cinnamon toast will always hold a place close to my heart. And, Lee Farnsworth showed me a wonderful way to supplement my income when I was a little older, and a starving musician who didn't want a day job.

For years, I served as a middleman. Someone would come to me and ask for a load of pot. It started as a quarter pound, then a half. Before long, it was one or two pounds at a pop. I would run a couple of houses down the street, broker the deal with Lee, and then make a quick $500 or so.

Through this, I was able to supplement my passions. Music, concerts, chicks and all the things that go along with that.

Hey, it was the seventies. Consequences weren't a real consideration. Remember?

When I was thirteen, two things happened of great significance. The first involved Pete.

Pete was a stocky guy who had hands like canned hams. He worked at a bar; he drank like an Irishman; and he fought like a Scot. It really didn't matter who with, but my Mum and I were prime targets.

Now, despite my personal actions and life experiences, I'm really not a fighter. Well, not physically, anyway. So, when Pete would occasionally get crapulous, he would simply beat my ass.

One instance, in particular, when I was 15 or so, I came crawling into the house around four in the morning, as polluted as I've ever been. Pete and Mum were asleep.

I never made it to my room, and passed out on the couch.

When Mum came downstairs to find me on the couch, halfway to Heavington, she tried to wake me up and get me upstairs before Pete saw me. Noble, though her cause was, I didn't react well to being woke up.

"Get the fuck out of here! I'm sleeping." In hindsight, probably not a wise idea. She didn't take it well, and went to get Pete.

About the time I got to my bed and laid down, Pete hit the door, all piss and molten metal. He grabbed me up by the hair and punched me square in the face. All in all, pretty intense. Thankfully, I was still drunk-numb, so the full effect of it didn't hit until I woke up, later.

My face and lip were so swollen I could barely talk. My own damn fault, though. I got drunk and mouthed off to my Mum. Pretty much, I got my just deserts, so it wasn't really a big deal to me.

When Pete saw it, though, it was a different story. The guy felt like shit over it. My face was so bad that Pete gave me the keys to the car and let me take it for the day. Mind you, I was only 15 at the time, and nowhere near having my license. But, I'd been taking the car since I was 11. Pete knew it, and felt this was the least he could do.

The guy wasn't without his post-drunk remorse; not all bad, when you gave him a chance. But, we really weren't ever going to be best friends. He wasn't my buddy; and I wasn't his pride and joy. For the most part, we just tried to stay out of each other's way.

So imagine my surprise when Pete did the one thing that sent me on a speeding rail toward realizing my dreams.

He gave me a guitar and amp.

While music had always been a big part of who I was, it wasn't until Pete gave me the guitar that my path became clear.

It was a weird night. Pete comes into the house, about half lit. He was working at a bar at the time. In his hands, he's carrying a guitar and a small amp. I never knew where he got it. It could be that some guy at the bar owed him money, or he might have bought it on the cheap. Shit, he might have copped it. Who knows?

But, he walks in with it, looks at me and says, "You're into all this music and shit, so here you go."

Like I said, the guy wasn't without his moments.

My tastes in music had never changed, but new bands were popping up that I was really enjoying. Granted, most of them were still British bands.

Among them was Queen, David Bowie, The Sweet, Deep Purple, Humble Pie, etc. They were trash glam at its glammest. No question. They had the best make-up, the best bouffant ridiculous hair, and they wore pants so tight, we discovered Camel-Toe had an ugly little brother named Moose-Knuckle. Thankfully, The Sweet also had the best tunes.

Ironically, when they fell apart, they did it in a monstrous way. The whole thing ended in bitter acrimony, alcohol, arguments and early death. It never occurred to us that RATT would follow almost the exact same path until it was too late.

It's the wise man that learns from his mistakes, but it's that smart fucker who learns from someone else's. These days, I endeavor to be that smart fucker.

I digress.

Still, it was a time where clothes were ripped, make-up was caked on eyes with a putty knife, cheeks were pierced with safety pins, and nobody smiled anymore. The simple pleasures of glitter and gloss were easy to forget.

But there was that new music movement. Call it heavy metal, hard rock, arena rock, I don't give a shit. It was that hedonistic sound and balls out attitude, preaching sex, drugs and rock. And, it cut right to my guts. Right to that place that made me exist.

When I looked at that guitar, I saw that for myself. My possibilities wrapped up in six strings.

I sat and jacked around with this thing, trying to make sense of it the best I could, but I wasn't really getting very far.

I heard about a guy who lived in the same apartment building as me, named Harold Hawthorne. Harold was a guitarist, and I needed to learn how to be a guitarist.

I dropped by the guy's house and knocked on the door. His Mom answered, and I talked my way inside, and then went straight up to Harold's room where he was practicing.

Remember when I said I make fast friends? Harold is still a good friend to this day. He and Drew are both parts of my childhood that I've carried all through my life and still hang out with today.

But, unfortunately, the guitar wasn't meant to be. Not for me, anyway. Although, I still play, just not blistering leads, a la Warren DeMartini.

Harold was a pretty good guitarist. He took lessons and knew all about music theory and scales. Shit like that. I didn't seem to have it. Not the patience, not the talent, not the "mojo." Whatever it took to be an axe-slinging rock god, I didn't have it. And, it frustrated the hell out of me.

While Harold and I hung out and practiced, and the talent gap continued to spread, another kid in the neighborhood hooked up with us. His name was Marty Cory, and Marty was a budding drummer.

A drummer.

I hadn't really thought about it before. But, it sounded good.

It wasn't long before our little jam sessions began to evolve, but only for me.

I got into the habit of sitting on the drum kit and working the beats while Marty picked up my guitar. In short order, I had surpassed Marty in as a drummer.

We traded, straight up, my guitar and amp for his drum kit.

Harold continued to bloom on his guitar, but our sessions never really went anywhere as a group.

But, it wasn't four or five months later before I was playing band calibre drums. Joining bands was the next step.

Life was pretty good, for me. And, thankfully, it was being lived on my terms, for the most part. Naturally, this existence would lend itself to trouble, but I didn't care. It was my life, with my decisions to make.

School was no different. Drew and I were the designated offendees. Often times, we were guilty. Other times, not so much. But, I'd call it even, considering the number of things we didn't get busted for.

Drew was the first to go down. He was kicked out of Sam Levy, and sent to a "specialty school." It was sort of a special education / juvenile detention kind of place.

Honestly, it was the sort of place they sent the disposable kids. You went there, and your academic potential would be pronounced dead a week later.

Not to piss and groan about it, mind you. I mean, what else were they going to do with the kids they didn't know what to do with? It was just easier to sweep them under the rug than deal with them. The seventies were never that big on consequences. Know what I mean?

My own educational demise at Sam Levy wasn't far behind, and oddly enough, it was a fairly minor infraction that spelled the end.

One day, in 8th grade, we got to school a bit late. We'd been hanging out at the 7-11, smoking cigarettes and a joint or two. Needless to say, I got to class with a sinister case of the munchies. I'd have taken a bite out of the desktop if I hadn't found something to kill the cravings.

Fortunately, I found something.

In the desk belonging to the rather odd girl who usually sat next to me was a package of Dip N Sticks. For those who don't remember this shit, it was a foil package of a substance kinda like Kool-Aid. It was, basically, a bag full of flavored sugar. It even came with a little stick, which was white and made out of even more compressed sugar. You could eat the stick! I'm surprised they didn't make a way you could eat the fucking bag! It was a sinister sweet treat capable of leveling the typical educational experience with a few gritty swallows of packaged sugar high.

Needless to say, I was stoked.

I snatched the package up and gave it a shake. Sure enough, the familiar sound of granulated tooth decay Rattled back.

I unrolled it and upended the contents into my mouth.

In hindsight, I probably should have considered the oddness of the girl who sat next to me. Because, surprises in life are often very enjoyable. This wasn't one of those times.

It seems after consuming her package of Dip N Sticks, she saw the empty foil bag as a perfect place to hold spilled glue, and to her credit, the glue was still pretty fresh. But, it tasted like hammered shit, and I spat it all over the desk in front of me, gagging and choking. I was generally making a huge scene of the whole thing. The whole class ground to a halt, and watched me be a clown for a couple of minutes.

Never one to leave an opportunity unexplored, I thought I might be able to get out of the rest of my school day if I made like the glue had made me sick, so I milked the moment.

It worked a little too well. It got me out of that day, and all the ones after it.

The teacher took me to the office, and after several minutes of arguing with the powers that be, I was unceremoniously kicked out of school.

Generally, our teachers, parents, or any adult in a position of authority viewed Drew and I as troublemakers. We were rowdy, true, but we were kids. What did they expect?

Thinking about what I was like as a kid, and often times as an adult, I was probably A.D.D. / A.D.H.D. If I had been a kid in today's world, they would have had me medicated to the nines, walking around like I was on a lithium drip. But, being the times it was, no one had a damned clue as to what Attention Deficit Disorder was...

...and I preferred to self-medicate, anyway.

In the end, our only true crime was the music we listened to. Something happened in the adults of the seventies. I truly think they forgot what it was like to be young and eager to discover.

So, fuck em.

I told you that two things happened of great significance during this time.

The first was Pete giving me my guitar, which led to my first drum set.

The second thing was something that happens to every horny young guy. I met a girl.

Her name was Jeni Malara, and she was Carol's best friend.

Jeni used to come by all the time, hanging out, staying over, listening to music with Carol, doing all those Seventies teen girl things. Let's face it, I was always horned out. If it was female, I was going to give a once over, and my standards usually weren't that complicated.

She lived on 226th in Torrance, just up the street. There was something about Jeni and the way she was around me. I think she really dug me, but I was younger than her by a year or so, and getting into her pants (as hard as I tried) wasn't in the immediate future.

It's not like I thought she was "the one," but she had a quality other chicks didn't. Besides, Drew's super hot sister wasn't really working out for me, right?

My future with Jeni was set. It was only a couple of years later that we were living together...

...then getting married...

...and having a son...

...and stomping down the rugged road of life for another 24 years.

Stay tuned for more on THAT.

RATT in Pasadena 1982, Metallica opened for us on this show.

3

THE HIGH SPIRITS OF MISADVENTURE

"You don't need anybody to tell you who you are or what you are. You are what you are!" - John Lennon

My entire life is bound, wrapped and colored by music; both the music I listen to and absorb, and the music I've helped create.

There's something that happens when you're around music. Yours or someone else's. Something inside you kicks on, or turns off accordingly. Whether you're into whatever is playing, or not, your soul responds. And it's a different response for everyone. There are dudes in this world who worship the accordion. I don't know those guys, mind you. My guess is that most of them are middle-aged, virginal, and still living with their mothers. But, at least they have the accordion. Bless them for that, right?

I have been blessed in my own ways. One of the best is my memory. It's served me very well my entire life. I remember dates, events, experiences, almost at will. And, with really great clarity. I can remember most every concert or show I've ever seen. Even the shows where I'd abused myself in some fashion or form (chemically speaking, of course), I can pull up with near total recall. It's a gift that I cherish. It's also a gift that has saved my career, as you will discover a little later.

Once I'd been bitten by the creative process, I couldn't get enough live music.

I'd spent my childhood huddled around beat up record players listening to everything. I had my favorites, true, but I'd give a listen to most anything. Music even determined most of the relationships in my life. If you weren't into music, I wasn't into you.

But, when I started playing, and playing well, I tried to go to every concert that came through the LA area. The guys who manned the gate at the Long Beach Arena knew me on sight. I saw everything.

It was like music school, on the cheap. One weekend, I might catch Humble Pie, Spooky Tooth and Uriah Heap on the card at the arena, then catch a couple of local shows over in Hollywood the next night.

I was a machine, and each show I went to was a learning experience in some fashion. It wasn't about fame and fortune. It was about life. My life. And there wasn't anything else I was going to be able to do with it. I HAD to be a musician.

One night in July of 1975, I had one of my best moments at a show. It was the night that Aerosmith headlined a show at the Long Beach Arena with Mahogany Rush and Status Quo opening.

Actually, I had several "moments" that show. The whole night was just a little off center. It was one of those nights that could have ended in disaster at any given second, but whatever rock gods were watching over me, they chose to show me favor. I got away with some pretty cool shit that night.

To start with, I was hanging out with this chick named Debbie Daw. She was fun times, but neither of us had a car and both of us wanted to catch the show.

So, we hitchhiked.

We were picked up by a van on the corner of Artesia Blvd. and the 405. Turns out that the guy and girl in the van were also heading to the Aerosmith show, so the night was starting off well.

At this time, I was playing in my first real band; a group called Slicker. I was loving playing live and the whole vibe it created as a club act, starving for gigs was getting a bit old. And, Slicker wasn't really pushing to be anything beyond what it was.

So, I was looking for greener pastures.

A few days before, I had heard that the hottest band in the South Bay area at the time was looking for a new drummer. It was a group called Spike, and they were huge, so I had set my sights on getting that gig.

I felt really good about it. Everything was looking like the gig was going to be mine. Turns out that the bassist was a guy I knew from school; Juan Croucier, who would later play with me in RATT. Life was great.

Debbie and I hit it off pretty well with the guy and girl in the van. We were all really into music, and struck up quick conversations about bands, the scene, who was hot and who was not.

Somewhere in the midst of this conversation, I mentioned that I played in Slicker there in Redondo Beach. It was all right, but it looked like I was going to be joining this band Spike. They were looking for a new drummer, and I was the guy.

The conversation continues for a while. More music, bands, generic talky shit. Then this guy mentions, "Yeah, I'm in a band, too. Here in Hermosa."

"No shit?", says I. "Which one?"

"Spike."

Awkward. Just a little bit.

So, I sat there in my hip-hugger bell-bottoms, platforms, and Mick Jagger haircut with glitter around my eyes, and laughed it off.

In seconds, all four of us were laughing and having a good time over it.

You'd think that would be the most interesting part of the evening, but no. Not even close.

The show was great, and Aerosmith blew the roof off the place. The arena was emptying out, but Debbie and I weren't ready for the night to end. So, I get this idea...

Why not go backstage and see the bands?

Sure, I was just some random teenager. But, where's the harm in trying, right? So what, if they throw us out? The show's already over.

So, we did.

We snuck backstage and knocked on Status Quo's dressing room door. When it opened, we weren't fooling anyone. They knew we were just a couple of kids who talked their way past the security.

But they were really cool about it. They let us inside, and we got to hang out for a little while. It was my first real experience with "what happens backstage at a big concert," so I was completely soaking it up.

In situations like this, balls beget balls. I decided to check out the other dressing rooms.

I knocked on the door to Mahogany Rush's room. In a second or two, the door opens and there's Jimmy Ayoub, the drummer for the band.

"What the fuck do you want?"

Clearly, this wasn't starting as well. So, what the hell?

"Just thought I'd come by and say, hello."

"Go into fucking Aerosmith's dressing room and say hello."

BOOM! The door slams shut in my face.

He was an abrupt guy, that Jimmy Ayoub, but he didn't have a bad idea. I decided to give it a try.

But, as I rounded the corner to Aerosmith's door, I saw a couple of the biggest black dudes I've ever seen in my life. At this point, common sense came screaming to the front of my mind.

These dudes are paid to EAT kids like me. Maybe I better think this through.

I turned around and went back to Status Quo's room.

But, that was me, you know? I've had a lifetime of being in places I was not supposed to be, at times I wasn't expected to be there, and getting there in a fashion that I never should have been able to.

Nevertheless, there I would be.

For instance, I tended to ditch school a lot, and was always wandering around. Even at an incredibly young age. I'm not sure if it was just the fact that my parents didn't give a shit, and didn't care what I did, or if it was just the time and era. But, back in

Pittsburgh, I was literally six or seven years old, riding my bike all over town, miles from our house!

One time, I went to my grandfather's work. He worked in an auto repair shop, and I just showed up in the garage. My granddad freaked out and called Mum.

"What the hell? Bobby just showed up on his bike! How did he get over here?" My Mum, pissed to the gills, rushed over and picked me up. I was a nomad from birth. A very independent nomad.

That's probably why I loved dirt bike riding so much. It was a kind of independent freedom where anyone in authority had difficulty keeping a thumb on me. Pete got me a dirt bike for Christmas, but as luck would have it, the sky dumped rain on us for a solid week! I wasn't allowed to ride it in the rain, so I rode that fucker in circles in the garage.

When it finally cleared up, I took the bike over to a big field by the school and rode there. I was busted by Pete while riding in the street, which was another big no-no. I saw Pete coming around the corner in the car, hit the kill switch, and tried to make it look like I was pushing the bike along with my foot, which was total bullshit. Pete had been following me for four blocks, and he took the bike away for a couple of months!

I'll say that Pete and Mum had their hands full with me.

The South Bay hangouts at the time were the bowling alley, and a place called the Smokestack. Van Halen played the Smokestack early on. Come to think of it, so did I; in Airborn with Don Dokken.

The other hotspot was the local mall.

We hung out at the arcade a lot; complete mall rats. Drunk, stoned, hanging out and trying to get chicks to do stuff with in the various nooks and crannies of the mall were the cheapest forms of entertainment at the time. That, and house parties...A lot of house parties. Life was about getting laid and having fun.

People who know me, know that my voice is a bit gravelly. It gets a lot worse, the more I talk. I've got a theory as to why.

One day, we were hanging out at the mall, and some wise-ass calls in a bomb threat to the arcade. So, they emptied out that whole area. We had all been drinking, and that probably had a little something to do with what happened next. As soon as the cops gave the clear, we rushed back in to get all the free, unfinished games on the pinball machines. Some of the security guards were yelling at us, but, fuck them. We completely disregarded rent-a-cops.

They chased us down and literally started beating the shit out of us! This guy was choking me on the mall floor, banging my head into the tile. It was crazy.

I couldn't breathe, thought I was going to die, and ended up going to jail. What for, I'm not quite sure. Being drunk and a teenager, I guess. My neck was scratched and raked up, and I think my windpipe was fucked up, because my voice has been like this since.

I'd like to say that was my first scrape with the law. I'd like to say that.

I had skipped school one day, and was busted stealing an 8 track tape of the Allman Bros. Band - Live at the Fillmore East.

Of course, they called Pete to come get me, which got me into a new world of trouble. He put me on restriction, and whacked me upside the head. He didn't rough me up too bad. But, it didn't matter. There was no way I was going to stay cooped up in the house when there were other things I could be doing. I always had a plan.

Whenever they put me on restriction, I would just make it so unbearable for them, they'd let me go. I'd be banging around, wherever they were, tapping on stuff, hovering, fidgeting. Total annoyance. They'd have to cut me loose and let me go.

Pete might bellow, "You're on restriction for two months, Bobby!" And, in the back of my mind, I'm thinking, "Fine. I'll be out by Thursday."

Another scrape with the law wasn't my fault. Carol was supposed to watch Michael one afternoon, and she wanted to go out with one of her friends instead. She told me that if I stayed with Michael until Mum got home, her friend would give me the key to her mother's car and I could use it. So, I agreed. When Mum got home, I immediately split and thumbed down to Redondo where the car was. But, I couldn't get the goddamned door open.

A friend of mine and I tried to break into the thing, which we did. But, the key we were given was a house key. What the hell did I know about keys? I was thirteen. So, my buddy and me were walking back to Sepulveda Blvd., looking to thumb back home when the police whipped in and got us. They took us to jail because they thought we were stealing the car.

The coup-de-gras was in 1976. I was 17 years old and a friend of mine and I had been at a party with a couple of chicks. The party ended, and we wanted to keep going, but there was the problem of booze. The two of us dropped by this store and went inside. What the fuck we were thinking, I have no idea. It's funny how when your dick gets involved, dudes will do some stupid shit. I know what I'm talking about, too, because, I'm the original horn-dog.

My buddy and I decided to do a smash and grab. Each of us grabbed a six pack of beer and bolted. We were laughing it up, driving off, thinking we had gotten away clean. Alas, it wasn't to be.

A few blocks from the place, the red and blues start flashing behind us. We were stone cold busted. The cops got us and took us in. The fine was $125, which I didn't have, so I got an extension. When I went back, and the fine was still $125, and I still didn't have it.

The thing was, I was only 17, but my license said I was 18. In those days, you could get your license three different ways: through school, take the test, or provide proof of age. I had my baptism certificate that mis-listed my age as a year older, so I used it to get my license. And, I was afraid that if I told the cops I lied about my age, they would take it away.

What I didn't quite comprehend was that adults went to county jail, and at eighteen, I was an adult. At least, according to the state. Going to county was enough to break me from every wanting on the wrong side of the cops again. There are people in LA county jail that are barely fucking human. Pot and drinking aside, I would never do anything to put me back in there. You get a quick idea of what humanity is capable of in a place like that. It's very scary.

But, other than that, most of my existence was chasing chicks, getting loaded, and not giving a shit.

At fifteen years old, my life was going pretty good on one level, but was sucking balls on another.

I was working my ass off, trying to put together the beginnings of a career in music. School had pretty much become a non-event, and whether Pete and my Mum just didn't care, or it was a sign of the times, I got away with it with little or no grief.

Pete and Mum were struggling. I remember some horrendous fights. Just hideous battles, with shit breaking, glass flying, and anyone or thing caught in the middle taking damage.

It was only a matter of time, but when it actually happened, it came as a surprise to all of us.

One night, Mum simply didn't come home.

The majority of their fights boiled down to jealousy. Pete was really jealous of a guy they had both been hanging out with. A big cowboy named John Ray.

They had met him at a bar called the Tiki Hut, where Mum tended bar. Every weekend, they would hang out, and apparently, Mum was enjoying the time together a little too much. Because they would come home afterward and the battle lines would be drawn.

The fights seemed to last forever, and the whole house became like a mine field. You never knew which step you took was going to set off an explosion of some type.

Pete was never the easiest guy to get on with, so looking back at it, I guess he pushed her away. It wasn't exactly a loving atmosphere toward the end, and John Ray was probably just the first safe haven to come along.

Finally, push had come to shove, and Mum simply didn't come back to the house. We didn't know where she was, or if we would even see her again. That's how bad it had gotten.

Pete looked all over for her, but she was nowhere to be found. Two days passed before he found out she was gone for good. She sent a friend to the house to pick up all her shit.

Pete flipped out. He worked hard, and begged her to come back, but Mum refused.

Michael was the only one of us four kids that was Pete's. And, in a rage, he decided that he was going to take Michael and move back to Pittsburgh. Fuck my Mum, and fuck Carol and I too, right?

The next thing we knew, he was gone.

Mum had her new guy, who didn't really seem to be interested in kids, and Pete was completely over us.

Carol and I were on our own. She was eighteen, and I was sixteen. Just as well, I guess. I'd already been looking for a way out for a while, so this simply was the shove that I needed.

Carol was always my closest sibling. We were kindred spirits, especially when it came to music. We were tight, and still are. When Pete and Mum split, it was Carol and I who gravitated to one another for protection. We just moved out into a tiny little house in Torrance where we had a "Loco Lobo" Mexican neighbor who would terrorize us nightly.

He was this crazy-assed, drunk who would get loaded up on Tequila and just plague us. We were scared shitless of the guy. Those few months we lived in that house were some of the weirdest of my life. We didn't know what we were doing. We were so young. Just sixteen years old.

When Pete moved back to Pittsburgh, he had taken Michael with him, and the scene quickly got to be too much for Carol. She wound up following them.

I moved in with the Gonzalez family.

Tom Gonzalez was a bro, and his family was good enough to give me a place to stay. Bonnie, Mark, Pierre, Alfonzo and Rudy. They were really great people, and were good to me. It made the transition into premature adulthood a little easier to deal with, I'll tell you that.

I lived there for four or five months, before me and Marty Cory got an apartment together.

Mum had started giving me the social security money from my dad's death that she got every month. It was supposed to be for living expenses, but being like most things involving the government, it was never enough. It was only like $211 a month, but it helped. I got it until I turned eighteen, and back then, rent was only $190 per month for an apartment. Today, that same place probably goes for $1800. Utterly unbelievable.

So, I'd have a hundred bucks for rent, and another hundred for food, gas, and beer. Whatever else I needed.

The apartment with Marty didn't last very long, and when I was eighteen, I moved in with Mum and John Ray. I was there for maybe a year, but after all that time on my own, moving back in with her was not a good existence. She wanted to tell me what and when, and that obviously wasn't going to happen. So, it was really short lived.

And that's when I moved in with Jeni, Janet McCormick and Nancy English. We got this nice place in Torrance. Three girls and me in a two story, really old house. This was in 1976. It pretty much laid the groundwork for the rest of my life.

Nancy's boyfriend, a guy named Dennis O'Neil, grew up over in Culver City with a singer named Stephen Pearcy. I had known Pearcy from house parties and such, but didn't really meet with him until we had a party at our place. So, Nancy is to thank and to blame for all the shit to come. Right?

Sounds logical, I think.

I wasn't working at the time, and hadn't finished school, so it was time for some heavy decisions.

But, I was on my way, and I knew it. The decision made itself. My home away from home was going to be a mile and a half stretch of Sunset Boulevard, in Hollywood.

The Sunset Strip.

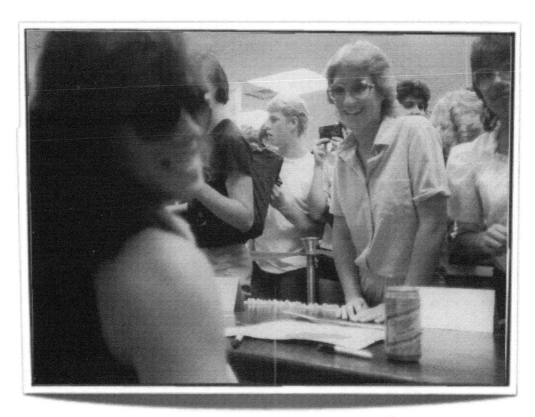

In store autograph signing in McAllen Texas, 1984.
Over 3000 people showed up! Absolute Chaos!

Stephen conducting class backstage, 1984.

4

THE GAUDY, TAWDRY MECCA CALLED SUNSET STRIP

The Strip in the late Seventies was something to behold. It was all music, women and seedy brilliance flooded in too much neon and pretension. This was the place I had imagined when Pete moved us out here in 1971. It was everything that it promised to be.

The Strip stretches from Crescent Heights Boulevard at its eastern end to Doheny Drive on the west, and it was the place where the best music of the time was being played. Every major player who went on to become part of the early 1980's music scene made a run through the Sunset Strip.

Van Halen, Mötley Crüe, Guns N' Roses, Metallica, RATT, The Doors, The Byrds, Bruce Springsteen, The Seeds, Frank Zappa, and Elton John played at clubs like the Roxy, the Starwood, the Whisky-a-Go-Go, and the Troubadour.

At night, the Strip was a grotesque slash of neon, where the giant billboards, clubs and sidewalk bars hover over a traffic jam of kids, people-watchers and celebrity wannabes. Everyone was an up-and-coming rockstar, a movie star, a star-fucker, or the kind of kid living in denial who eventually winds up a casualty of the scene.

I was in the middle of this machine, doing anything and everything I could to make that scene; hanging out at the Rainbow, where you could eat downstairs, then sneak upstairs to the super exclusive club where all the stars and rockers hung out. This was the place where John Belushi ate his last meal of Lentil Soup.

There was the Whiskey-a-Go-Go, where go-go dancing was born when a chick working as a DJ started shaking her ass in a cage above the floor. It was one of THE places to play if you were a band on the edge of breaking in.

The Viper Room used to be a club called The Melody Room, and was a gambling joint run by Bugsy Siegel in the 40's. It's also the place where River Phoenix overdosed and died on the doorstep.

The Roxy was a celebrity water hole that spends most of its time stroking the egos of the people who live just up the street in the Hollywood Hills.

There was the Starwood, The Troubadour, Gazzarri's (where Mickey Cohen was shot), the list was endless.

Every night, there were dozens of shows at these clubs, and they were always about the scene. But I took them as a chance to study, too. My new school was the Strip. What equipment were the bands playing on? What was the stage presence like? What was their style?

It was all about who you were meeting and where they were going. One of the coolest bands on the Strip that never went anywhere was The Wheeze Show. They had a lead singer called The Big K. Dumb name, but completely amazing singer. That whole band was unbelievable. But, they just disappeared into the Sunset scene, and I never heard what happened to them. That happened quite a bit, actually.

By the time I turned 18, I had already been in a couple of bands, in addition to Slicker. I had been jamming with Juan Croucier for a couple of years at that point. Despite the fact I didn't get the gig with his band Spike, he and I were fast friends. Most of the music scene viewed the two of us as THE new hotshot talent as far as rhythm players.

I was playing in a band called Airborn, opening for acts like Van Halen, Quiet Riot, A la Carte, and Wolfgang (which later became Autograph). We played the Starwood when Van Halen was still playing cover songs, right on the edge of breaking in.

Airborn was a pivotal point in my life from a friendship point. It was where I first met and worked with Don Dokken.

It's a funny story, how I met Don.

I was delivering pizzas one night in my 1961 Falcon station wagon, and needed to take a piss. So, I stopped at this donut shop on the corner of Aviation Blvd., and the Pacific Coast Highway.

I recognized one of the dudes inside as the singer from Airborn. I was still in Slicker at the time. The guys name was Don Dokken. We chatted each other up for a bit, and Don said that Airborn was looking for a new drummer.

It was tempting, but I had to think about it for a while. I mean, I wanted to leave Slicker because it had gotten stagnant and wasn't really going anywhere. But, here was another band, and true, they were playing bigger gigs. But, Don Dokken was twenty-two or twenty-three at the time. He was so damned old! To my seventeen-year-old mind, he was fucking Methuselah! In my opinion, if you hadn't made it by the time you were twenty, you weren't going to make it.

I went down and jammed with them anyway, and it really clicked. I joined.

We enjoyed some really strong success in the LA area in that band. There were shows at the Starwood, the Troubadour, the Whisky, and all the Strip hotspots. It was the end of 1976 or 1977.

I went to visit family in Pittsburgh in Feb. 1978. I came back to find out that I had been replaced in Airborn with another drummer. No phone call. Nothing. Don and I were like brothers. And, I mean that.

Airborn lasted for about a year and a half. My friendship with Don Dokken lasted for twenty-two years, and it ended badly. More is the loss, but we'll explore that mess as we go, okay?

I was back to splitting time between my domestic issues, finding enough money to make a living, and looking for that perfect band that seemed to constantly be eluding me. It wasn't easy.

There were some brilliant musicians in the LA basin, but there were a hundred times as many wanna-be's with no real vision.

When I was 21, I started going to Pier 52. Mick Mars was in a band called Vendetta, and Don Dokken and I had shared a rehearsal space with them. The guys in Vendetta were all eight to ten years older than me. They were a cover band, and we were originals, doing our best to get a deal.

They played Top 40, four or five sets a night, six nights a week, to pay their bills. It's a last ditch effort for a serious musician, cover work. But, I was just about to that point.

Mick was a good guy, but really reclusive. He has some sort of degenerative bone disease that's just getting worse with time. Tommy Lee set me up to see their show not long ago, when I lived in Houston. When I saw Mick on stage, I was stunned. I don't know how he was even able to tour. My gut hurt for the guy. It really did.

Anyway, I had been bumping around after Airborn, looking for a new gig. Desperate for one, actually. Juan Croucier and a guitar player named Ron Abrams pulled me in and created this power trio called Firefoxx.

Great band. It was in very short order that we started playing up around Hollywood in some of the bigger rooms. At the time, Airborn had been a pretty big act, and Juan had been in Spike, so we were able to use some of our popularity to our advantage. We started playing places like the Starwood and the Whisky. In fact, The Knack opened for us at the Whisky. That was in the summer of 1978, and by the end of 1979, those guys were huge.

Firefoxx was a hot act, but was pretty short lived. The reason being, I let Juan and his girlfriend Shelly, this unbelievable bitch from Palos Verdes, move in with me.

This chick was an absolute nightmare. A spoiled rotten, rich kid from Palos Verdes. Her parents had flipped out when they found out she was dating Juan; this longhaired, musician Cuban kid; and they forbid her to see him. So, I let them move into the apartment with Jeni, Nelly Herron and me.

On a side-note, I actually introduced Nelly and Don Dokken in 1976. They started messing around and continued to do so for almost 30 years. They have a great, beautiful daughter named Jessica.

I never got along with Juan's chick, Shelly. To give you an idea of what kind of person Shelly was, I came home one day and she had rearranged all of the pictures on the wall. So, I moved them back, and bitched her out. She was just staying there. She didn't own the place.

It was becoming evident that this arrangement wasn't going to work, but I did try to accommodate them. With Jeni and I, we were clean people. We weren't neurotic about it, like Helga on the tour bus, but we liked to keep our stuff nice. When it became clear that Juan and Shelly were slobs, I left a nice, friendly note for them.

"Let's all help clean up after ourselves, so that the place stays nice."

I wasn't an asshole about it, or anything. I was just trying to get my point across without creating tension with a face-to-face discussion.

I found the note wadded up on the floor later that day.

It wasn't long after that I came in, and the kitchen was in a total upheaval mess, as it had been many times before, with her and Juan not cleaning up after themselves. I told her to get in there and clean up the shit, or pack up and get out. She went out on the front steps and waited for Juan to get home. When he got in, she was out there crying. I told him, "Dude, I don't know why she's acting like this, but I'll tell you like I told her. I don't mind you staying here, but clean up the mess you make, or move out."

So, he moved out. Then he quit the band. A successful band on the rise. But, that was Juan. He was completely unreliable. He would never show up on time for rehearsals, just a complete pain in the ass nightmare. All through the days of any band I ever played with him in.

We did go demo a tape in Firefoxx, and it was really good. The closest we ever came in that band was when the legendary producer Kim Fowley, who produced the Runaways and others, showed some interest in us. Kim was a trippy dude. I remember he was managing Helen Ready at the time. And, he always referred to women as "stink". We were all over at the apartment one night, and he gets a call. He starts fumbling for the remote, trying to find it. "What's up", we ask? "My stink's on the Tonight Show." We turned the channel, and there was Helen Ready talking with Johnny Carson.

In the summer of 1979, cash flow had reached critical mass. I started playing in a cover band, called Rocket 88, named for this old Oldsmobile one of the guy's had, just to pay the bills.

In the end, it was a good thing. It really helped my playing. You just can't overplay when you're doing five or six sets a night. You'll have nothing left in the tank, come the fifth set. Jeff Naideau, who passed on about three years ago, was the singer / keyboardist; Bruce Bossert was on bass; and Steve Conrad was on guitar. And, we did cover shit. That was the first band I ever went out of town with.

We went to Albuquerque, NM in Jan. 1979 and did a two-week stint there at a place called Bo Jangles. We stayed at this hotel that had this weird bar across the street with transvestites and shit in it. I'd never seen anything like that, really. Maybe a little, up on Sunset. But even that was still pretty tame. We came back and played all over LA, then went to Flagstaff, Arizona. I was gigging more than I ever had. At five sets a night, I'm lucky my arms didn't fall out of socket.

Fire Foxx 1978. RATT Bassist Juan Croucier (left),
Me, Lead Vocalist and Lead Guitarist Ron Abrams (right)

Rocket 88 in 1979. We were playing in Flagstaff Arizona here.

Brother-in-law took this picture while working as an interpreter in Russia 1984.

5

LEAN INTO THE STRIKE ZONE,

AND TAKE ONE FOR THE TEAM!

Be careful out there. There are things that go bump in the night. Actually, there are things that go 'Give me your wallet or I'll kill you' in the night. - John Larroquette

It was through Rocket 88 (named after the old car from the 1950s, Rocket 88) that I wound up sacrificing a full year of my life to the court system.

We were finishing this two-week run at a biker bar called the Hard Rock Saloon in Long Beach. This was a really rough neighborhood, and our look in Rocket 88 was that of a bunch of skinny rocker guys. Usually, that would have made us targets for some abuse, but the biker's never fucked with us. I guess they figured that skinny rockers are better entertainment on stage than nothing at all.

In this particular place, there were seldom any fights. They were a "locals" kind of place, and there might be arguments once in a while, but nothing like what I was about to witness.

It was the final show of the second weekend. We did four sets a night, Wednesday through Saturday, for a two week stint. That week, during the Friday night show, some random black dude came walking in and was dancing at the front of the stage. That was *really* odd, because normally black guys don't like being around bikers, and vice-versa.

This guy, it turned out, had a saxophone with him, so he actually got up and jammed a Stones song with us. I think it was "Brown Sugar" or something. He wasn't very good, but it was funny and we were enjoying it, so everyone had a good time.

As I'm looking out at the club, the bar is straight ahead, and at the left of my vision is the entrance to the front door, and to the right are a couple of pool tables.

I noticed these two dudes hanging out at the pool tables. One of them really stuck out to me, because he looked like Chuck Daw. Chuck was my bro, but Chuck had an unfortunate habit of getting into trouble with the law. He was a really sharp guy, but not sharp enough to keep his ass out of jail. He had a drug problem which led to him stealing shit and getting collared for it.

When Chuck would get out of jail, he would just be ripped! He was always a big guy, with huge arms. My bro had some major guns on him, and could flat out fight when he wanted to. But, when he would get out of stir, the guy was a monster. All he had to do while inside was lift weights, and it showed.

Chuck was a total nice guy, you just don't want to be on his bad side. He would always wear those wife-beater T-shirts and have his hair cut real short.

There was this guy in the bar, and he had that exact same look. Fresh, prison reject.

For whatever reason, these two assholes caught the black guy outside after the show and beat the shit out of him. It really pissed me off when I found out about it.

The next night, those two guys were back. They really stood out from the bikers. The bikers looked like they were bikers. These two guys looked like jailhouse Arian Brotherhood.

It was at the end of the night. We always started out the evening with "Hello, Ladies and Gentlemen" by Cheap Trick, then we would close our last set with the same song, but change it to "Good night, Ladies and Gentlemen." We were in that song when this all went down.

During the song, I was watching this fight break out over by the pool tables. It started, then worked it's way around the bar and toward this fake doorway that was made by the entrance. The thing had been built out of 2X4s and drywall, and was used to guide traffic into the club. When those guys hit that thing, I could have sworn it was going to come down, the thing shook so hard.

We finished the song, and the ambulance chaser in me came to life. I went outside to see what was going on. The bikers were looking out, and I worked my way to the front by weaving in and out of them. I was a lot smaller than they were, to say the least. When I got out there, I was shocked by what I saw.

There was a really big guy sitting on the curb, with his arms behind him, holding him up. These two assholes were kicking him in the head, over and over! It was bad enough that the bikers went back inside. They were too scared to do anything. That's how un-nerving the thing was.

The Chuck Daw look-alike was a guy named David Lee something-or-other. He was the one who was really going off. He was kicking him in the head with everything he had, going, "You motherfucker! Don't you ever touch me!" His buddy kept going, "Come on, man. We gotta get out of here!" He kept trying to pull the dude down the street. David Lee broke away and delivered one more brutal kick to the victim's temple!

The guy on the curb looked like he had a bucket of blood dumped over his head! It was unbelievable. I thought he was dead, and just hadn't fallen over yet.

I had this moment where I was looking at the guy sitting there, and seeing myself in his place. Having my head kicked in, with literally no one raising a finger to help. It was a very weird scene. I could honestly feel myself sitting in his place.

There was nothing I was going to be able to do for him.

I ducked up the street and followed these two guys on the sly. I'd hide behind cars, or trashcans and wait for them to round the corner, then I would rush up and look around the thing to see where they went. Eventually, they got into a car, and drove away.

I got the license number.

I went back to the Hard Rock Saloon and started packing up my drums. By that time, you could hear the cop cars and ambulances coming to the scene. The guy on the curb was alive, how, I have no idea. That man was a fucked up as I've ever seen another human being. The cops came in and I pulled one of them to the side. I told them what I'd seen and gave them the license number. They thanked me, and I went back to packing my gear.

I was getting ready to pile into the van and leave when the cops came back. They asked me if I would go with them. They had the car pulled over with the two guys still inside, and they needed me to identify them.

"You're kidding me, right?" Those two guys were animals. They just didn't care, and they had destroyed a man who was easily twice my size, no exaggeration. I told the cops that I felt I'd done my civic duty. I followed them and got the license plate. I'd rather not get any more involved.

The problem was, no one else in the club could accurately identify them. Without my help, they were likely going to walk for what they had done. Civic duty can be a bitch, folks, let me tell you.

The cops talked me into going with them, but the agreement was that the two guys wouldn't be able to see me. The lights from the cop car would be in their eyes, and they wouldn't be able to make me out.

That turned out to be total bullshit.

The cops were nervous about these two guys, so there's no way there were going to have them get out of the car until they absolutely had to. I had to actually get out of the cruiser and walk up to their car to look in.

It was them. They looked right at me, and I looked right at them. It was a pretty scary lock of eyes, there.

I told the cops, and off they went to jail. They were both out on parole, and now they were under arrest for attempted murder!

The district attorney interviewed me, and I told him the whole story. Surprise! I was going to be their number one witness. I was the only one who followed them to the car. I saw the whole thing. So forth, and so on.

I was concerned, because now I've got my nuts up on the chopping block should these two ass clowns beat this charge. They didn't seem the forgiving types.

When they started the trial, I'd go down there, get on the witness stand, and the first thing they would tell me to do is, "State and spell your name, and give your street address for the record." They did that every day, with David Lee and his buddy looking on. It got to a point where I looked at the judge and went, "Should I just give these guys my apartment key? Would that make it easier for you?"

It was reaching a point where if these guys walked, I was going to have to take my family and move someplace no one ever heard of me. It was that kind of a situation.

I had been to the court so many times for testimony. Each time, they had to read the transcripts of the last appearance, I started getting a little more ballsy and irritated. I was getting a lot more matter of fact with everything.

I remember the first time the guy who took the beating was in court. I remember him being in the club, because he was a pretty big guy. He was probably 6'4". He reminded me of a friend of mine named Crow, because he had the same kind of curly hair.

This guy comes up to me in the hall.

His mouth is wired shut, because his jaw had been broken in several places, his nose was broken, he had contusions and stitches all over the place, broken arm, concussions, it was unbelievable what the guy went through.

But, that dude never fell! I remember that like it was this morning. He sat on the curb with his hands behind him, holding himself up, and he never fell. THAT was amazing, considering the beating those two jack-offs threw him. He would just take the force of the kick, but not fall over where they could stomp him. I can visually picture this right now.

He came up to me, and through his clenched jaw, goes, "I want to thank you for what you're doing." I looked at him, and he was soooo skinny. He'd lost so much weight because of his wired jaw.

I go, "What the fuck happened that night?"

He says, "Those two were going off on a guy with a pool stick. I just stepped in and stopped them, saying, 'Hey, you don't need to do that. If you gotta fight, do it without the stick.' Then they both turned on me."

The guy was just trying to stop some random guy from getting his head beat in with a pool cue.

One of the witnesses was a waitress. One of them was the club's owner. But, I was the focus for the prosecution.

At one point, I got into an elevator with one of the guys who gave the beating. Not the David Lee character, but the other one, and his family. I didn't knowingly get into this elevator, mind you. I was rushing to catch it as the doors were closing, and I caught the door and got in. Then I noticed that it was them in the elevator with me. It was a really uncomfortable moment, because they looked at me, I looked at them, and then he goes, "Let's take another elevator," and they all got off.

I went down in that elevator, and I was going to my car. I was looking around, all nervous and shit. It was a tense time for me. I was scared shitless.

One of my last trips to court, I had been out the night before to Pier 52 with a bunch of friends. We finished the night off at my place, partying and drinking and snorting blow. The party went all the way into the morning.

I called the lady at the prosecutor's office and told her that I was sick, and my car was broken down. I wasn't going to be able to make it in. Please let the District Attorney know.

The D.A. called me right back. I don't know if he could tell that I was loaded, or not. Most likely, he could. But, he goes, "You have to be here today. This is one of the last days of testimony. You have to get here. It's a very crucial day."

I told him, "Well, I don't even have a car, and I don't have money for a taxi!"

He goes, "Hey! How would you like to be in jail with your buddy, David Lee? You think that would be cool?" He wanted to put me in a cell with that fucking Neanderthal and his partner? Thank you, too, asshole!

"Are you kidding me, dude? You're threatening me with jail? After all I've done to come down there and testify?"

"It's against the law to refuse to come down and testify, Robert."

I told him, "I'm not refusing! I don't have a means of transportation. You want me down there, then send a car to get me!"

I was pissed off, but not so much that I wanted to go to jail. They sent a court car to get me, and down we went. I went back in for the last day of testimony, and bottom line, those two guys got sixty years each for that, and I hope they forgot my name, because that was thirty years ago. Parole is going to be an issue soon.

There you have it. Rock N Roll.

After Rocket 88, I left and joined a band called Romeo with this guy named Roger Romeo. He had been the lead guitar player for Legs Diamond in the mid-70's. It was me, Roger, and Juan's brother Tom Croucier on bass. It was like a power pop band, that thing was. We did shows around LA, and cut a demo.

It was a good time, and I enjoyed playing it. I had known Tom since I was a kid, because he was Juan's older brother. Tom was a great musician; great singer. He was one of the guys who never got his due in this business. He just wrote amazing songs and was always trying to chase the deal.

I was in Romeo for that whole year. 1980. Which was the hottest summer I've ever seen. Hell in August would have been cooler. We played gigs all over town, sweating like whores in church the whole time, completely miserable from the heat. Cars littered the sides of the road at any given time, all overheated and baking in the south California sun.

I remember when I met Roger. I hooked up with him through an add in The Recycler, a local Los Angeles magazine that you can put adds in for various items or services. Musicians who are looking for new gigs use it all the time, because it's free.

I went up to Roger's house in Hollywood, and he answers the door wearing these big purple sunglasses, and this ridiculous mini-skirt looking bathrobe kind of thing.

I was thinking, "What the fuck is this?" I had my kit in my van, so I brought it in and we jammed. We clicked, so the next day we had the bass player, this guy named Liberty come in and join us. That was the band at first; Roger, Liberty and I. Then we got rid of Liberty and got Tom.

It was a great fit. Tom and Roger played and sang really well together.

Once again we were off to conquer LA.

6

BEATLES FOREVER!

"Everybody loves you when you're six foot in the ground." - John Lennon

Things were really starting to get lean for Jeni and me. At least on the music

front.

I was finished in Rocket 88, and while Romeo was still gigging, it just wasn't enough to pay the bills. I had to find a job, and soon. I had done it before. Pizza delivery; painter; I started to work with a steam cleaning company in 1977, and eventually bought a couple of machines. A friend of mine, Chuck Daw, and I worked them, but it was never meant to be my "real" income. For the first time, I had to sit down and seriously consider the immediate future.

Then I got the opportunity, through Chuck Daw's mother, Iris, to go to work in Manhattan Beach at the Ford dealership. Let me just say, I love Iris Daw. She's like a second mother to me. She really cared for me, too. It's like I was one of her kids.

At the time, Manhattan Beach was a pretentious, "too-much-money" kind of place. Still is, actually. There is a kind of hierarchy to the beach communities of southern California. It starts to the south, in Long Beach, and then moves through Palos Verdes.

Those places are pretty loaded. Then you get into the "middle beach / family beach" areas like Redondo and Hermosa. Then, Manhattan Beach is the next community north.

North of Manhattan Beach just gets richer and richer. El Segundo, Marina Del Ray and the Venice Beach Boardwalk, then there is Santa Monica and on up into Malibu. But, regardless where you are, if you're on the beach, money drips everywhere. I've just always felt that Manhattan Beach thought a lot higher of itself than it should have.

If you want to make money on the straight, you gotta go where the money is. So, the beach communities were it to me. Manhattan Beach had one of the strongest dealerships in the country at the time. Manhattan Beach Ford. And, with Iris as my ally, I was able to meet with the management of the place. I knew I could do that job, and do it well.

I've always been a good salesman. It didn't matter what, really. I did it in the steam cleaning business. Always upselling the add-ons, like Scotch Guard, menthol, and conditioners.

The next thing I knew, I was a moonlight rocker, selling cars in one of the richest communities in Southern California. I would put a little gel in my hair, slick it back to make it nice and tight, and no one was the wiser. You'd have thought I belonged!

That job was going well. I was making money, and they gave me a demo car. A brand new, 1980 Mustang. After having my 1966 Dodge Van, and every other piece of shit car I had owned up to that point, that Mustang was awesome! Believe me.

At that time, Jeni and I still lived in the apartments on Vanderbilt Lane in north Redondo; The same place that Juan and his psycho chick from Palos Verdes were staying with us in.

Nice cars, good house, plenty of cash, but that doesn't do it for you when you're still chasing your dreams. I hadn't made it as a player. I was playing gigs every once in a while, not making a lot of money at it, and I wasn't getting any younger. At twenty-one, I was almost as old as Don Dokken was when I met him. And that's too old, when you haven't been discovered yet!

Something had to give.

Romeo was still playing gigs, but they were coming fewer and fewer. Roger Romeo is a great guy. A really good friend. But, at this time, Tom and I were getting very itchy. Romeo just didn't seem to be advancing.

On December 8, 1980, I had gone to work like normal. Sales were still really good, and I was driving a nice, new Mustang demo car.

It was sometime late-evening, only a few minutes before we closed, and I was on the showroom floor, working with an elderly couple. We got a lot of elderly who would come in late, and just look around. They were bored. So, they would come in and just grill you about different things on the cars. They weren't really there to buy, just to pass the time. But, I approached everyone as if they were going to buy, even at ten minutes to close.

They were asking me questions about an LTD. The car stereo display was about 15 feet away, and it was on. No one ever paid any attention to it, really. But, then it said:

"We interrupt this broadcast to bring you breaking news."

That immediately grabs everyone's attention.

"We are receiving reports that moments ago, outside of his New York City apartment, controversial music icon, John Lennon, was shot."

I couldn't believe what I was hearing. I was stunned. My gut immediately wadded itself into a fist, and was struggling to punch its way out of me. I've never felt quite like that since, and I don't think I've ever been the same.

It was time to close, so I took my cue. I asked the elderly couple to come back the next day, and I went home. I had the radio on the whole way. I'm dialing through stations trying to find out what happened. Initially, they were saying that he was shot by a pregnant woman, which was disturbing. What the hell did he do? Knock some groupie up? Have an affair? What?

Up to this point, no one knew he was dead yet. The stations were only reporting that he had been shot. Then, I turned to a station, and they were playing "Imagine." I knew then, he was gone. I got home, and Jeni and me were watching TV on this the whole night.

To say that John Lennon and the Beatles are icons doesn't do it justice. Lennon and McCartney were the teachers. Not just for me, but for everyone. They taught how to write classic, beloved songs the whole world over. They taught me music through every Beatles record I'd had since I was five years old. I'll challenge anyone to come up with another band, other than the Beatles, who have had more of an impact on modern music. And, who among the Beatles or any other band was more powerful than Lennon, other than McCartney?

I'm always irritated when I hear the media compare someone or some band to the Beatles. Especially Nirvana. But, we'll get into that more, later.

It sickens me when someone comes along and compares something like "The Back-Door Boys" or the "Spice Whores" to the Beatles. Anyone that musically retarded should be hog-tied and beat with a bamboo cane!

It's almost like they are forcing these others on us in an effort to replace what was probably the greatest musical force since Mozart. It's fucking asinine! There is only one Beatles. Only one John Lennon. Only one Paul McCartney. Only one Beatles! There will never be another, so deal with it and stop trying to shove some other second tiered talent down our throats. We're big enough to make our own judgments about who is genius and who isn't.

Lennon, McCartney and the Beatles were genius. Jimi Hendrix was a genius. He transpired talent, and completely changed the way the electric guitar is played. Led Zeppelin was genius. Again, few modern rock bands are untouched by Zeppelin. Maybe The Rolling Stones. Maybe Aerosmith.

Everyone else is a copy, or a variation of what those guys did. And, just because you can play like Hendrix, does not make you Hendrix. If you mimic a genius, it doesn't make you a genius by association. You're a fucking Doppelgänger, bro. And, if you don't know what that is, go look it up, learn from it, and then go out and be something original and brilliant.

Maybe, then, we'll call YOU a genius.

But until then, shut the fuck up with calling someone the next Beatles, or the next John Lennon. Give me a break with that shit.

When I heard that Lennon was dead; that he had been murdered by a cowardly bag of shit like Mark David Chapman; I was crushed deeper than anytime in my life. What this miserable fucker did was steal one of the beacons of music from us. From everyone. He's a miserable, urine stained shit-streak on the face of humanity, and I can only hope that some dude in prison takes a barbell in his hand and does to Chapman what they did to Dahmer. Bust his goddamned head in. This guy deserves it, on behalf of the world.

How could something like this happen? Where is the rhyme or reason to it? None of it made sense. The whole event shook me to the foundation, all with the radio still droning on about Lennon bleeding to death in his wife's arms.

The next day, I was due back at work. And, I couldn't get out of bed. No other figure, beyond my own family, was more important to me than Lennon. He and McCartney were more important to me than the President or the Pope.

I called Jeff, my manager and told him, "Listen, Jeff. You've seen the news all over the place. John Lennon was murdered. I just can't come in today, and try to concentrate on moving units. I just can't."

Jeff was one of those 50's kind of guys who grew out of that, and into someone with no real understanding of music. He had been to a couple of Romeo shows, and once you got a couple of drinks in him, he knew how to have a good time. But the next day, it was all about the car lot. That was who he was, and it was who he expected me to be. Needless to say, he really didn't get it.

"Bobby, you're a good salesman. I know you're a musician and everything, but you've got a future here. I really need you to come in, and I can't give you the day off because of this. You need to decide where you're purpose lies. I need you to come down here and work."

"I can't do that. So, where do we go from here?"

"I just need to tell you, Bobby. Either you come in to work today, or your job is on the line."

Wow. I couldn't believe they were going to do that to me on the day John Lennon was assassinated. So, I got in the car and went down there.

I dropped the keys to the demo on his desk. No hesitation.

"See you later. Beatles forever."

Then, I walked the three miles back home to Jeni, where we spent most of the next week in near total seclusion, mourning the loss of one of our heroes in life. John Lennon.

Don McLean wrote a song in the early Seventies called "American Pie." It was a tribute song to Buddy Holly, who had died years earlier in a plane crash in Iowa. In that song, he referred to that moment as "The Day the Music Died."

I've heard that statement used several times over the years when talking about other events. Hendrix. Morrison. Joplin. Most recently, I heard it used to describe Hurricane Katrina and it's destruction of New Orleans.

But, for me, that statement will always be best used for the day Lennon was assassinated. I just couldn't imagine music going on without him at the epicenter of it.

But, I was wrong.

In the midst of this social and emotional funk, I got the phone call that started everything changing.

Don Dokken called me and said, "There's this project that Dieter Dierks is putting together with Vic Vergat. They need a rhythm section. You and Tom interested in auditioning for it?"

I didn't know that much about Vic, but I'd heard a little of his stuff, and it was pretty good. Plus, the guy was recording in Germany with Dieter Dierks! Dierks is a legend of a record producer. He's most famous for being the guy who did all the Scorpions albums, and for working with Accept. The chance to do some recording with that guy at the board was too good to pass up. So, Tom and I went down and auditioned.

We saw a lot of the usual suspects there. Frankie Banali was waiting in the wings for his turn, as were a number of other LA noticeable. Tom and I did the audition, which went really well.

I was still really down over the loss of Lennon, so I can't say I had any real good vibes that week, but on December 12, four days after the worst news of my life, I was told that Tom Croucier and myself were the new rhythm section for Vic Vergat.

We found out we got the gig, and what it paid. A whopping $400 a week. That was less than I had made at the car dealership, but I was on my way to Germany, and was playing music with a platinum producer. Fair trade, say I.

The problem was, how do we tell Roger that we were quitting Romeo? Roger is a great guy; a great bro. He was at my house for the Super Bowl this last week. So, he's a lifelong friend. When we told him, he took it really hard.

We had the core group of followers, ten or fifteen chicks who followed the group Romeo, and we agreed to do one last show at the Madam Wong's in Chinatown. When it was over, Roger broke down, as well as our fans. That was a really hard scene for us. It was raining that night, and the whole thing was very sad.

I had a tough time with it, because on some level, you feel you're letting your friend down. There's a part of you that questions your loyalty in a moment like that.

However, we had to pack our shit, because it was off to Europe. For me, the music had certainly not died. Not yet.

I had a really good time playing with Roger Romeo.

7

BOMB SHELTER REHEARSALS

"If my answers frighten you then you should cease asking scary questions."

- Pulp Fiction

Europe, for anyone who has never been, is awe inspiring, and a little overwhelming. It's like John Travolta says in "Pulp Fiction", "It's the little differences. A lotta the same shit we got here, they got there, but there they're a little different." My first experience in Europe was one big, "Royale With Cheese" moment. Literally.

I got off the airplane, and went to a McDonald's to get something to eat. I wanted a Quarter Pounder with Cheese and french fries, and I got a Ziffel flunder mit Käse, und Pommes frites. I hope it was the same thing. Who the fuck knows? But, I was able to get a cold beer with my Ziffel flunder. A fucking beer at McDonald's. That would explain the grin on the Hamburgler's face.

Before we left for Europe, the Vergat management group gave us each $500 to go buy our "rock clothes." So, I boarded the plane on that trip in a brand new pair of blue suede boots. Eat your heart out, Elvis.

I proceeded to get totally shit-faced on that flight, not realizing that when I got off, I had to read signs and billboards that were not in English. Not so easy to do when you're hung over. It was a pain to figure out where the hell I was going.

We lived at the Hotel Trost in Cologne, Germany. Let me say, Cologne is one of the most amazing cities on the planet. Just a stunning, fucking cool, really interesting city. The Cologne Dome was built in the 8th century, and the magnitude of that place, this monolithic structure, is mind-boggling.

Cologne Dome is a giant, Gothic cathedral. You'd expect either the Pope, or Dracula to come out the front door, depending on what time of day it was. I remember standing there thinking, "How the fuck did they build something like this in the 8th century?" It's insane. Just crazy.

During World War II, Cologne was leveled by the Allies and their bombs, twice. But, it was pretty obvious that our boys were told, "Do not bomb this thing." It's that kind of a place. Even war shouldn't touch it.

The only other place I've ever seen like that is Edinburgh Castle, in Scotland. We played a date there on the Vergat tour. The castle is built on top of a 300' cliff, and seems to be built right into the side of the thing. It's amazing that men could build something like that so long ago. Absolutely awe-inspiring.

The Trost Hotel was a trippy kind of place, too. It had, like three floors of just bedroom suites, so it was pretty small. Then on the main floor was a bar, a big monolithic -looking oak bar. Real old world German stuff.

I remember I would always spend time with Mrs. Trost, but I could only talk to her through her son, because she didn't speak English. She was a great lady, really sweet, but would chain smoke like a fucking demon! She'd walk around this room with a halo of smoke above her head all the time. Her teeth, fingers, even her fingernails were a dull yellow, and she smelled like an ashtray. But, she was a really sweet, old world lady.

During down time, I would hang out with her in her apartment at the hotel. She was an absolute fiend for American movies, especially the older classics. Actually, considering the place, it was probably all she could get.

So, she would have her old television set on, and we'd watch movies on video tapes with the likes of Gary Cooper, Bob Hope and Bing Crosby, or John Wayne, together.

It was hysterical, because every one of them had been dubbed into German, so I was watching movies that I had seen many times as a kid; but I couldn't understand a damned thing they were saying. But, watching her light up with that twinkle in her eye and laugh hysterically at Bob Hope movies was genius. It made for a very bonding moment between the Yanks and Krauts.

Imagine having four or five German beers in you (which is like drinking a case of the watered down American stuff, I swear!), listening to John Wayne saying, "Hallo, kleine Dame. Sie sicher schaut ziemlich heute an," to Maureen O'Hara. All the while, trying to figure out what he said, and if that lame assed line was enough to get in her pants!

To add to the random enjoyment of hanging out with the Trost matriarch, she had one of the all time greatest laughs. And, the best thing about it, is she would just bust out with it at random moments during whatever movie we were watching. I'm sure something was done or said on screen that she thought funny, but I haven't a clue as to what it could have been.

Her laugh would start out as the classic, old lady smoker's laugh. It was deep and raspy, but without warning, she would suck in a blast of air and let out with this high, warbling giggle. It sounded like the love child of Celine Dion and Ernest Borgnine on crack! I would laugh my ass off, not at the movie, but at this insane Joker giggle she had!

When we weren't watching movies together, and her son was nowhere around, I would still try to talk to her. She didn't understand a word of English, so, for some reason I would use my hands a lot more. As if my wild American gesturing would somehow get my point across. After all, everyone understands the sound of English, right? It's the body language they don't get! Right?

All this would do is make her laugh that wacky laugh of hers, which pleased me to no end. She was a cool woman, that one; despite her occasional, random piece of Nazi memorabilia.

Her son, Wilhelm, used to hang out with me while I was there. Wilhelm loved to tell Jewish jokes. His eyes used to really light up if he heard a new one. He would laugh really hard. It was bizarre, and pretty fucking creepy, to tell you the truth. It was 1981, so that stuff had happened a long time ago, but it wasn't THAT long ago!

In school, you'd read about the events and effects of the Holocaust and stuff. So to sit and listen to this otherwise cool dude tell Jewish jokes with such glee...it was like talking autopsies with Dr. Kavorkian. It made for some very strange vibes and moments in that place. We were still old enough that our fathers had been in WWII and shit.

You would go down the stairs and through a doorway, and that would be the bar and restaurant. Then there was another door in the far wall. You'd go through there, and there was a bowling alley. Not like a real bowling alley, though. At least, not like an American bowling alley. It was Middle Ages sort of shit. They had these little bowling balls, about the size of a cannon ball, that you would throw toward the pins. The alleys were really narrow and small, compared to what we would have at home. You could tell it was really old. Way older than Americans have a mental grasp on.

Mrs. Trost would show me pictures of SS guys down there hanging out in that bar and shit, you know. So it was really bizarre. I was 21 years old, and in a whole new world.

We rehearsed in the basement. Well, really the basement's basement. You'd go down these stairs into this really cold, damp, stone-walled room, and that was the basement. But, then they had dug out this other, subterranean thing below that to use as a bomb shelter during the war. So you'd get to this basement, which was really trippy and old, with it's creepy stone walls and shit. Then, they had dug a hole, and there was a track that ran all the way down where they would run supplies when they had to hide in the shelter. There were spigots all the way along the walls, and the place was domed shaped. That's where we rehearsed. We had our PA and gear, and we jammed out in a subterranean bomb shelter beneath a centuries old German bar.

Bizarre.

We got to know the guys from the Scorpions really well. They were really tight with Dieter Dierks, and would come by and pick us up to go party. Matthias Jabs and Herman Rarebell would cruise up in their Mercedes, and off we'd go. We'd go out and get loaded, then check out Whitesnake or whoever was playing in Cologne. Or, we'd just go out to the local bars and drink. I'm a good friend with those guys to this day. Cool bunch of dudes. In fact, I have a great story involving Matthias and a flying fish while taking a trip to Catalina on my boat. But, that's later.

Speaking of driving in Germany, if you've never seen the Autobahn, you've got to check it out! It is an experience unlike anything I've ever had. You hear the phrase "no posted speed limit", but it doesn't really sink in until you are on the thing.

The label had given us a driver, and this little Citron for him to carry us around in. It's a Swiss car, that can really scoot when you need it to. We would have our driver take us on the Autobahn where we would be going 80 or 90 miles an hour. Just flying along. And, every once in a while, our driver, who had a huge German accent, would go, "Oh, 'ere zay come again!"

We'd look behind us, and see a Ferrari or a Porsche gaining on us at 180 miles an hour. We were doing 90, and this thing would roar past us like we were standing still. Fucking amazing. Then, just a few minutes later, "Oh, 'ere zay come again!" And another one would appear.

Amazing place, Germany.

Band Romeo Greg Mastrogiovanni (guitar), Tom Crucia (bass),
Roger Romeo (vocals) and Me, 1981.

Vic Vergat band, TV show shot in Bremen Germany, 1981.

1981, The Vic Vergat band.

Vic Vergat group; Tom Croucier, Vic Vergat, and Me in Basel Switzerland 1981.

8

THE CURIOUS CASE OF A CONSUMMATE HUSTLER

Around this time, I get a call from Don Dokken.

First off, let me say that he's a bit neurotic, our Don is. We were like brothers for so long, almost twenty years. I got him out of so many jams, mostly because he was, and still is a pathological "story enhancer."

The guy was ALWAYS on the hustle. ALWAYS.

At any given time, Don had five or six girlfriends who all had money, and were always funding him. He would be juggling them around, but, sooner or later, he'd get busted. It always fell to me when they needed someone to call, crying and upset. I'd wind up spinning them a story to bail Don out of trouble and get them calmed down until the next time it happened. Just say that Don has some pretty serious baggage floating through his gene pool.

He calls me, and is like, "Dude, I swear to God I'm about to fucking lose it! I'm gonna have a nervous breakdown. I gotta make it. I gotta make it right now. Fucking, you and Tom are over there. I got you that gig. You know, Vic Vergat, fucking going on tour with Nazareth. I'm sitting over here fucking dying." He didn't have a band put together at the time.

I'm like, "Don, why don't we do this. Let me talk to Dieter Dierks (who Don introduced us to) and see if he'll let you come over here and record your demo. Tom and me will play on it. See if you can get a deal over here."

So, I did. I set the thing up with Dieter. Don scrounged the money up to come over, but he had absolutely NO money while he was here. He slept in my bed, in my little hotel room in the Hotel Trost. I remember that I drew a "Line of Death" down the center of the bed with pillows. I said, "Don, if you cross this line in the middle of the night, you fucking die. I swear to God! Don't even poke your FINGER at me."

His first night there, I made him put his socks outside the window because he'd been wearing them forever, and they smelled like a demon's crotch! Not that I've ever smelled a demon's crotch. It's a point of reference.

Don is a strange guy. As I said, he had these weird habits, like the "story enhancing." He'd tell stories to people, and I'd know they were total bullshit. I'd know, because I had been there to witness whatever story he was elaborating on. Then he would look at me and say shit like, "Isn't that right, Blotz?" And, I'd be going, "No, dude. Not really."

But, for all his bullshit, Don and I were bros, even though he fired me from Airborn. We used to always be able to talk about our careers and that incessant journey to "make it." I had my bands, and he had his bands. We were just two guys trying to grab the brass ring. Neither of us were going to give in, and that sort of made us brothers-in-arms.

I've had a lot of really good times with Don. Lots of good memories, just none coming to mind at the moment.

He was a really good mechanic, and would always help me out with my cars.

So, Tom and I wound up going in and rehearsing with him. We had stopped rehearsing in the bomb shelter, and had moved to this theater where all the seats had been removed. We would work on the stage show with Vic, and then rehearse the stuff we were working on with Don, right after.

We cut 3 songs. "Stick to Your Guns," "Paris is Burning," and some other song, I forget. Something Young. Young something. "Young Girls," I think it was. They were all on the "Breaking the Chains" album.

Tom and I wrote on some of this stuff. "Paris is Burning" was one of George Lynch's songs. He was in a band called The Boys, and it was one of his songs. Don and I used to play gigs with them when we were in Airborn together. We used to always jam this song of theirs called "Paris is Burning" at Airborn rehearsals, because it was a cool song. Don said he had acquired it from George; bought it or something. So we worked it up, and I wrote the last lyrics in the song. Tom did some writing on it as well. We put everything together. We worked our ass off on all this tape we did with him. It was so good, that the songs went onto the Breaking the Chains album untouched.

Michael Wagner is the famous German engineer who has produced Warrant, Skid Row, the White Lion records, on and on. The guy has skins on the wall. He engineered the work, and this demo with Dokken was fantastic. Absolutely kick ass work. Don took the demo, telling Tom and I, "Look, if anything happens, you guys are getting half the publishing on these songs." It wasn't a big deal. We felt we were just repaying the favor. You know? He put our names in the hat, and we got the gig and were off on a major arena tour. So, it's the least we could do for a bro.

So, Don goes down to Hamburg and he comes back with a briefcase full of money! And, we're like, "What?!?" He got his deal, you know? Then, he gives Tom and me a hundred bucks each. That was it. We never got any writing credit. No publishing. Those songs went on the Breaking the Chains record just as we had recorded them. We were uncredited, and by then he had gotten George Lynch, Mick Brown and Juan Croucier in the band.

Typical Don.

9

"YODEL-AY-EEE-YODEL-AY-EEE-YODEL-AY-EEE OOOO"

"Mary had a little sheep; With the sheep she went to sleep; The sheep turned out to be a ram; and Mary had a little lamb." - Steven Tyler

After being in Cologne for two months, we boarded a train at the Cologne Station, heading for Switzerland for the beginning of the tour.

While we were over there, Tom and I were in a hotel in Basil, Switzerland. We had just gone out on tour. We were listening to some Beatles stuff, and playing backgammon with the television on and the sound down. I happened to glance over and catch a map of the US with a big red spike stuck right in Washington DC. I was like, "What the fuck?" I turned the sound up.

That was when we heard about President Reagan being shot. They showed the footage over and over. It was a very strange, disturbing feeling to be in a foreign country when someone tries to murder the President. Then, not long after that, some wackjob tried to kill the Pope. First Lennon, then Reagan, and then the Pope. It was a weird, disjointed time.

Most of the holidays are the same, with a few exceptions. April Fool's Day is NOT one of those exceptions.

While we were still in the hotel in Basil, I had this fax sent to me, and faxes were new then. I had never heard of a fax.

"What the fuck is this? A fax? Okay… "

I'm reading this fax, and it's from Eddie Van Halen. It says that Alex has been injured, and they need a fill in drummer to finish out the tour with.

I was freaking out! Was this real?!? This was Van Halen! The biggest band on the planet. It seemed like a possibility! I mean, I'm here in Europe, about to go out on a major arena tour. Maybe I'm coming into my own, you know? They knew me from when I was in Airborn. Maybe they knew I was making records and out on tour? I was going to play with VAN HALEN??? This better be fucking real!

I called Jeni, and was like, "Did anyone from Van Halen call and ask for the contact phone over here, or something?" She said, "No". I told her what was going on, and then we were both freaking out! The mighty Van Halen, and I was going to play with them!

I rolled with this thing all the way into the night, calling and trying to find out any information I could. The end of the fax had a little blurb saying they would be in touch with all the important info. Then later that night, we were all liquored up in the bar, supposedly celebrating, when Vic starts laughing. He and Tom had set up the whole thing.

"April Fool's, fucker!" The bastards…

I got him back, though. After we got back stateside, we had a couple of weeks off before we went out on the road again. We were going to do a couple of rehearsals, just to tighten things up before heading out again. Vic was waiting for us down at the rehearsal studio.

He had been staying at the Oakwood Apartments in Burbank at the time. So I got hold of him through Pricilla, the girl who worked the front desk at the Burbank rehearsal studio.

I threw a bunch of bass in my voice and said, "Yes, Mr. Vergat? This is John Sweeney (or whatever name I made up in my head) over at the Oakwood Apartments, and we seem to have some problems over here. Apparently there has been a burglary and your apartment was broken into. Everything has been turned inside out and there's a lot of damage done. Are you a musician, or something?" He's like "Yes, I am." And you can hear the crushing doom in his voice. "Well, the people who did this were seen leaving the apartment with guitars and things. Did you have instruments in there?" He's like "Oh my God, yes, I did!", with his Italian / French / Swiss / German, only Americanized, accent. "Well, the place has been ransacked. Some of the guitars have been smashed, and are in pieces in the room. You should probably get here as quick as you can."

So, he's hauling ass the 5 or 10 miles from the studio to the apartments, just sick to his gut.

I specifically waited for this moment, so I could be late. When he got back, I was already at rehearsal. He comes walking in and I'm like, "We're even, motherfucker! From Basil?" It was completely hysterical. A huge laugh.

I haven't seen Vic in years and years. He surfaced at my house back in 1994, and stayed with me for a week. His hair was all white. I mean, really white. "Albino with a bleach habit" white. Completely tripped me out. The guy was ten years older than me, and in great shape; just white headed in his mid-forties. He's back in Switzerland, as far as I know. I heard he was working in a studio over there. But, who knows?

After we had finished rehearsing, and Don had scurried back to the states with his briefcase full of money, we went on tour with Nazareth in Europe.

Incredible. Absolutely one of the highlights of my life. Packed to the rafters at the arena shows every night. Just a huge sea of people each night.

We had a couple of guys in the crew who were monumental assholes. The label had hired these guys, and sort of shoved them on us. One was the soundman, Night Bob, who had cut his teeth for seven years on the road with Aerosmith.

The guy was a New York type. The tour who was a New York attitude on wheels was Rabbit.

Because they had finished a couple of tours with some names, they had all these stories to tell, and that was pretty cool. But, they always talked shit. Always. And, they would do it in that really condescending New York way, like they wanted to fight.

I tended to just shine them on, but Night Bob was rolling on me one night, when we were touring the U.K. He was just giving me nonstop grief, and Tom got sick of it. He walked up and called the guy out. It was a thing of beauty. Night Bob just caved. The guy went down like Heidi Fleiss with cashflow problems. A total pussy moment. I gotta give props to Tom for that. It was a beautiful thing to behold.

Touring with Vergat had some interesting moments. Most of them coming from Vic himself.

Vic used to have a habit of washing his ass in the dressing room sink before each show. That's right. You didn't misread it. He would wash his ass in the sink.

Tom and I would be laughing our ass off at this. We'd be going, "Vic, what the fuck are you doing? Why are you washing your ass in the sink?"

He'd say, in his funky Euro-accent, "I don't want my ass to stink while I'm on stage!"

"Who the hell is going to be smelling your ass while you're on stage?"

"I don't know, but if they do, I don't want it to fucking stink!"

There's an odd logic to that, especially when you've been stuck in Europe for weeks on end. But, logic or no, Tom and I were not going to wash our asses in the sink. Let them stink! If they were dumb enough to sniff our ass, they deserved what they got!

Those damned ass-sniffing Europeans!

FUCKING WITH THE ROOKIE

10

FUCKING WITH THE ROOKIE

"Do me a favor. Just kick my ass, okay? I'm not asking, I'm telling with this. Kick my ass." - Artie Fufkin - Spinal Tap

We came back to the states and toured over here, also with Nazareth, and then the Joe Perry Project was added. I was playing huge arenas, at only twenty-one years old. I was sure that I had made it!

Rock music is racked with its touring traditions and superstitions. One of those traditions is for the headlining act to prank the opening acts on the last night of a tour. Our last show of the tour was in San Antonio, Texas.

However, this was not to be a traditional closing night. The crew, bastards that they were, decided to fuck with the rookie, meaning they fucked with me. They told me that it was customary for the OPENING act to prank the HEADLINER, not the other way around.

I didn't know! I was a kid on my first tour!

But, never one to buck tradition, I was told to put baby powder in Darrell Sweet's hi-hats. When he came on, he hit the hi-hats, and baby powder exploded out of the thing!

A huge cloud of this shit completely encompassed the stage. Pete Agnew, their bassist, was so completely pissed off that I thought he would stroke out on stage. The guy was spitting at me! He was ready to kill!

By the end of the first song, Darrell's glasses and beard were solid white! He looked like he was ready to be tossed into a frying pan. The whole room stunk like baby powder, and, dear God, they were so fucking pissed! I'm lucky they didn't beat the shit out of me. But, again, I was a kid! What the hell did I know about it? I was just doing what I was told!

You can never trust a road crew. Not ever! They're pranky little pricks who would love nothing more than to get you beat to death by a gold record artist!

The guys in Nazareth did come hunting for me after the show. And, I did plead my case.

"Those dudes told me to do it, man! I didn't know!"

Nazareth was a great band, and obviously they had a good sense of humor. At the least, they were forgiving, as evidenced by my ability to still breathe. Either they were forgiving, or their lungs were so permeated with baby powder, they couldn't breathe enough to stomp the shit out of me.

Jeni was pregnant with Michael during the American leg of the tour, so she was coming out with this huge belly with Michael in there.

Oddly enough, it's when things are going the best that the worst shit tends to happen. The American leg of the tour was done by late November of 1981. We were gearing up to do it all again. We went into the Capital Records Studios, which are in the basement of the world famous Capital Records Building, and cut thirteen new songs. We were looking for a producer, when suddenly, there was no more money.

The band was funded by a guy named Yurig Margward. He was a filthy rich, publishing type who had pieces of Penthouse Magazine, Poprocki Magazine, which was a European version of Metal Edge, and tons of other things. The guy was the principle financier for Vic, along with the label. He just decided he didn't want to pay for the Vergat thing anymore. The label picked up an option at EMI Europe, but dropped the new record stateside. Vic wound up going back to Europe and releasing the new album, but I didn't make the trip.

Tom was still in as the bassist, but Frankie Banali replaced me on drums. I never got the straight answer as to why, but in hindsight, I think it worked out for the best

At that moment, though, it completely sucked! Just like that, I was done. No more band. No more answers.

I was, out of a gig. I had been touring Europe and America with Nazareth and Joe Perry, playing to 10,000 to 13,000 people a night, just a few short weeks before. I had gotten my Ludwig Drums endorsement, and my Paiste Cymbals endorsement while in Europe. Now, I didn't have a job, and a baby coming in a month. Jeni was still working, we took in a roommate to help with the bills, and I started looking for a new gig.

It was all the way back to square one.

11

INTO THE CELLAR

Some of them want to use you. Some of them want to get used by you. - Annie Lennox

I was trying to get into a band called Bruiser. I was talking to Rick Ramirez (not the serial killer, don't get excited) about the gig. Vinnie Appice (Carmine's brother) had recorded a monster album with these guys, but he wasn't going to tour with them. So, I was jockeying for the gig.

Ramirez kept me on the line forever. He was always telling me, "Yeah, yeah, yeah, we're going to do it. Any day now." I learned the whole record, was ready to go at a moments notice, but they still kept me hanging for months.

During this down time, Stephen Pearcy had started coming around, and he was really pushing for me to join RATT. I had met Stephen through a guy named Dennis O'Neil, who was dating one of my roommates. So, I went to see RATT, and I didn't like it. I thought they were okay. It just wasn't what I was looking for. So, I turned him down.

About five weeks later, Stephen buzzed me up again, and was like, "What's going on, man. Did you get that thing?" I had told him I was trying to get the Bruiser gig.

"No, dude, they're still not doing anything." So, he tells me that they're playing another gig, and they have a new drummer, but they don't really like him either. So, why don't I come down and check them out again?

I went and saw them a second time, but it wasn't that much different from the first. Same music with a different drummer who wasn't very good. But, I was sitting around doing nothing, so I thought, "What the hell. I'll join these guys until something better comes along."

Thank God nothing better did, because it's fucking RATT! It's my life, now. And, it has been since that day. March 1, 1982.

Dennis O'Neil's mother's house was where we rehearsed; right in her garage. Juan Croucier drove me down there with all my shit in the back of his truck to play. Then he was heading off with this Top 40 band he was playing in.

The chemistry came pretty quick. I was a good drummer, and had a lot of experience. They could sense that, I think. Plus, we were all influenced by the same bands; Aerosmith, in particular. We were all close to the same age, and had the same influences, and that became a launching pad. We were just like, "Well let's have at it. Let's fucking do it." And, that set the tone for the band.

At rehearsals, the bass player really wasn't good. I was trying to get him out of the band. I wasn't being malicious about it, or anything. I was just trying to get him tightened up some; more in sync with me as a drummer. I was trying to get the rhythm section of the band going so there would be a foundation to the music.

The first gig we played together was at the Country Club in Reseda. Our bassist took a hit of acid before the show, and was just gone; completely out of it. He couldn't play any of the songs. So I told those guys after that, "Hey, it's him or me. I'm not playing with this guy anymore. I've got Juan Croucier. We've been playing together since we were seventeen. He is great. He's great on stage." So, I brought Juan into the mix.

Suddenly, RATT had elevated its music several notches in one big step. Juan and I were rock solid as a rhythm section.

I write songs, and I've learned to do it pretty well, but my strengths were always in arrangements musically. I could come up with parts. "How about going from this, to this to that, and maybe add this chord..." That sort of thing. So, instead of sitting down with a couple of guitars in a writing session, like those guys had been doing, we would take those sessions as a group and turn them into tunes. It wasn't that Juan and I "fixed" everything wrong with RATT. We simply brought out the potentials.

Warren was really young then. Seventeen or eighteen. And, he and Stephen used to butt heads a lot. It got so bad, that at one point in 1982, with Stephen's prodding, we actually got rid of Warren. Marq Torien, who's the lead singer for the Bullet Boys, came in and played guitar for us for a couple of months. He was an absolute wackjob, and we did not dig the whole thing.

Robbin Crosby, Juan and me, I can't remember if we really wanted Warren out, or if we were just tired of all the bullshit fighting between he and Stephen. It didn't matter, because we went out and got Warren back, then just continued on like nothing happened.

Our mentality was not so much a family mentality as it was just a gang. It was "us", out there to get "them". "Them" could be anything from an individual to the world, depending on the moment.

We were out to plant our flag and take what's ours.

Back in the early days, Stephen and I pretty much handled the booking. And, we were playing the same places, a lot. It wasn't like we had 35 venues that we circulated. For that matter, we weren't playing 30 shows a month, either. We would do anywhere from 3-5 shows a month, then we would go up north, or something. We weren't playing a lot, mostly weekend stuff, then occasionally during the middle of the week. But, we pretty much played every weekend.

Promotions was interesting. Stephen was a fanatic about it. We had a group of loyal fans, which they call street teams today, who would go out and flyer the gigs of other bands. Whatever was happening, at the Troubadour or the Whisky, we'd have someone there.

Pearcy was really into all that stuff. He'd always be out putting posters on poles and stuff. Me, I never did that kind of shit. I was just way to jaded. I was like, "I'm not going out into the cold, or whatever, to put posters and handbills up on telephone poles." It was pure laziness, I'm sure.

It wasn't long after that we played with Glen Hughes and Pat Thrawl. They had the Hughes Thrawl band. We headlined there a handful of times with bands like Steeler opening. Tons of others.

One of the first big gigs that RATT did was at Magic Mountain, the amusement park. May 27, 1982. We did two shows there in this huge amphitheater, and Great White played with us. It was completely packed for both shows, and that was a huge crowd. We were like "Ho, boy. Here we go. This shit's on!" That place held well over 3000 people.

Then we did a gig at the USC Mardi Gras. Which had close to 15000 people. It was really weird. Everyone in LA was just freaking out over RATT at that time.

Beyond that, those early days were on the Hollywood Circuit. Sunset Strip. The Roxy, The Whisky a Go-Go, the Troubadour, all of those places. We did some gigs up in Northern California. And, beyond that, we really hadn't ventured outside LA yet.

To my recollections, Marshall Berle was the first real manager to come out of the woodwork when we started to get a bit of a name. That was around August of 1982. Let me put it this way, we were meeting with him in August, and after all the meetings and shit, we probably went with him about a month and a half later. So, by fall of 1982, we were with Marshall Berle.

When Berle first saw us, we had been doing much better at the live shows. We were a lot tighter of a band. It had reached a point where we obviously had to get a record out, and, Berle saw that. Almost immediately after signing with him, we were in the studio recording our self-titled EP.

Music Man Studios on Melrose was where we recorded and mixed. It was really cool, because you'd walk out and Melrose is just like the streets of New York; Stores, clubs, restaurants. It seemed like it was overnight, but in very short order, RATT was selling out shows all over the LA club scene.

Suddenly, this thing was getting exciting. Musically, it had stepped up significantly. RATT was no longer the so-so band it had been when I first saw them, and the crowds were eating it up.

I had been in popular bands around LA a number of times, but it was never like this. Literally, you'd pull up to gigs we were playing and there would be lines clear around the corner. We'd sell out two shows a night, that sort of thing.

Like most things in this business, when you start making a little noise, you tend to draw a lot of attention. We made a lot of fucking noise! Before we knew it, we started having agents, and managers sniffing around us, looking for that next big band. Mötley Crüe was already a monster on the club circuit, and we were right on their heels. In fact, we were becoming fast bros with those guys.

We got a call from Marshall Berle, Milton Berle's nephew. Everyone on the Strip knew who Marshall was. He was Van Halen's manager when they got their deal, and through their first couple of tours. And, now, he was managing the Whisky a Go-Go.

Marshall wanted to manage the band. He thought we were really good, and he and a partner were going to put some money up for an EP. Robbin, Stephen and I took that first meeting with him.

I never really had a good feeling about Marshall, and I told Robbin and Stephen about it.

"I don't know if I trust this guy."

Marshall would never look you in the eye when he talked to you. That's always a bad sign. A person's eyes reveal too much, so if they're hiding them, that's bad news. But, like so many young bands, we were so eager that we signed a shitty deal. Marshall and his partner basically owned everything on the EP.

The recording of the EP was a whirlwind. We did all six cuts on the record in five days, working an average of eighteen hours each day. The engineer was a guy named Liam Sternberg, who is most noted for his work with The Bangles during their "Walk Like An Egyptian" days.

The EP was released on Time Coast Records, which was Marshall's record label. He had ties with Alan Niven, who was working for Enigma Records at the time. Enigma's distributor was Greenworld Distribution, so the deal was made and Greenworld distributed the record for us.

It was such a blur while recording for that record, that we really didn't have a chance to fuck it up. It couldn't be over-produced, because there wasn't time. There were no marathon runs of retakes, because there wasn't time. We couldn't risk screwing up and having to do it all again, because, you guessed it, there wasn't any fucking time!

As a result, the work on the EP is one of the truest representations of RATT that there is. It was raw, lean and nasty, just like the band. That's probably why it did so well, and put us on the map. It didn't have time to be pretentious. It just "was."

We finished that record around 8:00 am on Thanksgiving morning, 1982. I remember walking out into the morning sun, feeling like I was being released from a solitary confinement prison cell; emerging into the light after years in inky darkness.

We each crawled off in our various directions. My day was just beginning. I got home, got a shower, and helped Jeni get the kids ready. Then we were off to Jeni's parents house, as we always did on holidays. I spent the whole of that day sleeping in the back seat of the car with my feet out the window. I was a daylight zombie.

But, we had an EP in the can, and it was a kick in the balls! I could hardly wait.

When the EP came out in 1983, we had a single being played on KMET *and* KLOS at the same time, which was very rare. Usually, it was just one or the other. KLOS had a show called "Local Licks", and they started playing "You Think You're Tough". They got such a response for it, they put it into rotation. I heard it on the radio while driving my Datsun B210, and had to pull over to the side of the road, I got so excited.

There was an immediate reaction in LA We started selling a lot of records. One thing I can promise you; when you sell a lot of records on your own, the labels that didn't want anything to do with you suddenly come around and started bidding.

RATT was on the edge of breaking in.

But, the dysfunction that would prove our undoing in later years was already starting to bubble up. Juan was still playing with Dokken. He had signed some stupid deal that kept him bound to that band in return for a slave wage regular paycheck.

Dokken had signed with Electra, but they weren't doing anything. So, it became like a race. Who would break first? RATT or Dokken? Juan was playing both against each other, not wanting to leave one and commit to the other.

We got into the studio first and recorded the RATT EP. Juan played on it, but he still wouldn't leave Dokken. The thing with Juan is that at his core, he is only interested in himself. Everyone has a selfish streak, and I understand that. But, he's a total mercenary in this business, for sale to the highest bidder. I understand that you've got to look out for #1, but he puts people through pain in the way he conducts his business.

On July 27, 1983, we were playing at the Beverly Theater in Hollywood. Lita Ford was the opening act. She was so pissed that she was opening for RATT, she decided to show up late. In fact, she was so late, that we wound up just bumping her from the show, and went on. The show was completely sold out.

There were label reps scattered all around the place, all wanting to meet with us "for a couple of minutes." We were making the most noise around town, and everyone knew it. Doug Morris made it through the door before anyone. At the time, Doug was the President of Atlantic Records. He had heard of us through one of his A&R guys, Kenny Austin, who's father, Moe, was the legendary boss at Warner Brothers.

Now days, Doug is the top dog with Universal Music Group. He's probably the second or third most powerful person in this business. Just an incredible dude. This is the guy who signed us. He walked into our dressing room with Beau Hill at his side, and that was the night we got our deal with Atlantic Records.

We left the show that night, and were immediately on the road up to San Francisco to play a show. We drank the entire way there, celebrating our new deal with Atlantic. We arrived at the hotel in Frisco around six in the morning, and as we poured ourselves out of the van, exhausted and hung-over, I noticed something on the sidewalk.

Some enterprising member of San Francisco's best had written into a square of wet cement the words "MEN LOVING MEN." I turned to Stephen and just shook my head.

"Dude, we're not in Kansas anymore."

Back when I first joined, and Joey Criss was still playing bass with us, we played a gig that was so low paying, it was crazy.

We stopped at a Floyd's Market, a little grocery store. We'd made something like $50 as a band, before the split. Joey and I were trying to get some food, and Joey tried to steal a thing of cheese and a package of meat.

They caught him.

The clerk knew me, because I was coming in there all the time, and they guy was like, "Man, what's up with this shit?" He was just glaring at Joey, and wanting answers from me.

I just looked at Joey and shook my head. "Fuck, dude." He was embarrassed as shit. So, I look at the clerk, and go, "Bro, we're musicians, and we just did this gig where we got paid $50 among us. I didn't know he was THAT hungry, but we're putting our money together to get some food. It will never happen again."

The guy was like "Yeah. I can let it go. It's cool. It's just not cool to come in here and do something like that, you know? But you come in all the time, so I'll let it slide." I go, "Duly noted, so no worries."

We get outside and I look at Joey. "What's up? Why'd you do that?"

Joey's just whipped by the whole thing. He's completely humiliated.

He's goes, "Complete fuck up, man…"

I reach down in between my waistband and pull out a thing of cheese, and a thing of lunchmeat, and we both start laughing. "Okay, we're alright, then."

Not to say that we were thieves or shit like that, it's just that when you're really hungry, and it's food, you gotta do what you gotta do. I don't steal. I don't want to steal. But, hunger is a motivator of stupid things, you know?

Juan had been so incredibly problematic with the Dokken / RATT, dual band thing, that we had parted ways with him, briefly. Joey Criss was playing bass for us, at the time. But, Joey wasn't cutting it. He was a great guy, but was really timid when it came to the music and performance. He didn't have that nasty, edgy punch that Juan did musically. Plus, he just wasn't as tight a bass player as Juan. I was REALLY missing that, musically.

So, we went to Juan and said, "Look man, here's the deal. We signed with Atlantic, so you're either in or you're out. Right now. Because we're about to start recording." He was in. Dokken was out. The rest is RATT N' Roll.

August of 1983, we started working with Beau Hill at the Village Recorder. We demoed "Out of the Cellar" with Beau. We needed to see that it was going to be a good pairing, which it worked great. Subsequently, we went back to the Village Recorder, which is on Santa Monica Blvd. in west LA.

The Village Recorder had a lot of albums come out of there. Most notably were a couple of the Fleetwood Mac albums. I remember we went in, and Kenny would be coming in with pockets full of blow. He brought Stevie Nicks in, one time. It was a trip, you know?

We were coming into another world. We demoed three songs, "Round and Round", "Wanted Man", and a song called "Reach For the Sky" that didn't make the "Out of the Cellar" album, and had nothing to do with the album we did later by the same name.

Those sessions were sort of a match making session to see if we liked Beau as a producer. It turned out great, so we were like, "Dude, you're the guy." Beau was our producer for five records after that.

Juan and I were the only ones who lived in South Bay. The rest of those guys lived up around Hollywood. So, Juan and I would carpool to the session everyday. I remember we would be arguing over who was going to pay for gas each trip.

We were pooling change and shit, just trying to get us there. That's how broke we were; buying fuel with pennies. It was the irony of our lives. We were bitching with one another as to who threw in the most quarters to get gas, and then going to a recording studio to do a record that would go on to sell five million copies.

It was an exciting, virgin territory for us. We had just signed with Atlantic. We had this new album we were working on, and we got this little taste of money, about $7500 each. Then, about a week later, our manager called us and says "We gotta give this money back!" We were like, "What the fuck do you mean, give it back?"

I never really got the straight answer on it, but there was some sort of protocol, bookkeeping thing involved. We eventually were paid the money, but they did make us give it back. I think I told them, "I've spent most of mine already", and only sent back a couple of thousand. It was a complete lie, but what the hell.

RATT Mansion West. That was what we called Stephen's apartment. It was located in Palm, a little spot between Culver City and Hollywood. Stephen and Robbin had that place. It was a little one bedroom, and they would alternate who got the bed. The other two guys took the mattresses that were thrown in the corners.

We would all hang out there and get drunk, get loaded, write songs, fuck chicks...I mean, all the groupie types would bring food over there and take care of them. I was a little different. I always had a nice place, a wife, and kids. Jeni and I were living in a nice apartment in Redondo, then we moved into a house in Manhattan Beach. We lived comfortably, so I never really was a constant participant in the squalor and mess of the usual LA rock band.

Stephen actually lived with Jeni and I for a while right after I joined the band. It was shortly after Michael was born, Stephen rented a room from us. He was the complete opposite of Juan when it came to being a roommate. Stephen was a clean freak! We never had to worry about a mess with that guy in the house, that's for damn sure.

For a while, Jeni and I were forced to downsize in money a little. We left our $950 place in Manhattan Beach for a $700 place in Redondo Beach. It wasn't a month later that Don Dokken called me and said he had this fantastic duplex in Hermosa Beach. One side was a 3 bedroom, multi-level spread with a full ocean view. The other side is a two-bedroom tri-level, as well.

I went over to look at the place and was just freaking out at how nice it was. It was a brand new place. Don was like, "Yeah, you can get your side for $700 a month, with a two year lease." So, I had to get out of my lease in Redondo. I had to talk my way out of it. I had talked my way into it, and then talked my way out of it. The landlord let me. Like I said, I've never had a problem selling something.

So Jeni and I moved into one side, and Don, Alan Niven (manager of Great White / Guns & Roses) and Guenella (his wife) moved in on the other.

So, that was interesting. Especially when, six months later, we found out Don had lied to us to get in the place himself. The lease wasn't a two-year, it was only six months. And, at the end of it, the rent jumped from $700, to $1400. We wound up having to move out, because of Don's bullshit.

But, for a time, the rest of the band were living like slobs in RATT Mansion West, and I was living in a great house, with an ocean view.

While we were living in Hermosa, in the duplex next to Dokken and Alan Niven, George Lynch moved in with us. We rented him a room for a couple of months.

He was cool. He's a trippy person to live with; a trippy guy in general. We used to sit around and play his guitars quite a bit. He gave me a few lessons, stuff like that, but he moved out owing me $30 on a phone bill.

He still hasn't paid it. It's been almost 30 years, and every time I see him,

 like at a Christmas party a few years back, I mention it. "I'll get you, dude. No problem!" Then he doesn't pay me. It's become this big running joke.

That's okay, though. Because after 30 years, the interest has that shit juiced up to around $300.

None of that mattered, though, because we were all pirates, or Pi-RATTs, as we called ourselves. So invariably, I'd end up at the RATT Mansion West getting lit and doing what Pi-RATTs do.

My first gig with RATT at the Whiskey late March 1982, Looking Mick Jaggeresque.

Engineer Jim Farachi during the recording Invasion Of Your Privacy 1985.

12

15 Months: A Lesson In Debauchery

"Every city in the world always has a gang, a street gang, the so-called outcasts." - Jimi Hendrix

In the beginning, I had a hard time picturing RATT headlining arena tours. We had some really good songs, but something was missing. The successful bands, the bands who went on to be huge; Van Halen, Mötley Crüe, Bon Jovi; they all had that "thing." I don't know what that "thing" is, but, it can't be learned, only discovered. You gotta have that "it factor," or the group never gets out of the gate.

Stephen has a cool voice, but when we started out, to me, he didn't seem to be a great frontman. Given our success, it's safe to say that I was shown wrong, but only to a degree. I always felt, and still do, that Stephen has another level to his ability. It's right there beneath his surface, and if that guy ever tapped into that, who knows what would be accomplished. He had some great hooks; some great music; but there was more to be had with his voice and lyrics.

Stephen and I have always had a tumultuous relationship. I was seeing other front men who were just taking control of a show. They dominated. I knew Stephen had that in him. I knew it was there. But, that's not Stephen's style. He's never been a "run around the stage - high energy" front man. He stalks around the stage, sort of like Rob Halford in style. He isn't Vince Neil, Jon Bon Jovi, Bret Michaels, Jani Lane; sprinting around all over the place. I guess he's more traditional. He's more old school. I just didn't recognize it. I saw all our contemporaries out there stealing our audience with very energetic, calculated front men who knew exactly what the audience wanted, and then giving it to them.

Stephen has that air of mystique about him, but his vocal performance and live image often wasn't as compelling. There was too much cigarettes, too much weed, and his voice really suffered as a result. However, this last tour we did in 2007, he was as professional and driven as I've seen him. He wasn't drinking. He watched a lot of old tapes from past arena tours and tried to dial in to where his strengths were; trying to bring it to the stage, and suddenly, it was almost like old times, which is good for us all. The guy has a immediately recognizable, franchise voice. You hear him, and you know it's RATT.

These days, I can listen to the radio and hear a song, and I can't tell who it is. All the singers sound the same, and so much stuff isn't discernible from the other songs you hear. Stephen is discernible, that's for damned sure! But, he's old school, and you'll never teach the proverbial old dog anything. He's a complicated underachiever.

Back when I first met Stephen, all the way back in 1977, he was just another random rocker guy with a party band from San Diego. I think he was still trying to figure out what to do with himself. So, I didn't really pay much attention to him. We were really young, and just starting bands. But, having spent time with the guy, I'll tell you this. I don't think Stephen has EVER figured out what to do with himself.

It's interesting to watch what this business does to people. Some of the things it brings out of a person are surprising. In Stephen's case, it brought this sort of neurotic, paranoid, isolationist thing. These things weren't there in the beginning, as much. But, as we went on, they surfaced quickly. He became so unreasonably difficult to do business with, but, I think it was just the effect of fame. Everyone was out to get him. So, he would get them first. The response from the rest of the band only seemed to fuel that separation.

Starting out, we all hung together. We'd go to parties and shit, but that gradually stopped. While we tried to stay close, it was a struggle. By the later years, it was near impossible.

A good example is on Warren's 25th birthday, I threw a surprise party for him. It was a complete success! The surprise was huge! But, the surprise was ... Warren never showed up! I had all these different rock stars there, all our friends. I tried for hours, but I couldn't get him on the phone. There was tons of food, drink, a cake. Little did I know, he pulled an all nighter and missed his own birthday party. and he missed his own 25th birthday.

It was pretty humiliating for him, really. He was really embarrassed. He actually had one of his signature snakeskin guitars at my house, and told me, "You can just keep the guitar, man." He felt so bad. I was like, "I'm not taking your guitar, dude. That's your gig."

I felt really bad for him that he missed that.

It's a miracle that we've gotten to where we've gotten, because, at our base level, we're all a bunch of lost superstars who just can't seem to find ourselves. Jesus! Who would RATT have been if we could have just found our identity and KEPT it? I think about that. I think about that more than I should.

During that first tour, I was the only guy who had ever done an arena tour. So, for a little while, I was a little bit of the elder statesman with the band. It was short lived, though. Especially once we were into the meat of the tour. Everyone was an expert by that time.

But, in the beginning, the guys were really inquisitive. Especially since the Vergat tour spent some time with Joe Perry, and we were all major Aerosmith fans.

For me, it was amazing to be on the same stage with Joe Perry. Even though he was so loaded on that tour, he was hard to talk to. Joe was out of his mind and weird. He would go up to the microphone, loaded out of his skull and sort of mumble into it. "Yeah, I used to be in Aerosmith." That statement would just be dripping in sarcasm. Then he would throw his guitar up in the air and let it come smashing down.

WHANG!

He was really fucked up on that tour. Self admitted, too. He talks about it a lot in the Aerosmith bio, "Walk This Way". That's a great book. It's really revealing about this industry, and them as a dysfunctional bunch, just like us.

So, I couldn't see us doing it in the early days. But, I was proven wrong. The audiences really started responding. When we started getting popular, we evolved.

We had gone from being a band on the rise, to recording our first full-length album, within a few weeks. An album that would go on to sell five million copies worldwide. We were signed in mid-August of 1983 and formed our plan. By mid-September, we were in the studio. There was no "cooling off" period where the label tries to pump up the name and buzz of a band before recording them.

It was Slam! Bang! Here we are!

We started getting into the meat of the recording on "Out of the Cellar" around the middle of October. It took a couple of months to get it done, but the album was finished by the end of November, early December. By the time it was released, in February of 1984, we were heading out on the road.

RATT's creative process started out just like other bands. It was a normal writing session. At first, Stephen had a lot of songs that he had written on his own, but they needed some help. Robbin was the guy who really jumped in and took care of that. At that time, Warren was really young, but he was a guitar riff machine. So, Warren would come up with a great riff, which Robbin would work the melody up around and Stephen and Robbin would write the lyrics. Then we would all work on the arrangements. That's the way it ran up through the EP, and the writing sessions for "Out of the Cellar."

After that, things started heading south fast. Juan became this egomaniacal rock-beast. He was a pain in the ass to work with before, imagine what it was like when we were famous. Stephen became a problem, too. He was a rockstar! Suddenly, our work ethic became something to be compromised, and he wouldn't show up to rehearsals or writing sessions. He would come down after we had been working on music, then he would take home a cassette, and be writing lyrics and melodies. We had no idea what he was doing.

But he is driven! No doubt about that. Unreasonable to a fault, but definitely driven.

By the time we reached that first show was in Denver, Colorado at the Rainbow Theater, the flood was building behind the gates, and we had no idea what was about to happen to us. The album had just come out, and we had just shot the video for Round and Round. I.C.M. The flood gates were about to open, and it was going to be swim or drown...for a long time.

Every move was huge. Every step was epic. Every thing we did was a gigantic leap forward, and as much as we thought we were ready, we really weren't. Fame is like that. You fight and fight; struggle and starve; lose faith, then find it again. Suddenly fame hits like a wall of water, and you've become that "Cheers" episode where everybody knows your name.

I was the only one in the band with home life commitments. I had Jeni. Michael was just a little toddler, and Marcus was a newborn. So, that pulled at me. But, the rest of the guys weren't married, and didn't have kids. I had cemented in my head exactly how I wanted to be a father, and while my job was one that dictated me being away from home for long periods of time, my family, especially my children, were crucial to me. It made it very difficult at times.

I remember a time on the "Out of the Cellar" tour where we had a vote. We were deciding whether or not to go home early. It had been almost fifteen months, remember.

Juan was talking down to me, saying, "Look, Blotz, I know you miss your kids, and everything. I really miss my dog, too."

I just looked at him and went, "You're comparing my kids to your fucking dog?" The prick! The balls on that guy, man!

Turnabout is fair play, though, because it was Juan who made a huge deal about the European leg of that tour. His wife, Debbi, was pregnant, but wasn't due until November. We were touring the UK in October, and Juan wanted us to not do the tour because he was afraid he would miss the birth.

I could understand his feelings, wanting to be there for the birth, but we weren't going to cancel the tour because she "might" drop. We had business to do, and a record to support. He rightfully needed the time off, though, so we were going to get Jeff Pilson, the bass player for Dokken, to fill in for him. That completely freaked Juan out, and he did the tour.

He stayed, but he bitched and complained almost non-stop about having to be there. It was constant whining and moaning about how we fucked him over! In the end, we finished the tour, went home, and Debbi didn't have the baby for another two weeks.

And, that was that.

I was home in Hermosa when Michael took his first steps, which was an incredible moment for me. But, when Marcus took his, I wasn't there. I was on the road. It's been little things like that all through my career that have given me a dual existence of pleasure and pain. I made an incredible living for me and my family, but it has come at a cost. Like the song says, "Nobody rides for free."

Don't misunderstand. I'm not saying that Jeni and I would have made things work out, had I not been on the road so much. In fact, things probably would have deteriorated a lot sooner with me around more. But, there's always that thought in the back of your head when you have a family. That thought says, "They don't even know you." It's a cold-faced liar, of course; but, there's times when that thought can be really fucking convincing.

We were on the road so much during those early years. "Out of the Cellar" was the longest tour we did. Fifteen months. But, the "Invasion of Your Privacy" tour, with Bon Jovi opening, *immediately* followed. That thing was 8 months in the states, then we went to Europe and Japan. All of our 80's tours were over a year each.

I love the road. I don't want to sound like I don't. Playing gigs every night in front of 13,000 people is a physical rush. Better than any high you could achieve. I know, because I've tried a few in my day. In fact, playing live is very much like a narcotic. You can ride it, but it can hurt you in the end.

On the Cellar tour, our managers kept us informed of the album's progress, at first. But, we watched the Billboard Top 200 every week. We would take the charts page and hang it up on the wall of the bus. When we did that first video, "Round and Round," it really started to go sky high. MTV was rotating that video in half hour increments, so we got *tons* of airplay. Then, we really watched the album really fly up the charts. Around May, June, and July, we were moving 100,000 albums a week, which was unbelievable. It was exciting for us, as a band, to see our work start catching on like that.

We were headlining clubs up through April of 1984, and then went out for a while, opening for Ozzy Osbourne. After Ozzy, it was back to headlining the clubs; then a month opening for Blue Oyster Cult; then it was back to clubs again. We bounced back and forth like that up until the summer months. By then, the album was doing so well that it was time to headline some big shows.

We did 222 shows on that tour. By the end of it, we were spent! We were so shot, that we were having problems remembering what city we were in. It reached a point where I quit looking at the itinerary. It was just a long list of dates, yet to play. All that did was remind me the end of the tour was nowhere in sight. It was an indefinite thing.

On the other hand, you're completely excited. We were building this monumental momentum as a band. I remember the first big payday, $15,000 to play a festival in Kalamazoo.

That show was amazing for a number of reasons, money not withstanding. It was May 27, 1984. Ozzy, Triumph, Accept, RATT, Quiet Riot, and Mötley Crüe were all on the bill.

Kevin Dubrow, from Quiet Riot, kept trash talking Mötley Crüe, RATT and just about every other band who was popular at the time, in the media. In every interview, he would be talking shit. I guess what he didn't realize was that their fans were our fans, too. When he started talking shit, the fans picked up on it and saw it for what it was. Total bullshit. Kevin Dubrow killed Quiet Riot with his mouth. They took a huge fall from grace because he couldn't shut up and keep his jealousies under control.

The Kalamazoo show was a time when Kevin Dubrow was at his worst, and Tommy Lee was hell bent on beating his ass. Tommy and I spent most of the festival walking around and looking for Kevin.

It had gotten so bad with Quiet Riot that Kevin had to be walked in surrounded by security. I looked on in astonishment as his contemporaries taunted him! These are the other bands, other rockstars, and they just wanted to rip this sorry cocksucker apart.

I couldn't believe what I was watching. It wasn't just Tommy and me, although, we both wanted to get our hands on him, too.

We actually went around to Quiet Riot's side of the stage, and Tommy had planned to go on stage, in front of the crowd, and kick the shit out of Kevin. People knew he was going to do that, and security met us at the bottom of the stairs. They let me up there, but they wouldn't let T-Bone up there.

I see Tommy squaring off with this huge bone-snapper of a bouncer, so I cut back in. "Come on, Tommy. Let's just go back down."

We're on our way back down, and Tommy is pissed! There was a little trailer at the bottom of the stairs. It was the guitar tech trailer where they would tune up the guitars. Tommy took a bottle and fired the thing at the trailer, sending it smashing through the window, and right into Jake E. Lee's lap. Jake was tuning up for his set with Ozzy.

One of the bands, I'm not sure who, took the sign off of Quiet Riot's door and put it on a porta-toilet door. That's what the other stars were thinking about Quiet Riot. They were shit.

I felt really bad for Rudy Sarzo and Carlos Cavazo. Those guys were good guys. Good players. Good people. And, in all honesty, they couldn't stand Kevin Dubrow either. It must have sucked ass for them, because they had to be associated with the guy. Frankie Banali was always on Kevin's side, but the others were just caught up in the mess. Guilty by association.

That was a long, long feud between the Quiet Riot camp and the RATT camp. It was all started, perpetuated, originated and created by Kevin DuBrow. We toured with them in 2005, but that one show in Kalamazoo was the only thing we did with them in the 80s, which was a good thing.

I knew that this part of the book was going to be difficult for me. I really haven't looked forward to talking about this. And, you'll see soon enough, there are other stories that are equally as painful and conflicted.

Kevin DuBrow was notorious. He constantly had bad things to say about the people around him; especially if it was another band. He was an extremely negative person.

As much as I couldn't stand the guy, when he overdosed on cocaine at the end of 2007, it really affected me. He had made so many people's lives just pure misery. Utter hell! But, when the guy died, all that hatred and animosity seemed to lose some steam. I couldn't stand the guy, but the reasons suddenly weren't as important.

I started having really weird, disturbing dreams, after I heard about his death. I was losing sleep. I don't know if it was a sign of me struggling with my own mortality, or if it was just the thought of mortality in general, but I was having some problems with it. Kevin was only three years older than me. I was remembering playing clubs at the same time as those guys; working the same circuit; back in 1976 and 1977 when Don and I were playing together in Airborn.

I've never gone as far as to publicly call the guys in Riot dicks, but Kevin and Frankie really were. There's no other way to put it. They were downright cruel to the people around them.

They had calendars on their bus walls, and when we were touring with them they would draw a big rat on our individual dates, and then put a red circle and line through it. Just petty, juvenile shit like that, nonstop; and for no real reason. They wouldn't let their crew hang out or talk to anyone in the RATT camp. You'd think we were going to "infect" them somehow.

Anyway, a few nights ago, I ran into Frankie Banali, the drummer for Quiet Riot. We were at a club called "Howl at the Moon" over in Universal City. It's a hangout for a lot of the guys from the 80s, and a great time. Especially on Wednesday nights. I'm in there, just sort of soaking up the room, when Frankie walks in. It's only been a couple of weeks since they found Kevin in Vegas, so the wounds of his death were still really fresh for me, but Frankie was a bit of a wreck.

Keep in mind, Frankie and I were caught on opposite sides of this feud. It's not that we couldn't stand each other, as much as we simply defended our own camps. We didn't get along, even though none of this bullshit started with us. So, when he came up to me and started talking, I was a little taken aback.

We immediately started talking about Kevin's death. It was clear that Frankie was pretty much devastated by it, and I really felt pain for the guy. It was hard to have that talk, just because of all the emotion involved. He told me that he would never take Quiet Riot back out on the road. Not in any form. That made sense, I guess. We'll see how the future financials for Quiet Riot work out without DuBrow.

With RATT, we had learned that something gets lost when you change your front man. It's like the face of the band changes, and people don't recognize you anymore, yet, you're still trying to be who you once were. That would be double so for Quiet Riot, because Kevin had been so outspoken and notorious that he *was* the identity of that group.

Frankie said he wanted to bury the hatchet. Which, I was willing to do, but I couldn't help but think that it took Kevin DuBrow killing himself with cocaine for us to get to this point. Frankie and I went back all the way to 1979. We were two very similar drummers with similar styles and influences. We always knew we were both pretty equal in ability, so, there was always somewhat of a rivalry based just on that.

When he came up and started talking to me, it was the olive branch that could have and should have been extended years before. Honestly, either of us could have done it at any time. So, hopefully, that whole thing is behind us, and there's a friendship to build on there. It's just unfortunate that it took someone dying to make something like that happen.

I've always respected Frankie as player, and I know he respected me. We told each other that in the early days. When we hit it in 1984, I was buying a house, and I knew he had just bought a house off of the "Metal Health" album. So, I called him up, and was like, "I've got no idea how, or even a concept of what to do when it comes to buying a home. Do you have any tips?" It was a two-fold thing. One, I needed his advice, but two, it was sort of announcing that RATT was there, too. We were in the same vein again.

Then, I ran into him after the 1984 tour at some bar in Universal. This was after Kevin had been running his mouth about everybody on the scene. I was like, "What are you going to do about your singer, man?"

He just exploded! "You fucking worry about shit in your camp, Bobby! I'll worry about shit in mine!" He was real heavy.

I just put my hands up. "Don't shoot." Frankie was getting pretty weird about the whole thing. We were never the same after that.

When I would see him, it was still pretty cool for a while. We'd see each other occasionally, and it was still hugs and shit. Then, on a website called Metal Sludge, he did a 20 questions kind of thing, and they always ask you to rate other players, on a scale of 1-10, you know?

When they asked him to rate me, he goes, "I'm not going to even answer that. Because Blotz knows I think he sucks just like he thinks I suck." I'm like, "What the fuck? Where's he get off going out on me like that?" I considered e-mailing him about it. But, again, I'm not an innocent peach in this. There have been a few times where I've said shit, and he's said shit. Although, it was almost always about Kevin DuBrow, not Quiet Riot itself.

We toured with them in 2005, and I saw how Frankie had become. He was unscrupulous. I thought he was just brutal. There was a side of Frankie that I didn't know and didn't like. The "bro" side was still there, only it was laced with a crocodile smile. It was the kind of smile that promised to hurt you if you turned your back.

When we patched it up a few nights ago, he said, "This is business, bro, but I always knew where your heart was. I want to bury the hatchet with this right now."

I didn't really understand that, coming from him. It's almost like he was saying, "Blotz, you're an asshole with the way you do business." But, whatever.

"That's good with me, Frankie. Just remember that none of this bullshit started with me. We didn't perpetuate it." And, that's where I left it.

I've never envied his position in having to deal with Kevin. We both had our "singer demons" to contend with, so I'm not shining myself in a better light. But, it couldn't have been easy for Frankie. We just got mired up in it, and sooner or later, that shit has to get to you.

The night Frankie and I spoke, it was the first time he had been out since Kevin's death. He was pretty down. The guy was in mourning. That was obvious. Plus, his gig just went away. He still has the rights to the band name, and there's ways he can make a living off that, but he made it clear to me that touring was over. Touring is where they made their money. It's not a good time for him. Not right now. All of which made me think, "Thank God for RATT."

The morning that the story had broken about Kevin's overdose, my phone started ringing with text messages at 4:00 AM from people back east who were already up and heard it. The whole thing affected me in a very strange way. I despised Kevin! I couldn't stand the way he was!

I couldn't help but think, "Jesus, dude. How could you be such a fuck up? You fucked it up for yourself, and everyone who loved you! What the fuck was wrong with you, man?"

It was anger. I'd watched this guy ruin his life for almost 30 years, and ultimately ruin everyone else's life around him. But, I could have done that, too. I could go out, get drunk, and kill somebody on my way home. It happens all the time. It happened to Vince Neil, and Vince was a good friend.

I would never do that, though. I drive perfect when I drink, as ridiculous a statement like that is to make in this political climate. Flipped out "mothers against anyone who drinks" political climate. But, it's true. I'm focused when I'm behind a wheel. I've never been close to an accident while drinking. But, it still was possible.

Every time I think about drinking and driving, I think of Sam Kinison. "It's not that we WANT to drink and drive! It's just that we don't have another way to get our fucking car home!"

I heard another comedian say once that 33% of all road deaths are caused by drunk drivers; but, that means 67% of them are pulled off by fuckers who are completely sober! Take that for what you will (by the way, send all your hate mail about these statements to my manager. He'll love that!).

Hopefully, we've put all the vicious, vindictive Quiet Riot vs. RATT shit to bed. I would like that. And, while Frankie and I aren't going to be picking out curtains together, we might be friendly again.

We'll see.

We went out with Motley in 1984, while on the Cellar tour. That was...that was when history became legend.

Our history with Mötley Crüe is colorful, to say the least. But of all those guys, Tommy Lee is my bro! Tommy and I go way back. Back in the day, we hung out a lot; Did a lot of dirt bike riding, things like that. We don't see each other as much, these days. Being who we are, life simply gets in the way. But, when we do get together, it's like we see each other every day. T-Bone is rocker family.

Heather Locklear's sister, Laurie, was married to this guy Terry Ahearn, who I still see from time to time. Terry, Tommy, Vince and I used to go dirt bike riding, along with Mickey Diamond who was a champion motorcross rider. We used to have a lot of fun together like that.

Tommy and I were out together the night he met Heather. We went to see REO Speedwagon, and we were hanging out at the Forum Club, which was an elite type of place at the Forum where you had to have a VIP Pass to get in. We were at the bar, hanging out with all of our friends who were there, when I saw Heather Locklear and Scott Baio walk in.

I was like "T-Bone, check that out. It's Heather Locklear."

Tommy went, "Aw, dude, she's fucking hot! She is so hot! We have the same dentist!"

"That's awesome, bro. Really."

Tommy's all giddy, and he's already loaded with liquid courage, courtesy of Mr. Daniels.

He flashes this troublesome grin he has, and goes, "I'm going to go talk to her, dude."

I was like, "Don't even go over there, bro! Not right now. She's with Baio."

He's like, "Naw, man, I'm going to do it right now. I'm going to call my dentist and get her number."

And, he did. He called me a few weeks later and went, "Guess who I'm going out with?"

I'm like, "You motherfucker!" So, I couldn't wait to hear about the first time he fucked her.

Took him a while, too. It was something like three months before he closed the deal. I don't know who was more impatient about it, T-Bone, or me.

Over the years, Jeni and I did a lot of hanging out with Heather and Tommy. There was one time where Heather, Tommy, Jeni and I were out on the town all night, then went back to their place and spent the rest of the night partying.

She was great; a really great girl. Great to hang out with, and a fantastic personality; she had a fun sense of humor, just everything a guy could ever want in a girl. I loved her to death, and she was so unbelievably hot, too!

That night, she was up showing Jeni her jewelry chest. It was this wacky looking pirate's chest full of jewels and baubles. She was showing it off.

Tommy and I were downstairs in the kitchen trading shots, snorting lines, and telling stories of how much we both hated our lead singers! Meanwhile, outside, it's turning blue. The sun is about to come up. Then Tommy, in mid sentence, kinda looks through me and just falls forward.

It was almost like a joke. You know, when you're cutting up, and you're going to act like you're falling forward onto your face, but at the last second, you don't? It was just like that. That's what I thought he was going to do, but at the last second, he didn't stop. He hit, face first, right in the middle of the kitchen floor!

BOOM!

He landed with a big crack of a thud, and never moved!

I went upstairs, "Uh, Heather? Guys? Tommy's, like, out of it down here."

We picked him up and managed to get him over to the couch. The whole thing was a little scary. I'd not seen anyone that fucked up before. Even when I was touring with them.

That turned out to be shades of dark things to come for T-Bone, and the rest of us in the 80s music crowd. It seems that drugs and alcohol had their crosshairs on us, and it was only a matter of time before we were shot down by them in some fashion or form.

But, that's something for another chapter.

On a fun note, New Year's Eve in 1987, Jeni, Heather, Tommy and me all took a leer jet to Vegas for New Year's. And, in typical Tommy fashion, he got the pilot to do barrel rolls!

Only T-Bone! That dude is a breed unto himself.

Oddly, on the list of groups that we opened for on that tour; Motley, Night Ranger, ZZ Top; there was only one that gave us any grief. Billy Squire. Not Billy himself, but his production people. They were just a pain in the ass.

We were already headlining arena shows by that time, but we had agreed to do a tour with Billy Squire as the headline. It was a little awkward. I don't think anyone anticipated us taking off so fast, so when the tour was booked, it wasn't a big consideration.

By the time it made it's way around, we were already huge. The Squire leg was less money, less stage space, and a huge pain in the ass. But, management insisted we do it, because they didn't want us developing a bad reputation of leaving tours hanging.

Our first night with Squire, there were no lights. There was very little space on stage for us to use, and Squire had this huge, round thing in the middle of the stage that made it even tighter.

By that time, we were the big band on that tour. Squire was big, but we were blowing him away in the merchandise sales every night. Squire was cool about bringing out the new up-n-coming bands on tour with him. He had us, Def Leppard, and others, that he had run tours with.

We tried to do something similar to that when we were headlining. When we took Poison out with us, no one knew who they were. But as they started to break, we had discovered a formula that works really well. The opening act actually helps the bill.

We got along with the Squire guys pretty well, all things considered, but the tour was a tough one. We should have been headlining, and everyone there knew it. It made for tense relations, because, clearly, RATT-mania was in those crowds.

I did a lot of partying with the late, great Bobby Chouinard, who was the drummer for Billy Squire. He was a great guy.

Bobby passed away a couple of years ago from a cocaine overdose. I can't say I'm completely surprised by that, considering the amount of blow that I witnessed him go through. The guy was ALWAYS on that shit. It was one of those things that eventually catches up to you.

Bobby Chouinard will be sorely missed.

These days, my rituals are set. I'll show up to the gig about an hour before. I'd drink about 3 Coors Lights and start to warm up by stretching, and playing along with my favorite CD's. I'll just tap along on any surface, because going and getting a drum pad would just be too fucking easy! I always use the bus as my dressing room. Especially today. Robbie Crane and I would be in there getting ready. After the show, if I drink, it's red wine. Sometimes I like to throw a Jagerbomb with the guys every now and then, but not very often. My days of hard liquor consumption are behind me, for the most part.

We finished the U.S. leg of the Cellar tour in December of 1984. We all went home for Christmas, which was really great. But, before we could call an end to the tour, we had to hit Japan.

We were all really tired by that point, but nothing prepared us for the Japanese fans. They were maniacal! It was complete "RATT-a-mania", and we were mobbed everywhere we went! Plus, the culture is out of this world, so, it was a whole new experience for us, after 15 months of nothing but whole new experiences!

We finished the Japan tour, and shot the RATT Longform Video over there, you know, us on the bullet train and stuff. It was a platinum video.

It was a great way to end the tour. The band immediately took a sabbatical to Hawaii where we ran and hid in Maui. We all had these condos on the beach, and a little portable recording studio. Our job was to write the "Invasion of Your Privacy" album.

These were tough times. None of us were given a chance to relax from the tour, and we were already back into the mix with a new album. Management was really cracking the whip on their platinum recording show pony, believe me.

Little rifts were already forming in the band. Mostly between the band and Stephen, but a little with Robbin as well. Of course, we brought our families, otherwise we would hardly see them before we went back out on tour with the new album. I think that created more tension in the band, because, instead of working, we took a lot of personal time. That's too bad, but what did they expect? It's our families.

We were in this little restaurant in Lahaina one night when I get a tap on the shoulder, turn around, and there Billy Squire.

I was like, "What the fuck are you doing here?!?! Are you following us?" We got a big laugh out of it, and hung out with him for a few days, having a good time.

Maui was where I learned to play golf. Kapalua. Our manager, Marshall, was leaving every day to go play golf, and one day I was like, "Hey, let me go with you."

He's goes, "You ever played before?"

"I've played baseball, dude. Golf is baseball for fags. I think I can fucking handle it."

So I went to one of the greatest courses in the world to learn to play. I bought the shirt, shorts, shoes, hat, glove the whole fag uniform. I didn't buy clubs over there, though. I rented clubs. But, immediately I was hooked. For life!

Hawaii was where "Invasion of Your Privacy" happened. We went out there together, with the intent of hammering out the new tunes and getting back to the mainland for recording. But getting Stephen to show for rehearsal was virtually impossible. He was simply never available. Too much sun and sand, maybe, but I'm amazed anything happened beyond that second album.

The fracturing was already starting to form.

Of course, it did happen for us. When we got back, we immediately started recording the record at Rumbo Studios with Beau Hill producing us again. There was absolutely no time off, but if you've got to do it, do it when you're young, right?

We were young, in more ways than one. We had just become multi-platinum recording sensations, and none of us knew the "rights and wrongs" to the business, yet. We were all too naive to realize we were being severely overworked. By the time we caught on to that fact, it was much too late to stop the nose dive.

During the recording of Invasion, things seemed to gain their focus again. Stephen wasn't yet at the point he would be after the coming tour, and he showed to the sessions pretty consistently, and he sang along as we were tightening things up. So, it wasn't bad... yet.

Consequently, we literally got this record done and out in four months time.

For all the huge, grandstanding groups that came out of southern California in the early and mid-eighties, we were still a very tight community. We all knew each other, and most of us had played in other bands together; and were really good friends, with very few beefs. There were exceptions, most of which involved the various lead singers, but for the most part, we were all bros.

So, I'm both nostalgic and mournful with a lot of the stuff I'm reading in other books and bios of the time.

A lot of these rockstar bios are hitting close to home. I'm sure that this one won't be much different for the guys who read it. Those guys were friends, or at least, good acquaintances. Tommy's book, "Tommyland." Slash's book. Motley's book, "The Dirt." Even "The Heroin Diaries" that Nikki put together.

I've never had a real great love for Nikki. I respect his business acumen, and his song writing skills, but, he's a difficult person; a complete egomaniac. Stephen and Juan pale in comparison to Nikki's ego.

His book, "The Heroin Diaries"... Jesus. I read a few chapters, and it really started to feel real. It was really unsettling in my gut. I was close to them when all that shit was going on. I've seen those guys amazingly fucked up. That first tour with them is a big example of that.

There are a lot of memories that I've kept buried, but, that book conjures all that shit back up. Sixx wrote a very dark tome, and I was in that circle of darkness at that time. I can really relate to a lot of that shit. I had a hard time reading about the total meltdown of a guy I once ran with. It's depressing as hell.

On this subject, I never saw Nikki or Robbin doing smack. Come to think of it, I've never seen heroin. I knew something was probably going on with those guys, but again, I sort of exist in two worlds; my family world, and the band world. Luckily, I never really partook of the lowest of lows like some of these guys have. I never hit the extremes one-way or the other. Not very hard, anyway. The responsibilities of one side always trumped the other. So, I never noticed those guys were doing that shit.

We worked as a democracy as a band, but that was about to become very difficult. We had to fire Robbin on the Detonator tour. He was so buried under alcohol and heroin that he began to really fuck up on stage. Shit like, putting the wrong guitar on and playing the whole song out of key. It was horrifying.

It was at the Sun Plaza, in Tokyo. He just didn't change guitars between songs, and we started into "Lack of Communication" with him playing completely the wrong chords. We actually had to stop the show and make him change. That was the end.

I missed some big signs with King. He was always throwing up on the side of the stage. I just thought it was nerves, you know. I didn't know he was smoking heroin!

I don't remember when it finally clicked for me and I learned of Robbin's problems, but it was late. Really late. Like I said, at this point in the game, we were all leading decidedly separate lives. From the beginning, the core debaucheries were a little outside my world. I had my wife and kids going. They were the priority in my life, and while I would party with the best of them, my responsibilities as a father made me look at my professional life differently than the other guys.

It was probably after the 1989 tour that I realized what he was doing. That shit was scary, man. To watch Robbin go out like that. Supposedly, Robbin had been an addict since 1985.

To say that Nikki Sixx introduced Robbin to heroin, I don't know how true that is. I wasn't there. But, they roomed together early on, so, I guess it's possible.

In the end, Sixx turned out not to be a real friend to him. Robbin, in his last days, turned on Sixx. He didn't like him at all. Sixx wouldn't come see him. And, those two were really tight bros for years.

Robbin was in the hospital for almost two years, and Nikki stayed away. He didn't even go to Robbin's memorial down in La Jolla. That friendship didn't end well.

I never see Nikki anymore. I think he heard I went out in an interview and blamed him for King's death, but that's bullshit. I never said that. King decided to do heroin. It didn't matter if he got it from Nikki or Joe Smith the midget. King killed himself. He could not conquer his demons. Seeing that, Nikki is lucky to be alive, himself. Everyone knows that. Him most of all.

Nikki has a problem with me, but he's also got a problem with all the 80's bands. He tries to remove Crüe from that scene, but he can't. They are the center of the 80s metal universe. With their Theater of Pain album, it was Nikki in fucking polka dots and Vince in pink chiffon and shit. They were the originators of glam metal.

A lot of people look at those years, and knowing that I ran with that, they aren't going to believe me when I say I didn't know. Maybe it's denial. I'm not sure. But, when I finally heard the stories about Nikki, and saw the horrible results with Robbin, I was genuinely surprised.

Heroin scared the fuck out of me. I was too smart to get sucked in to that. But, the guys in Mötley, that's a different story. They lived the most depraved, ragged edge existence of any band in the 80s, possibly any band in history. I don't know. They were so desperate to get loaded, that they would drink cooking sherry if they had to. They snorted Halcions, for Christ's sake!

Mötley Crüe was an incredible display of reckless debauchery. I'm amazed any of them made it out of the 80s alive. They all came really close to punching the clock; Nikki most of all. When you hit drugs so hard that you are periodically declared dead, it's gone to far.

Mötley were way more over the top than RATT was. We weren't one of the big drug bands. That was Mötley and Guns. We were all pretty harmless with drugs. Stephen and Warren smoked weed; Stephen, almost constantly. Hell, everybody smoked weed! Everybody snorted blow after the show, and no one thought anything of it. It was just something you did.

Even Robbin, who wrecked himself with smack, did his fix on the sly. We weren't privy to it. It was his dirty little secret.

It was the invulnerability of youth and wealth. We weren't the poster boys for it, but we certainly hung out with those who were.

Mick Mars and Me backstage during
the Mötley RATT tour 1984.

Last night for Mötley and RATT tour party, 1984.

Me and Tommy Lee at
Namm Show in 1985.

Stephen, Ozzy, and Me at 4 AM in Ozzy's suite, 1986.

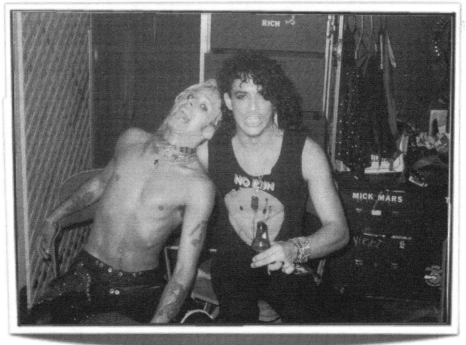

Vince and Stephen comparing notes, 1984.

Warren and Kathy and Me having some late night tea in my room in Tokyo, 1985.

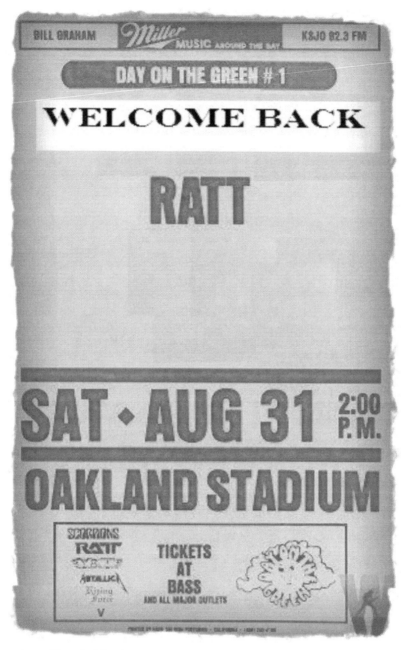

Scorpions headlined this show. RATT was special guest. Opening bands were Metallica, Inva Malmsteen, and WNT.

13

ALL HAIL THE MIGHTY KRELL!

"Cocaine is God's way of saying you're making too much money." - Robin Williams

Cocaine (or *KRELL*, as we affectionately called it) and I go way back. While I might have gotten close a time or two, I was never addicted. I drank like a fish, and A.A. probably had me on their radar, but that's bullshit. When I wanted to quit hard liquor, I did. And, weed is just an old friend; weed, cinnamon toast and Black Sabbath.

We used to love to snort on tour. Again, we never saw a problem with it, unless you completely abused it and stayed up all night with it. At times we had done that, of course, which sucked, but for the most part, it was just a recreational thing.

This one time, in 1985 on the Bon Jovi tour, we were playing a show up in Montana. There's no krell in Montana. None. Zero. The only snow in Montana is the kind the dog pisses in.

Somehow Hugh Horn, my drum tech, had acquired some blow.

We were playing the show, and I feel a jab in my leg. It's Hugh, down in my dollhouse with a drumstick in his hand. He's jamming me in the leg, trying to get my attention.

Where I sat on those tours was pretty high up in the production. We all had our little places behind our amps, which we called our dollhouses. Most of them were pretty tight, but mine was fucking huge. It was big enough that I had a full bar in there, with posters and things all over the wall. I used to invite the opening bands back there to drink and check out the show.

Any given moment, it could be Bret Michaels, or someone from Kix or Queensryche, just hanging out back there and enjoying the show. It was an open door. There was so much booze on our rider, and besides, I thought it was really cool that I had a full bar right behind my drum kit. So did the other bands, when you get right down to it.

Anyway, I look down, and Hugh is jamming my leg. He's holding a small, folded paper, and he's shaking it back and forth. He's got about a gram of blow inside it. When they sell coke, they'll sometimes fold it up in little paper pouches, and give it a seal. That's what Hugh was waving at me.

Needless to say, I was pretty excited!

It was the last song, which meant we would take a quick break and then jump back on stage for an encore. I immediately hopped down into my dollhouse.

I said, "Give me a bump!

Hugh goes, "No man, just hold on for one more song."

I'm like, "No, fucker! Give me a bump! Now! Hurry up!" I was jonesing. What can I say?

He's like, "Alright. Wait." He's got his flashlight, and he opens up the little pouch. He rolls up a $20 bill and passes it to me.

I'm like, "Don't bother cutting out a line, I'll just do a snort from the pouch."

I take the bill and put it to my nose, but as I lean over the pouch to do my snort, a huge river of sweat runs from off of my head, down my nose and plops down dead center of the gram of coke! It immediately soaked all the powder in the pouch.

"NOOOO!!!"

Anyone who knows what happens to krell when it gets wet, you know what I'm talking about. It's done. No one will be snorting any coke that night.

I pass the pouch back to Hugh, and go, "Oh, my God! Fix it!" Then I jump back up behind my kit to play the encore. He's back there in the dollhouse with a fucking blowdryer trying to fix the greatest disaster in Montana history... at least in Blotz-World.

The show ended, and that shit looked like a yellowish cottage cheese sitting in the bottom of the pouch.

That shit sucked.

Drugs weren't big players in RATT. Not until we realized what Robbin was going through, but by then, RATT was falling apart for a multitude of other reasons. I can't place our abuse of Krell or weed, or even alcohol as the primary reason for our initial breakup in 1992.

I think, with respects to social position within the band, I was the voice of reason and responsibility. Robbin was like that too. He was just a really sweet guy. Really nice. But, Robbin would call it like it was. I tend to be a lot like that, as well. Stephen has always been unrealistic and difficult. Warren, while not as bad as Stephen, was the same. Warren is a purist; an artist. I'm a businessman. The two tend to conflict. Juan was only interested in Juan. He could give a shit about the rest of us. Juan was an island unto himself.

Robbin was the kind of guy who would bust out after a show with truth and honesty.

"God, we fucking sucked ass tonight. That sounded like shit!"

Stephen was the total opposite. He didn't want to hear anything about it. Didn't want to talk about it. It's like, if he didn't acknowledge it, then it never really happened.

Having Bon Jovi out with us in 1985 was going to be a little bit of a payback. We had started the 1984 tour with those guys at a club in Portland, Oregon called Starry Nights. They were real shitty to us that night, and then the next night when we played up in Seattle at the Paramount Theater, they were even worse. They had all their gear shoved way up, so we had virtually no stage room.

In Seattle, we found out that we got the Ozzy tour. Naturally, we completely bailed from the Bon Jovi thing and immediately flew down to San Diego to go out with the Prince of Darkness on tour!

When Bon Jovi came out with us in 1985, it was time for a little payback, so we thought. Instead, an oddity of the rock world happened, and we became quick friends. Most of us were, anyway.

Stephen always fucked with the opening acts. He went out of his way to make sure everyone knew it was HIS stage, and no one could put their feet on HIS monitors, etc.

Of course, standard procedure is that no one goes on the headliner's production anyway, but, Jon kept climbing up on our shit. We kept having to pull things from them, things from their dressing room rider, stuff like that. It made for some friction, but almost all of it was between Jon and Stephen, which made for some entertaining road drama.

Stephen told me a story about that tour.

On Christmas, just before the end of the tour, we were in Albuquerque, New Mexico. Stephen had the balls to walk into Bon Jovi's dressing room and say, "Merry Christmas." Jon looks at him and goes, "You're a fucking hypocrite! Fuck off!" Stephen was really stunned.

They finished the tour out, which ended on New Year's Eve of 1985 in San Diego, and then they went on to superstardom, absolute superstardom. That tour was greatly received. It was a huge sell-out and a lot of fun.

Jon really resented Stephen, after that tour. But, surprisingly, when RATT split up, and Stephen was playing in Arcade, they opened ten shows for Bon Jovi. I never understood that. Someone must have owed someone else a favor. Either that, or Jon has a very selective memory.

We used to hang out a lot and play poker on that tour. Usually, it would be me, Richie Sambora, Alec John Such, and sometimes Tico Torres, but that was rare. We'd play cards until all hours, you know?

There was one game that seemed to last forever.

We were up north, somewhere around the Dakotas or something. The game was in my room, and started as poker, then went to blackjack, and finally wound up as Acey Deucy (also called Hi Low).

With Acey Deucy, you bet between the cards. Say you lay one card to the right, and it's a 9 of diamonds, then you lay another card to the left, and it's a king of spades. You then can bet on whether the next card will fall between the two cards. So, when you start the game, everyone puts ten bucks in the pot. On each turn of the card, you can bet anything up to and including whatever is in the pot. If you turn over a card that's between the two showing, you pull from the pot, but if it isn't, you lose your bet.

So, this game can quickly get out of control. At one point, with our Dakotas game, the pot was over $7000. I remember Alec kept trying to bet the pot when it was around $5000.

I'm like, "Dude, show me where you have the ability to pay ten grand if you lose, and you can bet the pot." Reason being, if Alec had lost after betting the pot, he had to pay double! He just keeps going, "I bet the pot! I bet the pot!" Alec was a quirky, Jersey kind of guy. He had this tiny, little derringer pistol he would leave out on the table, and thought he was really cool, smoking cigars and weird shit like that. I thought it was kind of geeky.

Jon had been in the game earlier, but he had tapped his cashflow pretty quick and didn't want to buy in for any more chips.

Our tour manager's banging on our door at five o'clock in the morning going, "We have GOT to go! We got a five hour drive ahead of us." So, we had to write everything down, and keep track of it so we could continue the game later.

It took us about four days to finish that game! I don't really remember who won it all. I think Richie got a big chunk of it, Alec took a big chunk, I don't remember. I just know that I didn't win it.

That's okay, though, because I was making all the money on the tour. Those guys were only getting something like $500 a week salary.

I remember that Richie Sambora and I were in my room one night drinking. We were starving, so I'm thinking, "Let's go down to our bus, we've got pizza down there."

So, we scurry down to the bus, and all the pizza is gone. I did find a box in a bunk that had some two-day-old pizza in it. Hard as tree bark, but we tried to heat it up and eat it, anyway. It just wasn't very appetizing.

We kept talking about business, mostly merchandise. He asked how much we were getting, and I told him. He was blown away! I asked, "What about you guys? What do you do?" He's like, "Fuck if I know. I don't get any of that."

I was stunned. Are you kidding me?

I go, "You don't get anything on merchandise? Wow, dude. You wrote the songs with Jon, from the very beginning." We talked about it until he was pretty worked up.

He was worked up enough to go in and insisted on a piece of it, I guess, because he came up to me later and said, "Thanks for sticking up for me that night, because I went in and recut my deal." Now, he's got something like $80 million in the bank? So, hey, Richie! Send a brother a little love, will ya?"

I had my rituals on the Invasion tour, as most of us did. I used to go out every night and watch the opening bands, especially if I really liked their music. I'd go out there and have a couple of beers, watch Bon Jovi, and hang out at the soundboard.

We had a Veri-Lite system on that tour, and our lighting guy was a big golfer. He knew I was too, and he had a golf game in the computer. We weren't using the Veri-Lite system during their set, so I'd be hanging at the board, playing on the golf game during Bon Jovi's show. People would be looking at me like, "What the hell? Is Blotz mixing lights for those guys? What's that all about?" I'd be hunched over the board with a mouse in my hand, looking all serious.

Pretty funny.

By and large, that was a great, fun tour. It started in April, and ended New Year's Eve. They were with us the whole seven months. We kept in touch with one another for years afterward. I was in touch with Jon up through 1992. Sadly, when grunge hit, everybody went their own way.

14

LOVE & CONSEQUENCES

'Life is like a jar of Jalapenos. What you do today, might burn your ass tomorrow...'

Moon Zappa came out with Dweezil while we were on tour in 1985, and we were running with us for a while. They were friends, and we just hung out on the bus.

Moon was always wanting to play games, and have fun. She had this child-like quality to her. This sort of eternal youthfulness that I couldn't get an understanding of initially, but it was cute and charming. The guys all really enjoyed them hanging out. At the time, she must have been 21 or 22.

One night, we were all partying, and things got a little out of hand with Moon and I. We had a little overnight tryst.

It was at this point that I discovered the source of her kid-like nature. Moon Zappa, daughter of Frank Zappa, born and raised in a musical family, and around over-sexed rockers her entire life, was a virgin. Not only was she a virgin, but after that first night, she was pregnant.

Anyone who tells you a virgin can't get pregnant needs to go fuck themselves. I'm here to testify.

When she told me, I tripped out in a big way. It was a huge, life-changing moment for both her and I. The only reason i'm discussing this is because I know she speaks of it when she does her spoken word shows. She tells me that I have to go and tell Frank and Gloria.

Frank Zappa.

I'm going, "There's no fucking way!" I couldn't go in front of Frank and tell him that I had knocked up his baby girl during a one-night stand! That's like going in front of Don Corleone and telling him you won't do business with him, right after you've shown him your prize race horse!

Only, it wasn't going to be a horse's head was going to wake up next to!

I couldn't do that. There was no way that was going to end well.

Moon and I were good buddies. We cut up a lot, and talked about random shit. She was a good friend. Then, somehow, we get drunk one night and our lives are turned on their asses.

I haven't talked to Moon in many years, but Moon is a beautiful person.

"Invasion of Your Privacy" was a chance for us to solidify our position as one of the dominate bands of the era. We did that, I feel, but it fell a little bit short in terms of super-stardom. Our egos were getting bigger than the reality of our press, and as a consequence, we were falling short of our potential.

You can blame the management for cracking the whip so hard and so often. You can blame the general discourse and bickering that was soon to come. You can blame the sheer burnout that was the result. But, somewhere along the way, around the end of 1985, RATT became something different. We weren't the raw, lean and nasty band we were on the EP, just TWO YEARS EARLIER! We were becoming something else. Something cannibalistic in nature. Something that was slowly, and deliberately destroying itself with its own success.

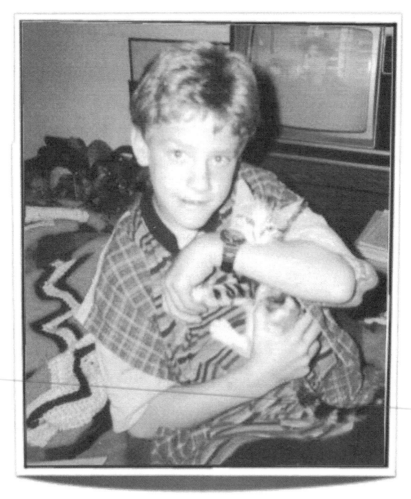

Marcus, and our cat Meeka, Marc was 7.

Marcus, Michael, and Me, skiing Mammoth, 2008

Marcus, Me, Michael, my good bro Mike Smith at Dodgers game, 2008.

15

BACK FOR MORE

"I'm just a musical prostitute." - Freddie Mercury

I always said, "If I ever get a gold record, I'm buying a Trans-Am." I've always loved Trans-Ams. We were home for four days to shoot the "Back For More" video, and Out of the Cellar was gold.

I went down and bought a Trans-Am. It's odd, thinking about it. My dad died in a Pontiac. Interesting, how my favorite car was also a Pontiac. Thankfully, the omens didn't carry over, because I sure had a hard-on for Trans-Ams.

I remember going down to the lot and doing all the stuff that goes along with buying a new car. I don't remember what the financing was, but I put down something like $5000. They took pictures and everything, then called me back later in the day and said they couldn't do the deal.

I was like, "What? That's bullshit!" But, they wouldn't sell. So, fine. Fuck 'em.

I went to another place and got another car. I didn't care. In the end, all I wanted was my red Trans-Am.

That was when we were shooting the "Back For More" video. We were in off the road just long enough to do the video. In fact, my car is in the "Back For More" video. If you watch, when Warren and Juan leave the restaurant and get into the bright red Trans-Am, that's my Trans-Am. Robbin and me were in a Mercedes, and Nikki Sixx and Tommy Lee were playing cops. They drag me out of the car and act like their kicking the shit out of me on the curb.

So, I had my first official "toy" as a result of RATT. There were many more soon to come.

Of course, I didn't get to drive that Trans-Am much before we were back out on tour. Which was fine. It gave Jeni a good car to drive. That was nice. We'd never had nice cars, or anything like that. I mean, we had a couple that were good. There was the demo Mustang from Manhattan Beach Ford. That one was nice. I had a Cougar that wasn't bad. But, we had never owned a brand new car. That Trans-Am was our first one.

Jeni was a good woman. She made a lot of sacrifices during those early years, and when we made it, she kept it tight. She didn't overspend, or anything like that. I bought her a BMW, and some other nice shit, but we didn't get extravagant. Except for cars. When we got back from that first tour, I went car nuts.

When we were home shooting "Back For More," it was the summer of 1984, and we were home for four days. Two of those days, we were shooting the video. One of those days, I bought the Trans-Am, and on the fourth day, I saw Dokken for the first time.

Don Dokken was having a party. He calls me up, and is like, "Yeah, me and the guys from Great White are having this party. Why don't you stop by?"

So, I came by and parked my "pretty, red cock on wheels." Don knew I was getting the car, and of course, he had already told everybody.

"Man, Blotz just went out and bought a brand new fucking Trans-Am!"

So, everybody was coming out to look at it. There were a lot of people at this party that were fans. I didn't even know most of them. The fans were "RATTING out" in very short order; coming by to say hi; professing their devotion to the band; all those things that fans tend to do when they see their idols.

This one chick pulls "Out of the Cellar" out.

Now, mind you that Don Dokken was out of his mind with envy. His band hadn't broken yet, although "Breaking the Chains" had been released and had minimal success, and he wasn't dealing well with the fact that RATT had. They were signed with Elektra, but they weren't yet headed where we were. I was in the middle of a huge tour while he was sitting at home. We were all over MTV every half hour, and he wasn't. He was just eaten up with jealousy.

Then this chick puts in the "Out of the Cellar" cassette. Don comes into the room, and just flips out.

"Who fucking put that in?!? Who put that in?" This poor chick is like, "I did." He looks at her like she just took a shit on his carpet, and he wants to rub her face in it.

Don pulls the cassette out of the player, and starts yanking the tape out of it! He's flipped! This tape is ruined, and piling up on the floor around his feet.

I just looked at him, like, "Are you out of your mind? What the fuck is wrong with you?"

I split the party. It was just too damned weird. Don was my friend, and had been for years and years. And, it wasn't like I left with him not being my friend anymore. Not at all. It's just that when Don has an episode, like Don tends to do, it's better to call it a day, and try it again, tomorrow. You know what I mean?

Don is, and always will be, a little bit crazy.

A lot of people were freaked out that Don would have the balls to do something like that right in front of me. But, with Don, if you know him, you sort of understand.

It's like watching a shark go into a frenzy. Their eyes roll back white, and they just lose all rationale. That's Don! He couldn't have time to think, "There's Blotzer, standing there while I do this jack-assed, juvenile, off the wall act." He simply descends into an absolute reckless abandon.

In a way, I actually savored that moment. Especially in light of what happened in 1998 with Don. Because, it was like, "You fucking little geek. Everyone just saw you do that in your prissy little jealous rage, and all it did was make me look better. What the hell are you thinking?"

So, I just left, which made him look even worse. I didn't make a big scene. I didn't act all pissed off. I just said, "Hey, see you later!"

That night was a pretty shitty night, all things considered.

When I left Dokken's party, I went up to Hollywood to hang out at the Rainbow. When I was getting ready to leave, the valet pulled my Trans-Am up to the front door.

I looked up and saw Blackie Lawless from WASP standing there. He was walking by with whatever chick he was banging in his coffin that night. He takes a look at my car, then at me, and he squints his eyes, as if to say, "You fucking cocksucker."

What's he do? He jumps on my car, drops an elbow on it, and puts a dent in my brand new Trans-Am! I jumped out of the car and came around swinging, but people got in between it. He squirted away to his ride and took off down Sunset Blvd.

I jumped back into the car and took off after him. I chased him down Sunset and was doing everything I could do to get him pulled over. We were flipping each other off, and yelling. Granted, Blackie is probably 6'4" or 6'5", and could probably kick my ass, but I didn't care. I was going to get a piece of his sorry ass one-way of the other. I could have chewed his fucking eyeball out. He never did pull over.

I was really disappointed that.

Irony of ironies, it was probably Don who popped that dent back out for me.

Go figure.

1984, in a limo going to the Grammys in a pink suit.

1984, New York City. A shoot with Mark (Weiss guy) Weiss, for Faces Magazine
cover for New Years Eve. Photo by Mark Weiss.

1985, the "weird" backdrop shoot.

16

Everybody Loves A Porsche

...Some More Than Others

The Trans Am was my baby through the end of the Cellar tour. But, after I came

home from the 1985 "Invasion of Your Privacy" tour, I wanted a new baby. So, I bought a

Porsche. Which was stolen in 1986.

That's right. You read it. My Porsche 944 was stolen.

The story goes like this: It was 1986 and we were having a bunch of friends over

for a big bar-be-que. We're hanging around at the house, and the party was off to a slow

crawl. So, we started talking shit about golfing.

There was this little par 3 course right in the middle of the neighborhood; 9 really

short holes. We decide that we're going to run over there and shoot this course. It only

takes about 35-40 minutes to do the whole thing, so we'd be back before anyone even

noticed we were gone. No problem.

We got some beers, and a bag; put some ice in it, and we're off! We jumped in my

Porsche and were gone. I say we jumped in, but there were four of us, so it was more like

we "wedged in."

We pulled into the place and see a couple of carloads of kids getting ready to go inside. So, it's like, "Shit, we gotta get in there quick!" Now, understand something. I'm a very impatient person by nature. If I get in my mind that I want to do something, it needs to be done 10 minutes ago. That should make what happened next a little more believable.

I left my keys in the door of the car. I know! Don't start with me! I'm impatient, remember?

What I did was when I opened the driver's door, I pushed the hatch button. The 944's had a button hatch that was supposed to pop up with the press of a button. My 944 sort of struggled with that concept.

My keys were in the door to lock it, and I had pushed the button for the hatch to get the clubs. The guys are going, "Dude, this thing isn't opening." So I shut the door and went back to get the hatch up, leaving the keys hanging. The hatch opened fine, so I pulled out the clubs we were going to share (all we needed was a wedge and a putter), and slammed the hatch down.

I was standing there with the clubs and looked up to see the other people getting out of their car to go inside. I'm like, "Come on, we gotta jet or wait in line", forgetting that my car keys are still hanging in the door.

I'm guessing you know what happens next.

While we were shooting 9 holes, someone took my goddamned car with the keys just sitting there. My wallet was in there. Everything. The little cocksucker who stole it charged up a bunch of shit on my credit cards. It was a miserable nightmare.

So, first off, we finish golfing and I call Jeni from the parking lot. She had been giving me shit, "You're going golfing? We're having a bar-be-que party!"

I'm like, "It's no big deal. It'll take an hour, tops. We'll be right back." She's like "I can't fucking believe that. Whatever."

I'm there, calling her from a payphone in the parking lot. Because, cell phones in 1986 were the size of a briefcase. I know, because I had one. It was in the damned Porsche.

I call her. "Very funny. That's really cute. Now, get over here and pick us up. We're done."

"What are you talking about?", she says.

"You know what I'm talking about. You came over here, took the Porsche. Very funny. Now, come back and pick us up."

She goes, "I don't know what you're talking about. I don't have the Porsche. Are you telling me the Porsche is gone?"

Suddenly, I was getting a bad feeling right in the pit of my stomach. I started in. "Jeni, I'm gonna say this one more time. Did you ... "

She said, "I don't have the car."

I was like, "FUCK!" I was really close to rolling over a little myself.

Jeni came over and picked us up and I called the police. This is at the end of summer in 1986 after the tour. The top quality law enforcement of the time really stepped up...and did nothing. To them, I was just another spoiled superstar with too much money.

At this point, I decided to start calling the cell phone that was in the car. Little fuck-stick probably didn't even know what it was, but it was worth a shot. He never did answer.

Christmas morning, I get a knock at the door, and it's the neighbor's kid from across the street. He was a good kid; nineteen years old. He's kind of shuffling around, and I can tell he's got something important to say.

"Hey, Bobby. What's up. Merry Christmas."

"Merry Christmas."

He's like, "I just came over to give you a Christmas present."

I'm looking, and he's all empty handed. "Okay. So, what is it?"

He says, "I was at a Christmas party last night with a bunch of people I know and went to school with and stuff. All of a sudden, a conversation came up about a friend of ours. I was asking where he was these days."

I used to know the guys name buy heart. Knew it for years, but I can't remember it now. Anyway, my neighbor continues his story.

"They were telling this story where he had been talking shit about how he had stolen this rockstar's car. His wallet and everything was inside, and he went shopping and bought a bunch of shit on the guys credit cards."

So this kid had been telling my neighbor's friends about ripping me off! I couldn't believe it! My neighbor kid had found the dude who took my Porsche. Ultimately, the little prick had taken my car to Mexico and torched it.

The idea of getting ripped off was bad enough, but to think of my beloved Porsche roasting in a Mexican desert? It drove me crazy!

The insurance had settled with me on it, but I got like a grand less than I paid for it and everything. It was bullshit. It just sucked. It completely sucked.

To add insult to injury, I called the cops and gave them this kid's name, address, everything. They never did fuck-all, and I never understood why. I called all the credit card companies and reported it, but nothing. I finally gave up trying. By this time, I was back out on the road.

I kept calling this one detective going, "Why aren't you guys doing anything about this? What is the problem, here? I gave you this thing on a fucking platter."

It was so bad, I almost got to a level that I could never let myself do. But, I was really contemplating having this kid fucked up. I had a friend named Chuck who goes, "Brother, give me his address. I'll take care of shit."

Chuck Daw is a very tight, very long time friend of mine. We worked together when I had that steam cleaning business in 1977. As a matter of fact, his sister Debbie was the girl with me at the Aerosmith concert. I always had a big crush on her. In fact, for my sixteenth birthday, she gave me a birthday present I'll never forget.

We've talked about the Back For More video shoot, but we have a total of 18 music videos.

Video shoots are all the same old shit. Every time, it's the same thing. You get there and stand around with your thumb in your ass. It's a really overdrawn, over produced thing.

I've always complained about video production from the get-go. I see a lot of people standing around on those things, just milking the time, since that stuff is paid by the hour. That always costs us money.

When we did "Nobody Rides For Free", we shot on Zuma Beach, where you're only allowed to shoot from ten in the morning to ten at night. Which is perfect.

Everything gets done in a single, twelve-hour day. Unlike our normal video shoots, which were twenty hour, three day shoots.

"Nobody Rides For Free" was in the movie "Point Break", and they intercut scenes from the film throughout the video. That made it even nicer!

Nonetheless, my point was this; if you can't shoot two hours of footage of each guy, and still not have enough to put together a three or four minute video, then use what you've got!

I always thought videos were a big, over hyped rip-off. We would spend six months cutting a new record, and the production would cost $250,000 - $300,000. We'd spend three days shooting a music video, and the cost was $250,000 - $300,000. That's insane. For ending up with three or four minutes of footage, we could have produced another album?

Bullshit.

I've enjoyed some of the video productions, though. I just hate that they cost so damned much. The "Nobody Rides For Free" shoot was good, because it was outside, on the beach. You know?

The Detonator videos were fun, although they turned out to be kind of stupid to watch. "Loving You's a Dirty Job" turned out okay, but in "Shame, Shame, Shame" they had me doing some stupid, comedic shit.

They shot me jumping out of a plane with no parachute, grabbing onto some chicks underwear as she hangs from her parachute and pulling them off on my way down. I did this stunt for filming, where I jumped off of this plank in between Juan and Robbin, and landed in a giant airbag below. That was cool. But the end result looks gloriously retarded.

The director thought I was funny, as did Marshall, our manager, who directed most of our early videos. They both loved doing shtick, which is why I wound up doing the comedic stuff in the first place.

The video for "Slip of the Lip" was fun, because we shot it on location while out on the road. It's a complete live shoot. I've always liked those. It was down on Bourbon Street, with all the live stuff out on the road.

"Wanted Man" was a kick in the ass! We had just played a show in Tucson, Arizona. Our wake-up call was for 4:00 in the morning. Absolutely brutal. We drove out to Old Tucson, where they shoot a lot of cowboy movies and westerns. We shot all day long, and then had to get on the bus and go play a show in Phoenix. We pulled into Phoenix literally ten minutes before we were supposed to be on stage. So, it was completely chaotic.

But, "Wanted Man" was a killer video, a lot of fun to shoot. All of us had cowboy and Indian fantasies as kids. Gunfights and bar brawls and all that. That video let us kind of play along to those kid charms.

My horse was a bit of a pain in the ass, though. He kept pulling away from me, and just not wanting to do what he was supposed to. It's funny, because people who know horses, and have seen that video always bring that up to me. I guess you can spot those things a mile away, when you've had to deal with them. I kept wanting to "run it out of him", but they wouldn't let me.

None of us in the band were expert horsemen, but I think all of us had been on horseback enough times to know what we were doing, and have a little confidence. For me, I just wanted to go fast. I'm not jumping it, or doing tricks with it. I just wanted to get that rowdy urge the animal had going, and run it out. Plus, I like high speed. Cars, motorcycle, horses... women. I don't give a shit.

I don't have a lot of fear, anyway.

The horses were the only real thing they let us do. We didn't get to do the brawl, or anything like that. Just the horses and the gunfight at the end, where I got my few moment of fame by catching a bullet in my teeth.

They did teach Robbin to throw a stuntman, which you get to see during the brawl. Yea, for Robbin!

The show in Phoenix went off pretty well, despite the complete lack of sleep. So, the video was worth it, plus it turned out to be one of our best.

Phil Collins did a music video where he emulated four or five other videos. "Wanted Man" was one of them. Flattering, in a back handed sort of way.

We get a call to come down for Sam Kinison's "Wild Thing" video shoot. We knew Sam from around town, and as everybody knows, he was a fabulous, hysterical comedian, and a notorious party animal. We get invited to be in the video that he's shooting. He's doing a cover of The Trogs song, "Wild Thing."

He's got Jessica Hahn, who is most known for sucking and fucking Jim Bakker, the televangelist. Now, she emerges with these new, giant 38DDD tits. So, she had gone from this scandalous church thing to romping on the floor with Sam Kinison for his video, showing her tits all over the place, and wearing barely there clothes.

We get there, and the people in tow for this video are Joe Perry and Steve Tyler from Aerosmith; Tommy, Nikki and Vince from Motley; Jon Bon Jovi and Richie Sambora; Slash and Duff from Guns N Roses; and finally us. Me, Stephen and Robbin. I think Warren might have been there too.

So, we get up to this sound stage in Hollywood at Zoetrope Studios, which used to be Charlie Chaplin's studio. They still use the place for movies and stuff. We go in, and they have this ring set up, with a big pit in the middle of it. They're shooting scenes of Sam boxing Jessica, and wrestling around with her, and we're all hanging around the top of the pit just cheering them on. Great fun! I got to hang out with all my friends that day, which back in those days, we all kept in touch. All the time. It was very different from today, where most of us have licked our wounds and gone our ways. We weren't really creative friends with Aerosmith, but obviously we all idolized them.

Aerosmith knew who we were, and were incredible guys. Joe Perry came out and jammed with us in Boston at the Centrum Arena in 1987. He and Tom Hamilton and Joey Kramer came to our show. We got Joe to come up on stage and play "Walking the Dog" with us. That was a trip.

So, that day at Sam's video shoot, I had to go take a piss, which took me back to this decrepit men's room. The thing didn't have urinals, just this really long, really old looking trough. Really old. It reminded me of the schools I went to back in Pittsburgh. So, I'm standing there, taking a leak. This trough has to be thirty feet long, and I'm the only person in there.

I hear someone come into the room while I'm standing there, having a piss. There's all sorts of room at this thing, but the guy comes in and stands RIGHT BESIDE ME, shoulder to shoulder.

My proximity warning is blaring!

There are unwritten rules about the men's room. You don't make eye contact. You don't look down and to the side. And, if there's room, you always leave a space with the guy next to you. That's just the way it is, you know. So, I'm uncomfortable. I look over, and it's Steven Tyler! One of my childhood icons!

What can you do? I said, "What's up, dude?"

Tyler looks at me and goes, "Hey Blotz!"

I about flipped out when he said that. Not only is this a one on one encounter with an icon, but he called me by my nickname! I couldn't believe he knew my name. Much less my nickname! If he's said, "Hey, Bobby", I would have been giddy, but "Hey, Blotz?" Fucking awesome!

Now, let's keep things in perspective, here. I'm standing next to one of my heroes, and we both have our dick in our hand. That's a little weird, giddy or not. So, we both finish recycling our beer, then I'm talking to him and telling him about my days of learning to play drums to "Get Your Wings" and "Toys In The Attic", and how at the gig in 1975, backstage at the Long Beach Arena I had my first backstage moments.

He really got a kick out of hearing those stories. It was one of the cooler, more interesting meetings I've ever had

A lot of amusing things were going on in the 80s. But, one of the weirdest was the whole PMRC thing. Parents Music Resource Center. Tipper Gore.

It's common knowledge that the best thing you can do to sell something is to tell people they can't have it. Especially kids. Then they HAVE to have it, just to rebel, if nothing else. We never needed that kind of publicity, because our sales were strong regardless. And, they never really took a lot of interest in us.

The only thing I ever heard them call us out about was the cover of the "Invasion of Your Privacy" album. Something about looking through a window at a hot chick in her underwear made Tipper and her friends tighten all up. But, that was tame. We were never going to be on their "Filthy Fifteen" list. Not for lyrical content.

I never really gave them that much thought. I thought it was stupid, so it was in one ear and out the other. Of course, when you get acts like WASP out there, and they record the crap they are known for, whether it's "Fuck Like A Beast", or whatever, they need all the help they can get.

That band is one of the worst bands I've ever had the displeasure of watching. So, I couldn't have cared less if they were going after Blackie Lawless and his crew. I'm like, "Go get 'em. Knock yourself out."

A lot of bands used that whole thing to get airtime. Quiet Riot is a prime example. Those guys were never a target, but they got out there and did everything they could to make some noise and get some attention. I don't know. It seems pretty pathetic.

There were guys out there who were using every means of shock they could to sell their records, and then going up there and claiming it was a first amendment right. It's pathetic. They were covering for their lack of talent by being a sideshow attraction.

"Hey! It's Blackie Lawless, the Bearded Lady of Heavy Metal!"

I knew the dudes who were going in front of Congress and testifying. Some of them were great, like Dio and Alice Cooper. Some of them, not so much.

Of the big three, John Denver, Frank Zappa and Dee Snyder, I think Zappa and Denver made the biggest impact. I could have done without Snyder, with his vampire teeth, representing me as a rocker and an artist. But, a lot of people really dug what he had to say.

Zappa? It's not like he's going up there all buffooned out.

Zappa was genius when it came time to fight the PMRC. Nobody could hold an argument with Frank Zappa. It's impossible.

Rock N Roll has always been pigeonholed, poked and prodded at. If that were me, I wouldn't have been nearly as worried about Prince's "Darling Nikki" and her magazine masturbation. I would have been more concerned with "The Exorcist" and Linda Blair as a little girl masturbating with a crucifix! Yelling out the words "Let Jesus Fuck You", and shit like that.

That would seem more damaging, and it happened fifteen years earlier!

Then again, people are entitled to their view, even though some of that lyrical content was completely ridiculous. Some of that needs to be regulated, I guess. You can't have a twelve-year-old girl reading lyrics from WASP, talking about how Lawless likes to fuck chicks in coffins. That's improper. There's some accountability to be had with that. But, no one likes to be told what to do. Certainly, not me!

For some acts, they were desperately trying to get on that bandwagon. No one would have paid them any attention, otherwise.

Personally, I think Tipper and her brood just needed to be laid one time...REALLY WELL. Then all that shit would have fell to the wayside.

RATT's Dancing Undercover record 1986-87 billboard on Sunset Blvd.
Look at gas prices!!!

Tommy Lee, Me and Nikki Sixx on the set of Back For More shoot. They beat the shit out of me in the video, and I mean REALLY punched the shit out of me, fuckers, 1984.

On the set of Wanted Man. Jeni on the left. June 1984.

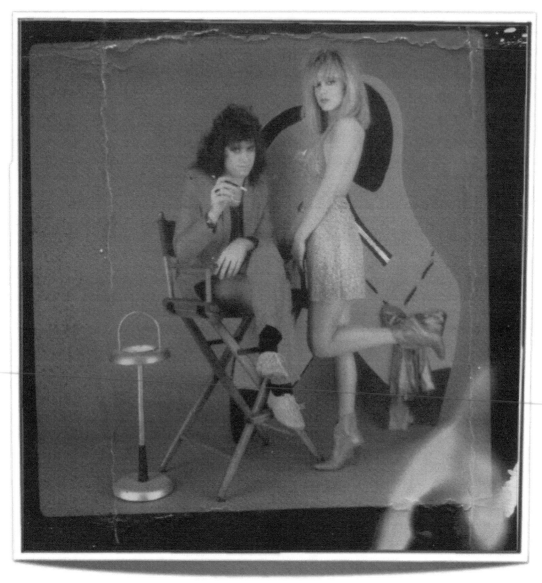

Photo shoot 1985 with a hot blonde model. Photo Courtesy Mark Weiss.

Osaka Japan, 1984.

Tommy and Me, playing a little Poker. Photo courtesy of Neil Zlozower.

17

THE NEED FOR SPEED

I got invited to race for Dodge in the Celebrity Circuit in 1987. They flew me out

to Mid-Ohio Race Track to Skip Barber Racing School. The Circuit was sponsored by MADD. It was a program called "Think before you drink or use drugs and drive." So, I went up there and took the driving school course and was issued an IMSA racing license. Then our first race was out there at the Mid-Ohio Race Track.

That first race had Ted Nugent, me, Craig Chaquico from Starship, one of the guys from .38 Special, there were so many people in that field. I had the pole position for that race. I've always loved to race, and I've always been really good at it. I'm a really good driver. I've raced off-road, and with dirt bikes; I know how to hit my apexes and such; and I have very little fear. So I was really good.

We did the race, and I fucked up. I was looking at the wrong tower coming up to get the green flag. Ted Nugent was fucking with me pretty strong while we were following the pace car. Ted is an out of control nut! He really is a crazy kind of dude. Fun loving as hell, and about three degrees left of center, if you get my drift.

Anyway, Ted guns it, and I'm thinking, "What's he doing? We haven't gotten the green flag yet?" That's when I see all these other cars coming up. I looked in my rearview and went, "Oh shit…"

I saw the flag guy in the opposite tower. "FUCK!"

So, I stand on it, trying to catch up to Ted. I tried that whole race, man. I was right on Ted's ass the whole time, but I could never overtake him. I finished second.

My next race, I had the pole position again. This time, it was in Indianapolis, and Lorenzo Lamas beat me on that one.

But, on my final race, down in Del Mar, California, on my 30th birthday, I finally won. These races were all warm-ups for actual Grand-Prix races; big time GTP cars. I won the very last one, which meant they gifted me with any Dodge car I wanted.

I asked them if I could let my sister pick out a car for her, instead. They agreed, and so I was able to get Carol a brand new van.

That last race was really cool. They gave me this big two-story suite, right on the San Diego Bay. There was a big party with a birthday cake, the whole nine yards. Great time.

On that last race, I had gotten Vince, Tommy and Don Dokken into the Circuit as well. On the final race, they pick the best of all the previous races to pit against each other. All of the first and second place finishers were in this race.

Again, I had the pole, and Vince was right behind me. He kept trying to get in on me while we were following the pace car. So I kept running him off the side. He was getting really pissed! I couldn't hear him yelling, or anything, but I could see his eyes whipping around in his helmet.

I kept flipping him off, and shit, screaming, "Fuck you, dude!" He couldn't hear me, of course, but I didn't care. "After the race, Neil! I'm kicking your ass!" It was good times.

At one point in the race, I spun him out, which really flipped him. He was yelling and banging on his steering wheel. It was worth a good chuckle on my part.

Don Dokken crashed his car on that race. So did Stephen Pearcy. Tommy was trying to keep up and Ted Nugent kept bumping me and shit. But, I held the line. Wound up winning the race. I loved running that circuit. Racing was a rush.

They were asking me to race with them on a team race called Scout Racing. It's where you and your team rotate drivers. One of you races for three hours, then someone else, then another, finally you all take another turn. This goes on for 24 hours.

But, I couldn't do it.

We were on tour, and there just wasn't enough time. It just never happened. I wish it would have, though, because the adrenaline factor is amazing.

I've got a picture from that last race, where Tommy and I are sitting side by side with Stephen and Vince. I laugh about that picture when I talk to Tommy, because it was just a few days before that Jeni and I were at his and Heather's house partying.

It was the night that Tommy and I were talking about how much we hated our singers... then Tommy fell out in the floor.

Yet, there we were, days later, laughing it up with those two guys at a Celebrity Grand-Prix race. Go figure.

There are so many weird assed stories when you're a celebrity. Chuck was always working over at my house. I was doing a lot of remodeling. We bought that house, and I put like $250K into remodeling it. From the curb to the end of the property in the back, anything that could be changed or upgraded, I did. There was new tile, flooring, everything. Even the public walkway in front of the house was new. It had buckled up and cracked and looked like shit. So, I had it all torn out, and relaid so it looked nice and level. Then from where my front walkway started, all the way to the house, everything was brick and tile. I even put in a Koi pond, a pool, a Jacuzzi, and like 40 palm trees.

Of course, I didn't do all this by myself, so Chuck was always working there.

I had to keep changing my phone number, because people would get it and start calling all the time. I had just changed to a new one, barely a month before. But, I started getting this call. Same guy, every time. Just talking shit. Taunting me. "RATT sucks!" Stupid shit like that. Literally anything you could think of to get a rise out of me.

I remember saying, "Look, fucker, if I ever find out who you are, I'm fucking you up so bad!"

"Oh, you are, huh? Fuck you, dude! Come on over right now and do it!" But, of course, he wouldn't say where he was. So it was a bunch of juvenile, high school bullshit.

I'd get the call a couple of times a day, going back and forth talking about the band and the musicians, my wife, all kinds of shit. So, as this went on, I would try to keep him on longer and longer, trying to recognize the voice. I'd just keep him talking.

Then one of the times, I had been trying to figure out where he could have gotten the number. Who could have gotten access to this number? It was so quick after I had it changed. Then it hits me. This vision of me driving through one of those one-hour photo labs places. The kind where you drive up to a window and drop your shit off then come back later and pick it up again.

This memory pops into my head and I bust out with, "Are you that fucking little dude? That little prick at the Photo Mat, down there by Ralph's?"

And, while he had been all talking big and shit, he suddenly stopped in mid-sentence. Busted. I could tell by the quiet that I had got it right.

I go, "You motherfucker! Dude, I'll be down there tomorrow. I'll see you tomorrow." CLICK. And I hung up.

I went down there the next morning. I pulled up and jumped out of my car, and the guy inside immediately started in with, "It wasn't me! It wasn't me!" He's shaking his hands and shit.

I'm like, "Open that window!"

"It wasn't me, man. It was (this other guy who worked there)." The guy was really scared.

"Oh, really? When's he coming in?"

The clerk goes, "I told him not to do it, man. I recognized your name when you came through, and I told him not to do it. But, he took your number off the bag." Anyway, the guy told me when he came in again.

The next day, Chuck and I went down there together. Man, this jack-off was in tears. I mean, Chuck has some huge guns. He's a good-looking guy, around 6'2", but just looking at him, you don't want to fuck around with Chuck. So, this dude was shitting his pants. We didn't harm him, but we did get with the guy's manager.

Call it a "civil dismemberment with minimal bloodshed."

In 1985, we were offered a slot on the "Top Gun Soundtrack." It was easy money, but Warren didn't want to do it. He thought it would alienate our fans; make us look like we sold out. That record went on to be the highest selling soundtrack album ever. Its sold somewhere around twelve million records, and it's still selling!

When we brought it up to him, he'd be like, "The Stones wouldn't do..."

"Warren, we're not the Stones!" We probably lost two million bucks in income for passing on that deal.

To make it worse, we wouldn't have had to work on it. We were going to use a song that was already recorded; demoed for the "Out of the Cellar" album when we were taking Beau Hill for a test drive. It was called "Reach For The Sky", hadn't made the cut for the Cellar album, but was perfect for "Top Gun." We weren't going to have to record for it. The song was already in the can! He convinced the band not to do it, and every one of us had resentment toward him because of that. It was a bad move and a dumb-ass decision!

A couple of years later, we were offered "Iron Eagle" with Lou Gossett Jr. We turned that down as well.

Finally, we were offered Eddie Murphy's "The Golden Child." That was in 1987. And, it was pretty cool. "Body Talk" was in the movie during the scene where he was fighting the bikers. They gave us $150,000 for the song, and paid for the video. At that time, we were spending $200,000 a video, so to me, that song made us $350,000. And, we were in the Eddie Murphy movie! It wasn't his biggest commercial success, but it put us out there in association with Eddie Murphy. At the time, that was a very cool thing for the band.

I've always had this work need, or want. For Christ sake, it's not ditch digging. It's not that hard. It's hard being away from the family. It's hard getting up and moving every day. But, we're musicians, and we're making music. All I want to do is golf during the day, and rock out at night. That's my tour ritual. If it's the right season, I'm on a golf course.

There are so many shows that stick out to me. But, when we went over to England and toured with the Monsters of Rock show, I remember we played at Castle Donnington in 1985.

Ozzy was headlining. Metallica, RATT, Accept, and a bunch of other bands were on the card as well. There were about 125,000 people there, and somebody threw the head of a pig on stage while we were playing. THAT was goddamned disgusting! Then I was told that somebody threw the pig's pussy onstage during Ozzy's show, and Ozzy ate it out. I don't know if there was any truth to that or not, but if it is, it makes for a pretty funny, repulsive rockstar moment.

Given the grand scheme of things I've seen and heard Ozzy Osbourne do ... let's just say that scenario isn't beyond the realm of possibilities.

We toured with Deep Purple over there in 1987, again on the Monsters of Rock bill. That was amazing. 150,000 people a day at these shows, making for absolutely killer dates.

Being a major Deep Purple fanatic, I was especially pumped. After all, Ian Paice is the reason my drumming style is what it is. He and Joey Kramer from Aerosmith, as well as John Bonham from Led Zeppelin. Those three guys combine to formulate my style as a drummer.

But, hands down, my worst moment as a drummer was in Cleveland in 1987. If you read the introduction to this book, you already know the story.

We always started our show on that tour with me standing on my drum throne with this big wash of mood lighting and shit behind me. It made for a nice silhouette thing for the crowd, but for me, it was pretty dark. It's a wonder I didn't kill myself on that throne a lot earlier.

I would be standing up, with the devil horns held high, then I would hop down and do a "four count" on the hi-hats to start things off, and BOOM, we explode into the first song of the night.

My family was in town for that show, so I really wanted it to be great. I hopped down to do the hi-hats thing, and my foot caught on the leg of my drum throne, turning my ankle onto it's side, and sending my foot into an angle it was never meant to bend.

It completely destroyed my ankle. The thing was the size of a grapefruit in a matter of second, and I had to play an entire show with this thing! I had my drum tech getting me glass after glass of Jack, and I couldn't get it in my gut fast enough. I was doing anything I could to numb the pain. Let me tell you, that pain was the worst I've ever felt. Mountainous, monstrous pain!

The tour had just started, really, and by luck, we had four days off in a row. That's something that NEVER happens on the road. Because, any idle day just bleeds money in production costs; especially on arena tours, where you have five semis, four tour busses, and fifty people on the payroll to go along with that. So, for us to have four days off was bad for the tour, but helpful to me.

I spent the whole time with my foot immersed in ice water. Then I had to play for about a month with my left foot as my lead bass drum foot. The hi-hat was another story. For those of you who don't know what a hi-hat is, it's the two crash cymbals that are mounted on a stand, one on top of the other and are clashed together using a pedal. It usually sits to the left of the drummer, and it requires the use of your left foot.

In my case, that wasn't an option.

I had to adjust the thing to where it barely had a gap. Just enough to give it some sizzle, but there was no real hi-hat play. No cutoffs, nothing like that. That was painful as fuck! The shows got pretty blurry after a while, because I had to get loaded beyond belief to just get through it.

Anyone who has ever experienced a severe injury to an ankle, or wrist, or finger, will tell you the same thing. That lightning flash of a burn is followed by complete shock at what just happened. Then it's on! The pain is ruthless! Couple that with being on stage in front of 15,000 people who paid good money to see you that night? Fucking horrifying.

Absolutely scary beyond anything I've ever experienced, because I knew it was bad. Just the jolt that went through my body when it happened.

"Oh, my God. I'm in trouble." I'll never forget that.

It got to the point that I would go out on stage with my crutches so the crowd could see, "Okay, he's fucked up. So if this sucks, it's not his fault."

You just feel such a responsibility on an arena tour. The pressure is unbelievable, and to have an accident that could jeopardize the whole thing??? That busted ankle could have cost 100 or more people their jobs!

Then there was the time that I put out a hotel fire in upstate New York. That was pretty exciting.

What was weird, was that I had been watching "The Towering Inferno" at the hotel in New York City, the night before! If you remember that flick, it was about a huge fire in a skyscraper, and everyone trying to find a way out. It was a classic 70's disaster flick with Steve McQueen. I'm a sucker for movies, especially old flicks that I hadn't seen in years. So, I'm just laying around, after our show at Madison Square Garden, grooving to this old movie.

The next day, I drive up to upstate New York for our next show. I get to the hotel, and get settled in, just in time to go to the arena for sound check. I'm cruising down the hall of this hotel, and I smell smoke! And, sure enough, there's smoke all in the hallway!

No way! So I'm calling on all of my fire and rescue training that I'd gotten from Steve McQueen. I'm feeling doors, and shit, trying to find the blaze. And, I actually find the room that's on fire!

Smoke was pouring out from under the door. I'm beating on the thing, and there's no answer. So, I do my best Hollywood Action Star move and kick the door in. The carpet was totally engulfed in fire! I took towels from the bathroom, threw them in the tub and wet them, and was smothering the thing.

Then I called the front desk and told them their hotel was almost burned down. The whole thing made MTV news and all that. I guess, because I told everyone on the tour about it, that it made it's way back to management. They thought it would be a good idea to publicize the whole thing.

So, for about 15 seconds, I was a hero on MTV. Of course, for 10 years, I was a rockstar on MTV. Take your pick, because they were both pretty cool.

Given the penchant for the average LA band to self-destruct in the drug scene, RATT was managing to avoid that. Don't get me wrong, we were by no means drug-free. We all did blow.

I had done blow for years, well before I joined RATT. In the Seventies, no one could understand why cocaine was illegal. All it makes you do is talk too much, feel good, and it's perfectly fine...right? Well, maybe not.

But, as much as I did, I never got hooked to it. Never. There was even a point at which I was dealing some blow. A gram sort of thing. It was just to make extra money. I needed money. It was laziness, or whatever you want to call it; and, it wasn't my proudest moment. That doesn't change facts, though. Krell was a part of the scene back then. It was viewed with the same casual humor as weed is today. I mean, I used to have Vince Neil coming over at three o'clock in the morning.

"Dude, just two or three grams, that's all."

One night, we all went out. Me, Jeni, Vince and his wife Beth. We went to the Comedy Magic Club in Hermosa Beach to see Gallagher, the guy who smashes watermelons with a giant mallet. Bill Kirkenbauer was there too.

I don't remember how we were introduced, but they knew the guys from Mötley and RATT. They all came back to our house where we were snorting blow and drinking. It wasn't long before Vince started being Vince, getting all weird and shit. He started accusing these guys of looking at his wife's tits and stuff. Then Vince and I started wrestling around and fighting in the living room and just blew those guys minds. They looked really uncomfortable and not sure what to do with themselves.

Of course, that was around the time I first met Vince and Tommy. Those guys came out to a party at my house after the Foreigner / Scorpions show at Anaheim Stadium.

The guys from Scorpions rode back to the house with us in my little Datsun! I remember backing that thing down into the guts of the baseball stadium, piling those guys in, and driving them out in this little piece of shit 1977 Datsun B-210. They had just finished playing in front of 50,000 people!

The guys in Mötley and RATT came over and we partied all night. I remember Matthias Jabs looking at me and with his thick German accent going, "Bubby! You need to change zee name of zis band! No vun is going to buy a record from a band called RATT!" I remember laughing and going "Yeah, Matthias, 'Scorpions' is a little less threatening of a name." It was pretty funny. He's probably changed his mind about it, since then.

We partied all night long, and that was when I first got to know Tommy. He was just a kid then. Let's face it. We were all kids, but when you're 21, 18 seems a huge difference. But that didn't matter, because Blotz and T-Bone were fast friends. Mötley and RATT did a lot of partying in those days!

In 1986, while we were recording the "Dancing Undercover" album, I bought a boat, which tripped the guys out.

After I had finished all my drum tracks, I went with a buddy of mine, Mark Valdez, down to Long Beach at this place called Marine Stadium where you could water ski. It was this giant, intercoastal, just off the ocean, lake kind of thing. And, Mark had a little ski boat down there.

So, we went down there, and I wanted to drive the boat. I'd never driven a boat before, but I drove all over the place in this thing. It was great! As we were leaving, the guys were like, "Hey, dude, there's a boat show down in Long Beach by the Long Beach Arena. Stop and check it out."

I went down there, and I bought a yacht.

The king of the giant impulse buy, remember! It was completely retarded. I had just driven a little tiny ski boat, and I came back with something that had bedrooms and a kitchen and all that. So, I came to the studio the next day with the manual brochure and showed those guys. And they went, "You're fucking kidding us, right? You bought a fucking yacht?"

My boat was the source of MANY interesting stories. But those are yet to come. I'm getting ahead of myself again.

During the 1986 tour of the UK, we met up with Motley. They were coming in to play, and we were getting ready to leave, but we were staying at the same hotel for a night.

Tommy and me went out on the town partying. We went to all these clubs, finally settling at this strip joint. We were big shots at home, but we were only "sort of" known in Europe. Barely. You know, just in certain clubs, that sort of thing.

Well, we settled into this strip club. And, they figured we rockstars of some kind, because T-Bone was ordering bottle after bottle of Cristal. I'm drinking what I usually drank, which was Jack and Coke, and, we've got all these girls sitting around us. They were sitting on our laps, hanging out and giggling. It was pretty cool.

At the end of the night, they bring us the bill, and I see Tommy just shoot his head around at the guy who gave it to him. And, I can see he's pissed! His face is all like, "Dude, what the fuck is this?" I'm across the way, and I can see him pointing at the bill and gesturing wildly. Then he starts chewing on a strand of his hair. That was the sign.

Anytime Tommy started getting nervous, he would chew on his hair.

So, I go over to check it out. I'm like, "T-Bone, what is that?"

He's really worked up. "Man, it's our bill."

"Okay, so what's the deal?"

"Well, it's in pounds, but the guy just told me how much that it is in dollars, and it's three grand."

I go, "WHAT?!?" We get the guy back over, and find out that he's been charging us for the girls just sitting there, and all the champagne.

I'm like, " T-Bone, bro? I was drinking Jack and Coke all night. Figure out what we got going here."

I think I picked up about $800, and he got the rest on his AMEX. I had to kick in on some of the chick thing, which sucked, because we never asked for it, and were never told! We went back to the hotel, I've got this on videotape, and we were partying in my room.

I had to be up at seven o'clock in the morning, because RATT was going to Abbey Road Studio! This is the place where The Beatles recorded so many of their albums! This place is Rock N Roll history! They were going to shoot us playing in Abbey Road Studio, and beam it out via satellite, which was very new back in those days, to a television show in Japan. It's seven in the morning, but over in Japan, it's the dead of night, and we're going on a TV show that has fifteen million viewers a week!

I forget what the hour exchange is, but it's significant. My call time was really early, and Tommy didn't leave my room until about 5:30 in the morning. So, I couldn't think about sleeping.

I get up at 7:00, after I've dozed for about an hour, still half drunk. Then, we get to Abbey Road Studio. As a Beatlemaniac, to be at Abbey Road should have been a bright eyed, bushy tailed, sponge moment for me. I mean there's the crosswalk. There's the steps up. The whole kit caboodle.

We get there, and the Japanese are in there. They have us set up in the tracking studio; the big room. They have a train track set up around our gear, and a platform with a camera on it that rides around the track. I think it's called a dolly track. Anyway, it goes all the way around our set in a circle. And, they were zooming around on it while we played.

Anyway, while we were waiting for them to set up, there was this old guy there. I forget his name. This guy had been working there since the 50's. He was still there in 1985. So, I started telling him how into the Beatles I was, and how my whole family were fans, and yada, yada, yada. So, he gave me a personal tour of the place. Which was an amazing feeling, being in that room, knowing that those guys were in that room writing and recording and stuff.

So, after he gave me the tour, I slipped back into where we were going to be doing the recording for "Lay It Down." "Lay It Down" was the song they were beaming. Once I got back in there, it was "not ready", and it wasn't going to be "be ready" for the next ... "whatever." So, it was, "Just go hang out somewhere, and we'll find you."

I wandered back down the hallway that the old man took me down, and wandered into one of the studio rooms where the Beatles had recorded. I went into this room, and laid down and went to sleep.

They finally found me. It was one of those things where I was "missing" and "sleeping".

"Woah, oh, shit dude! Sorry, I was taking a nap."

"Yeah, no shit. We've been looking for you for the last 45 minutes."

It gave me a little extra nudge of sleep to help me do the performance better, I guess.

I called Tommy later that day at the hotel. Tommy was hurting from our party the night before.

He goes, "Fuck, dude. That was fun last night, but I'm hungover, and that BILL! What was up with that bill?!?"

"I don't know, man. That SUCKED!"

Eight hundred bucks was a lot, for me anyway. I mean, it wasn't like I didn't have money, but I never had bar tabs like that, not that high. Especially in those days. We pretty much would drink for free.

This was all at the end of the 1985 Invasion Tour. We had finished in the states on New Year's Eve, then went to Europe with Ozzy.

We had a lot of history with the Mötley guys. A lot of history.

Poison was one of those bands with a dubious reputation for getting along, but I never really saw that from them. They didn't come on to the scene until sometime in 1986. By that time, we had been on the road seemingly forever.

When we got back home, all I wanted to do was hang with the kids, golf and ski. I really wasn't into checking out the local bands. So, we didn't meet Poison until they opened for us in 1987.

Our first gig with them was at Reunion Arena in Dallas. RATT, Poison and Cheap Trick.

I remember during sound check of that show, we were in this huge arena, and there were four random dudes sitting in the fourth row all right next to each other. We had no idea who they were. But, at the end of every song, they would be clapping. At one point, I stood up and shouted to them.

"Sound alright out there?" They were all thumbs up and grinning.

"Yeah, cool, great!" Turned out that was Poison.

I watched them that night, and my jaw was just hanging open! You've got to be kidding me. These guys are comical! It was Barnam & Bailey retarded. They couldn't play. They were just … so … goofy!

I was like, what the hell is going on? I think Stephen knew them, or something. It was obvious that we were doing them a favor. I don't want to sound down on them, because they were cool guys, but their stage show was sideshow ridiculous.

I remember that Ric Neilson, from Cheap Trick, and I would go out and watch them every night and just laugh our asses off. But, after a few shows, they started to get tighter, and they were out with us for months!

When their record started to do really good, and we could tell. Because at first, the audience was like, "What the fuck is this?!?" Then the record started taking off and you could hear the applause and could tell they were really starting to make ground. It wasn't long before they started wanting a little more production up there, which we accommodated for them.

It was a good tour. Lots of fun. It was cool to watch those guys evolve in front of us. We did months and months with them, and it became very successful for us. Not as successful as our 1985 tour with Bon Jovi opening, but still a very good tour.

But, true to form, the break after Poison didn't last. We were right back out on the road, again.

In 1987, we were on our way to tour Europe with Deep Purple, and we were on a flight that was taking us over the North Pole and Canada. During the flight, this older man had a heart attack, and our production manager, Charlie Hernandez, this giant Puerto Rican, muscled the seat out to get to the guy and do CPR.

He revived the guy, and the plane had to emergency land in Canada. So, Marshall, being the kind of manager that he was, took the opportunity to get a little publicity out of it, and made a big deal to the airline that it was one of our guys who saved the old man's life. We had to be in Europe to start a tour immediately, and we weren't going to make it. That was bullshit, of course. We had plenty of time. But, nevertheless, you'd have thought we were transporting organs for transplant the way Marshall sold it to them.

Before we knew it, we were all on the Concorde, flying to Europe.

Concorde flights were something like $10,000 per person. It was amazing. Flying at Mach 2, somewhere around 68,000 feet, I'm strolling through this plane with a video camera, talking to the flight crew and the pilot. It was pretty wild.

That plane is extremely tiny inside. It looks huge from the outside, but it isn't. For anyone who has ever been in a leer jet, or a turbo-prop plane, you have an understanding of what it's like on the inside of the Concorde. Tight as it was, though, it was still badass to make it all the way across the Atlantic in three hours. King had to duck his head to walk down the aisle of that thing.

We played the Los Angeles Sports Arena in 1989. RATT, Kix and Britney Fox. Tommy came down with Heather, got up and jammed with us. We played an AC/DC song. So, I enjoyed the hell out of that show.

By 1989, we were all pretty fashioned out. Some were really flamboyant with it, too. Even Mötley was, to an extent. Everyone except Guns N Roses. They were tattoos, leather and denim. That sort of thing.

After the show, I had just gotten showered up and dressed. I was wearing this really hot blazer thing I had bought on Melrose. It was a purple, satin kind of jacket. Really sharp looking with the sleeves that would cuff up. The inside lining was a pinstripe look. It really looked cool. Especially for the time. Padded shoulders and everything.

Tommy and Heather came backstage.

T-Bone and Heather walk through the door, and fuck all if she isn't wearing the exact same jacket!

I was like, "Okay. That's that." I immediately took it off.

I never wore that coat again. It really was a gay looking jacket, now that I think about it.

It seems that most of my notorious stories always had Tommy involved in some fashion or form. There was the time that T-Bone and I were out on the town with Ozzy and Sharron Osbourne.

Imagine this picture. Ozzy and Sharron, Tommy and I all crammed into my Porsche. We had been partying all night, and were finally making our way back to Ozzy and Sharron's hotel room. They were in the penthouse of the hotel, and there were only two rooms on the floor. Theirs and some random CEO's.

Outside the CEO's room were a pair of very expensive shoes, which had been set out there to be shined.

Ozzy, being the anti-establishment kind of guy that he is, is like, "Quick, piss in the shoes!"

"What? What are you talking about? I'm not going to piss in them."

He waves me off, and looks at Tommy. "Then, quick, shit in them!"

Tommy looks at him like he's flipped out. "I'm not going to shit in them. You shit in them."

Now, Ozzy is a reactionary kind of guy. He's quick to embrace whatever gauntlet has been tossed out. Ozzy grabs the shoes, drops his pants and hovers, then pinches a shit off into them!

Oh my God! It was the most putrid stink. Fucking hideous. Mind you, we had consumed A LOT of alcohol that night. This stench was like a physical thing, just kicking the hell out of our senses. How we kept from puking, I have no idea.

The CEO should have been honored. He had the Prince of Darkness drop a deuce in his shoe! He could've had that thing bronzed, and sold it to some random fan for three times what the shoes were worth. I know he could have.

I've met the fans who would buy a bronzed shit!

Afterward, Sharron came up. She had been downstairs, waiting for the guy with the room key. We went into the room and partied out for the rest of the night.

Pearcy showed up late at night. I have no idea where he came from. I finally left there at, like, eight o'clock in the morning. I was on my way back home to Redondo, and we had snorted so much blow that night, and I hadn't had any napkins. My nose had been running really badly, and I kept using my shoulder to wipe it off on.

I got pulled over for speeding, and how I managed to not go to jail, I still don't know. Because, I had white dots all over my shoulder and arm from where I had been wiping my nose.

I had crusted cocaine snot all over me. How's that for a sexy rock star look? I'm so lucky. Yet another stupid thing you do when you're stupid and young.

I ran into Sharon again in 1998 at the Wilshire Theater in Hollywood during the Mötley show. I hadn't seen her in a long, long time, but it was right after their Behind the Music on VH-1.

She's like "Hey, Bobby! Hi!"

I told her that I was really touched by her story in Behind the Music. She is so sweet and nice. People like to trash talk her in the media, but I'm telling you, she's as good a person as I know. Those people are full of shit.

We're laughing up the old times, talking about the VH-1 episode, and she goes, "Wouldn't it have been great if they had put "the shoe" in there?"

I about fell out laughing. "Oh, my God, you remember that, too?"

She goes, "Oh, God, are you kidding?"

I guess a rancid shit in a shoe is hard to forget.

I'll give you another example. My 32nd birthday. 1990.

One of my neighbors, and really good friends, was Alan Niven. Alan was the manager for Guns N Roses, and it so happened that on the night of my 32nd, Guns was playing the Los Angeles Coliseum, opening up for the Rolling Stones.

I'm a huge Stones fan. Alan knew it, and suddenly BAM! There I am with a laminate pass around my neck, watching the show.

It was awesome! A great birthday present. And, the Stones were really knocking it out during their set.

I couldn't resist getting a closer look.

Gradually, I worked my way to stage right, where the bands are led up. In a matter of minutes, I was standing on the stage, just out of sight of the crowd.

Mick Jagger kept looking over at me, confused. It was pretty obvious that he had no idea who I was, or what the fuck I was doing there. Everyone else around me was personnel working on the show.

After about 20 minutes, this guy taps me on the shoulder, and with a thick English accent goes, "Excuse me. Who the fuck are you, and what are you doing on my stage?"

I tried to calm the guy down. I told him that I was a friend with Alan Niven, manager of Guns N Roses. My name was Bobby Blotzer and I'm the drummer for RATT. It's my 32nd birthday, and I'm a huge fan.

The guy's like, "Happy birthday. Now, get the fuck off my stage."

He wasn't having it.

"Yeah, yeah, yeah...keep walking." He led me down the stairs at stage right. By the time we got to the bottom, I'd convinced him I wasn't just some guy who wandered up there, and I kinda belonged.

So, he mellowed a bit. At least he didn't try to have me tossed from the place.

From there, I figured the best place in the house to hear the show was going to be from the sound booth, since the guys mixing the damn thing were all sitting right there.

So, I made my way through the crowd to the sound booth. Again, a place I shouldn't have been allowed.

But, there I was. Standing there at the board, sharing a beer with Barbara Streisand.

It was a great show. And for 20 minutes, I was on stage with the Stones. Very memorable for me. And Babs hardly backwashed at all.

The night ended with just as much surprise as it began.

It's two in the morning, and I'd just gotten back to the house. The show is still buzzing in my ears when the phone rings.

It's Alan Niven.

"Dude, get dressed. I'm taking you somewhere."

"Where?"

"Just get dressed. I'm sending a car."

Sure enough, a big limo pulls up in front of my house a few minutes later. They won't tell me where we're going, but by three o'clock, I'm standing on the tarmac of a private airport next to a leer jet.

Alan shows up, we board, and by sunrise we're on the East Coast, making plans to see Great White.

I don't remember much after that.

Thirty-two was a really good number!

Stories like these don't happen with the same frequency anymore. These days, we just don't hang out much anymore. Everyone is off doing their own thing, having evolved beyond the 80s. So, it's more of a matter of just running into each other every once in a while.

I still have all the same friends that I always have had, and for that, I'm thankful. I just don't see them much.

I see them when I see them.

Back in our early days, when we were rehearsing at Dennis O'Neil's mother's house. Our chemistry came pretty quick. I was a good drummer, and had a lot of experience. The others could sense that, I think. Plus, we were all influenced by the same bands. Aerosmith, in particular. We were all close to the same age, and had the same influences, and that became a launching pad. We were just like, "Well let's have at it. Let's do it."

Our mentality was not so much a family mentality as it was just a gang. It was us, out there to get "them." "Them" could be anything from an individual to the world. But, we were out to plant our flag and take what's ours.

Of all the guys in the band, I was probably tightest with Robbin. He was the most sensible. He was pretty well educated, and had an even, cool temperament. Juan and I were pretty tight, too, though. Because we were close while growing up. But, then Juan started having some serious ego issues, especially when we really started to get famous. It just got to the point where I really couldn't stand him. I didn't want to be around the guy, and he had been one of my closest bros.

Warren and I were like brothers who, when you see them, it's great, but when you don't see them, you don't see them. It's no big deal.

The Invasion tour finished off in the United States in San Diego; Stephen, Robbin and Warren's hometown. Then we *finally* got three or four weeks off. It didn't last long, though. A month later, it was off to Europe with Ozzy and the Monsters of Rock Tour. After that, we were off to Japan to wrap things up.

We had been on the road nonstop for almost four years. The strain on the band was very evident, and for me, all I wanted was to get home and be normal for a while.

The thing never seemed to end. Not that I wanted the BAND to end, mind you. I just wanted a chance to be a dad and a husband for a while. But, every time we would get home, it was immediately back into the studio, then right back out on the road.

The Show Pony Express, that was us. Atlantic Records and our management were driving our asses, whip in hand. I wanted any chance to see my family, and when they came, I jumped on them.

I was the first one in the band to buy a house. Paid $248,000 for it. It was right on Torrance beach, in a neighborhood called the Hollywood Riviera, right at the beach. And, in the tradition of the booming 80s, my interest rate on the loan was, brace yourself, 13%. Fucking Reagan Era, baby! Yuppies ruled the Earth, and greed was still good!

I put $50,000 down on a $248,000 house and my payments were still $2300 a month. At the time, I was getting rich, so I didn't give a shit, but, Jesus! Today, you get that house at 5%. It's nothing.

When we got back, they tried to shove us right back into the studio to record "Dancing Undercover." But we weren't anywhere close to ready for it. Our manager was giving us shit because there was a deposit on the studio, and we were going to lose it if we didn't get in there. So, there was a lot of pressure.

That album was winged together so quick. Pearcy was at his worst. The guy wasn't at a single rehearsal. There was really a lot of dissension in the band by that point. Lots of bad vibes. I got to say that most of that blame falls right at the feet of the label and management. They worked us right into the ground for three straight years, and now they were "back for more," to not put too fine a point on it.

There's some good stuff on it, too, but by and large, it wasn't my favorite. Especially side B. There are songs on there that are musically cool, but the lyrics are a waste and it blows it for me.

One night, somewhere around 1988, Jon Bon Jovi calls me up. He was in town, and he goes, "Hey, Blotz. You wanna go to this Keith Richards listening party for his 'Cheap Winos' record down at the Whisky. You want to go?"

"Yeah, bro. That sounds pretty hot."

So, Jeni and I pick Jon and his wife, Dorothea up at their hotel. I was really surprised when I saw where they were staying, too. I was giving him shit about it. I'm like,

"Jon, you've sold 20 million records with that last album, and you're staying in this place?!?"

He was staying in a Ramada Inn. It was in the Wilshire area, but a really old, kinda dumpy Ramada. It was WAY below what he was used to.

We get to the Whisky, and they're playing the record over and over. We see Keith come in, surrounded by bodyguards and make his way to the VIP area.

We were all in the balcony area, sitting at a table. Keith walks right past us on his way upstairs.

"Well, there he is! Keith Richards!" I figured that was the only time we would get to see him. He looked well guarded and unapproachable.

A few minutes later, a guy comes up and says, "Jon, Keith would like to meet you and take some pictures."

I was like, "Shit." I really wanted to go up, too, but I didn't want to intrude, you know.

So, I sat there with Jeni and Dorothea, just shooting the shit for about a half hour. Jon comes back, and I was asking him all these questions. He was a little star-struck by the whole thing, and I can't say I blame him. It's fucking Keith Richards!

A few minutes later, Keith came back down, being escorted out. So, it was over. He had made his appearance and the evening was done.

At some point, Jon decides he want to go, so he's like, "Man, if you want to stay, that's cool. I'll just jump a taxi." So, he and Dorothea were off. So, Jeni and I, along with my buddy, Krell-Gar, Phil Soussan, the bass player for Ozzy, and this chick that used to be with Mick Brown, the drummer for Dokken are all sitting on the back stairs at the Whisky, just inside the back door. We're just talking and having a good time.

All of a sudden, the back door opens, and in steps Keith Richards without a bodyguard in sight. I look at him, and I'm like, "Holy fuck. Keith, what are you doing, man?"

He's like, "How you doing?" In his raspy, vice-addled voice. He looks around, and goes, "Ah, shit. I thought I gave this place up in 1963!"

I go, "I'm glad you're still here." I introduce everyone around, and he's hanging out, talking to us. I was telling him what a Stones fanatic I was, since I was old enough to walk. He's being real polite, but has to get upstairs.

He stops on his way by and looks at me. "You want to have a drink?"

I'm like, "Hell, yes!" It was clear he was talking to me, but Phil Soussan latched on to our belt loops and joins us.

We get upstairs, and Keith pulls out a bottle of Jack Daniels. He pops the cap, and we're passing this thing around for a while, just taking a pull and handing it on. I was completely tripping out. I'm thinking, "This is never going to happen again, so definitely enjoy it. Milk it for all it's worth."

I'm asking him questions about old Stones songs and records. I told him that "Exile on Main St." was my favorite Stones album of all time. A double album, and every single song was fantastic.

He's like, "That was a good one, that was a good one."

I go, "How's Charlie doing these days?"

He takes a long drag off of his cigarette, sucking the most he can get out of that thing, like he's the masculine version of Bette Davis; blowing a long cloud of smoke out like it's never going to hurt him.

He looks at me, and goes, "Ah, Charlie's great. That Charlie loves to buy cars. He's got a whole stable of them, there in his garage." With his English accent, garage came out as "gay-rodge". Pretty funny. "He never drives them. He just starts them up and stares at the dash. He loves to play with them."

Jon was tripping when I told him about it.

Another instance with Jon, the day before they got their American Music Award for "Slippery When Wet", we were over at Doc Mahgee's house for a bar-be-que party.

Some of the guys from Mötley were there, and the guys from Bon Jovi. I was the only one from RATT who was there, but a bunch of people who worked for Doc were hanging around. It was a pretty big party.

We stayed well into the evening, long after people started to fade away and leave. Jon and I were shooting pool, and doing shots of tequila; just shooting the shit. It got to where it was just the two of us.

I had sent Jeni home with the car, because I wanted to stay and hang out. Doc told me, "You want to stay, hang out. I have a limo outside. I'll have it take you home."

So, me and Jon were getting completely crapulous on tequila. That was Jon's drink back then. Tequila, the bitch whore of all hard liquor. So, we're polluted pretty bad, and I go, "Jon, I'd never ask anyone this normally, but I've had enough to drink, so I'm going to. What was your take on that last tour and record?"

He goes, "You mean as a whole, or what I pulled myself on that?"

"What was your take?"

He thinks for a second, then says, "I don't usually tell people stuff like that, but since I'm as shitfaced as you are, I might as well. Right now, it's sitting at about eighteen."

I grin, and all tongue-in-cheek, I go, "Eighteen hundred bucks? Odd, I would've thought you would have made more than that!"

He starts laughing, and goes, "Yeah, eighteen hundred bucks." I'm thinking to myself that this guy who opened for me last year made $18 million.

I go to leave, and the limo is gone. Doc comes outside and goes, "What are you still doing here?" I told him about the limo, and he calls them back to take me home. The guy picked up the bill on it, and everything. Doc's a great guy. I just crashed out in the back of the limo.

The next day, I was SO hung over. I was hurting all day long, and kind of laughing to myself, because I knew Jon had to be hurting too, but he had to get up in front of a huge audience at the award show and look good!

Sucks to be him, right? Mister "I made Eighteen!"

So, I watched it on TV, and they kept showing him on the camera all night. He looked all right, but I know different. No way was he was in good shape. No way!

Two nights later, there was an Aerosmith show at the Forum. I was at the sound board with the laminate pass, and I feel this tap on my shoulder. It was Jon. We immediately started pointing at each other, laughing. I knew exactly what he was going to say.

The first thing he does is hand me my wallet. I'm like, "What the fuck are you doing with my wallet?"

He goes, "You left it at Doc's the other night."

"And YOU have it? Alright, whatever."

He goes, "I am never drinking with you again!"

"Yeah! I'm the bad influence in this. You're the one who drinks tequila, bro. I was drinking tequila with YOU! That shit was YOUR fault."

So, we had a big laugh about that. Then, all matter-of-factly, he goes, "Hey, I'll be right back. I've got to go up there and jam with these guys."

The bastard! Go ahead and rub my face in it!

About ten minutes later, Steven Tyler is bringing him out on stage to jam.

These are the ways and days that we lived at that time. Life was a fairy tale, written by the Brothers Grimm!

There's really not much to talk about on the Dancing Undercover tour. It was just another tour. We had a good time, with Cheap Trick and Poison opening for us. There's some good friendships from that tour, but while it was well attended, it was becoming mundane. It was our life; almost our entire life. We set them up with a huge stage, a giant lighting truss and all the bells and whistles, but, we had been crushed under touring and recording.

We were numb.

After Dancing Undercover, we made a point with management. DO NOT BOOK A THING! NOTHING! WE WILL TELL YOU WHEN WE ARE READY! After the deposit fiasco at the studio for the Dancing Undercover record, we weren't going to deal with that again. That's why that album was so forced. That's why it doesn't really fit with the rest of RATT's catalogue. We had to throw it together overnight because our dumb-ass manager dropped a giant deposit on a studio. We were nowhere near being ready.

This band is not a band that writes well on a tour. I don't know why that is, but it is. Warren has to sleep during the day, because he stays up all night on the bus. On the road, it's always, "Oh, my head's not in the right place to write." That makes no sense to me. Get your head on straight. Let's get on it, and make shit happen. We could bring a studio on the road. We could be totally self-contained. Again, artist VS. businessman. It's a volatile combination. I don't understand why it can't happen, but it doesn't with these guys. I don't push it.

The next album was "Reach for the Sky," and it was the same old same. RATT was slowly spiraling down. We went to a new producer, thinking that would cure our woes. Mike Stone had worked with Queen and Journey, and a bunch of others. He, unfortunately, had a pretty bad alcohol problem, but he was still getting really good sounds in the studio. But, Stephen did the same thing again. He took these songs and wrote some really weak lyrics.

When we finally heard what he did, we were in shock! We were in trouble. The situation was bad enough that Atlantic made us go back and rewrite it all, with Beau Hill taking over the production helm. Stephen had no choice. For once, it wasn't the band criticizing him. I'm sure he felt like the whole world was ganging up on him, and it was, to a sense. But when Doug Morris, the president of Atlantic tells you that your work isn't good, so do something, you do it, or you likely won't get a chance to do it again.

Around 1989, I built a studio in my house, and started working up my own material to bring in for the "Reach For The Sky" record. There were a handful of ideas I brought in. But, it's hard when you have those four guys writing songs. First off, there's a greed factor involved.

Originally, the band split everything five ways. That's the way it stayed until 1984, when the other four guys got together and voted my split of the writers share out. From that point on, we split all publishing five ways, but publishing would only account for 50%. The remaining 50% was the "writer's share".

I'd do a ton of arranging on the songs. I've got a gift for arrangement. We'd all contribute to that, but there was never any writing credit for working up the music.

Warren would be against it from the start. "That's an arrangement. Not writing." But, when you write the song out on a chart and compare it to what it was before the "arranging", clearly my parts are in there, contributing to the writing of the song.

It's a sore spot, especially for me.

They didn't consider me a writer, and I had no say in the matter. That's the bitch about a democracy. You can get ganged up on. They didn't want to split up that song writing pie, and from that point on, I made half of what everyone else in the band made.

For my part, I just wanted to make records I could be proud of. I'm not saying our stuff was getting bad. It wasn't, but when you've got to look for reasons to like something, it usually means it's not good enough. In 1989, I had to look for reasons to like what RATT was doing.

We did what we were told, and "Reach For The Sky" was completed. The only problem was, we still didn't have a good single on it. Nothing that was radio friendly, with a great hook.

At the last minute, "Way Cool Jr." was brought in and worked up off a riff that Warren had been fooling around with. It was a song we had worked on before, but it hadn't gone on the record. Beau heard the riff and got onboard with Stephen and Robbin writing the lyrics. We had our single.

The "Reach For the Sky" tour consisted of us, Kix and Brittney Fox. When that tour wrapped, we got into working with Desmond Child on writing. During the writing sessions, he quickly saw the dysfunction in this band. Helen Keller could have picked up on that! It was really a hard time, creatively. Stephen can be hard to work with, especially when he isn't happy. And, Stephen hadn't been happy in a long time.

It became impossible to get things done. Add to it the fact that the rest of us were developing some serious burn out issues, and our personalities were starting to reflect that. You can do the math. RATT was on life support.

Once we got famous, Stephen had his own dressing room on tour, while we were all in another dressing room. It turned into an "us against him" sort of thing. Lead singers, man. They call it "L.S.D." "Lead Singer Disease." They are a breed, almost without exception. Singers are not normal people. And, in truth, they can't be. It takes something beyond the normal thought process to stand in front of a crowd of people and perform with only your voice.

There are exceptions to this, though rare. Sammy Hagar is an exception, but then Sammy is a guitarist as much as a singer. He's got a good balance. But the others...

Our recording process changed significantly over the course of those first five records. When we put out the first EP, with Liam Sternberg producing, he really didn't do what most producers do. He would tell us that we sounded great, and he might make a tiny suggestion here or there, but he wasn't anything like Beau Hill. We already had the arrangements for the music. I don't remember him contributing anything there.

But, with Beau, it was completely different. He would have everything all charted out. He was just way more meticulous. You know? Making sure every bass drum pattern was the same. Just way more attention to detail.

With the EP, we did it all in two weeks. "Out of the Cellar" took two months. Originally, when we would record, it was me, Juan, Robbin and Warren, just working out trying to get a drum track. Once you had the drum track, you would go back, and set everything up in the room to do real guitar tracks.

It was just easier that way. In that studio on the EP, there wasn't really isolation rooms for the guitars. It was just a wide open space. There was just the iso-room for vocals. So, they would plug into the board and I could hear them for the parts. We did that for "Out of the Cellar," too.

On the Invasion album, I started playing alone. It was a lot faster, and I was just really good at remembering arrangements with no one else playing. Just me and a click track.

Beau Hill loved it. So did I. I was in and out of the studio in a week, and my work on the album would be done! It was great. It was days less of having to stop and restart because someone fucked up a part, or the groove wasn't working, or some shit like that.

Once I was done, I was done. I didn't have to come back in to record. Everything was built off of what I had done in the first week. I would drop by once in a while to listen, usually when I was heading uptown or during the day if I was bored. But, I'd just hang back and listen to whatever was going on. I had no responsibilities at that point. It was great.

I recorded in that manner all the way up until "Detonator." On Detonator, we all went in and tracked together. That album was a lot more about trying to spark some unity with the band. We all saw what was coming, but I don't think anyone knew how to stop it. Try as we might, I think the damage had been done.

Then on "Detonator", I had a lot of good ideas. Desmond Child saw that and wanted to do some of the tunes. "One Step Away" was going to be a single, and that's my song. Unfortunately, it never got to the stage. The times hurt us to the point that it never got off the ground. It was all about grunge. Radio wouldn't play anything but grunge, and 80s metal was brutally shoved to the wayside. Our fans were all still out there, and eager for bands to keep recording, but the radio stations abandoned us. The Seattle sound was the only thing getting play, so "Detonator" struggled as a result.

With Detonator, I brought my studio out to rehearsal, and we demoed all of that album at the rehearsals, with Desmond Child and Sir Arthur Payson. Sir Arthur Payson was this kooky New York engineer that Desmond made us use. And then we had Mike Shipley do the mix. Shipley had done AC/DC and Leppard and a lot of huge bands.

I like "Detonator." I loved the drum sound and think it's a kick ass record. Although, some of the others didn't seem to be into it. Especially Robbin, but by that time, Robbin's activity outside the band was catching up to him.

So, before "Detonator," I would wind up with tons of time on my hands during the recording of a new album. And, I'd do wacky shit.

I became the king of the giant impulse buy. I was a rockstar with money and time on his hands who didn't have a major drug problem. It's an interesting combination, because when you have time AND money, I guarantee you will discover your vices.

I was living the life, man. We were recording, finishing tours, I bought a Porsche, boat, koi pond, waterfall, just spending money. It was cool. But, in hindsight, I would definitely have managed my money a lot better, because it would come back and bite me in the ass, big time.

We made a lot of money in RATT. Over the course of my career with RATT, I've probably made over $3 million with them. Now, mind you that in the 80s, for every dollar I made, my accountant would take out $.55. That was a 50% tax bracket era. If you made that much money at that time, you paid 50% to the government. After your tax write-offs and everything, you probably walked out paying 35%.

I just remember getting checks in the mail, and having to send half to my accountant. Then, at the end of the year, you'd get back whatever was left over, and we'd start the whole thing over the next year.

But, to keep it in perspective, take that three million dollars and average it out over twenty years. After taxes, it isn't really that much. It's weird. We never really had a consistent, predictable income. I think the biggest check I ever got was $450,000.

That was a crazy day. My friend Tom Gonzalez, who I had moved in with when my family broke up in 1975, was at the house the day that check arrived. He was over, just hanging out, when a messenger showed up at the house with a package. I signed for it, opened it, and it was a check for $450,000. I showed it to him, and he just about fell over.

Here was a guy that I had hung out with all through my formative years. As a kid, and a young adult. Not so much after RATT, because I was just always on the road, in another world. But, I can remember the two of us being starving guys, going out in 1977 looking for a job. Getting dressed up and going "We gotta get a job!" It was insane. He sees that kind of thing, and simply can't believe it.

We had six guys in the pot when it came to money; the five in the band, and Marshall Berle. Our budgets on tours were in the neighborhood of $130,000 per week. Now days, that money would probably be around $250,000 or even $300,000, I don't know. We used to have to work for three days in a week, just to pay for the production costs. There was a crew of 48 guys; 5 semis; 4 tour busses; it was a massive, expensive thing.

While we made a lot of money, and came home with a lot of money, it wasn't like when Mötley hit it in 1990 on the Dr. Feelgood tour, and were selling out multiple nights at arenas. That's when you're doing it. When you have a record that sells 5 million and you do multiple nights at an arena, you don't have to worry as much about set-up costs and travel expenses. You go home, and you have millions of dollars in your bank account. I had hundreds of thousands at all times, but never millions. I've never had, at one time, $1.3 million cash sitting in the bank. But, I'm proud of what we did. It would have been nice to have that, for sure. But, not very many people were at that level. Very few guys were in that echelon. Van Halen, Mötley Crüe, Bon Jovi, and Def Leppard. That was about it.

For some reason, I always judged our success against the guys in Motley. They were my litmus test. They always had about 20%-25% more success than we did. That's how I always looked at it; the number of records they sold; what they did in arenas; all of that, tended to be about a quarter more than what we would do. And, it was that way, pretty much until Feelgood happened. That record was a behemoth for them. That's when they all got into the mansion era.

It was odd to look at it, but when we started out, RATT and Mötley were pretty much equals. Over the years, we watched the gap slowly widen. It was confusing at first, but the older I got, the more I understood it.

Nikki pretty much ran the show in Mötley Crüe. He was the driving force that kept them moving. So, when it came to decision-making, there was only one real factor. Nikki Sixx. For RATT, we had five decision makers, all with different visions, and different drives. Too many cooks spoil the pot, right?

RATT was a democracy, but a flawed democracy. Mötley was a dictatorship. It allowed Mötley to surge higher than the rest of us. Dr. Feelgood blew the roof off for Mötley Crüe.

Interestingly, the Detonator album was poised to be our Dr. Feelgood. RATT was right on Motley's heels. But, our timing was just a bit too slow.

But the shine fell off that Feelgood penny really fast.

The Nineties hit. Seattle music became huge, and we felt the pain of it almost immediately.

From what I've been told, for all the money Mötley made, several of those guys were really close to going broke. I heard Tommy was in a real predicament when our manager, Carl Stubner took him over. He was two million dollars in debt, and then Carl started all that Tommy campaign shit. I heard that T-Bone made close to $20 million. T-Bone just bought a house for $6.5 million. It's out of this world to contemplate, but I'm happy for the guy.

I remember hearing when Nikki sold his house. Nikki's house was right below Tommy's there in North Ranch. When I went up and stayed with Tommy and Heather, after the "Nobody Rides For Free" shoot, T-Bone was showing me Nikki's house below. It was a 12,000 square foot mansion, and looked like a Four Seasons hotel. His plant lady, that came by his house a couple of times a week to look after his landscaping, was $2000 a month.

That's what my mortgage was!

It was a very flamboyant lifestyle. Lots of private jets and shit like that. Now, I had went on private jets several times, with Tommy and Heather, Alan Niven, and such. But, I couldn't spend my hard earned money on that sort of shit. I just couldn't.

Good thing, because we were all about to hurt, and the higher up you were, the further the distance you had to fall.

The famous shoes that Ozzy shit in.

Me, Stephen, and Ozzy hanging at the Rainbow 1986.

The late Jeff Naidu from Rocket 88(left), Herman Rarebell Scorpions drummer (center), Me.

Me, Tommy, Vince, Stephen racing for Dodge, 1988.

18

THE FALL OF A KING

When the game is over, the king and the pawn go into the same box" - Italian Proverb

I think back on Robbin, and try to pinpoint where everything went wrong for him. Back when Detonator was happening, Robbin went through rehab. He had gotten some of his tracks done for the album, but not all of them. He was just so out of it. Just fucking smacked out. Drinking and drugs. So, he checked into rehab and we kept working on the record. Warren finished up the guitar tracks for him.

When he got out, we did a twelve-city club tour as a warm-up for the arena tour. He came out on that thing straight. Some guy from AA was out there with him, sort of a baby-sitter, I guess. He was very preachy about it, and of course, we were all drinking and doing our normal thing. But, he seemed okay during that.

Then, when it came time to go to Europe, he started drinking a little bit. Not a lot, but some. By the time we got to Japan, he had started hiding and drinking. He was smacked out of his head, even though none of us saw him break out the kit.

He was out of his mind on stage. What sunk the deal for him was in Tokyo at the Sun Plaza when he didn't change guitars for "Lack of Communication" and "Lay It

Down". Those two songs are completely different tunings. You can't just put a regularly tuned guitar on it. It has to be an open D tuned guitar. So, you can imagine how that all sounded. It was a collection of completely different chords.

During the Detonator video shoots, Stephen went through Robbin's suitcase and found a gun, syringes, cocaine and all sorts of shit. He was supposed to be clean, and clearly wasn't. I can see it now, when I watch the Detonator Video Action.

During his interview portions of it, he's completely smacked out. I didn't know what you acted like when you're on that shit, but once I knew what he was like on it, I can look back at that footage and see it.

And that was the end of it. We had to let him go. Robbin never played with RATT again.

He didn't tour on the 1991 arena tour with us. And, as soon as he was gone, then the roles flipped, and battle lines were drawn within the band. It became Bobby and Juan vs. Stephen and Warren. It was only a matter of time before the whole house of glass shattered.

It became a war.

One day we show up to rehearsals for the American leg of the Detonator tour and there's a Hammond B3 organ sitting in the room.

Juan and I had rode over together, and we were like, "What the fuck's that?"

The guy at the studio went, "That's your new keyboard player's."

"What new keyboard player?"

"I don't know. Some dude that Warren...I thought you guys hired a new keyboard player."

"No, we didn't."

Warren gets there, and goes, "Yeah, we're going to use some keyboards on the tour." Juan and I were like, "What the fuck?" He'd hired this high school buddy of his to play keys for us.

This ridiculous B3 had flowers, and sunshine stickers, all sorts of psychedelic shit all over it! I couldn't believe they were bringing this into RATT. It didn't fit. It was a horrendous combination. The guy stayed for a bit, but we kept him shoved off to the side and hidden off stage.

It was ridiculous.

Warren assuming the role as music director for this band simply wasn't happening. So, we got Michael Scheneker to fill in for Robbin. That worked out pretty well, because he and DeMartini were a good complement to one another.

Even though Robbin and I had been pretty tight all through our days in RATT, I'd had my ups and downs with him; especially with the limelight hogging.

Stephen and Robbin really tried to dominate the spotlight, and Marshall Berle was only encouraging it. He'd have them as the focus of all the interviews and any broadcast opportunity. It really was becoming intolerable for everybody else.

Warren was always our lead guitarist, and Robbin was the rhythm. In the beginning, they tended to switch off a lot, and were billed as co-lead guitarists, but as Warren aged, Beau Hill really started to utilize his lead guitar skills. Robbin started, little by little, to be pushed to the side and out of the lead guitar parts. I think he probably resented that. But, honestly, it was what was best for the band.

When we would be working up new songs, a lot of times, the band would look at Robbin and go, "Why don't we let Warren do the solo on this?"

Robbin's soloing was very melodic and smooth. But, we wanted the razor sharp, flaring edge to the guitar solos. We needed a guitar god. Robbin didn't like it, but he went along.

Robbin's last days with the band were in Japan.

19

RAMBOAT: FIRST BLOTZ

"It's only Rock N Roll, but I like it." - The Rolling Stones

There was a really popular movie out when I bought my boat called Rambo:

First Blood. When it came time to name the boat, I was trying to think of names for my boat. My nickname is Blotz, so that had to be part of it.

I couldn't help myself.

Ramboat: First Blotz. That was what I named it.

When I bought my boat, I was this crazy ass rock star; this really flamboyant, attention stealing kind of guy. I had my boat in a slip in the Portafino Marina at Redondo Beach. Keep in mind that the Portafino Inn was where we lived when Pete first moved us out here. Here I was with a 30' yacht, a Cabin Cruiser parked in a slip there.

It's funny, thinking about that, now, I never really thought about that during the entire 7 years I had the boat there. I had come full circle, to an extent.

In any case, that boat was my own floating bar. It was incredible. I was so proud of that thing. Every chance I got, we would all pile in it and haul ass to Catalina Island.

A lot of my best stories are in that boat.

I remember, this was in the summer of 1986, the guys in Def Leppard were in town working on "Hysteria", and we were doing a lot of hanging out. I had been playing them the "Dancing Undercover" record, which wasn't done yet, and they were playing me "Hysteria", which was still in the roughs.

It was all drum machine, which confused the hell out of me. I was like, "Why isn't Rick playing?" I didn't know this, but "Pyromania" was originally done up on a drum machine. It wasn't Rick Allen playing. Normally, when you record a record, they rhythm boys (drums and bass) will come in and lay down their tracks first. Everything else would be built on top of that. But, not with Rick! This was just how he worked. With Mutt Lange, the guys would all come in and lay their guitars down to a drum machine, and Rick would lay his tracks last.

It was completely backwards from anything I was used to, and confused the fuck out of me. But, anyway. Whatever works, right?

I took Steve Clark, Phil Collen, Tommy Lee, and our good buddy Krigger, who was Ike Turner's drummer and also in Gregg Giuffria's band, on my boat for a trip to Catalina. Krigger's nickname was KRELL GAR, LORD OF KRELL! A nickname that I'm sure says it all to you. Robbin used to say his name in this super deep voice of his like it was Darth Vader announcing the arrival. We love Krell Gar! All hail the mighty KRELL GAR!

On a side note, that was one thing we absolutely loved about Robbin. The guy had this deep, booming voice, and he kept telling us he wanted to do voice over work. He had all of these character voices he would drop on us, completely without notice. It was so damned funny when he did! We would laugh our asses off at him. The guy did the best Jabba the Hutt, since Jabba the Hutt!

And now, back to our regular programming...

Those guys all showed up, and we're all heading over to Catalina on a beautiful, glassy, sunny day. We were pulling off the cliffs of Palos Verdes, with all the mansions overlooking the ocean. It's an incredible, impressive sight.

We left the slip about 11:00 in the morning, and anyone who boats out here knows that in the morning, the water is always calm. Completely flat. It's like cruising across a giant sheet of glass. It's really great to ride in.

Anyone that goes out there just looks around and thinks, "Thank God I'm on Earth." It's mind blowing how beautiful it is out there.

So, "26 miles across the sea, Santa Catalina is a-waiting on me", as the song goes. It's 26 miles from the point of Palos Verdes to Catalina Island. It's a little longer going from Redondo to Avalon, because it's at the other end of the island. Probably 39 or 40 miles from our slip.

On that trip, we come across this massive schooner. The thing had five or six masts. It was a giant! It was over a hundred feet long, and had tons of people on board. We just circled this thing over and over looking at it, completely blown away at the size of this fucking thing! No joke, it might have been 160' long.

The guys in Def Leppard were just mesmerized. They were saying they had never been out on a boat like that. They had been on ships, and out in a lake, but never out on an ocean in a mid-sized vessel like that. Small vessel, really. Especially in comparison to that schooner.

It was great. We kept motoring along, partying. Such a completely awesome ride. I remember that Steve Clark had this beard. I was looking at him, and for some reason, he looked like a leprechaun to me. My friend Jeff Ferris was there, and I'm like, "Check out Clarky, man. He looks like a fucking leprechaun!" So, we were calling him the "Def Leprechaun" the whole trip.

There's more about that beard here in a minute. But, we were about half way through the trip, just cruising and drinking beer when I ran across a school of dolphin. It had to have been 70 dolphin, they were just everywhere!

I knew from previous trips that if you just motor right into them at a slow speed (they won't let you hit them or anything), they like to surf the bow of the boat. They move like lightning through that water, too. So, by driving the way I was driving, it creates a big wake at the front of the boat, and the dolphins go to town on it.

I've done this many, many times. I'd be out there with family or guests, and tell them to get out on the bow of the boat, and then I'd create a big wave with the wake. If you lay yourself out and hold on to the rail, it's totally safe, you can reach down and pet the dolphin as they surf the wake at the bow of the boat. Now, while I'm resisting the urge to make a joke about the guys in Leppard "petting their dolphin" on my boat....I ACTUALLY had the guys in Leppard on Ramboat, petting the dolphin! It was great!

That stretch of water is one of my most favorite places on Earth. I've seen sharks, flying fish, all sorts of stuff. I've got a great flying fish story with Matthias Jabs of the Scorpions that I'll get into here in a minute.

So, we get to Avalon Harbor. I like to take people to Catalina and show them around, so I try to plan the whole trip out. They've got these golf carts that you can rent, and then drive all over the hills exploring the island. The Wrigley House, the Wrigley Mansion is on Catalina. The Wrigley chewing gum family owned Catalina Island, but they lose ownership in 2010. I'm not sure what happens to it. I think the state takes it over, or something.

So, we get into the harbor, and moor the boat, then call on the radio and get the shore boat to come over. A little taxi boat comes over and takes you into shore. Now, we really look like a Mötley crew, no pun intended with Tommy, but we all have hair down to there, and look like ... well, Pi-RATTs, to be honest. Let's just say that when we walk by, fathers hide their daughters. That's just the way it is.

Heads were really turning, as we walked onto the dock. Especially, when you have Mötley, RATT and Leppard, three of the most visible bands of the day, walking by you. We were garnering some attention.

We get to the place where you rent the carts, a place where I've rented these things a hundred times, and there's a little old lady working the counter. She looks up, takes one good look at us, and you can see the immediate concern on her face. I'm like, "We need to rent three, maybe four carts."

She looks me up and down, and goes, "I don't think so."

That sort of catches me off guard. "What do you mean you don't thinks so?"

She goes, "I just don't think we can make those available to you gentlemen. Damage could happen."

I start to understand, and, it kinda pisses me off. "What are you talking about? I've rented here forever. No damage is going to happen." And we start going back and forth.

She was older, so I don't want to get verbally brutal with her, but it was turning into a class-act bullshit moment. I'm like, "Listen, ma'am…"

All of a sudden, this guy who worked there walks up behind her. He looks at me, then at Tommy and the guys at Leppard, then back at me, just like she did, sizing us all up. But, where she was seeing "Lowlife, lowlife, dead beat, scumbag", he was seeing "Mötley Crüe, Def Leppard, RATT … Holy shit!"

He literally takes her by the shoulder and gently pushes her to the side. He's all, "What can I get you?"

"Well, we need carts, bro."

"That's not a problem, sir."

We cruised around that place all damned day. You can drive back up into the island, and there's a big bird sanctuary out there. Then you go up to the top of the hill, and you overlook all of Avalon Bay. They've got a big casino building out on the point, where in the 1940's, jazz bands like Benny Goodman, and Glen Miller, all those kind of guys would play gigs out there all the time. The "who's who of Hollywood" would go vacation out there and watch big band shit.

There's a really nice, 9-hole golf course up there. And everywhere you turn, there's a view that just takes you out, you know? You're literally stunned into silence with what you can see from the tops of Catalina Island. The guys were amazed by that place. It was a really good day.

Ultimately, we wind up back dropping the carts off. Once you drop them, you sashay down about a block and a half, and there's a cool little Mexican restaurant, Saldana's Taco Shop, which is called Coyote Joe's now days. You can drop in and eat and drink and look out on your boat moored in the ocean. I used to love that shit! I was so proud of that boat, you know? I never thought of having shit like that when I was younger. Its just amazing feeling.

Saldana's was the land of the giant Margarita. You'd get this giant sized glass of Margarita and stick 8 or 9 straws in the thing. There's a full bottle of tequila in these fucking things, so we're just having a great time. Not getting completely hammered, but just partying and enjoying ourselves.

We get back out onto the boat and start back to the mainland.

There's this thing that happens every afternoon called "afternoon wind chop" between the channel from Catalina back to the mainland. While we went out there with smooth, glassy waters, the trip back was different. The wind had really kicked up in the channel, and there were huge swells.

Those poor guys. When we first hit it, you could be looking back to Catalina, and the waters were pretty calm. But, when you looked back toward the mainland, it was like "Victory At Sea" on the A&E channel. Ten foot swells, and whitecaps! I've been through it before. It's not fun to drive. Intimidating as hell! But, we're heading home at this point. We were going out that night, and it was already 5:00. Generally, afternoon wind chop happens from 3:00 - 6:00, and then it starts dying down. I've made the trip back at night on that shit! But, as long as you keep your compass heading, you're good. Of course, now there's G.P.S. everywhere. Your watch can take you to Catalina!

So, I'm driving these huge swells, and there's a way you have to handle these things. You want to take the front side of the swell, and then try to come down as smoothly as possible on the other side. But, these were 10' - 12' swells, so going up the thing, we were seeing the sky off the front of the bow. No water, no land, nothing but clouds. It was probably a 30-degree rise, at least. Then we come crashing back down on the other side with your ass grabbing onto the seat, and your balls trying to find a place to hide!

Phil Collen was sitting next to me at the helm. He's having a good time! He's got two beers in his hand, and he's having a ball. He's trusting me. Steve is sprawled out on the bench at the back of the deck with his arms spread out on the seat back. But Tommy ... Tommy's struggling.

He is standing right behind me. The seat at the helm was a bench, and it would comfortably seat three people. And along the backside of it, there was a long, polished metal bar that you could hold onto for stability. Tommy has a white-knuckle grip on that rail, chewing the fuck out of his hair!

I'm looking at him, and my poor bro looks like he's about to shit kittens. I mouth the words, "Dude, we're going to be alright." You could tell he didn't believe a word I said, because his face never changed.

It was, "Dude, are we going to fucking make it?" He was like that the whole way back to the slip.

Now, there is genuine concern to be had in moments like that. If we had engine trouble, we would have been on the horn to the Coast Guard quick! I don't think those waves would have been enough to flip the boat, but who knows? At the same time, it's pretty thrilling to be in a boat, and climb up the face of a 10' swell, then come down the backside into a 15' drop, or so. It'll make your blood pump, I promise.

In the back, Steve was on a bench facing forward, watching us at the helm. And, it was such that every time we touched down on the backside of a swell, the water would splash back into his face. He had seafoam just drooling off this ridiculous leprechaun beard of his! It was the funniest looking thing. The Def Leprechaun beard was white with the shit.

Steve's catch phrase for the day was, "Is it working?" And, he would say it every 10 minutes with his thick English accent. Absolutely hysterical! We kept making fun of it, and shit.

At one point, he had to take a piss. So, he went downstairs. The trip back was beating the shit out of us, so we were just kind of idling; taking a break. But, the boat was still rocking back and forth pretty seriously.

When Steve came out of the bathroom, the boat took a big lurch to one side, and he reached out for my table that was mounted to the floor, and ripped the goddamned post clean out, mounting and all.

I was at the helm and heard this huge crack of breaking wood.

"Oh, fuck. What is this?" So, I'm like, "Steve! You alright down there?"

Steve's goes, "It's working!"

I'm like, "Oh, my god. No good can come of that." It was a fantastic day.

So, we finally made it back to the slip in Redondo, and everyone was quite ecstatic to be putting their feet on to solid ground. In fact, Tommy got down on his knees and kissed it!

One time, Tommy and I took the boat to the Long Beach Arena. This was back in 1988, I think, because Heather was off shooting "Return of the Swamp Thing".

In Long Beach, there was a restaurant with a dock right there, and I use to do this kind of thing a lot. I told Tommy, "AC/DC is playing Long Beach. Let's take my boat down there. We'll dock right there at the restaurant, eat and have a few drinks, then go across the parkway to the Arena." The arena was literally right across the street.

Tommy's goes, "Dude, isn't that a freeway?"

"No, it's just a parkway. It's where they do the Long Beach Grand Prix every year. Fucking AC/DC is playing! We'll just walk over to the backstage and be like "hey, we're here! It's Blotz and T-Bone!"

So, Tommy, my friend Larry Wilson, and my black lab, Gemstone all piled into the boat with me, and off we went. Larry would first mate with me all the time, because you always needed two people, at least, to run a boat that big.

Gem stayed on the boat, when we got there, and we went in and grabbed some food and drink. Then we go to the gig.

We walk up to the backstage, and security is standing there. They've got this list, and I'm like, "We're not on the list, bro. But, anybody in here will okay us coming in. I'm Bobby Blotzer, I play drums for RATT. This is Tommy Lee from Mötley Crüe."

You know how these security guys are. They get right up on you pretty quick. Especially since we just bolted across the freeway and were right there at the gate. Right in his face. So, he's like, "Hold on one second." And, just as soon as he turned around, someone from their crew recognized us. They had worked tours with both RATT and Motley.

We get backstage and check out AC/DC. It was a great show. We're hanging out with the guys, and they are just tripping over the whole thing. They kept asking us about the boat trip down.

Everybody was like, "What's this I hear? You two came down on your boat? At night?"

I'm like, "Sure! It's no thing. We just drive out about two miles and hug the coastline all the way down. Maybe twenty miles. I know right where it is. I can visually see it. There's no rocks. I'm out far enough I know where the buoys are. Piece of cake."

"Oh. That's fucking insane!"

We finish up with them and start to leave. Everyone is envious. They're all going, "Fuck, I wish I was on that boat with you guys tonight."

We head back. I've got my huge cell phone with me. My new cell phone, since that ass clown stole the other one! We've been partying all day long, feeling great, and Tommy decides to call Heather. "Hey, babe! I'm on the Blotz's boat! We're heading back from seeing AC/DC!"

She's like, "What? Put Bobby on!"

So I'm talking to her, and she's a little worked up. "Bobby, what's going on? What are you two doing?"

"It's cool, Heather. I come out at night all the time. It's completely safe."

She starts laughing her ass off. She was down in Georgia at the time, shooting that movie.

We made it back, no problem. I don't remember what we did afterwards. I think we went back to my home studio where I had my drums set up, and we jammed the rest of the night.

That's probably what we did.

I remember another time, also in 1988. It was when the Monsters of Rock tour was on with Van Halen, Scorpions, Dokken, Metallica, and Kingdom Come on the bill. I got a call from Matthias Jabs of the Scorpions.

"Hey, Bobby, I want to take you up on the offer of the boat. I heard you took the Leppard guys out!"

All the bands we ran with knew about Ramboat, and the invitation was just more of an excuse to go play on it.

Gregg Giuffria from the House of Lords also had a boat. So we would take them out together. He kept his boat in Marina Del Rey, I had mine in Redondo. But we would meet off of Redondo, keeping in touch on the phone or the radio.

We'd use the radio a lot, just to make it more fun. "Okay, people, sync up on channel 12. Okay, bro. Where you at?"

Then, we'd dual ride, side by side to where ever we were going. It's a total rush to do that. To look over at your boy's boat while you're both hauling ass through the ocean.

Just tearing up the water. It's one of the best feelings you can have. Making a huge wake behind you.

It's like skiing. I love to ski, when you get that giant rooster tail coming up behind you, or if you're snow skiing, it's the fresh powder. Awesome. Great feeling.

So, Matthias gets in his rental car and comes in. We decide to go to Newport. It's Matthias, my brother Michael, my dog, Gemstone, and me.

Matthias gets there just before sunset. So, we had this incredible sunset to drive through. I had the top down on the boat. There was a canvas top with fiberglass sides that would pop up or down as a whole system, so you could be open to the sky, or enclose the boat if weather was bad, or you were storing it or something.

But, it was summer. So, I unzipped the top and rolled back the three-foot wide section directly above the helm, so I could stand up if I needed.

We go to dinner at Newport, and have a ton of cocktails. We're telling stories and laughing our ass off the whole time. Just having a ball. That's how it always was on the boat trips. Beer, stories and laughing our asses off.

So, we're driving out there, and there's flying fish everywhere. They're a seasonal fish, so they only come around once a year. And, I'm like, "Woah! Did you see that flying fish?" Matthias is looking at me all perplexed.

He says in his dense German accent, "Vlying vish? Vhat do you mean? Vish do not vly!"

I'm like, "Matthias, you mean to tell me you've never heard of a flying fish?" And, you can tell he absolutely doesn't believe me.

"Come on, man. Vish dat vucking vly?"

So, I'm laughing, and the more I laugh, the less he believes in flying fish.

Finally, I'm like, "Bro, do me a favor. Just stare out over the water. Just for a little bit. I'm sure you'll see one." You see them every 20 minutes. I do, anyway, because I'm looking for them.

Sure enough, a few minutes later, Matthias sees one, and he is just blown away! It is a complete trip when you first see one. Because, they'll come up about 20' from the edge of the boat. They'll come up out of the water, with you going at 20-25 miles an hour. These damned fish are flying parallel to you for 100' or more! They pop up, cruise next to you, and then dive back down. With them matching your speed, you can see; IT'S A FUCKING FISH! AND IT'S FLYING!

It's completely bizarre. I trip on it. I still trip on it when I see them. They are amazing.

On the way home, Matthias and I are talking about everything on the planet. Michael is sitting in the seats behind us with my dog Gem. It's nighttime, and I've got all my running lights on; my interior lights, and the deck lights. It's beautiful out. Amazing trip. The boat at night looks bitchin', all lit up.

All of a sudden, Michael loses his fucking mind!

He screams, "Jesus Christ, man!"

My gut reaction was to immediately grab the throttle and pull it back. I whipped around and was like, "What the fuck?!? You scared the shit out of me! What the fuck is up?"

He's like, "Didn't you see that fucking flying fish fly between your guys heads, Bobby?!?"

Matthias and I were sitting on the bench at the helm. Maybe two feet apart. There's no way, right? I go, "Dude, there's no fish that flew…"

"Fuck that. Look!"

And, sure enough, there's a flying fish lying on the deck. It's about the size of a bonita, and has wings. It keeps buzzing around and shit. Gemstone, my lab, is losing her mind barking at the thing. It completely freaked us out.

Matthias looks like he just saw a ghost.

Michael goes, "That thing just flew right between your heads. I don't know how you could have missed it."

I gathered the thing up, and we tripped on it a second or two before I put it back out in the water. I didn't want to hurt it or anything.

Had that fish hit one of us, we would have been fucked. As fast as I was going, and that fish coming head first at us, that would have made that fish going like 40 miles an hour. It could've killed one of us. It was so fast, we never saw it go between us. I thought for a while that it might have gone over us, but Michael swears he saw it pass right between us.

Matthias was playing at the LA Coliseum the next day and, I was going to go see them. So, we get back to may place, and we're just completely jazzed from the trip. We played guitars, drums and jammed all night. I had my friend Brit come over with some blow. Needless to say, we were wired! Before we knew it, it was getting blue outside. The sun was coming up.

I'm like "Matthias, bro, you've got a gig in a few hours." They were playing Monsters of Rock and it was a day gig, at that. Those festival shows can get you going pretty early. One o'clock most of the time. So, I got him out of there. We're still drunk and krelled out, and he gets in his car, and is off to his hotel.

I got out on the street, and it's alive with birds chirping with a perfect morning about to happen. I've never had such a "Oh, fuck, It's morning" moment in my life. I'm blazing on coke. There's no way ... no way I'm getting to sleep! And, I'm supposed to go to the show.

It wasn't happening. I crashed around 1:00 or 2:00, and I couldn't get up. I had planned to be there when it started, because I wanted to catch all the bands and shit. Matthias gave me four tickets and passes, and I was going to go. It was terrible. I no-showed my bro.

I talked to him later, and he was like "Bobby, you should have fucking made it, man. It was great. It was tough as fuck at first, but then it was huge!" He was all up and jazzing on the day.

I'm all, "Matthias, I couldn't move. I couldn't sleep."

He's like, "Yeah, me neither." But he was in tour mode, and you can do that sort of shit in tour mode. You have an extra battery, or something. I was in home mode, and I just couldn't make myself move. That was that.

Enter, Jack Russell!

Jack Russell is the singer for Great White had been on Ramboat a ton, and completely loved it. He really wanted one. I brokered a deal between a guy named Wolfgang, who owned a boat down at the Marina and wanted to sell it, and Jack.

I had talked to Jack, and said, "I know a guy who's selling his boat, out at the marina. It's expensive, but what are you wanting?"

"I want the whole fucking deal!" He wanted something bigger than mine. Fishing, the whole thing.

Mine was big, but not like his. With mine, you walked down into the cabin through some L-shaped stairs, and there was a kitchen, bathroom, and a couple of bedrooms. That kind of thing. Jack's boat, you walked through sliding glass doors into a huge living room, and then you walked down into the cabin from there. It was quite a bit bigger.

Jack was a certified nut on his boat. He'd be up for days at a time, drunk, on coke and fishing. *Days* at a time. I remember he called me up one time, and went, "Dude, I'm going fishing. You gotta come out. I'm on compass heading 160 going southwest, just go about 10 miles out from the Palos Verdes point and call me."

Barry Edison, a friend of mine from Phoenix, came in to visit. When I met Barry, he was a security guy at one of our gigs. We're still friends to this day. I look at Barry, and say, "We're going out on the boat. We're gonna go meet Jack. Get your shit."

We took the boat out there at night. We had the radio, and we'd talked about what channel to look for each other on. Channel 11 was the Coast Guard, so we always went 1 channel up. Channel 12. I called him. "Jack! We're on our way. Be looking for us."

It took us a little time to get there, what with it being 10 miles out from the point and all. It wasn't foggy, or anything, I just couldn't spot his lights. Finally, we see them, and it's absolutely crazy. He's out there partying with all these guys.

They're "fishing."

They've got shotguns out and are shooting sharks with them! That's right. The crazy bastards were fishing for sharks with shotguns. Jack is a fucking freak!

He's the kind of guy who would take the bait and just chew into it to get a reaction out of somebody. He'd pick up a piece of squid and stick it in his mouth. Then just laugh the funniest fucking laugh in the world.

That night, the swells were rocking the boats a bit. Too much to tie the boats together without damaging them. So, I dropped the anchor and tied a long line off to Jack's boat. It was far enough away that my boat wouldn't bang into his, but we could pull it in if we needed to.

And Barry, God bless him. We had been drinking all day, and he was hurting. I'm like "Barry, you gonna go on Jack's boat?"

He's all, "Not right now, buddy. I think I'm just gonna hang here for a bit. I'm really buzzing."

"You sure? Alright. I'm gonna go over. Give me a yell if you need anything."

Jack was a complete train wreck that night! He was blasting away with this hand-howitzer of his.

Finally, I'm like, "Bro, put the fucking shotgun away. Do it, or I'm splitting." I could tell he had been up for God knows, and he wasn't quite all there. I've partied with the guy for years. I know the guy. This wasn't the time to have the shotgun out!

He's just laughing his goofy laugh, and puts it away.

After that, we were cool, and the party continued. Barry is still sitting on my boat. He's sitting at the helm, with his back to us, and he's kind of slumped over.

Jack's like, "Dude, Bobby, what's up with your boy? Is he coming over, or what?" Then he yells out to Barry, "Hey, dude! Fucking get over here and party! You're missing it!"

It was weird. He wouldn't look at us. Finally, I'm like "Barry! What's up? You okay?"

All he would do is just wave his hand in the air. But he wouldn't turn around. What the hell is he doing? Then I noticed him slumped, so I went down and started pulling my boat in to check on him.

I get him in, and I could tell he was in trouble. I'm like, "Barry? You're turning green, dude."

He goes "I'm sea-sick, dude. Bad." Then it hits me. This guy lives in the damned desert. This has to be a new experience, or at least an uncommon one. And now, he's going to puke all over my boat.

I'm like, "Oh, shit. Okay, man. Hang in there."

He was a ghost; as pasty white as I've ever seen another person be. So I looked at Jack and said, "I gotta get him back, dude. I gotta go."

So, we split. Barry didn't get sick on the 10 mile ride back to the mainland, but when we got in, he let go all over the place. He said he was still sick a week later! He could still feel the rocking of the ocean a month later, he told me.

I knew what he was talking about. I would go out on the boat for four or five days at a time. You'd sleep with that rocking motion, or cook dinner, or fish. Whatever you did, you'd be rocking back and forth. So, when you got home, or were up in Catalina playing golf at Avalon, you'd still feel yourself rocking back and forth. It's a trip.

My boat was certainly one of the "blessings" from RATT. I loved that thing. Every time I went out on it, there was a new memory, a new story to tell. It was great.

I couldn't help but to flash on the possibility, though. Particularly some of the grim possibilities, of what would happen is something had gone wrong on one of those Catalina trips.

Take, for instance, the trip with Tommy, Steve and Phil. I mean, the three bands with members on that boat, at that time represented probably 70% of the hard rock music industry profits.

I couldn't help but ponder, "If we go down, how much publicity would that bring to the bands?" Not that anyone would have died, or anything. But, what kind of story would that have been? If something HAD happened, and we went down, it would have been Buddy Holly, Richie Valenz, Big Bopper kind of shit.

You're talking three of the top five bands at the time! It was huge.

There was a clique within the docks down at Redondo, composed of people who lived on their boats down there. They felt that even though we all paid the same amount of money in slip rental, that they had some kind of superiority to the rest of us because they live down there. Not all of them, but it's definitely there.

One day, I had some friends down. We were out all day, having a great, great time. We get back and there's a bar at the marina. So, we go in and have a few drinks, put the boat away, just winding down a good day.

As we're in the bar, we look out. The sun is sliding toward the horizon, and it's just unbelievable, too good to not get back on the boat and just drive right into the mouth of it.

We get in the boat and go back out. When we were in the bar, people knew who I was. They knew I was in a big band, and the RATT thing was buzzing around all over the bar. This is where being famous as a rocker doesn't help. You could call it one of the "curse" moments.

Someone in the bar called the harbor patrol on us, and told them we were all in the bar drinking. We were all drunk, and we just went back out on the boat. So, after the sunset, we were pulling back into the slip, and the Redondo cops were standing there waiting on us. They were waving us back in.

I stop the boat, and I'm like, "What's up?"

They're going, "Bring the boat in. Bring it in right now!"

"I'm not saying I won't do it, but I'm just curious as to why?" The whole thing was confusing to me.

"Get the boat in here, right now!" It was obvious that they weren't interested in a Q&A period.

As soon as I went in, they gave me the sobriety test, which I failed. I got popped and had to go down with them. I had to go to jail. It wasn't a DUI, on the water, like it is now, but, it was similar to that. I forget what the thing was called. I told the cops, "I'm getting out of this," and, I did. I got a lawyer and it cost me a chunk, but I walked without so much as a slap on the wrist.

They didn't go on my boat, thank God! Because, when I went down the next day to pick it up, one of my friends had spread out weed all over the table. I was like, "Oh, my God! If they searched this thing? Fuck!"

I can't believe they didn't go down in the cabin, and at that point, they knew who I was. They were talking about RATT, and about Vince Neil and the wreck, he had down there on the Esplanade in Redondo where Razzle from Hanoi Rocks died. So, to them, I was a scumbag rockstar who thought he was better than the world. So, fuck me, right? I still can't believe they didn't search the boat!

...of course, I kept the weed...

20

GOLF COURSE OR INTERCOURSE

"Golf...my bitch mistress." - Blotzer

If I've ever had an addiction to anything, it's to this crazy, frustrating, humbling game called golf.

I've been playing golf since that day in Maui when Marshall Berle introduced me to it at Kapalua.

My opinion of golf as "baseball for fags" completely changed that afternoon. I love it. I don't play as much as I used to, unfortunately. I mean, I used to play three times a week. Now days, I might play once a week, or even once every two weeks.

I've discovered that the amount of time I spend playing golf is directly proportional with my urge to whack the shit out of some asshole with a stick!

When I'm on tour, I love it when there are a couple of guys in the other acts with us on tour who play golf. If there are, one of the first priorities in a new city is to find a course and shoot a round.

That's why I loved touring with Warrant. Those guys all play, so we'd be on a different course every day. We'd play the best country clubs in the world for free, and it makes the day pass that much quicker!

As soon as I got home from Hawaii, I started golfing all the time. At first, I sucked, but I refused to take lessons, either. Call me stubborn, or whatever, but I was self taught, much like in my music.

This is not, by the way, how I would recommend a novice golfer to go about learning. Once you develop bad habits with your swing, learning to do it correctly is like learning how to fuck without losing your cherry. It's pretty much not going to happen.

I started out playing Los Verdes Golf Course at the Palos Verdes Country Club. That became my home course for years. I'd play with an array of people; Jimmy Bane from Dio, Rod Smallwood, the manager of Iron Maiden, Vince Neil and Tommy, plus a ton of friends who weren't famous.

It was amazing to me how many of my bros actually played the game. You don't usually think of rock stars when you think of the golf course. Most people picture a bunch of stiff, white guys with bodies like biscuit dough and asses shaped like an office chair.

On the rare occasion that I hear people talk trash about golf, I just shake my head, because they don't get it. When you hit a driver 275 yards, which is three times as far as a baseball player can hit a baseball; when you drop a birdie from 40 feet away; when you take a 6 iron and punch it in on a par three, two inches from the hole; until you have done those things, don't talk to me about golf.

Golf is a sport that has changed the mentalities of our world. Let me explain. Go back a hundred years, before Americans really embraced golf. Back then, if you saw a bunch of white guys chasing a black dude, it's because they were fucking with him. Today, if you see a bunch of white guys chasing a black dude, chances are they're playing in a PGA tournament, and they've got a Tiger by the tail.

That's the beauty of it. It transcends all walks of life. Golf is the only sport where you can smoke weed like Tommy Chong (we call that "swing doctoring"), cigarettes like Keith Richards and drink booze like Dean Martin and still be brilliant at the game. It's an "everyman" sport.

On some of these courses, you're on a billion dollar playground! Some of the places sit on real estate in areas that sell for $3 million a quarter acre, and these courses are 18 holes, seven thousand three hundred yards, or whatever. But, think about it. You're playing in eighteen different parks, and for fifteen or twenty minutes each hole, that park is yours and yours alone.

There are so many gorgeous sights to be seen, and smelled, and just absorbed. I'm so happy that I got the chance to learn to play golf. It's a beautiful release, let me tell you.

I've played with Alice Cooper a few times, and that dude is the standard for all rock star golfers. He's good enough, he could survive in the PGA tour...well, maybe the Senior Tour. I'm not quite at Alice's level, yet. He shoots around a three handicap. Right now, I'm playing at about a seven. The lowest I've ever gotten is a five. Which means I've got to shoot a 75 or a 77 every round.

That's hard to maintain.

I could be having a great game for fifteen holes, and be three over; then double bogey the last three holes and kill my score. That will make you want to take some hostages!

Golf is a total mind game. You never know when you're game is going to go "hubcaps & lugnuts" and the wheels come flying off.

We had a group of golf guys called "The Braemar Cartel". This was around 1999 through 2003. That group included Tommy Thayer from KISS and Black and Blue; Ricky Phillips of Styx; Eric Turner, Jerry Dixon and Jani Lane from Warrant; my good friend, Glen Granat; Gary Ruddell and Robbie Crane, Pat "Gay-Day" Gaday, Barkley Martin; there were about fourteen of us, all total. That was great, because we literally had a game three or four times a week. I loved it.

After a while, everyone kind of pulled away and moved off, but we had a web site for a while where everyone would enter their scores, and get their handicaps. It was a lot of fun.

We came up with the name "Braemar Cartel" because that's where we played. When I was living in Encino, we played over at Braemar Country Club in Tarzana. For anyone that watches that Scott Baio reality show, "Scott Baio is 46, and Pregnant", he lives on that golf course. When you see him golfing, that's at the Braemar Country Club.

On May 27, 1994, down at Los Verdes Golf Course, I got every golfers wet dream. A hole-in-one!

I had just come off having the best round that I've ever shot. I shot a 75. We decided that we wanted to shoot one more round, and I was on my way to the second best round I've ever had. I don't know what got into me, but I was shooting lights out that day.

It was getting dark, and we were on the 17th hole. I drilled my shot, watched the ball sail in a perfect line, and drop a hole-in-one. I got the certification and everything. Absolutely amazing.

Of course, I've never done it again...YET!

Robinson Ranch, my main track out in Canyon Country, is one of my favorite places to play. My buddies Rick Smith, and Larry Atlas were big RATT fans. I met them about five years ago, and they both run the place. I enjoy playing so much, that I was ready to join the country club.

Rick goes, "Why would you join? If you want to play, just give me a call and I'll get you in."

I go, "Yeah, but what if I want to play a LOT!"

"Just call me, Blotz. If I can get you on, I'll get you on."

You gotta love having bros with connections!

There's a course in Pittsburgh called Diamond Run. I play there with my buddy "Big Joe" and this guy named Mickey gets us out there. It's an absolutely beautiful track. Very private and exclusive. Presidents play this course, and it's one of my favorite places. I go out there with my brother, Michael, my cousin Chuck, or Big Joe. It's good times all the way around.

I used to play a lot with Doc McGhee, who was Bon Jovi and Mötley Crüe's manager. I remember one time, I was playing with Doc, his dad, Frank, and Vince Neil.

We were playing down in Newport, at Bear Creek, where Doc was a member. Vince wasn't a very good golfer back then. I don't know what he shoots now, but then it was pretty bad.

Vince was getting so pissed!

He kept worm-burning everything. For people who don't know what that is, it's when you hit the ball and it doesn't get into the air. It just shoots across the grass. We call that a worm-burner.

He lost his mind at one point.

We were hitting over water to get to the green, and it was going to be the third shot. Everyone had laid up in front of the water, then took another shot to get on the green. I'm not sure where everyone's ball was. I think mine was a little off. Doc's was on, I think. I don't remember.

But, Vince still has to get over the water.

When Vince sets up to take his shot, he fires the ball straight into the lake! It hit so hard, it practically left a rooster tail behind it.

He screams, "Fuck it!" Then, staring at the water, he starts wailing on the ground with his club.

Doc goes, "That's alright, Vince. Just drop another one."

Vince regains some of his composure and drops another ball. He lines up, and sure enough, BOOM, he drills it right into the water!

He stomps off to the cart, pulls his bag of clubs off the back, and heaves them into the lake!

I was like, "Okay. This is good. I'm loving this." We were all just standing there silent, kind of shaking our heads in wonder and amazement at this total meltdown Vince is trudging through. I mean, I was laughing so hard inside.

I've seen some shit with the Mötley boys, but THAT was some SHIT! I've witnessed some classic moments with the guy. Vince is always good for some entertainment.

The rest of us went to the green, and finished out the hole. Vince is sitting in the cart, just steaming; he's so pissed off. We finish out the hole, and go, "Vince, you sure you don't want to...?"

"Fuck it! No! Leave them there!"

So, we drive away.

After about five minutes, he goes, "Son-of-a-bitch!"

He takes the cart while we're teeing the next hole, and drives back to fish his golf clubs out of the lake. We're just dying, trying not to laugh, which only would have made matters worse.

We go back to check on him, and he's standing knee deep in the water, fishing around for his bag with a club. You have no idea how painful it was to keep that laughter on the inside.

We watched for a few minutes, then went back to our game. I don't think he ever found the bag. Eventually, he just split, still fuming and embarrassed, I'm sure.

This next story I have on video. After we shot the "Nobody Rides For Free" video, I was over at Tommy and Heather's house in North Ranch, staying a couple of days with them.

Tommy was a member of North Ranch Country Club, which is very exclusive. In fact, he had to go in front of a board of directors to get approval to join. They had pictures of him in concerts where after his drum solo he would turn around and moon the audience.

They're like, "What's this?"

Tommy had to explain to them, "Look, that's a show. It's all about the comedy and entertainment of the moment. It's the end of the drum solo, and is just for fun."

He eventually got his membership and his gold plate with his name on it. His locker was right next to Frankie Avalon's. He thought that was so cool. So did I, for that matter.

We were out golfing at North Ranch. Tommy's just stinking it up, man. We're drinking coldies and having a good time. He hits this one shot, and shanks it as badly as I've ever seen a shot shanked. I'm video taping at the time, because it was such a scenic spot we were at. It was right by this mammoth, ancient oak tree. Just incredible.

On videotape, you hear me going, "Don't worry about the video camera, dude. Just keep your head down!"

Fucking hysterical.

He hits the shot, and hooks it. It goes ninety degrees to the left. I start laughing at him, and he goes, "Son-of-a-bitch!" He takes the club, and with two hand just wings it as far as he can throw! It's making this helicopter sound of "woosh, woosh, woosh, woosh" as it flies up into this oak tree and gets stuck.

"Uh, Tommy, it didn't come down!"

We all wind up standing under this tree, trying to throw clubs up to hit Tommy's 6 iron and get it down.

Finally, I go, "Tommy, we're going to have to climb up there and get it."

He's like, "Screw that, let's just go."

Of course, ten minutes later, Tommy says, "Stop. Fuck. I gotta go back and get my club." So he went back, monkeyed up this tree, and got his club.

He and Vince had something in common there. Who knew?

It's weird, some of the shit that will happen on the golf course. Here's a prime example of what I'm talking about.

At the time of the O.J. Simpson double-murder, I happened to be in Lake Havasu. I was up at the river, and heard on the news what had happened.

I had a great interest in that, because as a kid, I was a big fan of his. I always thought he was a really good guy; a superstar athlete; a really good example for the black community. The guy was really smart; a true businessman. So when he did that, I was stunned, and a little betrayed.

I followed that trial.

Well, let's be honest, it's not like you COULDN'T watch the damned thing. It was everywhere! It was a true example of the power of media, because that trial was held by the public. The whole world watched that thing, and made it's own mind up.

Second of all, I knew that Tawny Kitaen had fooled around with him for a while. Robbin had told me stories of what that guy was like, and what a complete whack job he was. They had a few run-ins over the years, and Simpson was a scary dude. He would show up at the studio lot and spy her out when she was working on her television shows. Then O.J. would drag her off on a break and go bone her somewhere while she was working.

I'm not sure why Robbin felt I needed to know this, but he did. Kind of weird, really.

When the trial concluded, a couple of weeks or a month later, I was up at Los Verdes, my home track in Rancho Palos Verdes, for a round or two. I had just cleaned out my garage, and I had one of my kid's old Halloween props; a machete, covered in fake blood!

So, reveling in my great and tasteful flare for comedy, I decided that this would be a great gag on the golf course! "The O.J. Club!" Everyone was talking about this guy, and I just couldn't help myself. I'd tell stories to the guys on the course, setting them up. I'd generally do it when someone was playing a ball that was stuck in the trees or something.

I'd go, "Hey, did I ever tell you guys that I played a golf tournament with O.J.?"

They'd go, "No, way! Really? I never heard that!"

I'm like, "Yeah, it was a trip. He gave me this club. Said it was great for making a 'low-cut shot out of the trees.' You wanna use it? I've got it in my bag."

They'd go, "No shit? Yeah, I'll give it a shot!"

Then I'd take that fucking thing out of my bag, with blood all over it, and go hack-slashing though the brush. It always got a huge laugh! It was so damned funny.

So, here we are, maybe a month after the end of the trial, and we're playing Los Verdes. We're on Hole 4, when my buddy, Gary, who worked there, comes over to us.

We're on the tee box, and he goes, "Dude, you are not going to fucking believe who in on the practice putting green."

"Who?"

He's like, "Take a guess."

"Barney Fife! I don't know. Who?"

He goes, "Dude, O.J. Simpson in warming up. He waiting to get out. He wants to play the course today."

I'm blown away. "What?!? O.J. is going to play Los Verdes?"

I jump into my golf cart and run over there, just to get a glimpse at the animal, you know? Sure enough. There he is. The Butcher of Brentwood, in the flesh, warming up on the putting green, with his other three, class-act standouts that make out his group.

I'm thinking, "Wow...look at that. It's the monster!"

Being right after the trial, he wasn't allowed to play private courses anymore. So here he is on my course, Los Verdes, in a very affluent community of Rancho Palos Verdes, with it's picturesque ocean views, but it's a county course.

I head back to the tee-box, and we continue our round. O.J. and his cronies are maybe 5 or 6 holes behind us. It was November or December, I'm guessing, and by the time we finished and hit the bar, it was starting to get dark. Really dark.

So, we're sitting in the bar, and they're about to close the place down. EVERYONE in the place is talking about O.J. being out there. I'm looking at the bartender, going, "Wait, wait! Don't shut down yet. Let see him walk through."

It's completely dark outside, and O.J. and his group come walking up the door. I guess they just barely got their 18th hole in before you couldn't see anything anymore. He tries the door leading to the parking lot, and it's locked. I immediately look to my boy and go, "Get that guy in here, man! We can't pass this up. Get him in here."

He runs over and waves them down. They come to the door, and he opens it up, letting the Juice and his Monster Squad come inside.

At this point, it's just me, a couple of my buddies, O.J. and his tribe in the bar. They've already turned out the lights, so there's only a couple of lights over the bar area still on. The place is dark and moody, and in the presence of a cold-blooded murderer, it's pretty damned creepy.

The bar is an L-shaped bar, with the long leg facing the room, and the short leg off to one side. I'm sitting on the short leg. He's sitting on the long leg.

I'm thinking, "This is just fucking weird."

People from the kitchen are coming out, and getting autographs and shit. Everyone is treating him like a novelty, and I'm completely repulsed by it. Everyone knows this fucking Frankenstein killed his wife and her friend! You'd think we'd be chasing his ass out of the room with torches and pitchforks! But, no. Everyone wants to get a picture, or an autograph, or talk to the guy.

Human nature. It's a macabre thing. What can you do?

I decide I'm going to make a move. I've got to talk to the guy, for some sick, fucked-up reason. I blame peer-pressure.

I have this good friend, Greg Begodee, who used to work for a moving company back before all the O.J. shit happened. One afternoon, he finds himself moving O.J. and Nicole Simpson out of their condo in Laguna Beach.

So, that's my in.

"How you doing, O.J.?"

He goes, "Hey, how are you?"

I said, "I just wanted to come over here and say something to you."

"Yeah? Okay."

"It's odd, but we've got a couple of acquaintances in common."

"Yeah? Who would that be?"

"You might not remember his name, but my friend, Greg Begodee, helped move you and Nicole out of your Laguna Beach condo. You went out and got footballs, and autographed them for him and the guys that were doing the moving. You wrote 'Peace to you' on it."

"Oh, yeah, man! How he doin'?"

"He's good. Doin' fine."

Now he's all personable and shit, so I decide to lob the coup-de-gras at him.

"Yeah, the other person is Tawny Kitaen."

His total demeanor changed! There were some dark clouds brewing, let me tell ya. I could see him sizing me up, thinking, "Who the fuck is this guy? What's this all about?"

I go, "I'm the drummer in the band, RATT. Tawny was on a couple of our album covers, and in a couple of our videos, and I know you guys went out for a while."

He completely clams up.

So, now, I'm wondering what his next move is going to be. He didn't get violent or anything, but he sure as hell got weird. Really fucking creepy. And, just like back at that Long Beach trial where I was the prosecutions star witness, I found myself locked in a dark, cramped area with a cutthroat killer type.

And then it hits me!

I could do more for RATT, in this very moment, than any publicist, record company, tour or new album could EVER hope to accomplish! All I've got to do is reach over that bar, bust a fucking glass, then jam that thing in this son-of-a-bitch's throat!

That's how fucked up I am! All I'm thinking about is how many records we could sell if I ended this asshole. Obviously, I didn't do it... but I sure would have been a hero to America if I did!

Meanwhile, all my buddies are in the back of my mind, goading me on.

"Dude! Show him the OJ Club! Show him the OJ Club!"

Some of these golf tournaments are pretty interesting. They get these strippers and shit to come out and visit you on the course. They're wearing dental floss bikinis and a smile. Pretty hot.

Those are always fun to do.

I've never done one of the Pro-Am tournaments, but I don't really want to, either. You can't bump the ball!

When we play, I don't care if someone bumps it or rolls it an inch to get a better lie. It's not the PGA, you know. But, sometimes you get stuck in games where the other players are Nazis with their enforcement of the rules. Especially if there's money on the game.

I used to have a crew of guys down in the south bay, at Los Verdes. They wound up being one of the reasons I moved. The first was my divorce. I needed to distance a little bit. The second was that our golf crew had become a gambling nightmare.

There was a lot of money being slung around, which made everyone follow everyone's ball. You'd go to take a back swing, and there's one of these guys in your hip pocket watching everything your doing.

It would be, "Get off my shoulder, man!"

It got out of hand really quickly. It was just too much money. Money darkens the game up so much that it can kill the enjoyment of it. I don't need the money that bad.

It's one thing if it's a friendly wager or something. It gives the game a little more interest. But these guys just got out of their minds.

Bobby Suer and this guy Jamie would play $100 or $200 a hole, and then they would have these little side bets. You couldn't enjoy your game, because they were always fighting with each other.

But, on the whole, there is very little down side to a good round of golf. It's relaxing, therapeutic, and, on occasion, they send out a hot chick wearing dental floss and a smile, carrying booze.

Golf life is good!

ACT II: THE DEATH

21

EIGHTIES METAL VS. NINETIES GRUNGE

"Hell is a half-filled auditorium." - Robert Frost

To call the transition to Nineties music a "surprise" is like calling Vegas a "party town".

I didn't realize what a maelstrom the grunge movement was going to be to the 80s bands, because when grunge was breaking, we were breaking up.

RATT was crashing and burning, and grunge had very little to do with it. Interestingly enough, Detonator still sold 800,000 records, even though Nirvana and those guys were dominating the radio.

Those numbers are a little off the mark, so I don't want to say grunge didn't have an effect on us. It certainly did. RATT always did between a million and three million plus in unit sales on each album. So, it was a bit of a letdown.

Atlantic was coming to hear the demos for Detonator, and they were loving it. They were saying, "Guys, Detonator is going to be your Dr. Feelgood. This thing's going to sell five million copies." That kind of optimism was comforting, and absolutely encouraging.

In the end, it just didn't hit the mark.

"Detonator" was released in 1990. That's about six months too late, because by the time it came out, the tides of music were changing. Had that record come out in 1989, we would probably have had our "Dr. Feelgood".

"Detonator" was a strong record. Musically, tune wise, lyrically; it was great across the board. "Giving Yourself Away" was going to be our huge ballad hit; something that RATT had never had before, and the label was really excited to have that to market.

We had always taken a lot of heat for not playing the power ballads on our albums. RATT was about the sex, not the love. So, here we go! A fucking fantastic ballad. It was too little, too late. The musical landscape changed so fast that none of the 80s acts had a chance to stop the bleeding.

Eighties metal slowly bled out, and by 1993, it was all but dead.

Good-bye, 80s Metal. Hello, Nineties Grunge. It became the world of Nirvana, Pearl Jam, Alice In Chains, Stone Temple Pilots, and Soundgarden. All these bands started flooding in. From a musical standpoint, it was like grinding the gears on a hot rod that you've driven for years! You know the thing inside and out, and in the middle of the race, you slip the clutch.

Suddenly, you're out of the running.

The Seattle movement really upset me. I mean, I liked some of the songs that were coming out, but those guys put us out of work, so they became adversaries. And, I took a very adversarial position.

I would go and check out some of the acts when they would come into town. I went to an Alice In Chains show, and those guys were hailing RATT and Motley! I was completely surprised when guitarist Jerry Cantrell and vocalist Layne Staley were talking to me about it.

"We played your stuff in the clubs for years! It's great to meet you!"

I was like "Thanks." It was very conflicting, because they were nice guys.

I guess it was late 1991 when I saw Pearl Jam at the Troubadour. Had no idea who they were. I was on my way to meet Roger Romeo. We were going to meet at the Troubadour to have a drink, and then we were going to go to the Rainbow.

I don't remember why we were meeting there, because I hadn't been to the Troubadour in years. There was this big bouncer guy named Ron that worked the door for years. He was there when we were in the circuit, and ten years later, he was still manning the door.

Ron was all "Hey, what's up, brother?" He was genuinely happy to see me again.

We were taking some time to catch up, and I asked him what was going on there that night.

He's like, "I don't know, some band called 'Pearl Jam'." And, he made the jack-off motion with his hand.

"Pearl Jam? Okay. That's very nice."

I hadn't heard of them at that point. I went in and checked them out. They were okay. Nothing I would have fallen out over. I couldn't imagine some girl throwing her panties on stage to it. But, whatever, you know? I didn't get it, wasn't really into it.

Suppose that's why I'm not an A&R guy?

I watched Eddie Vedder try to stage dive, and people just moved out of the way and let him hit the floor! It's not like the place was packed, or anything. There were maybe 150 people standing in front of the stage. He dove. They moved. He slammed face first into the floor.

I couldn't help but snicker a little when it happened. That was pretty funny.

In the end, I was way wrong about the new music. Those bands got huge, almost overnight, and we were out of a gig. It was very upsetting. A very distraught time in life for not only me, but the rest of the bands of the 80s era.

I think it hit the big guys like Mötley a lot harder, you know? They were the pinnacle of the scene for so long, and for it all to come crashing down like that? It's a long fucking way to fall when you've lived above reality for your entire career.

We were all king shit for years. Then, suddenly, everybody's broke up, and no one is doing fuck all. It was a bizarre time.

As I look back at the grunge thing now, I can respect it. It was a passing of the guard to a new generation of music fan. The Seventies had their fans; my kind and me. Then the 80s had their followers. When the Nineties happened, that was just the kids of the time finding their own.

It was the music that spoke to them, and I can completely get that.

One more thought on the 90's.

When I think of Kurt Cobain, I always think about how so much of the world was looking at him and his legacy as being the second coming of John Lennon.

...uh, oh...here I go again...BEATLES FOREVER!

Brother, let me tell you, that is a FUCKING JOKE!

It is a complete joke to me for him to be mentioned in the same breath as anyone in the Beatles. It's ridiculous. "Nevermind" had a few really good, really catchy grunge pop songs. I can see how the kids were latching onto it, because it was a different movement. A new generation was coming in, and this was their music.

The guys who were fifteen to seventeen years old when we were hitting it were now in their mid to late twenties. They were maturing, getting careers and families, and not buying albums and concerts as much, anymore.

For the new fifteen to seventeen year olds, this was their turn. This was their trip to a musical identity.

But, any talk of Cobain being on the same level as Lennon just drove me crazy! There is no comparison. To this day, I couldn't sit through a whole Nirvana record. By and large, I thought it was pretty obnoxious stuff, really. Everything sounded the same. It was all just too similar, song-to-song.

Some of my opinion comes from my personal taste in music, but there's a lot more to it than that. Lennon, McCartney and the Beatles changed music. Forever.

I'm sure that Nirvana has people they influenced, and music did change significantly after their music hit. But it wasn't a lasting thing. Grunge was all but gone just a few years later. It was like the disco movement in the Seventies. It had impact while it lasted, but once the novelty wore off, it was dead.

By comparison, you would be hard pressed to find a segment of modern music that hasn't been influence by what the Beatles did in the Sixties, and what Lennon did into the Seventies.

Kurt Cobain was a talented, tortured poet, but he was no John Lennon.

When I look back now, certain songs will always remind me of certain periods in people's lives. You can smell and taste where you were when you first heard that song. That's why I listen to the oldies stations, because I was a freak with the radio my whole life. I knew every song. I listened to AM radio, and I love those Sixties tunes. When I hear them, anything from the Sixties, Seventies, Eighties, Nineties, it immediately takes me back to that period.

That's why bands, not just ours, but all bands from those time periods, are still out touring. People want to be taken back to that.

So, that was that.

RATT broke up in 1992, and walked away until we reformed again in 1997.

The early Nineties became a HUGE wake-up call for me, especially financially. Everyone was out of work! And, not just RATT. I mean EVERYONE who had been a player in the 80s metal scene.

When the band broke up, the phone quit ringing. I wasn't hearing from our management, agents, or other guys in this MULTI-PLATINUM RECORDING BAND! Virtually no one gave the time of day. Suddenly, we didn't seem to matter to the music industry. They didn't care how many records we had sold.

I'd run into my rockstar brethren around town in the various nightclubs, or restaurants. They would all have the exact same look. It was a "deer in the headlights" kind of thing. Everyone was in old-fashioned survivor mode.

"Blotz, can you believe this shit, man? Can you believe what's happening to us? What the fuck is going on?"

It was stomach turning. I had to stop going out, because what was once a lot of fun, was now one of the most depressing things I've ever encountered.

One of the most valuable lessons I could teach about being a rockstar is this; PREPARE! Because, one day the phone stops ringing, and the money dries up. If you are not prepared, it will eat your ass alive!

In very short order, I discovered that I was living WAY beyond my means. Things were going to have to be sacrificed, and I wasn't going to like sacrificing some of those things.

The first to die on the altar of financial burden was the beloved and worshipped "Ramboat".

The thing about Ramboat is that, while she was a good boat, and ran well, I'd be gone for long periods of time, and it would just sit there in the slip. The salt water of the ocean can be incredibly corrosive, and just eats away at the engine parts over time.

If Ramboat just sits there, it's really bad for the motor.

That boat didn't have a fresh water-cooling system, like a car does. You didn't have a radiator and coolant that cools your engine. Ramboat pumped water straight from the sea to cool everything; so salt water had permeated everything in the guts of that boat. I didn't have a means of flushing the system out, unless I was taking the boat out of the water, which is a monumental pain in the ass.

As a result, I was getting a lot of mechanical problems with that boat. At a time where I couldn't be dumping tons of cash into constant maintenance, I was forced to sell her. I was sick of fixing things all the time, anyway.

So, in 1993, I had Ramboat detailed. I had everything working tip-top, so I put the word out. Drew Bombeck and I went golfing one morning, and then planned to spend the rest of the day on the boat down at the marina. I had two guys coming down to check out the boat later in the afternoon.

After our round, we stopped and bought a 12-pack, and headed to the docks.

The first guy came down to look at the boat. He came on board, listened to me fire it up and rev the engine so he could hear how well it was purring. He really loved it. Told me he would get back to me real soon.

I asked him if he wanted to take it for a quick little spin, just outside the breakwall. He turned me down, and said he could tell it ran great.

"Let me get with my wife, and we'll see what we're going to do."

Okay. No problem. I still had another guy checking it out later in the day.

The next guy shows up an hour later. He's like, "Yeah, this is really nice!" I offered him a beer, which he happily accepted. We're standing there, drinking beer, and talking over every little detail about the boat.

I go, "So, you wanna take it out for a spin?"

It was a beautiful day, with water like polished glass!

He goes, "Yeah! Hell yeah." So, I pull the boat out of the slip, motor out past the breakwall at the Portofino Marina, and head out into the bay.

All of a sudden, the engine was revving up faster than the boat was moving. Something wasn't right. The engine raced higher, but the boat was actually slowing down. I pulled the throttle back into neutral, and I'm thinking, "Shit. What's wrong with this thing, now?"

I tried to put it back in gear, but the thing wouldn't move.

"Son-of-a-bitch!"

Damn it. I was going to lose the sale. This fucking thing was going to take more cake to fix, which was going to put me further in the hole on the deal. Imagine that!

You wanna know what "BOAT" stands for?

B-REAK, O-UT, A-NOTHER, T-HOUSAND!

I get on the radio to Vessel Assist, which is like AAA on the water. I told them where I was at, and they said they were in Santa Monica at the moment, so it would be a while before they got up there. About two hours later, they show up and tow us in.

It was frustrating. I'd been going on and on all day about how the boat was in pristine condition, and there were no problems with it at all, then it promptly takes a dump in the ocean, miles from the marina, with a potential buyer on board.

I told the guy, "Look, I don't know what this could possibly be, but it will be fixed. Give me a call tomorrow."

He goes, "Sure. I'll do that."

I'm thinking, "Shit! No way I'll hear from him again." The pisser was, he really liked the boat. I had told him some of the more colorful stories about trips and things, and he was completely into it.

I took Ramboat in, and it cost three grand to get it fixed! I knew it was pointless, but, I called the guy and told him, "Hey, it's running like new. Now you have a brand new outdrive to go with your boat!"

Of course, I was thinking the guy would never want to buy it. But, in a surprising twist of irony, the guy came down, and Ramboat had a new captain.

I bought Ramboat for $65,000, and sold her for $25,000, seven years later.

Much like cars, boats DO NOT hold their value, I'm sad to say. That was the end of Ramboat, although the memories that thing provided will last forever for me and my friends and family.

Thus is the story of the demise of Ramboat.

RATT along with Atlantic Records Staff and Producer Beau Hill (far right) getting platinum awards 1984.

22

TIME TO TIGHTEN THE BELT

This was the beginning of a very lean time during the Nineties.

I had an intense need to downsize, because my monthly expenses were

significant, and it was becoming an issue to juggle everything. I had my mom's mortgage, my mortgage, credit card payments, which is how I paid off the remodel of the house after Stephen quit and the band broke up.

After we finished the "Detonator" tour in September of 1991, I started the remodel, with the knowledge that we would be back in the studio in a few months, and it would be business as usual.

I had budgeted $50,000 for the remodel. But, like a lot of things in life, it quickly escalated. By the time it was over, I had spent $120,000. Some of that overage was put on my credit cards, because I had huge limits on them.

To make this matter worse, when Stephen quit in 1992, we had already taken a big advance on a new record for Atlantic. The advance was for $350,000, half of the $700,000 we were getting per record at that point. But, it was an advance for a record that never got made.

Things like that don't go over too well with record labels.

I spent the first year after the break-up just relaxing and doing recreational stuff. I'd snow ski in the winter, Lake Havasu in the summer, and I golfed a lot. If you figure probably thirty days on the slopes, sixty days on the lake, countless golf rounds...the money was going really quickly.

That was much needed time off, believe me. Everyone was worn down to nothing. We had spent the whole of a decade on a constant, bullet train styled career.

I was tired, man. Dog dead tired.

But, I wasn't getting any calls for any work. No one was. Tired and broke wasn't an option.

After two years, I kept thinking the band would get back together. Meanwhile, I was spending $12,000 a month nut, just to pay my expenses. I was eating through all my money really quickly. Do the math, and after two years, I was hurting pretty bad.

I decided it was time to do something to generate some money, and fast.

So, in November of 1993, I decided I was going to go the entrepreneur route. None of the guys in the band were doing shit. Actually, none of the bands from the 80s were doing shit. Even Guns N Roses were pretty much done by that point.

So, as I sat, anxiously watching my bank account deplete, I decided I needed to explore career alternatives. You know, just in case!

Panic wasn't the exception at that point. It became the norm.

I bought a flower shop in Palos Verdes that my wife Jeni was going to run. It cost $90,000, and did really well, but it wasn't going to be enough to sustain us, should RATT never exist again.

It was a great little business, but you always ran one month behind on your bills vs. receivables. So, you had to keep a constant base of about $40,000 in the bank to operate on and keep things rolling tight. Jeni was good with it.

Funny story. I traded my Paiste gong to a good buddy of mine, Mikkey Dee, the drummer for Motorhead. The gong is a giant cymbal that you put on stage and hit with a mallet. I traded him my gong for this van that he had. We were going to use the van for deliveries for the flower shop. The very first day we had it, Jeni is driving it for a delivery, and the damned thing catches fire. It burnt to the ground.

So, Mickey, you still owe me a gong, ya cunt, ya!

Jeni eventually got sick of the flower shop, and finally sold it. We sold it to some people who defaulted on some of the loan. I had carried part of the note for them, another thing I wouldn't recommend. I wound up having to sue them to get the money, which I did, but it took a really long time to collect.

Thinking back, while I had a lot of jobs early on, the only one that I had for a really long time was a steam cleaning company.

It was a fairly easy, and profitable gig. You'd go into a place, and spend maybe an hour or two, and make a couple of hundred dollars for a three or four bedroom house. I knew it was easy money, especially if you could sell them "extras".

When I used to steam clean, I would sell them Scotch Guard for stain protection; pre-treatment for the carpet to eliminate pet stains; menthol for that "fresh" smell; the whole Canoli. I would go into a $149 job, and walk out with $250 or $300 because of all the extras.

There was an array of different things you could up-sell, most of which was a load of bullshit. Stuff smells good at first, but then wears off in a snap. But, that was the business I was in, and you sell the extras if you want to make any real money.

So, people, the lesson here is to never buy the extras from the steam cleaner.

It was an easy decision that one of the other businesses I was going to start during that 1993 period was a steam cleaning business.

I was looking for existing businesses for sale. Then, I found one out in Lawndale, California. Dan Hartwell, who was a good friend of mine for a long time, owned the company. He had 12 machines, which was much bigger than I was looking for. I was looking for something that would allow me to still golf, ski, go to the lake, but augment my income.

I would always receive my RATT catalogue royalties from my publishing and CD sales. That wasn't going to be enough, in the long run, but it doesn't mean I was looking for a sixty hour a week job. I just wanted something that would pay the bills. My royalties would run around $30,000 to $40,000 a year, and my monthly bills were twelve grand. You do the math. I don't want to think about it.

I wound up not buying the steam cleaner business from Dan, and opened my own, instead. His business was huge, and established. It was a lot to bite off in one shot. He was getting out of steam cleaning all together, telling me, "I'm going into the water damage business. That's where the money is at."

And, dude, did he know what he was talking about, or what?

Dan is this millionaire several times over. He owns "Emergency Service", specializing in water damage, and it's going balls to the wall. He's all over the place, now; San Diego, Frisco, Arizona, now he's moving into Texas. They're everywhere! He's really got this keen business savvy. The guys probably making a couple of million a month.

Dan's son was in a band with the son of another friend of mine, Shawn Brown. The boys were good kids, and for a while, I worked with them, showing some of the business ropes, and tweaking their musical style a bit.

They came to my studio at the house and recorded some stuff.

Today, these kids are un-fucking-believable musicians. They went through years and years of curriculum, and, myself, Mitch Perry, Don Dokken, we all had our hand in writing material for them. We were doing our best to show them the business while they were still kids, because, remember, this business eats it's young.

Dan started paying us to do this, which everyone was appreciative of. By this time, we were all VERY interested in anything that pulled in a little extra money. We all needed the extra income, and Dan was loaded to the nines, so compensating us for our time and expertise was a no-brainer to him. The band was called Beyond Control originally, but then they signed with Warner Brothers and changed to Dry Cell.

Shawn Brown and I will always be friends. He's like my little brother. He and Rickey Salazar. Tom Morgan. They were my brother's crew, so they came to be like family. I've been hanging out with them since they were little.

But, back in 1993, I was the only musician of concern in my life. We weren't destitute, mind you, but I've never been the kind of guy to let my family struggle. Not for any reason. So, we had flowers, steam cleaners, and finally...candy.

My third business, which I ran simultaneously with the steam cleaners and the flower shop, was a vending company. I bought 75 candy machines. Vending machines.

I had 70 locations, all around LA, with vending machines in them. The way I would run it, I would only have to work them three days a week. I would collect on a third of the machines, and load a third of the machines each day for three days. If you break up your territory correctly, you can maximize your work and still have plenty of time left over to dick around and do whatever you want.

I had those things in hair salons, gas stations, tire places. It wasn't bad. You'd go down to some of those spots, and the machines would be almost empty, so you'd know you had a shitload of quarters in there.

Thinking back on it, I would run around doing that and have bags and bags of quarters with me. I'd have thousands of dollars in coins. I'd run into CostCo and buy my candy, and then make my rounds for the day.

It was a good, little cash money business.

I didn't finish high school, much less have a college business degree, but I've always had a business mentality. Logic will tell you what will and will not work. It was slapstick entrepreneuring, but it did the trick. Those businesses brought money in. All of them.

When I bought the steam cleaning business in 1993, it was with the intentions of running it from afar, and having someone else work it for the day to days. But, like so many things in life, it didn't work out like that.

It was very sobering. I was a platinum selling rock star. But here I am, cleaning carpets. I was banking good money, but it didn't make it feel that much better. Honestly, I'm happiest with a couple of trees in my hand, beating the shit out of a kit in front of ten thousand people.

That's my home. That's where I can live. Steam cleaning was about survival. Nothing more.

Once RATT got back together at the end of 1996, I was like, "Thank God!" In 1997, I made about $250,000 in RATT, and it was like money from Heaven, let me tell you. But, who's to say? Am I a rock star who did some steam cleaning, or am I a steam cleaner who used to be a rock star?

It's a fine fucking line, my friend. Trust me.

To be honest with you, my friend Harold Hawthorne, who I learned guitar from, has been a steam cleaner for 25 years. Yeah, it's not glamorous, but he pulls down around $100,000 a year. Honestly, if you know what you're doing, you never make less than about $100 per hour. A one-bedroom apartment was $55, and it took you a half hour. And, that was back then. I don't know what it would run today, but there's money made in that business.

It's just humbling to do it after you've sold 12 million records, you know?

I worked with a property management company that kept me swamped with jobs, cleaning their vacant apartments. It was always a quick in and out, with no one there. Easy money.

They had complexes all over the place in Lawndale and Hawthorne. I could go in there and bang those things out all day and make $300 or $400 a day. It was really lucrative.

One day, they give me a call to go take care of some apartments they just acquired over in Inglewood. I really didn't want to go to Inglewood, or Ingle-Watts as we called it. It was a favor for them. I get over there, and damn it if it isn't a three-story building with no elevator.

Fuck me.

I had a method of carrying the hoses and buckets and everything, so I start lugging all this stuff up the stairs. I get to the apartment they needed me to take care of, and pull the key out. I open the door, and holy shit!

That place was just nasty, trashed out carpet. It stunk. The whole apartment stunk. I was like, "Shit."

I didn't want to do it, but Mr. Jenkins really needed me to take care of it. Jenkins Property Company was a big client, and I didn't want to do anything to jeopardize that. Nothing!

So, I get to work on it.

I'm cleaning this disgusting, nasty assed carpet in Ingle-Watts with the door open. My steam cleaner is outside the door, and I glance out toward it.

In the distance, over the top of the cleaner, I can see the LA Forum, and it hit like a sledgehammer between the fucking eyes! We sold the Forum out, with Bon Jovi opening up for us, in 1985. Here it is, 1993, just eight years later, and I'm steam-cleaning carpets.

That was a low point. That was my "where the fuck is my Jack Daniels" moment. I was as depressed as I've ever been.

But, I had to do what I had to do to take care of my family and my responsibilities. A lot of people would make fun of that situation, maybe even talk about how pathetic a fall from grace it would be to them, and they might be right...

... but, you do what you have to do.

I had been able to shave about five grand off my monthly nut. My expenses went from around twelve grand to just over seven grand per month. And, with the three businesses, I was able to hit on that...most of the time.

The pisser of this time was my house. I could have paid that place off several times. But, my accountant kept telling me, "No, don't do it. You need the tax write-off." I've regretted that ever since, because I wound up having to refinance my house, getting on a variable interest.

My house payment jumped to $4300 a month. But, things were tight, and I had to refinance the place and pull some money from it.

To complicate matters worse, the band was in a real situation with the label and our merchandise company.

In 1990, we had taken a million dollar advance against our merchandise sales for the 1991 tour; a tour we wound up coming home early on. Business wasn't good. We weren't getting along. And, when I say business wasn't good, we went from selling thirteen thousand tickets a night, to selling six thousand.

It was a fucking nightmare to look out there every night and see that. Almost half of the arena was empty.

Now, mind you. This day and age, selling six thousand tickets would be unbelievable, for most any band. It's just harder, now.

When Stephen quit, we still owed $750,000 on our merchandise deal. We had signed that deal in 1990. We all took our part of the advance and went off with it.

Winterland Productions was our merch company, and they were saying, "Alright, guys. You guys owe us this money." Now, it was time to pay.

We had fired Marshall Berle in late 1989, and Alan Kovac was our new manager. We found out that Marshall went to the label and took an advance on our behalf, then used it for something. We have no idea what he spent it on.

We fired him, and took, for life, his cut of any RATT royalties on anything. Alan Kovac was managing Richard Marx at the time, and now he manages Motley. He is a heavy hitter manager. But, he's also one of these guys who just wants to get the dollars now, take his commission, and not care whether things are going to be not as good next year, as a result. Get the money now, was his thing.

Alan gets us a publishing advance of a million bucks; a merchandising advance of a million bucks; we cut it; then Stephen quits and the band breaks up.

Now, the door starts pounding. I'm calling Del Ferrano on the phone. Del was the President of Winterland, and I'm going, "Del, listen, you guys have made millions. Millions and millions off of merchandising on RATT since 1984. This money will come back to you. You just have to be patient, because I'm not in a position right now to give you."

Each guy's cut was $150,000, that we had to pay them. "Just hold tight, Del. The band will get back together, and we'll make this good."

They hung tight, but only for about 9 months. Then they started sending us letters.

Legal letters.

Then they started proceedings. They were going to sue us.

I was backed into a corner. I had Winterland coming after me, putting liens on my house, thank you Stephen Pearcy. Atlantic stopped paying our royalties, because we took an advance on a record that never got started. So, till that was paid off, we didn't get a penny from them.

That took some time.

It was horrendous. I was led into a bankruptcy situation. I was advised that since I still had the credit card debt, the Winterland thing, Atlantic, mortgages, all of it, I had to declare bankruptcy. Not to mention my construction debt. I had torn out walls to put another story on the house, and I had to put it all back the way it was.

The house was a two story, built into the side of a hill, and I was going to put a third story on it. I had already done all of this work to it. Gone to the city counsel to file for a hillside ordinance because some of the neighbors didn't want me to build. I won, and the work had already begun when our whole house of cards came tumbling down.

Now, here I am, trying to hold all the pieces together, and there's just no possible way to do it.

I had to file for bankruptcy. It sucked. It was extremely humiliating.

My friend, Jay Freidman, my attorney managed to get me out of this thing with flying colors. I even kept my toys. My house, cars, our businesses. That pretty much wrote off about $212,000 on my slate.

All because Stephen quit.

Now, let me preface that by saying I paid Winterland about $30,000. Ten here, five there, trying to nickel and dime this thing down. Finally, I'm like, "This is ridiculous. I can't do this anymore. I don't have $150K to give them." Unless we get RATT back together and start making the real money that we were used to, forget it. So, bankruptcy was the way out.

I didn't want to do a BK, but it was a necessary evil.

The early and mid-nineties simply sucked balls.

My mom Lois, Jeni, Me, my sister Carol after a RATT show in Pittsburg 1984.

23

THE FOUNTAIN OF YOUTH, LAKE HAVASU

"Life may not be the party we hoped for, but while we're

here we should act like it is."

The mid-nineties were a crushing blow to any faith that the groups from the 80s

had of continuing careers. Some of the groups, like Bon Jovi, adapted their style and continued on with mixed success. But, even the mightiest of 80s icons became casualties for about a five year span. Mötley Crüe, Def Leppard, Guns N Roses, the list went on and on.

After filing bankruptcy, life got a little easier for me and mine. After all, I was still a rockstar. I just didn't have a band. I was a vagabond king; a wandering Pi-RATT without a crew. But, make no mistakes. A Pi-RATT without a crew is still a Pi-RATT!

Family recreation was always our escape. We had to get away, even if it was for only the weekend, and no matter what, Havasu was our haven. It was our secret port in the middle of the desert.

I bought a couple of Wave-runners. They were hardly an adequate replacement for the Ramboat, but they were fun as hell, nonetheless.

We had started spending weeks and weeks out of the year hanging out at Lake Havasu, a huge lake on the Colorado River, right on the California / Arizona border. It's an incredible, awe-inspiring oasis in the middle of a desert.

We tore that lake up on the back of those Wave-runners, just soaking in that arid climate and partying our asses off.

The first time I went out to that lake was in 1975. I was fifteen or sixteen years old, and I went out there with Chuck Daw and his family, Iris and Debbie and the others.

Lake Havasu was founded by Robert McCulloch of McCulloch chainsaw fame. He used to go out on the Colorado River to go fishing. When they dammed up the river at various points, they made all these lakes; Lake Mead; Lake Mojave; Lake Havasu. What he did, when they were getting ready to start damming everything up, was buy all of the land up that was going to become the Havasu shoreline.

He was a smart cat, I'm thinking.

There's a population of around 200,000 people out there, now. When I first started going, way back in 1975, there were a couple of hotels, maybe a couple of gas stations, NOTHING like it is today.

McCulloch dredged out a canal, which created a huge island on the lake. That's where they have the London Bridge. That's right. THE London Bridge. He went to London, to an auction, and bid on the London Bridge from the nursery rhyme, "London Bridge is Falling Down." It was all brought over, brick by brick, and reassembled to span the gap between the mainland and the island on Havasu.

On the island, they used to have the airport, but that's been moved. They have a really nice golf course out there; the Nautical Inn, which is my favorite place to stay when I'm in town; a few hotels; a big campsite; and all these homes that people live in or lease.

It's just unbelievable out there. There's all these coves that are absolutely gorgeous. It looks like the Blue Lagoon everywhere you go, with it's crystal clear, deep blue water.

You can go upriver from the bridge, you're in the heart of the Colorado River. The river meanders down from Laughlin where Davis Dam is, which holds back Lake Mojave.

You go up Lake Mojave, which is another incredible lake, seventy five miles to Hoover Dam, and on the other side of Hoover is Lake Mead.

There is a sixty-five mile stretch from Lake Havasu to Davis Dam, and it's nothing but incredible river canyon systems. The water is crystal clear blue, and ice cold year round. But, when you're on the lake, the lake runs really deep. So the surface water from June until October is somewhere like 82 degrees.

Just beautiful.

Back in 1975, when I went out there with Iris, Chuck and the gang, it was amazing, but there were a lot of bikers out there then. In those days, in Arizona, you could carry a gun. You could wear it on you; which attracted a certain kind of person.

Bikers had pistols in holsters, and some of these guys had rifles stuck down in their bikes. It was like the Wild West, so a lot of these guys were really intimidating. I didn't really like that end of it.

I went again in 1976 with some friends to the stretch of river south of Parker Dam. It's called the Parker Strip. Parker Dam, which is the dam that creates Havasu, is a huge, beautiful thing. The water gets sucked into the dam and pumped downstream. Parker Dam is about 200' high, and the stretch from Parker to the next dam is about thirteen miles. That's the Parker Strip, which was a crazy party scene.

My buddies, "Good Time" George, and Ron Welty, drummer of The Offspring, both have houses out on the Strip.

I remembered all of those sights, and when we needed to get away, Havasu jumped to mind.

I took the family out there in 1990 and fell in love with the place all over again. We started going out there all the time.

I had my Wave Runners for about seven years, just putting thousands of miles on those things. We used to run all the way up to Laughlin on the runners, no problem. It was just a great time.

My buddy, Mike Anthony, who was the bass player for Van Halen, has a townhouse up there on the lake, right by the London Bridge. He paid $143,000 for the place, and the things worth about $1.3 million now. I've done a lot of partying up there with him and his family over the years.

I've got my whole Havasu Crew that I run with up there. Mitch and Jenna, I've known Jenna since she was about sixteen years old. She's now been with Mitch Brandon for ten years, that's how I met him, he's one of my best friends. He bought a huge house out there, so we stay with him a lot. There's Mark and Christine Valdez and their kids; Joy Carter; Mike and Lisa Valdez and their kids; "Good Time" George Eastom and his girlfriend Summer; Ron Welty, the drummer for Offspring, who has a place right by the dam, so he can do the lake or the river. He's a great guy.

We do jam sessions at Mitch's house several times a summer. We just set up on the patio overlooking the lake and then have at it.

The sunsets are amazing, there. It's like the sky is on fire. Then, when you ride at night, the air is still around the low 90's in temperature. It's warm and soothing as you drive through it. That's a really comforting sensation as you watch the full moon rise at the bottom of the lake.

I've raised my children on this lake, that's how I feel about it. Cruising around that place, it's hard to imagine anything could ever be wrong in life.

I love it so much that upon the untimely death of my ass, they are instructed to take my ashes and scatter them in my five favorite coves in Lake Havasu. So, if I die next year, anyone who reads this and goes to Havasu, you'll be swimming in the Blotz's ashes.

How sexy is that?

One night, we were all partying over at Mike Anthony's condo. It overlooks the London Bridge and the channel. He's got a balcony, and outside the front door, there is a huge porch area where he has a Jacuzzi. We were all in the Jacuzzi, and were getting shitty, drinking. I was camping over at Crazy Horse, which is a big campsite out there.

We were talking about running on the water at night, because I had put lights on my Wave Runners to run at night.

Someone goes, "Blotz, go get them! I dare you to ride your shit through here at night."

"I'm sorry. Did you say you're daring me?"

Never one to turn down a dare, I hopped in the car and drove across the street to where my Runners were beached. I got on one of them, stripped down buck-assed naked, and rode all the way around the island back to the channel and Mike's place.

There's two ways you can enter the London Bridge area. If you're coming from the bottom of the lake, you enter one area, and if you come from the river you enter from another into Havasu.

I drove around to the top entrance. It's a "no-wake" zone, obviously, but there are never any cops on the lake at night. So I went by there, full speed, ass out in the breeze. I was flipping those guys off with one hand, and steering with ... well, imagine, if you will.

I went back and dropped the Runner off at the campground. I got dressed, and came back to the party to the sound of thunderous applause from all of my disciples, traumatized, though they might have been.

The Wave Runners eventually gave up the ghost, and it was time to trade up. At first, I got a 21' open bow Seaswirl lake boat. It was nice, but had limited partying capacity.

Now, I have a 27' JC Tritoon deck boat. It's really nice and seats 16 people. You're never going to set any boating speed records in the thing, but it goes as fast as you need it to, 38 mph, and it does it with a baker's dozen, plus three, of your best friends on board.

Every Fourth of July it's time to gather for the fireworks. They always shoot them off from the beach at The Nautical, there on the island, so you'll go out on the water, and there's literally hundreds of boats out there, just bobbing lightly. The red and green lights from the boats look like a huge Christmas tree floating across the lake. It's amazing.

When the fireworks start, you couldn't ask for a better show. They shoot them off right over your head.

That's the way to celebrate Independence Day!

There're so many party stories that you can't pick one over the other. But, that's what we do out there. We just stay clear of the cops. On busy weekends, they bring these out of town guys in, and they are just a bunch of neo-nazi assholes. You have to watch your step around them. But, that's the only rub to the place.

So that's it. I've been happily doing Havasu for the last eighteen years. But, I went to the boat show last week, and I'm getting the itch for an ocean boat again. So, maybe there will be a sequel to Ramboat: First Blotz.

Be that as it may, Lake Havasu will forever be my favorite vacation spot.

Commanding the SS-TriToon on Lake Havasu in June 2009.

Entertaining the troops, Havasu June 2009.

My dog, Jack the River, doing what he loves best; fetching anything that looks like a ball.

It really does look like a different planet.

24

RUMORS OF RECONCILIATION

AND THE KING WHO BECAME A PAUPER.

Wally Verson, who was our tour manager for years, was in management now.

In 1996, he met with Stephen, Warren, Juan and I at Warren's house about getting the band back together.

Wally was a strange bird. On one hand, he was pushing us all back together, which was good for our future, but on the other hand, he would pick at the wounds in the band. That kept old beefs from healing, which was going to absolutely be necessary if we were going to make another run at our music.

Wally really got into Warren's head. That kept Warren from wanting to jump back into it.

Stephen and I had to form some sort of strategy. We called Robbin, because we were going to do it with or without Warren. We were like, "King, we want to go out, do some business, play some RATT music and fucking live it again."

We weren't intentionally dealing Warren out, but we weren't going to wait around either. You know? If you're not wanting to do it, then see you. Step aside.

We figured that King would be able to step in and take care of the problem, then we could pick up another player.

We were horribly wrong.

In 1994, Robbin Crosby was a full on heroin addict. He was mainlining junk, and drinking so much booze, he hardly knew who he was. King was a man being rapidly consumed by his demons, and by a sickness, that in the mid-nineties was the plague of modern man. HIV.

He had this beautiful house in the Hollywood Hills that he was hanging onto by a thread, yet it was constantly being over run by these derelict, junked out friends of his. He had a crew of cotton shooters that would hang at his place for days and days chasing the dragon.

I was never up there with all those people, but I talked with a couple of the guys who had been, and I heard all the stories. It was sub-human.

In 1994, Robbin was asked to do an appearance on the Geraldo Show. It was an episode on drug addiction. While he was gone, these asshole gutter junkies cleaned him out!

They took all his platinum records, all his guitars, anything of value. He got back and this beautiful house of his was ransacked. There was trash everywhere, holes kicked in the walls, everything. It was something that Robbin, victim of his vices though he was, did not deserve.

It broke my heart when I heard about it.

He had a collection of guitars hanging on his walls that was worth a small fortune. There must have been fifty or more vintage guitars, all collector items and one of a kind, just lining both sides of the wall as you walk down the hall. They were worth ten thousand, twelve thousand, twenty thousand dollars each. It was sickening, and it drives me crazy every time I think about it. All that stuff was gone.

It wasn't long after that when Robbin finally crashed and disappeared to El Paso, Texas. I heard he was playing in a bar band, doing country music and shit. King Crosby, the Viking of Heavy Metal playing gigs in a country bar.

The night I found out that Robbin Crosby had AIDS, I was in a club the San Fernando Valley called FM Station. Jaime St. James, the lead singer of Black and Blue, tapped me on the shoulder and was talking into my ear, over whatever band was playing. He goes, "Sorry to hear about Robbin, dude!"

I thought I misheard him. "What are you talking about?"

"Robbin! You know. What's going on with his health!" Mind you that the music is cranking, so I was really struggling to understand what he was saying.

Finally, I'm like, "Come over here." I motioned him to follow me to a place where we might actually be able to talk.

"Now, what are you saying?" He goes, "Well, I heard that King's got HIV." I knew Robbin had some health issues, but holy fuck!

I go, "Where did you hear that?" Jaime looks at me, sort of confused, and goes, "I heard it from his roommate."

I got home that night and called Juan Croucier. "Juan, have you talked to King?"

He's kind of tentative, and goes, "Yeah."

"Have you heard about this rumor that he..."

Juan interrupts me. "It's true."

Fucking, no way. Juan filled me in on what Robbin told him. King had been feeling sick with the flu, and he just couldn't get past it. He went in to the doctor. They couldn't figure out what exactly was wrong with him, and finally they administered an AIDS test. It came back positive for HIV.

That was shocking.

When we first started talking about getting the band back together in 1996, none of us knew too much about King's situation, you know? We didn't have a lot of contact with him after he was let go in Japan, and what little time we did communicate with him, he didn't give a lot of details.

We knew about the HIV thing. But, we also knew that there had been advances made in the treatment for HIV. We were hoping for the best.

But, we got the worst.

No one knew that his condition was as bad as it was. His pancreas was shutting down on him, which just slaughtered his metabolism. He was swelling up like a balloon.

Robbin was a huge guy to begin with. Six foot five and about 230 in his prime, Robbin Crosby was a big motherfucker! But with his health in decline, he wasn't physically able to tour anymore. Honestly, it was a question if he could play the guitar again. I guess, at this time, he was up around 300 pounds or more, and his hands looked like baseball gloves. He was really puffy and swollen.

The really strange thing with Robbin's case was when you think of someone dying of AIDS, you think of someone who is really skinny and withdrawn, like they had the life sucked out of them.

Robbin was the complete opposite. He gained MASSIVE amounts of weight. It was hard to recognize him. There was no way he could pull off the work. His health and appearance were just not conducive to pulling off this reunion.

It absolutely sucked, because he really wanted to do it. It just wasn't possible.

God rest his soul, that guy. I love him. He knew I loved him, and I wish that whole thing had been different; you have no idea how badly.

But, wanting to do something and having the ability to do it are two very different things. Sometimes the game passes you by.

"The King" in Japan 1985. I miss you brother.

25

METAL'S PIED PIPERS RETURN!

In the end, we told Warren that we were getting Nuno Bettencourt from

Extreme to handle the guitar work. We hadn't talked with Nuno about it, mind you, but that's what we told Warren.

We knew that Warren and Nuno had a friendly rivalry thing with each other. They had lots of respect for one another, but it was a competitive, almost jealousy laden friendship. I never really knew the details, but we kind of used it to our advantage. It was manipulative, true, but when we told Warren that, he was suddenly interested it starting up again.

So, we put RATT N Roll back into business once again in January of 1997.

'97 and 1998 were odd years. We had been out of it for a while, and we had distanced ourselves from each other, so it was almost like starting anew.

Almost.

In 1997, when we were getting back together, people wondered why Juan wasn't getting back into the fold. I BEGGED Juan, fucking begged him to get on board with this. I tried to reach him through his brothers, through his friends and family, nothing worked.

Finally, I got him on the phone and said, "Look, man. We're getting this band together. You came out to that first meeting several months ago, and we're ready to roll."

He goes, "I don't know that I'm ready to do that."

I found that really confusing, since from a musical standpoint, Juan had been doing dick. It wasn't like he was blowing up the music scene. None of us were at that point. So, I go, "I don't know why that is, bro, but we're ready to rock."

He gets pretty raw about the whole thing. "Look, man, there's been a whole lot of shit happen to me because of Stephen Pearcy. I'm not ready to open that part of my life again."

"Yeah, but WE are, Juan. If you want to do this, which is the smart thing to do, because we're going to fire up the machine and go make some money, it's time to work, man. It's time to RATT and Roll again." I couldn't understand why he wasn't on board.

He says, "Look, Blotz. You and me own the name. As far as I'm concerned, unless I'm a part of the thing, no one is going out and doing anything with that band."

That stone cold pissed me off. I couldn't believe the balls of this guy. He's telling me that the band I BROUGHT him into, AFTER we were already signed; the band HE almost fucked off because of his love affair with Dokken; he was going to keep the rest of us from going out and earning a living? I was so mad.

I wanted to tell him, "When you're in that Palos Verdes house of yours, with the killer city view and the recording studio, thank Blotz for bringing you into this band, bro. Because you could be a pain in the ass from day number one!"

I didn't say that, of course. Juan is one of my brothers-in-arms, and I still wanted him to get back into the band. However, Juan has extremely thin skin. Fucking rice paper thin.

Back when he was playing us against Dokken, I went to his house because he wouldn't answer any of my calls. He lived in the same neighborhood as me, so I went to his place and said "Listen, are you in this band, or not?"

He kicked me out of his house! He came to his senses a couple of weeks afterwards, of course.

He tells me, "Maybe in two or three years…"

"Two or three years?!? Juan, the band is getting together. We're going to record and tour again. Either get on board or get out of the way."

I tried everything, for weeks, to get him to come around. He shot his own family down when they tried to get involved.

If Juan had told me that he didn't want to do it, but we could buy his share of the name and move on, that would be different. We would have worked out a price and cut our ties. But he didn't. He was a completely inordinate about it. He went and got a lawyer, and tried to sue us.

It cost us about $35,000 to defend the lawsuit. It never went to court. It never settled. It just sort of went away.

Juan didn't have the money to do it, and his lawyer was completely outclassed by our team of guys. The guy showed up to the first depositions dressed in a tweed suit, circa 1961, and was shot down in a blaze of glory. It was sad. He looked like he should be doing law out of the trunk of his car, or something.

We used the same firm that represented me during my divorce in 1998. It's this huge firm, with several departments, which sent in a full school of slick, pressed, and razor sharp sharks, and they could smell blood in the water.

To this day, Juan insists we stole the name from him. I firmly and morally believe that we did not. Our stance was this: When Stephen quit the band; he wrote a letter to our former manager, Alan Kovaks that wasn't written in a fashion that the bylaws of our partnership agreement would legally consider quitting. The letter stated, "I am no longer working with RATT, and you do not represent my solo interests." Then he signed it.

He never said, one way or the other, if he was completely out of the band, or if he was simply taking a hiatus.

When Warren quit, he did it through his lawyer. It was very concise and followed the letter of the bylaws, making it clear that he was no longer an owner of the RATT name.

Juan and I were left with the position of having the ownership of the RATT name and label. We were going to take legal action against anyone who tried to use it, even Stephen, despite the fact that his letter was sketchy at best, and it was going to be difficult to determine how a court would view that thing.

All the while when we were broke up, Juan kept sending Stephen letters from his lawyer stating all of this, and he kept trying to get me on board with it.

I wasn't going to spend a nickel. Unless I saw that Stephen was out there touring as RATT, don't count on me to contribute money to fire off warning shots at him.

But, Juan kept doing it on his own.

When it was time to get back together, and Juan decided to fight it "all the way to the Supreme Court" if he had to, it was my stance that Stephen had perpetuated RATT business the whole time we were broke up. He had taken care of clerical things dealing with trademarks issues and publishing and various other things that needed tending to.

I always felt that the time would come when this band would get back together. I wasn't going to go out and ruffle all the feathers. If it was going to happen, it had to be a smooth transition, so yeah, Stephen had quit, but when he wanted back in, he was in the band.

We used that as our stance. There were two owners other than Juan himself. We weren't going to allow Juan to come between the rest of us doing business and making a living.

Enter our Ritalin poster child, Robbie Crane!

Rudy Sarzo really wanted to work with us, and I really wanted him to do it. He was calling my phone daily asking about the gig. At the time, he had just come out of Quiet Riot. I was into the idea, but Warren wouldn't agree to it. He felt that Rudy wasn't a very good player, and had dealt with him during his Whitesnake run.

I'd never played with Rudy, but my good buddy, Tommy Aldridge had, and spoke highly of him. That's good enough for me.

Stephen brought in Robbie, and here it is, eleven years later. I'm glad the guy is here, even though he's so fucking hyperactive, I'm bringing a tranquilizer gun on the next tour, I swear to God.

Stephen recommended Robbie Crane, who had played in Vince Neil's band, and then played with Stephen in a band called Itronic.

Robbie was this young Mexican kid who was totally funny and fun to be around. Although, he was two hours late to the first day! I was ready to fire him right then and there before we met him. I was so sick of the years dealing with Juan's incessant tardiness. Juan's punctuality was painful. I wasn't going to deal with it again.

But, it was an honest mistake.

Stephen told him the wrong studio, so he didn't know where to go. When he finally got there, it was great. Robbie's been in the band ever since then. In fact, he has been in the band LONGER that Juan was. Now Juan was a writer, and Robbie doesn't contribute any songs, but he's really easy to work with. Really easy to get along with.

RATT was back!

The first thing we wanted to do was get some material out there that we could push. What we planned on doing was taking a bunch of songs we had in the vault, that were written and recorded for other records, put a record out when we toured and see what the climate was like.

That's what "Collage" was.

We basically put a bunch of songs that weren't good enough to make our platinum albums into a mismatched mash of a record. It was rehashed.

While I didn't really like the record, itself, it was one of the best things we could have done. We remixed it, recorded three new songs, and spent a total of ten thousand dollars on that record.

It was a collection of stuff that sounded like a polished demo, but we proved two things with "Collage."

First, we could still make money. We were still viable.

Second, we could still work together without killing one another.

Stephen loves that record, Warren loves it, and it actually made us a lot of money. So, I can't bitch. We got some pretty big advances for that record.

This is a picture of a fan with the band in 1997. Look how young we look in this shot.

26

RUMORS OF OUR DEMISE

HAVE BEEN GREATLY EXAGGERATED

We went out in 1997 and hired Tim Hyne and John Greenberg of Union Entertainment. Tim and John are cool guys. These days, they manage Nickelback, and before us, they managed Cinderella. They were two guys who had a stable of bands and producers at their fingertips.

Union Entertainment came on board and helped us whip our business into shape. Before we knew it, we were back in our vein and ready to tour.

We went out and started selling out everywhere we played.

That took us by surprise a little. Grunge had pronounced heavy metal dead on arrival a full six years earlier. We were proving that wrong, and it felt really good to be doing it!

As Mark Twain said, "Rumors of our demise have been greatly exaggerated."

I was thinking, "Oh, my God! Thank you! I'm back on stage rocking where I belong."

I hadn't been on stage since we broke up, other than little cover band things. But, of course, no one had.

It was hard to ride out those mid-nineties years, you know. Some of the other bands just refused to give in and kept plugging away on the road. The Warrants and Great Whites and LA Guns of the business were forced to fight through the bottom feeder aspects of this business.

When I say bottom feeding, I'm not slamming their talent. These bands were part of the royal court of 80s metal. It's just that, when you plug along like that, and you continually are available, you overexpose yourself. Your market value drops.

In contrast, we were doing really well. We were headlining the House of Blues sized venues. Come summer, we started doing some festivals.

We did this one festival called Rockfest. It was in Chippewa Valley, Cadott, Wisconsin. It's a yearly, three-day festival.

The day we were playing, we were second up to Boston, who was the headliner. We were being paid $35,000 for that show, so it was a very high paying show for us.

We were back where we belonged.

During our set, with the crowd amped up as hot as I've ever seen a crowd, Stephen disappears.

I'm looking at my tech, going, "Where the fuck is Stephen?"

I was getting pissed off, because I thought he was off drinking somewhere on the side of the stage.

Little did I know, he had fallen off the stage!

There was an ego ramp that went straight out from the stage. An ego ramp is what we called that long runway that allows the singer to get right out amidst the crowd. This particular ego ramp had a ten foot drop into a concrete drainage ditch all the way around it. There were no rails, no lights on this ramp.

You can see it in the footage from the show. I know, because we used the footage when we sued the city and the promoter.

Stephen had his hands up to his eyes, trying to see, and you watch him try to catch himself, with this look of complete, abject horror on his face!

Stephen fell ten feet, into this concrete culvert, and landed on his knee.

They had to take him away in an ambulance. All of this in front of 35,000 people.

It was really bad.

But, it could have been much much worse. We went to look at the spot afterward, and there were these fence posts with a pointed arrow tip sticking straight up. They were using them to tie the barrier fences around. A couple of feet to either side, and it would have been a case of "Mourners, please omit flowers. The Pearcy family thanks you for your thoughts and prayers."

Stephen could have died that night, impaled on a fence spike.

But, thankfully, he didn't. Nevertheless, he was seriously fucked up. His kneecap and been smashed and dislocated, then turned completely around the side of his leg.

He was a wreck, and in the hospital for a while. July 27, 1997, and the tour was immediately over. Backing up, July 27, 1983 is when we signed the Atlantic deal. 14 years to the day. Odd paradox, when you think about it.

We went to see him in the hospital the next day, and it brought me to tears!

I just couldn't believe it, dude. We had to leave him there in the hospital! He was there for about a week or so. We went back home, and we were off for the rest of the summer. Then, in October, we went back out doing clubs again.

Stephen had healed up pretty well, but he was never going to be jumping around on stage doing his high kicks anymore. Now, he had a legitimate reason for being a little stiff on stage.

We finished out the tour from October on, and that leg of the thing did really well, too. But, the fractures started to show again. It was getting heated out there, and, it was snowballing into something unstoppable.

In 1998, we sat down to do the "RATT" album, which was produced by multi-platinum producer, Richie Zito.

We were meeting with John Kolodner every two weeks with batches of new material. We literally wrote about 50 or 60 songs for consideration on that record. This went on for about eight months, and, surprisingly John kept picking my songs.

I was about ten minutes late to one of the meetings, and I came in all apologetic.

"Sorry, guys. I'm a little late. Traffic was crazy."

John looks at me and says in his raspy, nasally voice, "Congratulations."

He confused the hell out of me. I'm like, "For what?"

"You just wrote the first single!"

They had been combing through all of the new songs. It was a song called "Breakout." I wrote the music, and then Jack Russell from Great White came in and helped me develop the lyrics and melody.

There was another song on that record called "Live For Today" that I wrote with Jack. Over the phone, Jack and I were talking with Jack Blades from Night Ranger. We were having a problem with one section of the song, and Blades came up with the line. One line. But, he contributed, so he was listed as a writer.

Stephen saw that, and was like, "What the fuck? There's six writers on this song?!?" I go, "Look, you and DeMartini didn't do shit on this song, but you forced your way onto it. Jack Blades shouldn't really be on it either. He came up with one line. A couple of words. But, if you get credit, so does he." Jack Russell and I wrote that song. So, I don't want to hear it. It's a strong song.

I really liked that 1999 Sony release, but it was the wrong time for it. It charted, but didn't really perform.

In the end, I don't think Sony really gave it any kind of a push. There was virtually no marketing campaign. It didn't have a video. Nothing. But, it was our first jaunt back into it since Detonator in 1990. That's almost a decade of being out of the loop, and it took some time to get into the groove of things again.

RATT and Poison co-headlined on that 1999 tour, and it was getting exciting. People started getting used to seeing these bands out on the road again.

That was the "RATT" album, not to be confused with the "RATT" EP way back in 1983.

This was the "RATT" record...

Not the "RATT" EP...

...fucking retarded.

I hated the cover. I hated the fact we didn't title the record. We already had a self-titled album! Why were we doing another one? But, that's the bitch with a democracy. The majority rules. Now we have the bookend thing going on. Hopefully, we will get back into the studio and knock out another record. It's been 10 years since our last studio album, so it's time. I think.

27

OUT OF THE FRYING PAN, INTO THE FIRE

"Ah, yes, Divorce...from the Latin word meaning to rip out a man's genitals through his wallet." - Robin Williams

I'm not sure when it happened, exactly. I know that RATT's experiences through the Nineties were traumatic, and really took a toll on us all. However, the real impact, I think, hit us hardest in our personal lives. Maybe, it was because I was home all the time, where we had spent SO MUCH time on the road during the 80s. That's probably a big reason.

I guess it's easier to deal with a bad situation when you don't have to deal with it in your face every day. Relationships are no exception to that rule. My parents divorced. Mum and Pete divorced. Juan went through an ugly divorce, and it almost cost him his kids. King did it too, and his centerfold princess turned into a blood-sucking harpy who cried and moaned until the courts took everything he had and gave it to her. Laurie Carr was her name, and she was the quintessential gold-digger.

Jeni was no gold-digger, though. She was my wife, and the mother of my two sons. We had been married for seventeen years, and had been together for twenty-one. She was there when I was struggling to find the gigs. She was there when I landed my first break with Vergat. She was there when I joined RATT, and we marauded our way through the better part of the decade.

Jeni was always there, and our relationship had survived the best and worst of all those things. That is much to our credit, I think.

But, the one thing people tend to not understand about marriage, especially long marriages, is that things change. Sometimes, they change for the good. Sometimes, it isn't so good. But, make no mistake about it, who you are at twenty years old is a very different person than who you are at forty.

And, there's the rub.

I didn't see it during the 80s. I was always touring, or recovering from a tour, so Jeni and I were all right. We didn't see each other all the time, so the subtle differences weren't that noticeable.

When the Nineties hit, and grunge squashed the careers for a while, I was suddenly home all the time. All the time! We had become different people, Jeni and I. I expected the woman I married to still be there, but it wasn't really her. She was different. And, so was I. Add to that, the struggles of my music career, and the stresses of lawsuits and bankruptcy. It wasn't long before the battle lines had been drawn in the dirt.

Jeni and I were on life support as a couple for a long time. It had reached a point where I wanted out. I had been thinking of leaving as far back as 1992, right after the band split. Michael and Marcus, I felt, weren't old enough to really deal with that, yet. So, I kept putting it off.

I couldn't walk out on her and the kids like that. I remembered what that felt like, and while I survived the ordeal, I wasn't sure the boys could; not at their young age. My boys are my life, so we needed each other, at that point.

It was a fight, though. Almost constant conflict, and by 1994, Jeni and I were really battling hard.

I found my breaking point in the summer of 1997, after Stephen's accident where he fell off the stage. We were home, giving Stephen time to heal up, and then we were going back out on the road in October.

Jeni and I were fighting virtually all the time. We spent that whole summer in a constant state of battle. Jeni and I had always had an up and down relationship. She was a hot-blooded Italian, so she would get right up into my face and yell and scream. It would literally start the moment I woke up, and would last the entire day. We hardly spoke a civil word to one another, and any sort of positive comment was usually dripping in sarcasm and backhanded in nature.

By 1997, I finally sat down with her and said, "Obviously, this isn't working for us and has to end. Agreed?"

For once, we were both on the same page.

"We should start thinking about divorce, here. The kids are getting old enough to understand it. I'm back with RATT, making money again, so we can take care of things properly."

To my surprise, she agreed.

It's hard to explain how I felt about it. On one hand, there was this huge relief. I had to get loaded just to climb into bed with her, and we NEVER touched one another. It had been six months since we'd had the notion of sex.

On the other hand, I'd been with Jeni since I was seventeen. At this point, Jeni had been a part of me for more than half my life. You don't walk away from that without it having some impact on you. Even today, I find myself dreaming and thinking about Jeni, she was ingrained into my existence for so long...for life, actually.

But, it had to be done. Michael was sixteen, and Marcus was almost fifteen. The damage to them should be minimal, and we were both smart enough to see what was going on here. There was nothing of our marriage left to salvage. If we didn't stop this thing, we wouldn't be able to have a friendship, even for the sake of the boys.

So I said, "Look, when I get off the road, we'll figure out how to do this. We will split everything right down the middle. 50/50. No lawyers. No courts. Keep it tight."

We knew the outcome of lawyers coming in and taking everybody's money. We had seen it way too many times already.

She joked, "Well, that is, of course, unless you end up with some 23 year old blonde."

"Yeah, whatever, Jeni. Like that could happen."

Little did I know how prophetic she would turn out to be.

In October, we started the tour up again. Our first date was down in San Diego. Jeni and the boys came down for the show to see me off. When I got back in December, we would look at all of our assets, divide them up, then I'd get my own place.

The tour worked it's way up the west coast. We had a show in San Francisco, and then we were off to Seattle.

When we got to Seattle, I was hanging out on the bus, waiting for showtime, and looked out the window. There were three really hot chicks out there. Two of them looked like twins. I told Joe Anthony, who worked for us, "Go see if those chicks would like to come in and say hey." He did, and they all came on the bus.

That's when I met Traci and her sister. I was instantly mesmerized with Traci, who was all dolled up for a rock show, and looked as incredible as any woman I've ever seen.

It was a moment that would wind up costing me a part of my soul. I've been a rock star for a very long time, and, I've done a lot of rock star things; including women. As I've said before, we were Pi-RATTs out to pillage and conquer, so having a chick on the bus wasn't anything new.

It had been a LONG time since those days, and with what was going on in my personal life, I wasn't ready for what happened next.

Traci and I hooked up that night, and it was everything that I had been missing in my marriage. In one bat of her eyes, I remembered what it was like to FEEL. I was wanted by someone, and I didn't realize how much I had missed that feeling. Moreover, I was smitten and had a lot of love to deliver.

Traci started coming out on the road and visiting me, and I fell for this girl really hard, really quick. It wasn't planned. I wasn't looking for anyone. In fact, I didn't want anyone at that time. But I hadn't felt like this in a VERY long time. That's the way it was, and I was helpless to stop it.

I gave myself the usual, testosterone-laden explanations. Jeni and I were getting a divorce. We had verbally agreed to it. I wasn't doing anything wrong. Why should I pass this kind of love up? It didn't make any sense.

Pick your clichéd rationale, but honestly, I wasn't out to hurt my family, and I didn't see how it would end like that. I also didn't see some of the more obvious questions about Traci that most people NOT in love with her saw from the very beginning.

I was in love for the second time in my life. What are you going to do?

It was still an awkward situation, though, and the guys in the band picked up on it. They didn't understand. Traci was young. I was thirty-eight and she was twenty-three. Hey, it was what it was. We didn't care about the age thing, and my life was changing. Everyone needed to accept that. I had found my muse.

I guess my first mistake, the one that started Jeni thinking, anyway, was that my habits completely changed. I hadn't been calling Jeni from the road, which was something I always did. I was avoiding her because of Traci. I just didn't want to talk. Everything had been decided, as far as I was concerned, and I didn't want to address it.

I didn't want to talk to her.

This really bothered Jeni, I guess. I got the periodic calls of, "What's going on? Why aren't you calling me?" In the back of my mind, I started hearing that little voice of reason. The phone calls from Jeni told me that she didn't think our marriage was finished. Not completely. And, she was thinking that when I got back, we would pick up the pieces.

It couldn't be that way, though. I wanted this relationship over. I was done. Not to mention the fact that I was in love with the twenty-three year old blond that Jeni had mockingly threatened me about.

I started getting that bowling ball feeling in the pit of my gut. I had to be very careful how I dealt with the whole Traci / Jeni thing, or it was going to have lasting implications on the boys.

Making this issue worse was the fact that it wasn't a great time of year for this to go down. I got home off the tour on December 17, right before Christmas.

As usual, I made a substantial deposit into the bank, all of my tour income, and when I went to check it, the account balances were off by quite a bit. I called Jeni.

"I made a deposit into the account, and this is what's in there. According to my records, it should be this amount." She went off like a cannon; totally flying off the handle! Whatever. It was clear that two months on the road didn't change a damn thing. I just hung up the phone and headed for the house. I hung out with the boys, having a good time. Then when she got home, I was sitting on the bed and preparing for the maelstrom that was about to come.

She came into the room and tried to kiss me. That turned me off immediately. I was like, "Don't."

She looked confused, and completely upset about that. I looked at her and said, "We've got to talk, Jeni."

That dreaded "we need to talk" vibe.

"You know what we talked about before I left. I'm getting a place the first of the month. I'll stay through Christmas and make everything right for the boys, but after that, I'm done."

She was like, "What the fuck? You've got a girlfriend, or something?"

What's the old saying? The best laid plans of mice and men often go awry? Well, I don't know about the plans of mice, but a man's plan can get fucked like a Tijuana whore in about ten seconds!

I looked Jeni square in the eye...and lied. I told her, "No."

I didn't want to lie about it, but there was no way she was emotionally prepared for Traci. There was just no way. So, I thought I was doing...well, maybe not the right thing, but certainly the BEST thing. And, of course, like most things that begin with a guy's dick and end in his heart, it all came back to bite me square in the ass! But, I'm getting ahead of myself.

I looked at Jeni and went, "Don't act surprised. You knew this was coming. It was going to happen, and we made this decision two months ago. Let's not make this harder than it is."

It got real weird through Christmas. We went out to a party for the holiday, and I just couldn't deal with it. All the bullshit Christmas cheer, and the revelry spirit of the holidays sucked, and I missed Traci in the worst way. I told her, "Get a ride from someone. I gotta get out of here. I'm going home." She was fine with that, and I split.

It just so happened that the party was at Don Dokken's house.

Jeni came home that night, fully drunk-enraged. She was yelling, screaming and breaking shit all through the house. "I know about that fucking whore in Seattle!"

I was, needless to say, unprepared. What I had done in an effort to make this transition a little smoother had now come back on me in a big way. I looked like the typical, lying, cheating bastard that all of the movies on the Lifetime channel are about.

I wasn't that guy, though. However, no matter what I said, from that point on, I was never going to be trusted by this woman I had spent two decades with. She was never going to believe me again.

If I could get my hands on the cocksucker who told her...!

"Where did you hear this?"

I knew the answer, of course. She heard it from Don. I had confided in him while I was on the road. He was, after all, my bro. I thought I could trust him. I couldn't.

That was the second mistake I made during the course of my break-up with Jeni. I trusted someone I really shouldn't have. People like that will hurt you if they can; and Don Dokken could. He snitched me off.

It was really eerie how that whole thing went down with Jeni. That night, before she got home, the power had gone out on our side of the street. I ran an extension cord from our neighbor's house so we could power a few things, but it made for a very creepy night, given the way everything happened.

It was a really bad, really horrible night.

I moved to a hotel immediately after Christmas. It was really depressing. Really weird. I felt like complete shit. I finally found a townhouse in Redondo Beach, and I leased it. I remember buying furniture for it, because I had left everything behind. I took nothing other than my clothes when I left. I left a bunch of my gear in the garage. I just had to get out. The weight of the split was making it hard to breathe.

I had given Jeni $8000 in cash that I had from the tour. We hadn't done anything with the accounts, yet. Honestly, given how bad everything turned when I got home, I had no idea what we were going to do. But, I had assured her that everything would be paid for, and nothing would be neglected. It was going to be all right. She and the boys wouldn't want for anything. In fact, I'd just bought her a brand new car; a Ford Thunderbird, Anniversary Edition. It was a really nice, beautiful car.

Cars and money don't do the trick, though. In short order, people started getting into Jeni's ear. I was at Best Buy, picking up things for the townhouse, and when I got to the line, my bank card wouldn't work. I called the bank, and they told me that all the accounts had been frozen.

Panic began to creep up on me. The band was leaving overseas soon to continue the next leg of the tour. I had financial obligations, and without money...

"What do you mean, the accounts are frozen?"

"Well, your wife had the accounts frozen."

I'm calling her and going, "What are you doing? I'm leaving for Japan in a few days, and I've got to take care of my bills and expenses. You can't do this with the bank accounts."

She goes, "You're not taking the money!" Like I said, this woman was never going to trust me.

We had to split the accounts 50/50. Right there. On the spot. When I got back from the tour of Japan, we immediately started divorce proceedings, and it was a very morose time. I took a picture of this fax I got from her. I had one of those really old fax machines that didn't cut the pages, and the piece of paper stretched the entire length of my house. Un-fucking-believable. The thing must have been forty pages long.

As bad as things were with Jeni, it was the opposite with Traci. Traci moved to LA with her twin sister. I wanted her to move in with me, but she didn't want to leave her sister to live by herself. I wound up setting them up in an apartment right around the corner in Redondo.

Traci would stay with me every night, but she and her sister both worked at Fed-Ex. They drove to work together. They ate lunch together. They drove home together. They hung out together. It's like they were joined at the hip.

I had heard of twins who had separation anxieties, but I'd never seen it before. Traci and her sister had it really bad. It was really bizarre, looking back on it. Looking back on it, I'm surprised I didn't find the two of them walking the halls, hand in hand, and writing REDRUM all over the place.

There was no way I would have picked up on those vibes, though. Not at that time. I was crazy, out of my head, stupid in love with Traci. Believe me, when you're looking at the world with your "love glasses" on, you tend to miss the details. Jack Nicholson could have shown up at the door, all wide eyed with his axe in hand, and I would have thought he was there for firewood.

You gotta learn some lessons the hard way, folks. That's just the way life is.

I was only getting a couple of hours of Traci's time a day, and it was starting to eat at me. Traci was my sense of stability at a time in my life where stability simply didn't exist.

I was telling her, "I want you to move in. Let's get married as soon as the divorce is final." But, my voice fell on deaf ears. There was no way she would leave her sister.

Then I was visited by shades of the past. Traci got pregnant. Unlike Moon, who had been naive and sweet, Traci reacted very poorly to the news of a baby. She immediately wanted to have an abortion.

That bothered me a lot more than I thought it would. I don't know if I was really against it, or if I was starting to pick up on the underlying tone of our relationship, but the idea of her aborting our child kinda hurt. I told her, "If you do, you have to do it alone. I don't believe in that."

I ended up driving her down, because you can't let someone you love go through something like that alone.

I was starting to feel like I was in some UFC Championship Fight, and some big son-of-a-bitch was just beating me senseless. I was being hit from every direction.

The divorce was brutal. I'm paying my lawyer and hers. We're trying to hash this out, but it's not working out anything like we had planned. In fact, it was turning into something the total opposite. We were going to make a couple of lawyers a lot richer than we were making ourselves.

The reality of Traci came around full force shortly before the divorce was final. It was at this point that I realized my third mistake; the mistake that almost cost me one of my sons.

Per our agreement, I had the boys for two weeks and Jeni had them for two weeks. Traci had to get up at five in the morning to go to work, so she always went to bed early. About 9:30 pm, there's a knock at the door.

It's Michael.

"Uh… what's up, son? What are you doing here?"

He goes, "I left something for school in the bedroom upstairs."

Okay. Tense, but it was okay. I let him go upstairs to get his stuff. Traci was sound asleep in our bed, so it shouldn't be an issue, since his stuff was in his and Marcus' room.

When he comes back down, I can tell immediately that he's really bothered by something. I go, "What's wrong?"

"Who's up in your bed, Dad?"

"I thought you were getting something out of your room. What were you doing in mine?"

For whatever reason, he had to go into my room. So, I just said, "It's nobody. We don't need to discuss it right now. I'll talk to you about it tomorrow."

I had told Michael that his mom and I were splitting up back when I was leaving for tour. But, I think he completely blocked that out, because he denies ever having the conversation. It was becoming clear that whatever I had thought about my boys, Michael wasn't going to handle this split very well. Not very well at all.

But, I would talk to him about it at a better time. Maybe I could give him a better understanding of the what's and whys of the divorce.

I say good night to him and go back to the couch to finish watching television, thankful that I had dodged a potentially bad moment with my son.

A minute later, I hear this SMASH! SMASH! SMASH! from my front patio area!

I had all these potted plants out there. There were a bunch of palms and ferns that blocked people from being able to see inside the house from the patio. Jeni had come around the front of the house and started knocking those off and breaking them, screaming, "You fucker! Where's that whore? Where is she?"

I go out there, stunned by what I'm seeing, and say, "You've got to split. Right now. If you don't, I'm going to call the cops." It was an ugly scene.

Hell hath no fury, right?

I go out to make sure she had left, and she had written all over my truck in lipstick. Alright. I can deal with that. Mentally, she wasn't in a good state of mind. I feel bad that it happened that way. But, for years, we hadn't been happy. We were just raising our kids.

Unfortunately, the boys were there to see all of this anger and resentment going on between their parents. It was really damaging to them both, and again, I seemed to have no power in stopping it. The portraits had been painted, and I was the bad guy.

We finally get into arbitration. Her lawyer seemed like an emotionally handicapped, really odd person. She talked with a speech impediment, and she dressed really weird. I had talked to her lawyer on the phone a couple of times, which I shouldn't have done, but I couldn't talk to Jeni directly. Anytime I did, it turned into a whirlwind of hatred and aggression. But, this lawyer of hers struck me as really odd, even then.

When we finally sat down to start the process, Jeni's lawyer was completely intimidated by mine. They were on totally different playing fields. My guy was well known around southern California, and Jeni's lawyer looked like she was an outpatient from "One Flew Over the Cuckoo's Nest."

We struck a deal, and Jeni went pretty easy on me. They did this thing called Dizzo Master, which let's you put in what you make and what she makes, and then it goes back a couple of years. Based on what I had made, this fucking thing spits out that I was going to have to pay her seven grand a month.

I'm like, "Jeni, you're on crack. What am I going to do, sleep in the car? You know what I make in RATT right now. While it's decent, it's nowhere near enough to support that."

I ended up paying child support for each of the boys until they both turned eighteen. I don't know if she was just trying to be nice and go easy, or if she was just being naïve, but Jeni could have made my life much more difficult, and she chose not to.

Thank you, Jen. C.W.B.Q.

When you're married as long as we were, she could have gotten alimony for life. As it is, she gets half of everything I made in RATT, plus half of my publishing up to the time of the divorce, which does pretty well for her. I had to pay her attorney's fees, and mine, which was pretty costly.

Jeni and I keep in touch, via email, and she still makes it known that she loves me. I'm sure she would get back together, should that situation ever present itself. I love her too, for the boys and the years she gave. But, that love is a toxic thing. I don't feel I could get involved in that again.

She's gone through several different relationships to this point, and the one she's with now has lasted about three years. He seems like a nice enough guy, and I hope she's happy. She deserves to be.

Unfortunately, during a divorce, somebody's going to end up with the friends. Surprisingly, that was me, considering the light I had been painted in.

It wasn't that our friends didn't care for Jeni, it's just that when we broke up, she went on this quest to go to the gym and get super-fit, buffed up and got her hair done. She was showing "what I had lost", which she had every right to do. But, anytime she would be around someone, she would be talking about nothing but me.

It reached a point where our friends were like, "Give it a rest."

Then, on one visit to the house where I was getting some of my gear out of the garage, the phone rang and I answered it. I'm glad I did, because things came into razor sharp focus where one of our "friends" was concerned.

"Hi, is Jen there?"

"Who's this?"

"It's Don." You've got to be kidding me, right? The balls on this guy!

"Dokken? Dude, what are you doing calling Jeni? Don, stay the fuck away from my house and my ex! Understand? Go find another pool to swim in. This is my family."

That's when things really went south with Don and me. First, he ratted me on the whole thing with Traci, but now he's prowling around the remains of my marriage?

That's too much. That's way too much.

Traci and I were doing really well. We were completely into each other, and I desperately wanted her to move in with me. I wanted our relationship to progress further. I wanted this woman for my wife.

She still wouldn't do it, though. In fact, she wouldn't discuss it with me.

I had jealousies about her, you know? There were just certain things about her that I was starting to question. I was starting to not trust everything she told me.

When it was all said and done, most of what I was told ended up being true. Her sister, became involved with a friend of mine named Glen Granat. I met Glen through Robbie Crane.

Glen lived out in the San Fernando Valley, and her sister wanted to move there to be closer to him. Keep in mind that Traci and her sister are inseparable. They are married to each other; joined at the hip. Traci decided that she and her sister were going to move from Redondo and get an apartment in the valley.

Again, the warning bells should have sounded for me, but I was still in love. Everything had that rosy look to it, so I was still missing the details.

I guess I'd better move out to the Valley, too. At least if I wanted to see Traci on a regular basis. I mean, it's a hour from Redondo to the Valley with traffic. I didn't want to have that to deal with on a daily basis.

I bought a house out there. I was doing everything for this relationship that I could. She was worth it! Even if I had to jump through hoops!

Traci was going to be worth it...right? Why did people keep saying she was just a groupie? This was my love!

When it rains, it pours.

Me and the fans in Tokyo, 1985.

First RATT shoot with Neil Zlozower, 1982. Photo courtesy Neil Zlozower.

28

A BAD MOON RISING

Dark cloud gathering, breaking the day, no point running cause it's coming your way. - Deep Purple, Stormbringer

Throughout 1998, the band was writing the RATT record for John Kolodner.

John had signed us to Sony, which made us all very grateful. The guy was a legend in the business, and had made his name working with our rock heroes, Aerosmith.

We were touring intermittently throughout 1998, just making a living and keeping the wheels greased. Our drive seemed a little aimless, and while the new record was something that should excite us, I was starting to get a bad feeling from the other guys.

Something wasn't right.

My personal life was mirroring my music career. In 1999 we were setting up a tour with Poison, and Traci was still staying with me every night at the town home in Redondo. Not living with me, mind you, but staying every night. I didn't dig that AT ALL.

The personal wounds from the divorce were still very fresh, and the inconsistency with Traci only complicated that issue for me. My general disposition was changing, and I was getting a little confrontational; more than I usually would, or should, I guess.

The Poison / RATT tour became a co-headlining thing, and was shaping up to be a great tour. There were a number of bands slated for that tour, and one of them turned out to be Dokken.

I didn't react well to that.

What I did was harsh, and vindictive, and I'm not a bit ashamed of it, either. I called Bret Michaels and the agents who were handling the tour. I'm like, "Guys, I don't want to get too deep into this, but I can't have Don Dokken on this tour. He's involved with my divorce, and my ex-wife. If he's there, it will get very ugly."

They cut him. I had Don dumped from the 1999 tour.

About a month later, me and Traci, Mitch and Jenna, Eric Singer, we were all at the Motorhead concert at the Palace. This was April of 1999. We were getting ready to start the tour, which now consisted of RATT, Poison, Great White and LA Guns.

Don is at the Motorhead show, and backstage, right in front of everybody, he walks up to me and goes, "You fucking motherfucker! You cost me that tour! You had me thrown off that tour! Do you know how much money you've cost me because of that? $250,000!"

We were right in each other's faces in an instant. I was ready to start throwing! In fact, part of me really hoped it would come to that.

I go, "No, Don, it's not $250,000. It's probably more like $400,000 when you count merchandise. You damned right I had you thrown off! Fuck you! Stay away from my family!"

He's going off, screaming at the top of his voice. "I never fucked your wife! You hear me? I never fucked her!"

...whatever, dude.

I have known the guy for over twenty years. I know what he's like, and there's no way I can believe anything that comes out of his mouth.

Everybody moved away, and it was very intense; very exciting, and in the end, kind of funny. I didn't talk to him again until 2002. We actually wound up out on tour together. Enough time had past, and enough things had come about, that he was the least of my worries.

I was going to be able to co-exist, provided we avoided each other. The few times we did see one another, it was nothing more than, "Hey, how you doing?" But, it was very tense. Very stiff on my part.

Every once in a while, he would get that look in his eye, and I could see him about to extend the proverbial olive branch. I'm thinking, "Dude, don't even get it in your head. We're not going to dinner. We're not going to have drinks. I don't want to pick out curtains or whisper sweet nothings. Fuck you, we are not friends anymore."

Thankfully, it never got ugly. It was simple and cordial, and for the most part we successfully avoided one another. That guy will never change.

He's Dokken.

We finished the RATT / Poison tour, came home for a short break, and then headed back out on the second leg.

It was September, and we had the new record out, and new singles out, so we had to keep supporting it. We didn't do a lot of very good business. We were back in a lot of the markets we had just played with Poison, so most of our fans had just paid to see us a few months before, where we were playing in 16,000 seat venues.

Now, we're back, only this time, it's in shitty little clubs.

For whatever reason, the second leg of that tour wasn't doing very well. We fought through the thing, and went back home for a break before we started the final leg of the tour, which was Japan. Japan has always been a great place for us. We've always done really well there, so I was looking forward to it, and as a band, we really needed it.

I took that time off to finalize my move to the valley with Traci and her sister. When my townhouse was being sold, I moved in with them for a month. It wasn't a big deal, or so I thought.

One afternoon, I intercepted a phone message for Traci from some random dude up in Seattle. I was in Dallas, doing a show, and called home to check the messages.

I had no idea who the guy was.

"Hey, Traci, just wanted to say how great it was to see you up in Seattle this weekend. Thank you for keeping me warm. It was great." So on and so forth.

It was a complete kick in the teeth for me. I was freaking out. I was completely in love with this chick, and she pulls this? It was killing me.

I had never had a chick break up with me before, so I had never went through that sort of gut wrenching emptiness that hits you, you know? I mean, you're skinny from not eating. You can't sleep. You're a walking train wreck! You're just sick with the thing. It's really disgusting.

When I intercepted that call, I wanted to give Traci the benefit of the doubt. She swore on her grandmother, who she held dearer than anything in this world, that the only thing she did was kiss the guy. Nothing sexual ever happened.

I gave her the benefit. It felt like a payback was due for all of my years of piracy on the high seas. Call it karma. Whatever. I loved her too much to just throw it all to the side.

Then again, maybe I'm just a big pussy. She should have been given her walking papers right then and there, but that didn't happen. Instead, we decided to stay a couple, and in January of 2000, we moved down into the valley.

It was a bad time all the way around. At the end of the 1999 tour, when we got back from the second leg, Warren and Stephen were at it again, and Stephen and I hated each other.

Stephen and Warren were really hard to deal with on that tour. I want to be nicer about it than that, but I can't. There's no other way around it. We get back, take our break, and start gearing up for the third leg of the tour.

Three days before we were set to leave, on January 16, 2000, Pearcy quits the band...again.

Airfare had been bought; promoters had spent money; fans had bought tickets; busses were set; deposits were paid; salaries were expected; and it was to be only a five week tour, gleaning us each a nice chunk of change, plus merchandise! We were excited about it.

Then the whole house of cards comes falling down.

I'm stunned. "What the fuck do you mean, you're not going?"

"I'm not going, man. Don't fucking call me again." Again, thanks, Stephen Pearcy.

We did everything we could to get him back in. I was calling him on the phone, going, "Stephen, why are you doing this? To what end? Let's just go bang this stuff out, make our money, and take a break before the next album."

The guy was miserable. He was as unhappy as a person could be, and there was no working with him at that point. He wasn't willing to talk. "I'm out! I don't give a fuck! I don't care what you do, Bobby. Get another singer. I'm done."

Unlike back in 1992 when this happened, the music business wasn't changing. We were building our name back, had a new label and were making money. This time, a LOT of damage was done to the band's name and reputation.

I pleaded with Warren. "Let's not let him fuck us this time. Let's get a new singer and continue on. We still have the band together. We've got Robbie and Keri Kelli."

Before we could get to solving our singer problem, Keri defected to Warrant. Things were unraveling fast.

A new beginning, 1997. Photo courtesy Neil Zlozower.

29

Breaking The "Love Glasses"

After Stephen quit, I gave Traci an ultimatum. I told her "You gotta move in with me, 'cause, I've got to see you more. This thing with Stephen leaving is really fucking with my head. I'm out in the valley, you know. I've left my kids out in the South Bay."

She's shaking her head, and goes, "I can't do it."

I was fed up with it. This wasn't getting any better, benefit of the doubt, or not! "Traci, it's either move in with me, or that's it."

And, that was her exit.

She was able to use that as the excuse to finally get out. I think she wanted to, anyway. I guess the novelty of her rock star boyfriend had worn off. She went away. Not so far away that she couldn't keep tabs on me, though. Traci always kept her hooks in me. She still loved me, and I her, but she was never going to commit.

She had been gone for more than a month, and I had a girl that I was kind of seeing from Kansas City. I'd fly her out, and she'd stay with me for a while. Her name was Tamala, and she was this incredible blonde.

Traci just shows up at the house one morning.

I open the door, and Traci goes, "Let me come in. I want to see Leo and Phoebe."
Our cats.

I hadn't seen her in weeks. What the hell was she thinking? I said, "You can't
come in. Somebody's in here with me."

She's goes, "Open this door!"

There was no way I'm going to open that door. I mean, she's always been the one
that was getting on to me about being jealous. So, for her to do this was like "Sweet
Victory - Savior"!

We got into it pretty heavy, and she was going to break the window. And, in
shades of Jeni when Traci was the one in my bed, I told her, "You do that, and I'm calling
the cops." She was absolutely fuming! But, she left, or so we thought.

A little later, after we had shared an uncomfortable laugh about what had
happened, Tamala and I left the house to go get some breakfast. Traci was waiting
around the corner in her car. She started following my car and chasing us. It was a
complete "Fatal Attraction" moment.

I had to get away from her, as much for her neurotic behavior as it was my lack of
trust in myself. If the opportunity presented itself, I wasn't going to be able to shove her
away. She'd catch me when I was weak, and I'd be right back into the shit with her.

I had to move back to the South Bay. I just had to get the fuck away from it. I got
out of my lease at this house out in Van Nuys, and I moved back to Redondo. I rented the
guesthouse from a friend of mine, Tim Sullivan.

Then I was out every night!

I was out every night for three straight months. I'd wake up at about one o'clock
in the afternoon, take a Xanax or two, and then stare at the clock all day. I'd try to do
whatever business I had to do with the band, but I was just waiting for the night to fall so
I could get back into the city. Get into the clubs, and get drunk so I could forget about
Traci.

In the meantime, I was hitting so many different chicks, it was ridiculous. I was all
over the place. It was pretty cool in some ways, but I was still so gone, I just couldn't get
over it. It came to the point that all of my hook-ups and one-night became hollow

victories. I was trying to fuck Traci out of my mind, and there was simply no way to do that.

I was stuck in a downward spiral.

After Traci and me broke up in February 2000, after about two and a half years, I went through another really bad period. I'd been with Jeni since I was seventeen, and as bad as that ended, I made it out with my heart intact. I had prepared for that; built up to it over several years. But, Traci had been very different. For the first time, I felt like Jeni felt, because she took our break up really hard.

Traci played me like a marionette, and I was devastated. I had been completely in love with that girl. I just deteriorated into a mess.

I had Easter dinner with Jeni and the boys that year. Halfway through the day, I totally wigged out. I had to walk outside and get my shit together. I was FLOODED with guilt, all at once. I was thinking, "I left these guys for that WHORE? What was I thinking? Am I really that much of a bastard?"

I completely hated myself. Jeni understood what was happening, I think. She warned me when we were getting divorced. "Someday, you'll regret this move, Bobby. Someday, someone will do this to YOU, and you'll know what you've done to us."

She was right.

It wasn't so much that I regretted leaving, as much as it was how things ended with Traci and what that became. Traci transformed from this sweet, innocent Seattle girl that I always saw her as.

Everyone else that knows her, tells me the same thing. It wasn't that she was never the person she became once she got to LA. She was always that; but she kept it hidden when she was around me. When she came to California, she became Hollywood Rose.

It was embarrassing, and I couldn't deny it anymore.

Then I met Misty. She saved me from that nightmare...almost.

30

REPLACING THE VOICE

When Stephen left in 2000, we had to audition for a new singer, and it sucked!

I hated it like nothing I've hated in this business. It was just painful.

Traci was gone; Stephen was gone; and here we are auditioning all of these HACKS! The guy from Pretty Boy Floyd came down; guys that were just terrible. There was one guy, Jamie Row, who was a Christian singer. He was really good, but he just didn't look like a rock star. He looked like Billy Corrigan. Tall, bald, and with an odd shaped head. Nice guy; really talented; but, that's how that whole thing works.

If this business worked on talent alone, it would be easier, but it doesn't. You have to have a look, or a style, or some sort of hook to make you interesting to watch. I love watching American Idol for that reason. Lots of talented people, but very few of them have "it."

Look at "Jackyl". Jesse James Dupree had a "blip on the radar" career, but only because he went all "chainsaw redneck" onstage every night. Thinking about him, talent should count for more than it does! Alas...

Then we had Robert Mason come down. Robert had worked in Lynch Mob, and he was REALLY good! He was strong enough that John Kolodner paid for a showcase for us down at The Viper Room for the people from Sony. We were doing everything we could to save our deal, and Robert was up there singing RATT songs.

Sony didn't bite. They passed, which only heaped onto my depression.

Ralph Sanes from Atomic Punks, and Metal Skool came down. I really wanted Ralph in, because he's a genius front man. Testament to that is the fact he pulls in $30,000 a month in Steel Panther, playing cover shit! He's brilliant, entertaining, talented, and he's a great friend.

We probably went through thirty-something guys, trying to find the right mix. But, they all were clownish. It was really painful, trying to audition and keep the band moving and rolling.

So, Robert Mason was out. He thought we were going to get a deal, and he didn't want to go out and just tour for some reason.

We went back and got Jizzy, mostly because we didn't know anyone else, and we needed to work, because Stephen had filed a lawsuit against us.

But, we'll get into that in a minute.

However, NOT working wasn't an option, so we had to have a singer. Jizzy was the guy.

I like Jizzy. He's professional. He's easy to work with, although the guy is really introverted. He's a fairly sharp dude. By that, I mean the guy is booksmart. There's a little bit of something between his ears, and that makes life a little easier.

But, Jizzy's voice always rubbed me wrong for RATT, and I was never a "Love / Hate" fan. The guy fronted RATT for seven years, and I appreciate everything he brought. We did a LOT of gigs with Jizzy, man. We turned ourselves into show ponies.

Warren was impossible to do business with during that time. He really was. I didn't have his pockets, and he knew that. I didn't come from a wealthy family, like he did. So, I needed this money we were making to survive. We weren't recording new material, or anything, so all we had to exist on was the laurels of the RATT name.

Yet, he was constantly turning down fly out dates.

Dates where he and I would make five grand for a weekend worth of work would be turned down, simply because Warren didn't like the layover time for the flights, or the drive time from the airport, or some other piss-ant type of inconvenience.

It made me incredibly frustrated, especially at the end of the month when my bills were due, and the lawyers wanted money to fight Stephen. Warren could write that check. I couldn't. I feel like he got some sort of twisted amusement at having that kind of control over me, and I resented the fuck out of him for it.

Warren and I are like brothers. It's the "tormenting brothers" type of mentality, though. I'm sure that I torment him in my own ways, too. Although, I don't do that intentionally. Like I've said, Warren is the artistic purist, and I'm the businessman.

I make him crazy with the way I do things, but Warren can be painful to work with professionally. Ask anyone who has to do it. He's the biggest procrastinator you'd ever have to work with. The guy is an amazing musician, but getting things done with the guy is another thing entirely.

Enter John Corabi.

Around April, we had settled on Jizzy as our singer. We had intentions of hiring a rhythm guitarist, but the singer situation was the priority, and we hadn't gotten around to it. That's when I got a phone call from John Corabi.

"Hey, Blotz! How's it going? I hear you guys are looking for a second guitarist?"

I'm like, "Yeah, we are. You know someone?"

"Me."

"What do you mean, me? Me, who, John? What are you talking about?"

"I mean me, dude. I play guitar."

I'd only know John as a front man, which he was pretty good at. He was in a band called The Scream, which I knew nothing about, and then he was the guy who replaced Vince Neil in Mötley Crüe. It became John's job to steer that particular ship until it crashed into the reef.

I didn't really like the Mötley album he did with them. I liked his voice, and the production value was through the roof, but I just wasn't crazy about the material on that thing.

They had a really bad, failed tour with John. Fuck it, everybody was having really bad tours at that time. It was really fucking scary. I remember they played the Paladium to about 1300 people, and that was when those guys were slapped with reality.

Three years before, they sold out two nights at the Forum, two nights at the Long Beach Arena, and then two nights at the Irvine Meadows! That was summer on the Feelgood tour, and now they were drawing 1300 people just three years later?!? Mötley was on the skids.

None of that was John's fault, mind you. It's the curse of the lead singer, which is something RATT was about to learn.

There are two types of fans.

The first type are the fans who dig the music. These are the people who will show up to your shows regardless who's in the current line-up in the band. They like the music. These people will go see some cheesy-assed tribute band, all wrapped in spandex and Aqua-Net, just so they can hear your tunes played live.

Those fans will always be there.

The second kind of fan is the band worshiper. They are the purists who follow the band and the guys in it. These fans are fiercely loyal to you, and they defend you at every turn. They are the best kind of fan. But, you can't fuck around with these guys too much, because, like true love, when you hurt them, they'll turn on you.

Consider all the bands that have had frontmen changes. How many of them have actually survived the change, much less thrived with it.

Van Halen did it, although they completely changed their style when Sammy came on board to replace David Lee Roth.

AC/DC did it with Brian Johnson after Bon Scott died.

But, who else? Not many, that's for sure. Black Sabbath was never the same after Ozzy left. Skid Row became exactly that after losing Sebastian Bach. Journey without Steve Perry? Talented, but not "it".

The reason is simple. The frontman is the voice of the band. The other guys are usually colorful, and interesting, and all that, but the frontman is the guy in the band who talks to you. They communicate with the fan. As soon as you hear Stephen Pearcy sing a note, you know that it's RATT.

The singer is the identity, but that isn't to say that the sum isn't as important. It certainly is.

That's not to say the singer is more important. When a singer leaves a band, they seldom thrive outside of it. David Lee Roth didn't. David Coverdale didn't. Sammy Hagar did, but then Sammy was a solo artist before he joined Van Halen.

And, Stephen Pearcy certainly struggled without RATT.

So, it's a double standard. The fans want the original band. The REAL band. But, to do that, the bands have to co-exist, which is really difficult to do, sometimes.

John found that out when he joined Mötley Crüe and replaced Vince Neil. It was a lesson learned the hard way, because John is a talented guy.

I'd known John for a while, and he was always an easy going, laid back kind of dude. I knew he could write, and was a great singer, which worked well on the backup parts, and he was really easy to work with.

John became our new rhythm guitarist. He played great, looked great, sang incredible. With his backups, it sounded like the records again, with all these backup vocals.

We started a tour on July 29, 2000. The first show was the House of Blues in Hollywood. It was RATT / Warrant / LA Guns.

This tour actually got booked in a lot of big places! We did Pine Knob Amphitheater in Detroit, which is an 18,000 seat venue, which we drew 11,000 people. There were a number of those kinds of places on this tour. It was really successful.

It gave us a huge sense of optimism. We were going... okay, this is a trip. Maybe we CAN do this without Stephen.

Jizzy got drunk and started being a fucked up weirdo on the bus, and I lost it. I told the bus to pull over and I got in Jizzy's face.

"Drunk, or not drunk, you can get the fuck off this bus right now! If this is how you act, get the fuck off! We don't need you."

There was no way I was putting up with this whacked out singer bullshit again. No way.

He had gotten all ripped up on red wine, which he had only done a couple of times. But Jizzy was not a good drunk. He was really combative with people who were working for us on the bus. He deemed himself "Jizzilla" when he would get like that, which admittedly was very rare.

After that confrontation, he made a point to never be like that on tour again. He was really flabbergasted that I talked to him like that. But after eighteen years with a kooky singer, there was no way I wanted to relive it. I wanted to be very clear. No way.

That tour went through October.

It got real weird out there, because at one point, LA Guns wasn't able to sustain themselves on tour with the money they were making. Traci Gunns, who I'm not a big fan of, went to Robbie Crane and said that they needed us to kick some money down to them every night so they could survive.

Robbie came to me and said something about it.

I just started laughing. What did they want me to do, write them a personal check? And, where is this money supposed to come from? If they can't afford the tour, they need to scale back their travel expenses, and per diems, all of it. It's none of my business, and I don't want to know about it. It certainly wasn't my job to support those guys, although I liked the band.

Warren agreed with me on it. This is business.

I'm out here to take care of it. I've got bills and responsibilities, and they have nothing to do with Traci Gunns. We operate our tour on a very tight budget, knowing exactly what goes out and what comes in. I make a budget, and Warren makes one. Those budgets are usually very similar, and almost always land dead on in price.

To "kick them some money" because they can't take care of their own business would mean that it came out of my personal pocket. No. That's my mindset. I'm sorry. Our hands were tied. For them to be pressuring the other band on tour for a bigger piece of the pie was ludicrous. They've been around this business long enough to know how it works.

I knew what was coming down the pipe, and there was no room for RATT to be throwing them $1500 a night, or whatever they were asking, to keep them out there on that tour. We knew our bills, and we planned everything around them.

That was that.

They left the tour about a week later. I talked to Steve Riley after that, and was going, "Dude, this isn't a personal thing. I love you, you're a great guy, but there's nothing we can do to help this."

"I unda-stand, Bob. I unda-stand." With his thick, Boston accent.

When we finished the tour, about a month later, I ran into Traci Gunns at a place called Paladino's; a rock club out in Tarzana, California. I'm walking by, and he's passing me. So I go, "What's up, dude?"

He blows. "Don't fucking 'what's up, dude' me! I don't fucking like you!"

I'm a little taken aback. A little. "What, is this a joke?"

"No, it's not a joke, Blotzer. You left us hanging out there!"

I'm a guy who isn't quick to anger. I've got a pretty long fuse, and will let a lot of shit slide, even when I shouldn't. However, I get home that night, and Gunns is just eating at me.

Enter one of my nemesis. DRUNK DIALING! I called Gunn's cell phone and unloaded on the little shit.

I saw this kind of shit from him a few years earlier when I did the Contraband record in 1990 with him, Michael Scheneker, Sher Petterson from Vixen, and Richard Black from Shark Island. He pulled this sort of shit, then. I didn't know anything about it at first, but he threw his little temper tantrums and Hitler moves.

Since then, we've seen each other a couple of times. We're civil, and never let this thing go to war. That's smart on his part. Smart on mine, too, because I don't have time for that kind of bullshit.

When I got back, we had made some money. Not a lot of money, but enough that I could breathe for five or six months. Or, until our next tour because, that tour was done.

Contraband 1990 Michael Schenker, Share Pedersen, Richard Black (chair), Tracii Guns, and Me, 1991. Photo courtesy Neil Zlozower.

31

A VIRGINIAN ANGEL COMES TO THE RESCUE

I'd actually met Misty out on tour in 1999, but I didn't remember her. How that happened, I don't know. Because, this chick was certainly memorable!

I ran into her again at the Baked Potato when I was out on a date with a nurse. It was pretty funny. The nurse was completely loaded, and had no idea that I was checking out Misty.

I gave Misty my number that night, and told her to call me. I could tell that she was interested, and she was so fucking gorgeous! We just stared across the room at each other all night. When I first came in, we were looking at each other, and I'm mouthing to her "I want to talk to you" behind this nurse's head when she's not looking.

I didn't hear from Misty for weeks. I figured it was a bust. The next time I heard from her, I actually had Tamala back out from Kansas City.

I was starting to get pretty burned on her. She was getting to where she wanted to move out here and move in together. I flat didn't want to do that. Besides, there was something that just wasn't right. She was unbelievably gorgeous. We had such a great chemistry. But it didn't seem to be there for the boyfriend / girlfriend angle.

I'm mulling over all these things about Tamala, when Misty calls. I was out at the Coconut Teaser with Tamala, and the phone rings.

It took me a minute to realize who it was. I was like "You fucker! Finally! Where have you been? I thought you would have called the next day. I would have bet money on it!"

In fact, I came home that night with the nurse, and I saw Tim. I was getting ready to go and do my thing with the nurse, and I told Tim "I met this girl tonight. Misty. She'll be calling tomorrow, for sure."

And, then she never called. Typical.

Misty had moved out from West Virginia with her girlfriend. Her girlfriend liked me as much as Misty did, which caused them to get into this big rift. When I started dating Misty, her girlfriend got pissed. About a month after Misty and I started dating, the girlfriend left, and went back east, leaving Misty there by herself. She had no car, no furniture. Virtually nothing.

So I rescued her, and pulled her in with me. I was still renting Tim's guesthouse at the time, and that's where we lived. We were together.

I had to go back out on the road, so I told her "When I get back, we'll start looking for a place."

That whole time I was out on the road, Traci kept coming to mind. We started calling each other again. It was infuriating and enticing all at the same time. She would always keep in touch with phone calls and emails. I would catch myself saying that I loved her. People were saying that I was obsessive, but Robbie heard some of those calls, and he knows. Traci knew exactly what she was doing, because she went out of her way to keep that in me. She just wouldn't let me grow past her.

We almost got back together in the summer of 2000.

She was calling me all the time, going, "I still love you. I just want to hear your voice", all kinds of shit like that. The worst part is, it was working.

Traci made me understand the concept of addictions. You hate what you want, yet are powerless to stop wanting it. That relationship was an awakening for me.

She wanted to date for a while. My thought was, "I am not going to date. We've dated. We know what there is to know. If we do this, I want to pull in together and immediately go to the next level."

In the end, she still wouldn't do it. She simply wouldn't commit that far. I told her to forget it.

When I got back from the road, I got an apartment in Encino where Misty was going to move in with me. But, Traci was still trolling around, and as sick as it was, I wanted to get back with her.

I told Misty to hold off until I could get my head around what was going to happen. "Things are transpiring here. I think that Traci and I might try to get back together and try to work this out." I didn't want to hurt Misty. But, bottom line was, I wanted Traci back.

It was a very conflicting time, because I was really into Misty, too. I wanted to move on. I wanted to get past Traci, but I just couldn't seem to do it. It doesn't make sense when you sit and read this kind of shit, but believe me, when you live it; you completely understand the inner turmoil. On one had, I had this great new girl. On the other, I still had a chance to save the love that I had for Traci.

So, we went out and did the tour, and when we got back, I got an apartment out in the valley. I'm out in the valley again, because Traci and I were going to be "closer".

Shit went south immediately with her. She was stubborn, and overly independent. That same independence that was such a killer the first time around. The first several days I was back and in the apartment, Misty kept calling.

"I really can't talk right now, Misty. You're staying at Tim's. Just keep renting that place from him. Give me a little time to get my head around this."

She obviously wanted to keep things going.

I went out with Traci on a date, and she came back to my apartment to spend the night. It was a really odd night. Even though I was greatly tempted to get back with Traci, I still felt the burn from her fucking around on me. As weird as that sounds, I wouldn't do it.

The next morning, I'm lying in bed, and I hear the door open. I jump up and run out there.

Now, to preface this, Misty and I went and looked at apartments before I was going to move to the valley. The apartment that I was living in was in one of the buildings we had looked at. So, she knew where I lived, and came down to the building that day. Somehow, she convinced the manager that she was my girlfriend, and had lost her key to the apartment, so the guy gives her a key.

I hear the door opening, and it's Misty coming into the apartment. She was like, "I haven't heard from you in days. I thought something was wrong."

"You can't just fucking do this, Misty."

She wanted to come in and talk, and finally, I'm like, "Look, I'm going to just be honest with you. Traci is in there."

It wasn't cool, but as I told her then, and reiterate now, nothing happened that night with Traci. However, there was a pretty strong rivalry that started that day between Misty and Traci.

I found that really exciting, to tell the truth.

Shortly thereafter, the Traci thing was done. It was actually done when Misty dropped by the apartment, we just didn't acknowledge it.

I moved Misty in, and Traci was gone. Misty and I were together for five and a half years. Eventually, I bought a house over in Canyon Country.

I was going through a revolving door of women before I met Misty. And, during that whole time, I couldn't figure out what I was missing.

I was proud of all the time Jeni and I had been together. We moved in together in late 1976. While we were on top of the world in the 80's, there was never a time I would have considered destroying my family for something I found on the road. There were a lot of beautiful people out there, but this was my family.

Jeni was smart enough to know the Pi-RATT's life we were living on the road. After all, she came out there and saw it all first hand. I think she just turned a cheek to it. She knew what that was all about, and while there were jealous episodes, they were few.

I'd see my family at least once a month while I was on the long tours. Off tour, I'd see them every day.

I've talked about the damage done during my divorce from Jeni. During the breakup, Michael and Marcus suffered more than I ever thought they would. My thought was, "I went through a breakup when I was a kid. You'll be fine." I know they saw the battles that Jeni and I had, and they were smart enough to figure out how that would end.

But, Michael lashed out at the world. He was on crystal meth, and was very fucked up in very short order. I had to kidnap him and take him to the airport. I sent him back to Pittsburgh to be with my younger brother Michael, and let the kid clean up.

He's been clean since then, thank God. The guy has got a good heart, but that really fucked with him a lot more than I thought it would. I was sorry it happened like that. The boy defends his mother, and he thinks I fucked her over. I can dig that, but he'll understand one day when he has to deal with a breakup.

No one wins, and no one is innocent.

Marcus was a little different. When Marcus was a boy, he had clubbed feet. Both feet turned in sharply and he had to wear braces on both ankles in an effort to straighten them out.

Poor kid.

We struggled and struggled with that, trying to help straighten him out. At one point, we were going to have the surgery where they break his legs and reset the bones in an effort to straighten them. It's a brutal, extremely painful procedure, and I hated the fact I was going to have this done to one of my sons.

On the eve of the operation, at the hospital, some random doctor was talking to me in the hallway. He goes, "So, what's your son here for?" I told him about the surgery, and that we were going to have his feet straightened, because they were turned in so badly.

The doctor seems a little surprised, and goes, "This boy here?" He turns to Marcus and watches him for a second.

Then he goes, "Marcus, do me a favor. Go to the end of the hall and run toward me."

Marcus kind of grins, and then goes to the end of the hall. As he's running, the doctor is staring at Marcus's legs and feet.

"Okay, Marcus, now walk to me." Marcus does.

The doctor sort of looks at me, and starts to say something, but then goes, "You know, nevermind."

I look back at Marcus, then at the doctor, and go, "Wait a minute. You can't say 'nevermind' and then walk off! What were you looking at?"

"I'm just thinking, if he was my kid, I wouldn't do it."

"Seriously? Look, man, he goes in for surgery in just a couple of hours. You need to tell me what's going on."

He goes, "Do you know who John Elway is?"

"Of course, I do."

"When Elway was born, he had the same feet. The guy is a superstar quarterback today. When Marcus gets older, they'll straighten out on their own. There's no need to break them. He'll always be a little toed in, and he'll always have weird wearing on his shoes, but it won't slow him down."

That threw me into an emotional whirlwind. I immediately went in, packed all of Marcus's stuff up, and took my boy home. I'm really glad I did, too. That was going to be a brutal surgery. He was going to be laid up for a really long time. They had a party for him at school, and everything.

These are the things you deal with when you are a parent. There's an endless assault on your child from the moment they are born, and you're the only thing out there that can protect them.

Even then, things are going to happen. That's just the way nature works.

Marcus drowned in our Jacuzzi at home, in 1985.

I was coming home from getting my haircut, and an ambulance flies past me at full speed with it's sirens blaring. As it did, I got this profound feeling that something wasn't right. This was way at the top of my street.

When I get down to my house, Jeni comes running out to the street, crying. I'm out of the car in a flash, going, "Woah! What the fuck is going on?" I was in a total panic mode.

She goes, "Marcus fell in the Jacuzzi! He drowned! They had to resuscitate him!"

I almost fell out, right there. My boy had died, and then been brought back by a paramedic. Jeni went on to tell me that she had fallen asleep on the couch. Marcus got up while she and Michael were sleeping, and had made his way downstairs and to the back door.

He had only been gone for a minute when Jeni noticed it. She went looking for him, and when she found him, his stuffed bear was floating in the water. The water had been ice cold. If it had been warm, there would have been nothing they could do. Marcus would be dead. It was the dead of winter, and the water was near freezing.

I was always watching out for him. Precious little Marcus.

I remember one time, I was laying on the couch watching TV. I heard this sound, this sort of wailing sound that was getting louder. I muted the TV, and bolted up on the couch.

I ran outside, and here comes Marcus, crying. He had been riding in the street, and cars would come flying down that thing at fifty or sixty miles an hour. He came close to some car, and laid his bike down.

His tooth was stuck in his hand! He was scraped up and bleeding. It was a nightmare.

Again, that's what happens when you are a parent. You fight through the pitfalls and challenges, and if you're lucky, your children come out into adult hood with a healthy frame of mind.

Today, Marcus is full-time employed in the medical industry. He's gearing up for school to become an X-Ray technician.

Michael is a drummer. Michael is an incredible drummer. "A Chip Off The Old Blotz," is what we call him. They just fired their singer, and then the guitarist quit, so he's back to square one. He works a day job with a friend of mine at a company called Emergency Service. Dan Hartwell's company. He's making $2500 a month during training. But in about a year, he'll get his own truck. The guys doing that are all pulling in $100K a year.

Hopefully, he gets there really soon.

Both of those boys are the world to me. They are really tight, and really protective of one another, and absolutely convinced that the other son is my favorite!

That's another common theme with parenthood, and I've had to deal with that their entire lives. Marcus would know how to get Michael in trouble. Michael would know how to get Marcus in trouble. Then, when you bust them, it's all, "Yeah, dad. That's because Michael / Marcus is your favorite! You've always loved him more!"

"Look, I love you both equal, and you both drive me crazy equal. Now, who wants the belt first? You're both in trouble on this one."

Much to Michael's disbelief, I'm absolutely proud of them both, and it is a pride that I will carry with me all the way to my grave, and beyond.

I love my boys. I really do.

32

LITIGATION, MITIGATION, AND MENTAL MASTURBATION

"In this Rat-Race, everybody is guilty until proven innocent!" - Bette Davis

By the end of the 2000 tour, Warren, who was emotionally exhausted, told me that he wasn't sure he wanted to go back out and tour anymore.

I just couldn't deal with it. I became like, "Fuck this! Fuck musicians! I'm getting a regular gig, and I never want to see this shit again!"

That's when I went into the real estate business.

I wanted to become a real estate agent. I took a course for seven weeks, passed with flying colors, and by the time I got all of that done, Stephen was suing us.

In 2001, we found out that Stephen Pearcy was going out as RATT, and had filed a lawsuit making all of these ridiculous claims against us; misappropriation of corporate funds, unfair competition, breech of fiduciary duties, all bullshit.

When Stephen left this band, and left us losing all that money that we were going to make with the Japan tour, he stuck us with $6000 in incidental bills that he had run up and not paid for. Our tour manager had to pay for that out of the receipts of the tour, i.e., Warren and I paid for them.

So, battle lines were drawn. Worse, this was something that neither Warren, nor myself were expecting. Needless to say, we had to prepare for this on the fly. It was shaping up to be a knock down, drag-out fight.

It was Stephen and his disciples; his agent and his lawyer, who were putting this all together. Knowing the situation, it was probably Stephen's disciples that were pushing for the whole thing in the first place. They saw the bucks disappearing with him no longer a part of RATT.

Warren and I were in a position of "Where's all this money going to come from to fight a lawsuit?" So, we started having to gig, not only to survive, but also to pay for this fucking thing.

And now, things had to change.

There was no compromise to it. We had a lawsuit to fight, not only that, we also had to counter-sue and establish the reality of what was REALLY going on! Stephen walked out and left us holding the bag, now he's going to go out and promote himself as RATT? He's going to make the bucks? Nah. Don't think so. Not after he's quit the band.

I had just finished this real estate course, ready to dive headlong into life without RATT, but now Warren and I had this drama to deal with. So, the real estate thing had to go to the side. I just didn't have the time to do it. We immediately had to start booking gigs and touring again, as RATT.

Stephen had really stirred things up. He not only sued us, but he sued Tim Hyne, our manager, which was completely wrong! Tim Hyne did all kinds of things for Stephen, personally. Tim was good to us, as a band, so, for Stephen to sue Tim was a whole new level of betrayal. He sued Troy Blakely and APA, our agency. He was completely sue happy. Him, and his lawyer and his manager.

Then we got into the mechanics of mounting and defending a lawsuit. It was un-fucking-believable, the work, energy and pain that went into this thing. For three fucking years!

None of it was easy. Pearcy's camp started calling gigs that we were playing and threatening the promoters with lawsuits if they played us. It created such turmoil for the brand name in the marketplace that no one knew who to trust. Depending on who you talked to, we each took turns being the bad guy while everyone else was the victim. No one knew who to believe, and no one wanted to be sued, yet we were all trying to book our 2001 shows as RATT.

It was a total cluster-fuck, but we did manage to book some good gigs. Before it was all said and done, we played a ton of shows, and made a bunch of lawyers a lot of money.

We started out over in Scandanavia with Dio and Alice Cooper. That was a lot of fun, and really charged up the band. We'd never been over there before, and we were all really into it.

All along, I kept telling Warren, "Let's do some recording." But, he couldn't get into it. Not until we got all the lawsuit shit behind us. Which made sense. No need to record a new album, and risk having the profits tied up in court because Pearcy's delusions of grandeur were being manipulated by his handlers.

After Scandanavia, we embarked on a club tour in the U.S., which ran through the entire year of 2001. It was really hard to keep a steady, fully booked tour going, because as soon as we booked something, Pearcy's guys were on the phone to them, threatening a lawsuit.

It was that bully tactic bullshit behavior that cost Stephen in the courts. We wound up getting a court injunction against him that forbid him from contacting our promoters and venues. We also had the courts stop him from using the name RATT until the trial was over. We went back and forth for months with these injunctions, and it was a pure Hell on Earth.

We're out on the road, riding around in a bus and doing shows. Some of the shows were fantastic. Some of them sucked. But, at the end of the day, we were having fun with it the best we could. The tour was paying for our legal costs, and giving us just enough money to get by.

Unfortunately, we had to play a lot of shows that were beneath RATT. Stuff we would never play normally, dotted our itinerary throughout 2001.

In March of 2002, we went to trial, but it had been a long road getting there. The trial lasted a month.

The first attorneys we had were a complete joke, man. They just kept taking our money and not doing shit! So, we got this guy, Kyle Kelley, this little Irish drinking machine! Kyle was a bulldog in the trial, and just beat the shit out of Pearcy and his lawyer the whole time.

I remember being in the deposition of Stephen Pearcy. I was sitting there and listening to this, and it literally made me nauseous. He wouldn't look at us. He sat on one side of the table, and we were on the other. I just looked at him, and he would never make eye contact.

He would simply answer our lawyer's questions.

He did the same thing at the trial. He would just look straight out and answer, never over at us. I know. I watched him the whole time to see if he would.

I was sitting in the deposition, listening to him, and just feeling more and more disgusted.

All I could think of was the five of us up on stage at Madison Square Garden, playing our guts out to 15,000 screaming fans; or on the various stages on the Strip here at home, back when RATT was just finding itself; or the days in the garage above Dennis O'Neil's mom's place. The moments we've had. The good times. All I can think is, "What the fuck, man? What is this? Why is this happening?"

I literally got up and said, "I gotta split. I can't sit here and listen to this. Mr. Irish Drinking Machine, get shit done. Whatever you need from me, let me know and I'll be there. This is bullshit, and I can't deal with it."

We won the case.

We were there everyday for a little more than 3 weeks. Almost a month. I could tell that the judge liked me, and the lawyers could too.

I think the biggest reason was that I've always had this uncanny ability to recall dates. Almost any date. I still do, obviously, because I've ratted off several of them in this book. Although, I must admit that at this age, my memory isn't as keen as it was 5 years ago.

It's actually very easy for me to do. I've always associated events in my life with the music I was listening to at the time. I recall events from the past by relating them to the songs I hear. I give it a context of music.

It was a sad, depressing time. I would study the judge while Stephen was on the stand. Stephen would be tripping himself up, stuttering and just fucking things up overall, especially during cross-examination.

The judge wasn't being obvious with his body language, but there were times he would look over at me with an incredulous look on his face at something Stephen had just said. The judge and I would lock eyes, and all I could do was raise my eyebrows and shrug.

It was a joke that wasn't funny.

It reached a point where Stephen had, let's just say, brought his credibility into question so many times on stand that it was clear he wasn't being taken seriously. Honestly, I don't know that Stephen was intentionally lying. He's one of those people who will tell himself something in his head so many times that he begins to believe it. I really feel that this was one of those situations. He had convinced himself that this was the truth, but it wasn't.

Warren was uncomfortable on stand. He just wasn't good up there, so our lawyer made me the primary witness. We also had our agent come up. Our manager testified.

Stephen was buried, and we won the case, as much as you can win something like that, anyway.

We won the trial and were awarded $478,000 plus $300,000 in legal fees. To this day, that money hasn't been paid. Stephen went through a bankruptcy to get out of it. So, we made a deal with him.

We didn't want to have another trial where we grind him beneath our heel on this bankruptcy thing. The precedent was set so that anyone who had "willful intent" to avoid a court ordered fine by filing bankruptcy, the bankruptcy wouldn't apply. However, you still have to prove that "willful intent" in court. We were so sick of court and lawsuits that we told Stephen, "Look, we'll let you off the hook on this." We came to a mutually agreed to amount, and spread the payments over five months.

Warren and I had spent a fortune fighting that lawsuit, and all the pain and heartache it put us through couldn't get over with quick enough. At least as far as I was concerned.

As nasty as this whole thing was, even if we went our separate ways now, I don't think I could bring myself to go after him. It would cost him a million dollars before it was over, and the guy has had it pretty hard, already. Granted, he brought it on himself, but to his credit, he's trying to put himself back together.

Who am I to try and crush him? I'm not interested in ruining the guy's life. He's got one more payment, which will even us out for what we spent. After that, it's all Monopoly money, and I just want to forget all about it.

In truth, I don't care about it anymore.

With the trial finally behind us, 2002 was set to be a better year. But, that wasn't to be.

The Metal Edge Rockfest Tour asks us on. It was going to be us, Warrant, Dokken, Firehouse and LA Guns. That tour was booked through a very disreputable agency, whose name shall remain unspoken. Nonetheless, there was a lot of shady bullshit going on during that tour. They went with any promoter they could get, and with all those bands, it was a pricey ticket.

That tour was the first time I had to deal with Don Dokken since our little blow up at the Motorhead concert three years before. With all the names on that card, it was ripe with the potential of ego clashes. Complicate that with the shady promotion and my personal past with Don, and it wasn't looking like a fun tour.

When Dokken came onto that tour, they were really quick to DEMAND that they close! They were going to be the headliners! I figure it was a shot at RATT in general, and me in particular, but it was a non-event. We were only too eager to accommodate them. Truth is, we had played so many of those festival gigs in the past that we knew how they all went down. After sitting all day in the heat to watch bands, the crowd is pretty burned out by the time the last act takes the stage.

It's funny, because we never wanted to close that show, and we were prepared to fight so we *didn't have to*. Thankfully, Don made that easy on us by coming in with his grandiose demands. Because, sure enough, every night by the time Dokken went on, there was about a quarter of the audience left.

We had the best slot, because we were second up to Don. We would have the peak of the crowd's interest, so our shows were great. All these years, and the guy still hadn't learned the ABC's of this business.

We saw yet another classic Dokken meltdown while on this tour.

In Phoenix, during Warrant's set, Fred Coury and Eric Brittingham from Cinderella came up on stage to jam with those guys. They were playing some cover shit, like "Sweet Home Alabama", and some other stuff. Don storms up on stage.

The venue was "in the round", which means that the stage was in the center of the arena, with no backstage area. So the stage entrance was right through the middle of the crowd and up a long ramp. The style was made popular by Def Leppard during their "Hysteria" tour. The crowd sees Don stalking up on stage, and they think he's going to jam, so they start cheering.

He gets up there, and he's making the cutthroat motion. "Stop! STOP!" He grabs a microphone and starts yelling into it!

"I'm sick of you guys and all this fucking shit!" We watch Don have a nervous breakdown on stage.

It was a complete, "Oh, my God, I can't believe he's doing this" moment for all of us who watched it.

I mumbled under my breath. "He's fucking losing it."

Mick Brown left the tour that night, and the bass player from LA Guns finished the rest of the tour on drums for Dokken. It was really bizarre.

I don't hate Don. I just wish the guy would normalize a little more. You know? It drives me crazy to hear anyone continually lie and build themselves up with complete bullshit stories and try to incorporate you into them. I have respect for his songs and his music. He's still like a brother, just a kooky brother that I don't deal with anymore.

33

THE KING IS DEAD...LONG LIVE THE KING.

Contrary to some of the things that Juan has said in the press, we did, as a band,

try to take care of Robbin. There just came a point where his drug addiction was so out of hand that we knew anything we gave him, money wise, was going to go straight into his veins.

I wasn't going to do that.

I wasn't going to support the guy's habit, knowing what price he was going to pay. I had my own obligations at home, and there was nothing I could do that was going to help him. He had fallen out of touch with the band, and the only time we heard from him was if he needed money, or if we ran into him.

I did try to keep in touch with him through the 90's, but it was hard to keep track of him, which made it difficult to be consistent. Consequently, I didn't see his daily destruction, I only saw the graphic changes each time I would finally hunt him down.

Robbin was most put out with Juan. When Robbin was getting really sick, Juan wanted to put together a King tribute record. Robbin told me that he was really bent out of shape, because Juan was charging for studio time for the record.

Honestly, if what Robbin told me is true, that's bullshit. If you're going to make a tribute album for charity, donate the time. That's just common sense.

Robbin felt abandoned when he was in the hospital for so long. It's like everyone just forgot him. He felt betrayed that Nikki Sixx never came to see him, because those two guys were best friends for a long time.

It was a slap that Nikki ignored him like that. But, it was just so disturbing to go see King in that condition, man! I'd go and visit him, and every time I did, he was always up; always positive. He'd say things like, "Blotz, the doctors are saying I'm getting better. I'll get out of here soon, and I swear, I'm getting in better health. I'll be ready to get everything back together with the band."

I'd be like, "That's great, bro. I can't wait." But, inside, I'm just crushed for the guy, because I know… being up and being positive isn't enough to change what's happening to him.

He was so eager, but you could look in his eyes and know that he didn't believe it. It broke my heart to see him like that. I'd walk out of that place going, "I need a drink. NOW!"

King was this 6'5", larger than life, fucking Viking, and to see him in that condition was one of the most depressing things I've ever had to witness. He was a man's man. He just fucked it up. He fucked it up for himself, and he knew it.

I remember going to see him one time back in 1995, long before his two-year stint in the hospital. There's a tow truck on the street, and it's pulling this car out of the ditch. The thing looked like it had rolled out of Robbin's driveway and smashed into a tree.

I see Robbin come walking out of his house. He's got a huge out of control beard, and he's bare-footed. His appearance was shocking! He looked like a homeless dude.

I'm like, "Robbin, what's going on? Is that your car, man?"

He goes, "Yeah, the clutch gave out and it rolled into the tree. Just find a place to park over here." I was ten seconds from just jetting right then, because he was really fucked up.

Still, I went ahead and parked.

I went inside, and the tow-truck goes off with Robbin's car. We went into his apartment, and it was so dingy and disgusting. I couldn't believe it.

I'm thinking, "This guy is living like this, now? What the hell?!?" The carpet was just black with filth. There was a fifty-gallon, exterior garbage can that had been drug inside and was full of empty liquor bottles, wine bottles, and beer cans. There were dirty plates and pizza boxes all over the place.

On the wall inside that apartment, the only piece of artwork in the entire apartment was a "Platinum For A Decade" wall mount that Atlantic had given us in 1990, commemorating ten million record sales in the U.S.

In 1999, after he had moved back to LA from El Paso, King had a North Hollywood apartment, which was a really bad part of town. I was going by to give him some money. That place was worse than the one in 1995.

Robbie Crane was with me that time, and we were both stunned at the conditions of that place, and of HIM! How could he have let himself come to this? I didn't understand.

It was really hard to watch someone you cared about degenerate like that, and know that you were powerless to stop it. King suffered a series of major events that completely changed him and drove him deeper into depression and drugs.

He used to be married to this chick named Laurie Carr, some Playboy centerfold gold-digger. She completely ripped him off in the divorce. I won't go into it here, except to say that like a lot of women, they hook into someone with money, and then use him up. Then they utilize the courts to ream him for everything they can get.

I had been in to see him several times in this convalescence home. The fact that the guy was laid up in that place, flat of his back for almost two years is more than I can stand. I can't comprehend what he went through. Just recently, I was laid up in bed with the flu for a week, and by the end of that run I was getting nuts. I'm going, "I've got to get out of this bed!"

When I'd go in, there he was, putting on the face of hope. He did get out for a short while, but he went right back in.

I went and spent Christmas Eve with him the year before he passed. I brought my sons, Michael and Marcus with me. Misty was still my girlfriend, and she came along. We brought him presents and all sorts of stuff.

I had a bunch of photos of him from the glory days blown up and framed, then hung up on his walls. He was so happy to see the kids. He was just tripping. They hadn't seen him in a real long time either, and it was just really touching. Really moving.

Warren went to see him that Christmas, too. He hung out with him for a while, and made the guy feel great. Someone told me that he said it was the best Christmas of his life.

In the end, Robbin was afraid that he was only going to be remembered as a loser junkie, who threw his entire life away. King died an early death, of a vicious habit, and he owned nothing in this world. He was used up. But, all of that aside, Robbin "King" Crosby was a loved man, whether he completely understood that or not.

It's a shame that he's gone, man. Everybody loved that guy; my mom, our friends, my kids, everybody. He was a consummate gentleman. He went out of his way to make sure everyone was happy, treated them all great. Anyone who was around the band, he was always, "Can I get you something, dude? Help yourself to that. Do you need anything?" He always made people feel comfortable.

You were always welcome with Robbin.

When I heard the circumstances about the way he died, I cried. He had gotten out of the hospital clean. He was in a wheelchair most of the time, but he was clean. The apartment he lived in was this tiny, little one bedroom, but he was making due.

Then he let this asshole loser of a friend move in with him. The guy was a junkie, and that was something King was never able to deal with.

It only took him a month before he had overdosed. Most people thought he had died from AIDS complications, but that's not the case. It was a massive overdose of heroin that killed the King.

All those years chasing the dragon, and he finally caught it. His demons drug him all the way to his grave.

I went to Robbin's memorial, down in La Jolla. We all did. That was a very uncomfortable situation. Juan and Stephen were there, and Warren and I were there. Everyone was doing their own thing, trying to ignore the others.

They took Robbin's ashes out into the ocean on surfboards, and then scattered them. Afterward, at a club in San Diego, Warren and I got up and jammed with some of Robbin's friends.

A lot of people had hoped that Robbin's death might bring together the band, but it didn't. Juan and Stephen wouldn't get up and play with us. The whole thing was really fucking lame. It was a very sad event.

Long live the King, brother.

After King's death, it was a really somber time for Warren and me. We went back out on tour, still with Jizzy Pearl as our frontman.

At first, I thought that stylistically, Jizzy would be similar to Stephen. They both have raspy, scratchy whiskey voices. But, we've already talked about the curse of changing your frontman. Ultimately, I thought we had made a bad move.

But there wasn't an alternative. We were already underway with it, and Warren was like, "Bob, we can't just have a revolving door of singers." He was right, of course. All we could do was dance with the one that brought us.

We did about 50 dates total on the Metal Edge tour. It was a lot of nightmare shows. Not greatly attended. We got fucked over on our money, and right at the last moment, we started getting flack from Warrant's management. It almost made us back out of the tour.

In the end, calmer heads prevail.

"The tour is in a month and a half, bro, and I fucking need that income, and so do you!" Warren doesn't need income as much as I do, because he's a trust fund guy. Now, he's never divulged how much that is, but it's probably pretty decent.

I've been told he's related to the Mars chocolate family. He's always downplayed it, but I'll say this: During those lean years, he wasn't out working. Didn't seem to be concerned about it, either. He toured with Whitesnake in 1994, but that was about the extent of it.

In the end, we did this tour, and sucked "hind tit" to Warrant on some of the dates. It was all right. I had fun on the tour, because I was working. That's me. I have to keep working. I can't not work. I'll hang around and relax for a few weeks, maybe a couple of months, but that's it.

I always want to be playing and touring. Not year round, mind you, but enough to float my world, and to satisfy that artistic outlet and creative craving that musicians have to play music.

When I come in off the road, I like to relax for a couple of months and just chill. But then, after a little time, I start to get bored, and if I'm not working on a side project, or a new album, or band stuff, I don't function well. I used to be able to just golf that down time away, but I don't golf as much as I used to.

So, 2002 concluded, and things just went on their merry way. It was a tough, hard fought year, all the way around. We survived it, and the tour worked out pretty well. We were on nice tour busses. And the battle with Stephen was finally over.

Of course, there were still little skirmishes with him. We had to have him called back into court on two separate occasions for using the RATT name when he toured. Two times, he had to go back in front of the judge. Finally, the judge said, "Mr. Pearcy, I don't think you're understanding what I'm telling you. If you do this one more time, I will lock you up."

So, finally, Stephen got the point and quit the nonsense. He got to the point where he would contact us before playing and say "I'm doing a gig. I told them not to use any RATT shit."

Then, I ran into Stephen on my birthday in 2003. There's a local group called Metal Skool that I really enjoy and have followed for years. They're a glam rock parody act, and the longest running act on the Sunset Strip. Back then, they played a regular gig at the Viper Room, and Ralph called me up to play.

Stephen was in the audience, and jumped up there with us! Ralph looks at me like, "What the fuck is he doing, I was calling you." I got up there, and Stephen was already on stage, so, we jammed "Round and Round" and everyone was treated to a mini-reunion that most thought would never happen.

It went over really well. We got a huge pop from the crowd.

I remember it was a big thing, too. Everybody had been trying to keep us away from each other, keep each other on opposite sides of the Viper Room. I guess they were afraid we were going to have a go at each other, which is something I would never do.

I was standing up at the bar, and Stephen walks by. So, I tap him on the shoulder. He's like, "Hey". I go, "What's up?"

It was so loud in there. But, out of the blue, he gives me a hug. Right? And, in his ear, I go, "Dude, what the fuck are we doing? Why are we doing this? Let's put the band back together and go RATT and Roll. Yeah?" He gave me a kiss on the cheek, looked at me, and walked away.

I was encouraged by it. I actually hoped it would happen. But it was another four and a half years before Stephen stepped in front of the mic for RATT again.

April 2007.

House on Poppy Meadows street, Canyon Country, CA.
that Misty and I lived.

34

CALCULATING THE RISK

"Everybody knows that the dice are loaded. Everybody rolls with their fingers crossed." - Leonard Cohen

Thursday night, February 20, 2003.

That night was a really heavy evening for any human being with any kind of feelings, but for those who love going to rock shows with pyrotechnics, and going to see their favorite hard rock bands in a club environment, it would forever change their concert experience.

Obviously, I'm referencing the tragedy at The Station in West Warwick, Rhode Island.

The Station was a club that RATT had played a few times, so I was familiar with the place. They were one of those clubs that featured the glam metal and hard rock acts from the 80s and Nineties that were still touring.

On that particular night, my sister Carol was visiting me from Pittsburgh, and staying at the house. Carol, me, Misty, Robbie Crane and his wife, Melissa, and a handful of other people were at the Rainbow, having some dinner and a few drinks, then we were going to stroll down the Strip to the Cat Club. It's a tiny little club / bar, located right next to the Whisky a Go-Go and is owned by Slim Jim from the Stray Cats. There's a band called the "Star Fuckers" that plays there every Thursday night.

Before we left the Rainbow, I had slipped out to the patio bar to have a cigarette and was watching the TV. Then I saw this breaking news story.

"Another Nightclub Disaster."

About a week or so earlier, there had been a stampede at a nightclub in Chicago, where twenty people were killed. Tragedies like this are scattered through the history of this business. It's inexcusable that it happens, but every few years, we have another tragedy.

I'm watching this breaking news, and they're streaming live footage of a huge fire. It was total chaos. Just unreal. Then they flashed across the screen, "Heavy Metal Band, Great White, Performing." And, I just about lost it.

"WHAT?!? GREAT WHITE?"

I couldn't believe what I was seeing. I've told a lot of stories over the course of this book. Some of them are fun, and some are not fun at all. But, Jack Russell figures into a lot of them.

I've partied with Jack for years and years. I've written songs with the guy, and we were pretty tight for a very long time. I stood speechless watching the TV and seeing a nightclub consume fans, band mates and crews, and lastly, Jack's career.

It was horrific.

I watched for a few more minutes before finally tearing myself away from it. I went back to the table, there at the Rainbow, and got everyone's attention.

"Stop talking for a minute. You guys gotta hear this."

I told them what was going on. I told them about the visuals I had just seen, and who was involved. Their mouths just hung open.

When we got down to the Cat Club, I told Kenny, the bartender, to turn on the news. All night long, we were glued to the TV in that bar. We were trying to have a good time, but I couldn't help but rubberneck constantly, trying to figure out what was going on 3000 miles away. What was the latest?

They had visuals of people stacked up in the doorways and windows, trapped; literally burning to death, stuck on the inside of the club, just a few feet from safety. People around the world are watching this unfold before their eyes.

It's a terrible feeling, because the natural instinct is to do something about it. But you can't. All you can do is watch in horror and know that it was really happening. The footage ran over and over of people jammed in a doorway, with just their heads sticking outside, screaming in agony. It was the most graphic, spirit-cracking thing I've ever seen in my life.

True abject horror.

We went home that night, and I stayed up till dawn, watching this thing and talking to friends on the phone about it. Ty Langley, Great White's guitarist, was one of the guys who died that night.

Turns out that another of the people who died inside the club was my old drum tech. All of those people who died were fans of 80s heavy metal. They were RATT fans. It sat in my gut like a physical thing. It was a feeling of losing a lot of friends all at one time.

I was really stunned and taken aback by that whole ordeal. Not just by the nature of what had happened, but Jack Russell and I go back. I love the guy. He and Mark Kendall.

I couldn't believe they were involved in something like this. My first thoughts of it were just pure rage.

"What the FUCK were you doing using pyro in a small room like that? Are you out of your mind? Are things so bad that you have to rely on that, now? What is this?"

Not that it was totally their fault, but it's just reckless. What were they thinking? I mean, I couldn't help but to put myself in that place for a moment. RATT has used pyro in arenas our entire careers, but we would never use pyro in a club! It's crazy to do something like that!

Then you try to relate, and put yourself in their place. That's when you want to shrivel up and die. It's almost like Jack and Great White have branded themselves as baby killers, all because they used flash pots in a room with 12 foot ceilings. They have to deal with that for the rest of their lives.

I saw some footage of Jack being interviewed the night of the fire, and I was completely disgusted by his demeanor on it.

He was immediately trying to disassociate himself and the band from what happened, trying to put the blame on the club. I thought that was something he would have to do at some point, but not right out of the gate with the news crews! Come on, dude! There are ninety-six people inside that building, including members of his band and crew. They died one of the worst deaths you can die, and instead of openly mourning their loss, and the tragedy of the thing, he immediately starts pointing the finger away from himself.

That seemed very chicken shit to me.

I haven't seen those guys since then. I haven't talked to Jack. I haven't talked to Kendall. We've played a few shows with them, but frankly, the gigs we played with them were festival shows, and it wasn't our place to keep them on or off the card.

I know that Warren and Stephen will not play shows with Great White, strictly because of the Rhode Island thing.

Because of that fire, most promoters, festivals, and bands don't care to play with Great White, from what I generally hear. Then we were hearing allegations about misappropriation of funds from the tour they did that was to benefit the families of the victims. They've been blacklisted by their own hand.

It's a terrible thing, because Great White is a good band.

For me, just recently they were brought up as a possible opener for us on some off-season shows. I looked at Warren and Stephen and said, "We still like the Stones, and people were killed at Altamont; the Who had people die in Cincinnati in 1981, based solely on the fact that the Who had the venue hold the doors while the did an extended sound check. The crowd swelled at the door, and the people in front were crushed and trampled to death.

We were still fans of those bands, even though they were driving the shows when those tragedies happened. If a grand jury chose not to indict Great White, then how are you guys able to do that?"

But a few days later, on the anniversary of the fire, I saw on a website where someone posted raw footage of that night, where the fire was enveloping the people in the windows and doorways.

That just re-invigorated the rage in me that something like that was allowed to happen. I found myself siding with Warren and Stephen. Suddenly, disassociating from those guys was the right thing to do.

I respect Great White as a band, but it's still a little fresh. Those people died from someone's stupidity, probably several people's stupidity. And for what? The money on that show was made. The pyro wasn't going to change anything, so why do it?

The footage I saw on that website had the screaming and struggling of the victims on it. It's blood curdling, and those visuals will follow me for a long time to come. Who else in that crowd had I met? Had some of those people come to the RATT shows? Did I sign an autograph for them? Take a picture with them? And now they're gone for no reason at all?

I tell you one thing, though. That event scared me to the point that I don't go into any kind of a venue unless I know where the exits are. I'll position myself as close to them as I can without being obvious. Even to this day, I go to a place like the Magic Castle, the legendary Magic Castle, which is this old, Victorian looking building with several rooms and multiple floors where they do magic shows. The place is wood, and was built in 1908. One hundred years ago. It's a tinderbox!

That sort of stuff freaks me out, now.

That's how 2003 started for me.

The court case with Stephen was finally over with, and thank God for it. It was such an emotional and financial drain, that I just wanted to get back out on the road and build up the coffers again.

Warren didn't quite see it that way.

Maybe he was just too exhausted by what we had been through. Maybe he just needed a break. Maybe, even, he wasn't excited about making music anymore. For whatever reason, Warren simply didn't want to work.

We did a few club dates, but it wasn't much to exist on, and I was just sitting there with my newly acquired real estate skills.

So, what the hell?

I started up a business as a closing agent for mortgage companies.

I went to the classes, and got a notary license, then developed accounts with different title companies and banks. They would send me out when people wanted to re-finance or do a line of credit on their house. I'd work up all the closing paperwork, then go over and sit down with the customer, showing them all the details of the agreement. They'd sign it, I'd notarize it, stamp it and send it on its way.

Easy money, baby.

After about eight or nine months, I was pulling in around fifteen hundred to two thousand a week doing this, depending on how much I wanted to work. It was pretty exciting, and I enjoyed the hell out of it. It was a principle source of income all the way through 2005.

Again, it all started because so many fly out dates were being turned down by Warren.

At the time, we were still slugging it out in clubs trying to make a living. It was a pretty uneventful couple of years, other than the fact I did a solo record called "Twenty Four Seven."

My personal life was going pretty well. Misty and I were in love. My mortgage closing business was doing fantastic, and I bought a house.

Misty and I moved out of Encino and into a new house in Canyon Country.

Thanks to some of what I'd learned about real estate, I was able to get in for no down payment. Not only did I get in without a down payment, but I got another ten grand back, because I made the real estate agents add another point to the backend. My cut of the deal was a third.

That beats the hell out of the 13% I was paying back in the 80s on my mortgage rate. I was paying 7% on the Canyon Country house.

I was really proud of that place. It wasn't a big house, but it sat on a half acre, which in California is huge! Canyon Country was up near Valencia, just north of Los Angeles. There's a nice golf course out there, and Misty and I were very happy to have a home instead of an apartment.

So, to a degree I was back in the game. Won the lawsuit. Came off a good tour.

I was back!

Of course, I wasn't getting a lot of joy for my musical needs. We just weren't working as RATT very often, and as I've said, I have to have a creative outlet. Most creative people are like that. We don't function at 100% without doing that "thing" we do. In my case, it's making music.

I decided that if Warren was burnt out, I'd do a solo record. That should be a lot of fun. It was, but it was a disaster as well.

"Twenty Four Seven" was ambitious, enjoyable, and fulfilling, but it was also a train-wreck from a business prospective. It serves as a prime "you can't trust anyone" lesson for musicians.

The record was comprised of music that I had co-written with Jack Russell (before the Rhode Island tragedy), Ralph Sanes from Metal Skool, and John Corabi. I produced the record, and was playing all the instruments, Aldo Nova-style. John Corabi came in and did the vocals on it.

And, I was completely fucked over with that record deal.

I had signed with a cheesy little label called Metal Mayhem. There was this 6'8" guy named Ryan who owned it. The guy started out as an alright cat, but quickly degenerated into a creep, freak of a guy who ripped me off, and kicked me out of my own recording session!

It was incredible.

I was recording with this guy name Mike Viscera, who was a singer in Yngwie Malmsteen's band. We were doing all of the recording for the record at his house in his studio. It took two weeks, and I was staying in his guest room.

The record was coming along, doing fine, except he kept going off and doing his home thing, so I kept nailing him down to do work.

"Mike, look, from 10 in the morning to 7 at night, this is what we do."

Of course, he wouldn't listen. He would leave, and then I would do all the overdubs with Corabi on the vocals. He didn't know what to sing, so I was having to show him what to sing vocally, which was turning out really well.

My mistake was a small one, but it blew out of proportion in short order. I left my liner notes sitting on the table. Liner notes being the "thank you's" and special thanks and credits for the album.

Mike saw it. We had all the artwork done and finished out, so it was almost press ready. Mike sits down and is reading them. It said "Produced by Bobby Blotzer".

This Mike Viscera character freaked out!

He's like "What?? I fucking produced this album!"

I go, "Wait a minute, dude. You produced this? What did you produce?? You engineered it. I'm not the engineer. Even though while you were upstairs having dinner, I was punching in the overdubs. But, I'm not going to ask for engineering credit. What did you produce?"

He's flailing about, stuttering and fumbling for what to say. "When you fucking needed drums and amps, I'm the one who went out and got them for you!"

You gotta be kidding me. "That's producing? Look, you didn't arrange one thing. Not one. I came up with the vocal parts and harmonies. You know what? You're not getting producer credit."

Finally, he just throws his hands up and goes, "You know what? Get the fuck out of my house!"

I couldn't believe this clown. "Are you serious? Alright, man."

So, I packed my shit and Ryan came and picked me up. I was good with Ryan, until all this shit happened. He was just a little goonish, you know? He took me to his house, and was just tripping out that all this had happened.

I told Ryan, "Those are my masters in there. That's my music, my artwork. I want those masters."

We were getting ready to mix. I mean, it was just started. And, now Mike wouldn't let me in to mix, and he was saying he wouldn't give me the tapes. So, we're driving back to the house, and Ryan is talking to this ass-clown on the phone.

Things chilled out that night.

The next day, we were trying to figure out what to do. I said, "Give me the disks, and I'm taking them back to California and mix them."

Mike won't do it. Ryan comes on like, "He won't give them up, man".

I hung up the phone and called Mike. "Dude, I'm giving you one chance to give me my masters, then I'm calling the cops and we're coming up there."

I left that on the answering machine. Forty-five minutes later, I'm on the computer in Ryan's home office, and I hear the door slam open *BLAM!*. It slams open, and I hear this, "You motherfucker!" I hear this loud yelling, and I'm going, "What the hell?"

I go walking out of the room where the computer's at, and lumbering down the hall is this 6'8" freak, Ryan, and he's flipping out. "Get your shit, get the fuck out!"

Great...here we go again.

He continues, "You fucking call his house and threatened him?"

"I want my tapes, Ryan! That's my music!" I was pretty passionate about the whole thing. "You're the record company, not the producer. Those are my tapes, and I want them right now!"

He had me get my shit and had his brother take me to the airport and drop me off. He told his brother to just "Drop him at the end of the block." What a fucking cocksucker.

He never paid me the rest of my dough, AND put the record out. They kept the tapes and finished the mix without me. What the fuck am I going to do? He's in Connecticut. I'm in LA I was going to go bi-coastal on another lawsuit? Retain a lawyer there with a $10,000 a month tab? I didn't have the money, nor the wherewithal to go through another lawsuit.

So, I had to let the record come out. He said he was only going to print a few copies of it, and that was it. A lot of people liked that record, and have it. I don't know how many he printed. He said 3000, and he sold out of those.

And, that's how I rounded out 2003. Dealing with that nonsense. Lesson learned, right?

RATT did a short little stint with Vince Neil in 2004. Mostly fly outs, but that was about it.

It was and odd time, because we'd fly out on Thursday, do the gigs with Vince all weekend, signing autographs for fans, doing big shows, and living the rockstar life. Then we'd fly back home on Sunday. I'd then be up first thing Monday morning, doing closings, getting other peoples autographs.

Clients would spot me once in a while, which was always funny.

We'd be talking about various things. They'd ask me if this was my main job, and I'd tell them it was just a side gig. They'd find out who I was, and just flip out. I had people bring RATT records out of their back room and show them to me. They'd be pointing to my picture on the back of the album.

"Is that you, man?"

"Yeah, that's me!"

It was always a very big laugh, because these people would turn out to be HUGE RATT N Rollers. It was completely surreal for them to have one of their rock star idols sitting in their house or office and doing the closing paperwork on their new home.

Invariably, they would go, "What the hell happened, dude? Why are you here?"

It would take a few minutes to explain that the band was still working and touring, but this was just something to fill the gaps in time, you know? Most of them believed it!

It was a very strange, yet profitable point of my career.

I'd do five or six closing a day, on average. It was pretty trippy to get a look into these people lives. You'd find a contractor who makes $200,000 per month and lives in a giant house, and then the next guy would be an office guy who might make $40,000 per year.

It's interesting to see that cross section of American life.

In 2005, RATT went out on the Cinderella tour, so I had to put the closing job on the shelf for a while. It was a little upsetting, because I really had the thing dialed in. The agents and banks were getting used to using me, and I'd play the RATT card to get more work. If the scheduler was young, I'd always drop something like, "I'm going to be out on tour for a little bit during…" and they would get curious.

They'd find out who I was, and it would turn out they were big fans. Then I became their go-to guy. Once that's established, you work all the time. When you disrupt it, like I had to with the tour, it's hard to get it going again, because they've moved on to someone else as their go-to guy.

I shut it down for the summer of 2005, and started back up briefly when I got back, but it never reached the heights it had in 2003 to 2004.

During this whole time, Misty was my girl. We had been together for almost five years. August of 2000, when Traci and I were done, was the starting point for Misty and me.

But, by June of 2005, just before going out on tour, there were some serious problems.

All through 2005, my relationship with Misty wasn't getting any better, and we had such a tumultuous relationship to begin with!

She really wanted me to be something I couldn't be, and was very controlling. I was trying to make it work, but so many of the things that I had come to love were the things she had grown to hate. It drove her crazy being at Lake Havasu with my lake buddies, because we do what we do. We drink beer all day, have cocktails at night, and just have a really good time, running around with my crew and me.

While she would step out and enjoy herself, but she really didn't like the person I was when I drank liquor. She got really uptight about it. Same thing with Traci. Same thing with … well, obviously, there's a pattern here.

When I'm on hard liquor, I'm a completely different person, which is why I don't drink it anymore. Captain and Coca-Cola is as ballsy as I'll allow myself these days. I'm not violent, or anything, but I become a different personality. It's fun, but girlfriends don't deal with it.

So, a few Coors Lights, a little red wine, and I can still socialize and not be a fucking kook. Ain't life grand?

In 2005, I started giving her some signs. "Babe, it's March. We've been in this house for three months, and we've only had sex twice." I'm the kind of guy that needs to be intimate with the woman in my life. I can't sit stale, and just hope that's enough.

So, I told her, "This isn't going to work, if you can't be intimate with me."

"Well, the more you behave like this, the more you act..." giving me this ultimatum. Like I was in the wrong.

Misty and I had split for about three months in 2004, so this was not a new development for us. We managed to pull the thing out of the fire, and she moved back home. But, things were never tight again.

I guess it's like pulling a carton of spoiled milk out of the fridge, taking a drink and going, "Fuck! That's spoiled! Here, I'll put it back. Maybe it'll be better tomorrow."

Then Misty pulled some shit. She still won't admit to it, but it got back to me that she had been fucking around with some drug dealer type up in Hollywood. Everyone knew about the guy, and he's a total stain. She claimed that he had spiked her and her girlfriend's drink one night, and that she was totally innocent. She stayed the night there, but nothing happened, she swore!

You know, once you've been mauled by an animal, it's hard to really trust any other animal not to maul you, as well. I tried to take Misty's word as truth. I didn't want to think that she would go off and fuck this character, but thanks to Traci, I know how women can be, and things certainly hadn't been intimate around our house for a while.

In my experience, if nothing is happening in the bedroom at home, then chances are, it's happening somewhere else.

So, when it got close to the tour, I told her, "Here's the deal. I'm going back out on the road in a month. If you don't start acting like we're together, and not just roommates, I'm telling you, it's a bad thing. Me, on the road, having been emotionally deserted? I'm going out single, Pi-RATT flag flying high!"

So, that's the way it happened. When I went on the road, I told her, "We're done. While I'm gone, find a place to move."

Three months. But she wouldn't leave. She would not move out of the house while I was gone. I had to eventually get a friend of mine, Mike Smith, to go over and stay at the house. She couldn't stand Mike, and I knew that. He was my drinking buddy, so he was guilty by association, and I knew having him at the house was going to drive her crazy.

It worked!

Misty moved out the day before I got back from tour, and left the house completely trashed. I was really disappointed in her with that. We're friends these days, but that was a bad time for us. I'll always love her.

I love all of my ex's ... even if I hate them. That's just me.

While I was out on the road, I ran into a good friend of mine, who's name we'll call Misty2.

I met Misty2 in 2000 while we were out touring with Warrant and LA Guns, down in Austin, Texas. Misty2 and two of her friends were on Warrant's bus after the show. One of the friends was a guitar tech for Warrant. I was on the bus talking to Mike Fassano. These girls walked on, and I introduced myself as Bobby.

She has a smooth confidence about her, like she's been there before. She sort of laughs, and goes, "I know who you are, Bobby. My name is Misty."

To make things even stranger, they almost had identical last names. At least I wouldn't have to have worry about saying the wrong name at the wrong time or changing their luggage tag or Christmas card list.

At the time, I was with Misty, and I didn't mess around on her. Misty2 was married, and there was nothing going on between us. We were just good friends who hung out whenever we rolled through town. It was completely innocent.

In June of 2005, the tour got to Texas. Misty2 and I had been keeping in touch over the years. I knew she was going through a divorce, and she knew that Misty and I had split. But, she also knew Misty and I had split before, and then got back together, after a three months separation.

When I saw Misty2 in Dallas at the Smirnoff Amphitheater, I looked at her a little differently. She and a girlfriend picked me up at the hotel, and I was thinking, "Damn. She looks pretty fucking good right now."

I knew that since she had broken up, things were a little different. We had always been a little flirty. Not even that, just really friendly, but we never crossed the relationship boundaries. Never spoke of it.

Now, the gloves were off, and it was a different world. So, that night after the show in Dallas, I kidnapped her and took her on the bus. I took her to the mall the next day and bought her some clothes, and she went to Oklahoma with me on tour. We did a couple of shows, and then I flew her home. She started coming out, and we were a couple pretty quick.

When I got home from the tour in 2005, I started doing my closing gig again. But, the whole thing with Misty was really fresh, and it was everywhere I looked! Meanwhile, Misty2 was spending more and more time in California, and I was spending more and more time in Texas. It was coming to a place where we had to decide who was going to move, because the relationship had gotten to that point.

I finally decided to sell my house.

I had been looking around in Houston, and discovered something absolutely amazing about Texas. You can buy a huge, mansion of a home for $300,000. I'm talking four thousand square feet on an acre of land. Not only could I sell my place in California and live in a mansion in Texas, buying it outright if I wanted to, I'd still have money enough to start a business.

So, that's what I did.

I moved out to Houston, and bought a forty two hundred square foot home in Cypress, Texas with a giant yard. I loved that place. Cypress is a suburb of Houston, so I was right in a major metropolitan area. It was time to open my recording studio!

I had already met all of Misty2's friends, just in the time I had been hanging out in Houston, and I loved them all. They are a great bunch of people, my Houston crew.

Texas isn't all fun and games, though.

I got another DUI down in Austin, Texas July 6, 2006. Texas cops on a DUI are brutal. Totally lame. It's like that movie, "Smokey and the Bandit", only they don't have Jackie Gleason's comedic timing.

Trust me, Texas cops have NO sense of humor.

I was just leaving the 6th street area, which is the premiere party area in the entire state, and was sitting at a red light in 3 lanes of traffic waiting to get on the freeway.

The cop rode by on a bike, looked at me, and then doubled back. I wasn't wearing my seatbelt, which, in Texas, is the driving equivalent of clubbing baby seals.

I told Misty2, "I'm going to jail, so listen. Here's the checkbook, find a lawyer."

We'd been on Lake Travis all day, and out playing all night. I know that I shouldn't have been drinking and driving. I know that. But, in all my years of doing it, I've never had a fender bender. Nothing. I'm rock steady behind the wheel.

I've learned from it, to a degree. I just don't drink hard liquor anymore. They took me in, and it was all over the radio the next day. Nice. Really ugly. So, that was another ten grand in legal fees to make that go away.

This time, I didn't keep the weed. There wasn't any.

Somewhere along the way, I had met a guy named Gregg Gill. Gregg had a recording studio at his house, and he invited me over to look at all of it.

I had originally planned to do the studio at my house, because I had all of this expansive room. I had two full rooms set-aside for it. But, Gregg's stuff was pretty cool, and he seemed to really know his stuff. The down side, for him, was that he had a kid, and his place wasn't huge, so running a recording studio out of his home had become a bit of a drag. He had people there all the time, and it was kind of funky. He really wanted to get out and get his own place for the studio. So we started talking about putting something together.

Literally, within two weeks, we were on the drawing board. We had a place on Langfield Road, which was an industrial park there in Houston, and we were going to share the place with another friend named Jeff Diamont.

Jeff was starting an amplification company called Diamond Amps. It was going to be a real cheap date between what Jeff needed, and what we needed. It was a 5000 square foot space, and we had two full studios; Studio A & B. We got an architect to design the place, then had it all built within seven weeks.

We had a full studio, as well as the amp manufacturing facility. I decorated the place, which I have a flair for doing, and the business came out of the box really hot!

I started bringing bands in, and producing. Gregg was doing the mixing and engineering work, and Jeff would push his amps. It was a good combination. The property management company that ran the place gave us a buildup account of $25,000. We spent another $20,000 on top of that, and then I spent another $25,000 on equipment, in addition to the things Gregg already had.

We stocked up on stuff. There was a full, state-of-the-art Pro Tools set-up, and suddenly we were the hot new ticket in town.

Diamond Studios was born.

The first record we recorded at Diamond Studios was my Saints of the Underground record, which I produced, and sounds amazing. My production skills, which I was very proud of, hadn't slipped, and our studio sounded fantastic. I was bringing in bands that were digging it, and I was having a good time with it all. We were making good money, and I love Gregg like a brother. He and his wife, Alison and his child, Stone, were like family to me.

We opened doors in May of 2006. That's how quickly this all went. We had a great summer that year. But, in fairly short order, I started getting this vibe from Gregg. It wasn't really envy, at least I don't think, but it certainly had a dissension to it that I couldn't understand.

We were using my name to attract business, and I was getting paid well to produce records. Maybe that's what happened. Maybe that served as the root of jealousy that started driving the wedge in. At the time, I just chalked it up as growing pains.

I was making between $1500 and $3000 per song to produce. Then, on top of that, I was negotiating the rental fees for the studio, which he and I would split. Gregg might have seen that as double dipping, though he never uttered those words. But, he started getting really short tempered and such. I started feeling really weird when we were working together. I was producing and calling the shots. He was doing the engineer work. There were moments when I would wind up doing some of the writing for these bands; writing parts, and bringing out parts.

Gregg is a great engineer, and is really good to work with. He would sometimes contribute good ideas to the production, as well. The artists really liked him, and like working with him. It was shaping up to be a win / win deal for everyone.

Provided we could work our way past the dissension I was picking up from Gregg.

Act III: The Resurrection

35

ROUND AND ROUND: THE RATTS COME HOME

"Got one for the money, Two for the show, Three for my honey and four to let you know that I...Let The Music Do The Talking" - Aerosmith "Let The Music Do The Talking"

In late 2006, the RATT reunion started to become a serious consideration.

I was spending a lot of time on the phone with Stephen and Warren, along with our management, trying to get this thing done. This process was a good month and a half of daily phone calls, three or four hours at a time. It just went round and round ... no pun intended.

With Stephen, RATT's tours are doing very well. We're making really great guarantees per show as a band. Without him, we don't make as much. It's the same for him. His solo stuff doesn't go over very well, but with RATT, he's a king again. A twilight king, true, but a king nonetheless.

Simply put, we needed each other, and we all knew it.

RATT isn't RATT without Stephen, and Stephen has a huge hole he's dug for himself that RATT can help him climb out of financially. It was time to let bygones be bygones.

Juan was approached, as well. However, bygones were too much to get past for Juan. He was demanding things that simply couldn't be given. He should have been thanking the forces that be, Stephen, Warren, and myself, that we were even approaching him with this. He hasn't done shit, musically, since RATT broke up way back in 1992. My opinion on it was, "Juan, you want to go out and be a rockstar again? You want to go make some money? Then chill out, cap the ego, and let's go. Just play bass, sing, get along, and reap the rewards of the work we did back then."

He just kept stringing us along. Finally, I couldn't take anymore. I was like, "Guys, I'm not getting on anymore phone calls. This is the deal. He's getting even money. ONLY. That's all I'm going to offer. He'll get his part of the ownership back, but like with Stephen, we're not going to just give it to him. He has to prove that he's going to be a team player. He's going to get along."

Of course, Juan proved himself to not be those things before we got into a rehearsal room. THANK GOD! Because, I know how Juan is, and the problems he perpetuates. This thing would have imploded a month into the tour, if it even made it out of the rehearsal rooms.

So we moved ahead without him. We signed with Sanctuary Management, Carl Stubner and Jamie Talbot. They're a respectable management company, who handles Tommy Lee, ZZ Top, Fleetwood Mac, and several others. We signed onto the 2007 Poison tour, which turned into one of the best things we've ever done, and we're working out the details for our 2008 tour.

RATT is back.

RATT doing the Rockline radio show, 2008.

RATT playing Sweden Rockfest in front of 40,000 proper, 2008.

36

ANOTHER ONE BITES THE DUST

I'm definitely a co-dependent person. A lot of people mistake that as a

weakness, but it's not.

My friends always go, "Dude, why don't you just be single for a while? Go out and fuck chicks. Live it up." But, I don't want that! I've done that before, after I split with Traci, and it just isn't my thing.

I'm the kind of guy who wants to come home, have my chick waiting there for me, watch TV shows (there's a lot of shows I really like), and just be normal for a while. I like having someone to go to movies with. I don't want to be dating and shit. It's not my scene. It's too much hassle.

As a result, I fall into relationships pretty easily. I always figure, we'll eventually gel really well. I mean, how can you not, right? I'm so goddamned good-looking and irresistibly cute, and shit. How can the world not love me? Right? Right? Nevermind...

I'm obviously a pretty demanding person. Even my family says so. Carol, my sister, is always "Well, you know, it's always gotta be Bobby's way!" But, I'm a guy with ideas.

I'm like, "You got ideas? Let's hear them! Maybe they're better ideas than mine."

"Nah! You'll just shoot them down."

"No, tell me. I want to know."

"Well, I think we could..."

"Nah, that sucks! I don't want to do that!" Like I said, at least I have a sense of humor!

I've always been the kind of person that is the epicenter. Not in an arrogant or conceited sort of way, but there's always a core of people that spreads out from me. So many of my friends have other friends that they met through me. I mean, down to getting married and having kids, because they met while hanging out at the lake with me, or going out to Catalina with me, or hitting a club where I introduce them.

There are people who are lifelong friends of mine who had no idea the other existed until they run into each other at some sort of function I'm having. I'm a catalyst. I'm that radical stimulus that causes a chain reaction. I'm an impetus. That's right! I had to find a fucking thesaurus to describe what I am, but that's me. An impetus. So, go forth and befriend, for the impetus has spoken in your life. Whatever, right?

It's always been that way, though. It's a very interesting ride. A whole 6 degrees of Bobby Blotzer.

It's the end of the 2005 tour, and I've been flying Misty2 out, and flying to Texas to see her. We've been trying to figure out what the next move is going to be. Is she going to move to LA? Can she handle that? Am I going to Texas? The idea of moving to Texas wasn't on the menu until I went there and started hanging out.

I knew some of her friends, like Trey and Tanya Gabler, and Rick and Daphne Ward, and I just started cruising around the place while she was at work.

People tend to trip out a little bit when they run into you in those situations. Anytime I would pull up to an average situation in Texas, I was a celebrity. To them, they're meeting a rockstar that they grew up loving. In Texas, I got that a lot. Lots of people coming up and doing the fanfare thing, which I love. I've always loved that stuff when they're nice and cool about it. I love our fans. They put food on my table and make me feel that I matter.

Texas was a great place to experience that. I'd hang with our friends while she was working, enjoying the local flare, and before long I started cruising real estate. Are you kidding me? With the real estate prices in Texas, how could you not? I'm talking about a huge house by California standards. Four thousand square feet on an acre and a half of land...in the city and for less money!

I started thinking, I could go and cash a California house out, move to Texas, and be cruising in an amazing pad. I was looking at stuff that was comparable to what I had in California, and it only cost $190,000. That's a third of what I paid in Canyon Country.

I was seriously considering it. Then again, I do that a lot. Wherever I go in this country, I'm always checking out the real estate situation. California, Texas, Cleveland, Fort Wayne, Indiana. Doesn't matter. I'll check out the real estate. Anywhere in these great United States.

I got to thinking; the housing market in California was as high as it had ever been. I had enough equity built up that I could sell the place, move to Texas and have an even bigger place with a new life and a new girl, and, there would still be money left over to open a recording studio, which is something I've always been interested in.

To leave California was ludicrous. I'd always been there. My sons were there. Almost all my friends were there.

But, coming out of the Misty situation, I had to distance myself from it. I still love the woman, but it's a tainted, broken kind of thing. I missed the 5 and half years we were together, and the things we did. You build something like that, and you get accustomed to it. It feels comfortable, even if it doesn't work on any level.

In Texas, I had Misty2, and while I would eventually get into it with her as well, I still loved her. She was very good to me, and I thought we had a lot of growth potential there. I thought that if I opened the recording studio, business would come.

It did, too. Big time.

I sold my house in Canyon Country. I still had to pay off an equity line that I'd taken out to build a pool, and I spent a little elsewhere, but I walked away with about $220,000.

I was back in the real estate side of things.

I had a moving company drop a big trailer in front of the house, and I filled it top to bottom, front to back, then loaded up my truck and off we went. The company dropped the trailer off at my new place in Texas, and it was a done deal.

I was a Texan.

I bought a beautiful place on Villa Chianti Ct. in Cypress, TX, just outside Houston. Villa Chianti... just like the wine. Misty2, moved in, and it was pretty cool. The place was amazing. Four thousand two hundred square feet, on a fantastic piece of property.

I loved the house, loved the yard, and Misty didn't sweat me too much like the other wives / girlfriends tended to do. She never got on my ass about the drinking.

She was just, "God, you were a fucking piece of work, last night."

"Yeah, I know. Sorry 'bout that."

Misty2 was really good to me. At this point in life, I have aches and pains from years of playing drums, golfing, and my various other sport activities. She was always rubbing my back, or my hands, working the stiffness out of muscles that hadn't seen that kind of attention in a very long time. She was completely faithful, a great cook, and lovingly attentive. She kept the house tight, and worked a good job for good pay.

She had that "southern woman" mentality down to a science.

There's something about southern women that makes them stand out from the rest of the pack, and Misty2 is no different. They are very caring, loving, family oriented women by a rule, but the flip side of that is they are extremely possessive. They always want to know where you are and what you're doing.

That will get on your nerves pretty quick.

I'm the kind of person, that where my woman is concerned, I take care of things. I expect her to contribute to the cause, don't misunderstand. I'm not a sugar daddy for anyone. But, as long as she keeps a job, and chips in on the bills, helping to keep the house in order, I generally take care of everything else. I'm the lion; I'll take the lion's share.

Misty2 started getting a little weird, nonetheless. For instance, I bought this huge, sprawling house that had a game room upstairs in the front of it. Our master suite was downstairs in the back. Once or twice a month, I'd have the guys from the bar over.

We'd go back to my place and shoot pool all night. You know. Drink beer, and maybe do a couple of bumps of blow.

While I never buy blow, and I never possess it, occasionally if we're drunk and a friend has it, I do a bump or two. Like my friend "Good Time George." He's part of my Havasu crew,.

When I'm drunk, he'll make a gesture like, "Hey, you wanna do a snapper?"

"Yeah, why not?"

It wakes me up to do more drinking. That's all.

So, we'd be doing that sort of shit up in the game room, and Misty2 would come up with her arms folded and her frowning face, and the whole room would deflate. Such a killjoy.

At first, I would be, "Oh, what's wrong? What's wrong?" all concerned. She's like, "Well, it's really loud."

After enough times of her doing this shit, it turned into, "What the fuck are you doing up here?"

She'd make more hassles and bang on the ceiling. Finally, I had to sit down with her. "Look, I understand that you have to work in the morning. But, it's Wednesday night. I went out with the guys. We came back here to play pool. This is who I am. It's what I like to do. I bought a big house with a game room so I could utilize it. It's not every night. It's once in a while. So, go to bed, put on the headphones, or put a pillow over your head, whatever you need to do. But, do not come up to that room like that again."

It was all to no avail.

My phone rang constantly with calls from Misty2. She always wanted to know what I was doing. I could get up from the couch, and she would be, "Where are you going?"

"Nowhere. To take a piss. Stop asking me that all the time."

It was really kind of an insecure, squeaky mousy kind of approach, and my patience with it was wearing thin.

I'm sure that a lot of this is me, but there is something that happens in my head, and these women begin to get on my nerves. It's happened to a degree with all of them.

I feel bad that I hurt Misty2 with our breakup. She didn't understand, but it came down to a chemistry thing. I tried to explain it the best I could. We just weren't compatible. I love her as a friend, and would hate to kill that. In hindsight, I should have left our relationship alone, and kept it where it was.

As friends. Then she moved out to LA In October of 2007. Oh, boy! Is anything ever going to be easy?

In the end, we just didn't fit together. We were different animals. Even when things are progressing well, sometimes it isn't enough.

I don't think I was totally over Misty.

Because, just like my ordeal with Traci, Misty knew how to stay visible in my life. She knew how to keep just enough of my attentions that I couldn't completely let her go. I'm the kind of guy that when I love a woman, I love her forever. Regardless. To this day, I still dream about Jeni. I have dreams of all the women I've dated seriously. They may not be erotic dreams, if fact they never are, but it tells me that I love those women enough, that on some level my subconscious will never let them go.

I will say that Traci was definitely the worst. When I say worst, I mean that she epitomizes all of the deliberate, destructive things that people will do to kill a relationship. Despite all of that, though, I still have a glimmer of love for her. I seem helpless to end those things completely.

It is a curse. I'd love to be able to simply fuck and forget. Well...sometimes.

This was a tough time for me, all around. Misty2 and I were skidding, and not long before, I had received some horrible news about my Mum.

Around March 15, 2006, Misty2 and I were at a golf tournament in Houston when I got a phone call. They had just found two tumors on my Mum's brain, and one on her lung. She was in stage four on the cancer scale, and there are only four stages to be had. She literally had months to live, and likely it would be less.

I immediately got on a plane and headed for Pittsburgh. I brought my sons back there, but she wasn't coherent, which sucks, because they didn't get to say goodbye. After the boys went back home, I did get the chance to talk to her. She came around enough to communicate.

It was horrible to watch how she had become a withered, shell of herself. The cancer went so fast, it was terrifying. She had quit smoking five months earlier, and she was so proud of it, but the damage was done. She had been smoking since she was twelve, and she was seventy-three.

I'd had years to prepare for it, because I knew it was coming. She had been on oxygen for a long time, and I could see her slowing down over the years. I think she probably had those tumors a lot longer than anyone knew. It wasn't until she started getting dizzy and fainting that she went in. They did the CAT-Scan and found the cancer.

Both of my brothers and my sister were in the hospital at her bedside. While I did break down over it, obviously, it wasn't devastating like it could have been. It's not like when someone's mother, in the prime of her life, is killed in a car wreck. That's something that is sudden and crushing to the survivors. This was a little different. We had enough time to come to terms. It's absolutely painful, don't misunderstand. It always will be. That's my Mum, and better or worse, I love her with everything I am.

My other siblings, Michael, Carol and Ronnie, all felt the same thing. It was a huge loss, but an accepted one.

Speaking back on Ronnie, he had always been a bit of an enigma to me. He was the straight man, clean cut, and penny loafers. We called him "The Collegiate", and he was the total opposite of what I wanted to be or believed in. He was very much introverted, and pretty much mean as hell to my sister and me.

Don't get me wrong, Ronnie's my brother, and I love him, but we only recently started talking again after eight years of not speaking to each other at all. Even when we were all together this last April while Mum was in her last days (she died on May 7, 2007), Ron was anti-social, and he would hardly acknowledge Pete or even talked to him.

He's been better since Mum passed. It was really sad to watch him break down and cry back there, because he knew that he'd fucked it all up. All these years, he had successfully alienated his whole family, and now Mum was gone.

I had a falling out with him back when Mum moved from California back to Pittsburgh. I had always taken care of things with Mum, mostly because I had the means. I bought her house, bought her cars, paid the bills and the mortgage, gave her whatever she needed. No one else had to take any responsibility.

Carol didn't have any means to give. She was a single mother with three kids, so money was really tight for her. I understood that, and would never have asked her for money. Ronnie, on the other hand, he was a different story.

When she was moving back, I gave him a call and was like, "Hey, why don't you throw some money toward this move for her?" I had set everything up. She was going to drive her car back there, and we were going to send a bunch of stuff boxed.

Ronnie sent her $50.

I was infuriated. Considering the fact he would never make any effort to stay in touch with my sister, or my little brother Michael, yet he would always make time for me, I counted that as a slap in the face.

Mike was Pete and my Mum's son, so he was technically my half-brother, but that never made any difference. He's my brother. Ronnie never saw it that way, and he simply wouldn't engage. It used to piss me off. If you're going to talk to me, then make calls to your other siblings as well. At least ACT like the rest of our family exists.

When he broke down with Mum, I just looked at him with some sadness. "Well, brother, why don't we just look forward?" And that was the "new" that. Hopefully, Ronnie has walked away with a little enlightenment from all this. Hopefully, we all have.

The whole experience with the death of Mum caused me to quit smoking altogether. Part of it was the fact that I watched what it did to her, but another visual sticks out to me, as well.

I remember being at the hospital with my brothers. They would duck out into this alleyway to take a bit of a break, and they would light up a cigarette. I was really surprised they would do that, under the circumstances, but when I looked around, I got a shock.

There were several people out there, all of them working for the hospital, and they all had cigarettes in their mouths. Doctors, nurses, orderlies, would slip out, light up, and suck down a smoke. They would be dressed in their greens, with the mask they wear in surgery still hanging from their necks, and they were outside smoking!

I was thinking, "How stupid are these motherfuckers? They work around this shit everyday and see what it does to people. How can they do it?" But, there they were, nonetheless. They were overweight, pasty, freight trains puffing their way to their first heart attack.

Looking around at that, I thought, "I'm smarter than this."

I quit. I've quit for almost a year, now, and I've never had a puff. The weird thing is that I'll have dreams about smoking, and in my dream, I'm thinking, "Oh, fuck! What am I doing with this?"

Even in my worst state of drunkenness, I haven't succumbed to lighting a cig. That's what I always imagined would happen, too. I'd be out on the road, and having a fight with Warren where he's torturing me in that way he does, and I'd just go, "FUCK IT!" I'd grab a bottle of Jack and a pack of 'grits and I'd be off on a binge. Lighting up and going, "Fuck the world!"

Still hasn't happened, though. Mum's watching out for me.

While in Houston, I worked up a side project. It actually began as a jam band when I still lived in California.

Jani Lane had a band called "Jani Lane's Underdogs", and I was doing some gigs with them back in 2000. When Lane was off doing stuff with Warrant, I still wanted something to do, so me, John Corabi, Robbie Crane and Keri Kelli formed Angel City Outlaws, with John doing the vocals.

Angel City Outlaws was our jam band when we weren't on the road. We would go out and play covers of ZZ Top, Aerosmith, Zeppelin, Beatles, Stones, Queen, Bowie, et al. Basically, everything we grew up on and loved so much.

We were really doing a lot of gigs, and wound up being a great supplemental income for all of us. I was doing the bookings on it, and for the first three years, 2001 to 2003, we probably made an additional $15,000 each, just going out, drinking beers and having a good time.

I get a call on the 2005 tour from this guy named Sebastian Knowlton. He's a great guy. He's a young guy, 26, and his family is in oil, so he's got a lot of money to invest. He came to a RATT show, and is a huge fan of metal music.

Sebastian wanted to produce a Judas Priest tribute album. He hired a friend of his named Brian Clem, and a guy named Drew. They got Motorhead, Great White, Warrant, Jani Lane, and Vince Neil, all to do these Priest covers.

He came to a RATT show in Elko, Nevada. Right in the corner of Nevada and Utah. That's where I met him.

Sebastian used his dad's leer jet and flew in. He and Brian. They were totally funny, completely fun to hang out with. I liked them immediately. Then, a few months later, they called me out on tour and said they wanted RATT to do a song on the album. They were going to give us $10,000 to do it.

Of course, Warren, there he goes again. "I just don't like those things."

I'm like, "Listen, we'll go in, and do the thing in half a day. We'll go to Keri's studio, cut a cool Priest song, and drink some beers. It'll be fun. We'll make 3 grand each."

He didn't want to do it. So, not to pass on another easy gig, I brought it to the Angel City Outlaws.

I got to talking to Sebastian about it, and the conversation turns into, "Well, why don't Angel City Outlaws do a record?"

Just like that.

We had always talked about doing it. It just hadn't manifested yet. I'm like, "Is that something you're interested in?"

He's goes, "Hell, yeah!"

So we signed a production deal with Sebastian. We changed the name of the band to "Saints of the Underground", and we made a record. It took several months to get everything together.

John Corabi didn't want to make the record. He just had too much shit going on, and couldn't commit to it, which left us in a really tough spot. We didn't know whom we would use in his place.

We thought about Jani Lane, but didn't know if we could rely on him. We talked to him, and he was into it, but we started hearing a lot of horror stories about Lane.

Lane did an acoustic tour with Stephen Pearcy, Don Dokken, Kip Winger, and Firehouse. He was out of his mind on that entire tour. It was the clichéd "rockstar fall from grace" stories that were getting back to us, so we didn't know what to believe.

However, Lane is a fantastic vocalist with a signature style. It was worth the shot.

Keri Kelli and I were co-producing the record, and we were recording it at my studio in Houston in March of 2006.

Saints of the Underground is Jani Lane from Warrant, me, Robbie Crane on bass and Keri Kelli on guitar. Jani Lane was a crapshoot, a real unknown, and we were anxious to find out whom we were getting in bed with on this project.

Jani came to my house in Houston to do vocals, and it was a disaster. Booze was slowly consuming this man, and it was hard to watch.

Gregg Gill and I had built Diamond Recording Studios, and had her running like a machine, with Keri on guitar, and Chuck Wright of Quiet Riot playing bass, since Robbie couldn't be available.

By the way, this brings me to another reason I can't stand the guys in Quiet Riot.

Chuck played on the record, and Kevin and Frankie told him that he could not take a picture for this album because I was involved. They hated RATT that much, and it just pissed me off. I understand that Chuck had to protect his main gig. But, we paid him five grand to do that album, use his likeness, and be available for photo shoots, the whole enchilada. Then we were going to tour and split everything from there.

Chuck didn't get an even split on the deal, because I put the whole thing together, and me, Keri and Jani were the core of the band. There were a number of options available to us on this record, up to and including either Keri or I doing the bass work, or we could have hired someone else in for a lot less than five G's. We didn't. We jobbed it out to Chuck.

When Chuck told us he wasn't going to be involved, I was pissed. It was like, "Bro, you need to kick some of that money back this way, then."

I'm not going to say I lost a friend over it. He and I have been friends for a very long time, and we'll be friends again when I see him. But, we haven't been talking because of it. I was very much, "Tell those fucking guys in Quiet Riot to rot in hell!"

Of course, here I am regretting words like that since Kevin's passing. Not to say that Kevin DuBrow is in hell, but when he died, I immediately remembered saying that to Chuck. I was pretty distraught and pissed, but words like that are tough. I read somewhere that anger is a weapon that you have to hold by the blade.

That's the fucking truth, bro.

Robbie Crane became available, and is going to play bass when we tour, which is what I wanted anyway. So, prizes for me, right?

Jani shows up in Houston, and I pick him up at the airport for the sessions. Keri and Chuck had already come in June of 2006 and laid their tracks, so Jani was the last recording we needed to do before we started mixing the record. He was so fucked up, that he couldn't sing. It was as bad a situation as it could be.

Everyone who knows Jani knows that he's a lovable guy. He's a truly great person, but he's a person with some monster demons that just dominate him. They dominate him in ways that a man has a hard time overcoming. Lane had started doing crazy shit like leaving tours, and not being able to sing, or get on stage. He even pulled some stuff at my house, where I was like, "Dude, you gotta split."

Misty2 and I had taken a flight earlier that year, and one of the flight attendants was a huge RATT fan. The guy gave me a trash bag full of those little airline bottles of booze. You know the ones I'm talking about? The little single shots of hooch that they sell you for a ridiculous price. There had to have been a hundred bottles. So, when we moved to Texas and were unpacking, Misty2, dumped the bag of bottles into a cabinet drawer, thinking, "We'll be having parties and such, and when someone wants a drink, they can just pick their shot out of the drawer." There were so many cupboards in that house, just drawers for days with nothing in them.

Little did I know that Jani was filling his pockets with these things before we went to record.

He kept asking me to stop for tequila on the way to the studio. I'm like, "Jani, we are not stopping. We are working. That's what we're here for, is to work."

He kept trying to convince me that the tequila would warm up his vocal cords and help him sing better, but, brother, this ain't my first rodeo.

We spent five days in the studio, and, it was a fucking disaster. It just didn't work, and I wasn't sure where we were going to go to find a quality frontman.

Lane went away and did some soul-searching. He checked into rehab for a while.

The end of the story is that Jani got clean ... for a while. When he came out, he re-recorded the vocals out at Keri's house, which came out amazing! I'm like, "Alright. Disaster averted. That's a major difference." Jani has got an incredible voice. He's a great writer, great with melodies, and really good at stacking harmonies. He always has been.

As a producer, I was trying to tap into that, but it wasn't possible when he was sauced. Straight, he was everything we hoped he would be. His vocal work with Keri was fantastic, and Saints got a deal with Warrior Records through Universal Music Group. The record came out April 2008.

The plan was to get as many dates in as we could before RATT, Alice Cooper and Warrant start up their respective tours. Keri plays for Alice, and Jani was back with Warrant.

RATT in Japan, fall 2007.

RATT and Manager at dinner with support band Winger in Japan, 2007.

37

WHEELS OFF IN TEXAS

My last few months in Texas were tough. My Mum was fading very quickly,

semi-comatose in a Pittsburgh hospice center; my life with Misty2 was shot to shit, and

things were taking a down turn at the recording studio.

It was time to go back home to California.

When I was moving back from Houston to California, we were about 25 miles

west of El Paso, not far from Las Cruces, New Mexico. My friend John is following me in

my Mercedes, and I'm driving my truck, towing the boat. I was talking to my son Marcus

on the phone, and I kept hearing this noise.

"What the hell is that noise?"

I turned the radio down, and go, "Marc, hold on". Is it the road, or what?

Then I see John go wide from the trailer. And, almost simultaneously, I see the

tire from the trailer ease out into the lane, and begin to pass me! We were doing 70 miles

an hour at the time! Then it veered off to the left, bounced through the ravine, and

jumped into the eastbound lane of traffic on fucking Interstate 10!

If there had been a car there, it would have been catastrophic. That tire launched clear out into the brush on the other side of the freeway. The lugs had failed on the trailer, and shot the tire completely off the hub.

I have towing, including trailers, on my AAA policy. The only state that doesn't recognize that is, you guessed it, TEXAS! Yep. When I moved, I called them and told them "Hey, I'm in Texas now. Here's my address." Boom, it was changed. It became a Texas umbrella policy.

Had I kept my policy in California, instead of changing it to Texas when I moved, I would have just called them, and they would have sent someone to take us back to El Paso and get us fixed up.

But, it wasn't based in California anymore.

We set on the side of the road for three hours before someone got there to take care of us. Big 18-wheelers were flying by, freaking us out. I had barely been able to get the truck and trailer over to the shoulder, so these fucking big-rigs were flying by at 80 miles an hour less that four feet from us. Really un-nerving.

The tow truck shows up with a flatbed, and loads up the boat and trailer. Cost me seven hundred and fifty Hondo to get that done. We had to stay the night back in El Paso. I was going to stay at Bret Michaels' house when we went through Arizona. He had called and lived in Scottsdale.

By the time we got our stuff fixed, and were on the road again, plans were adjusted. We were on our way to Lake Havasu, and that was far more important than Mr. Michael's and his headband, or hairband. Whatever the hell he calls that thing.

I gotta give him shit. He's so fucking lucky. Because of that wacky assed reality show of his, he's getting $30,000 to $40,000 per night on his solo gigs when he was only getting around $10,000 before! And, in the world of living vicariously through your colorful singer, Poison's asking price just jumped from $60,000 to $100,000 per show, or so I'm told.

"Rock of Love" has struck gold for those guys. That's got to "rock his world" better than any of the pseudo-stripper chicks that compete on that damned show.

They're good guys. I just gotta give them a little shit. Lucky bastards. This year, Poison headlines the "Rock Of Love Tour!" Get your panties ready, ladies!

I'm going to do a reality show. It's going to be called "Bobby Blotzer presents: Fuck Love! Give Me A Chick With No Issues!"

Every week, I'll eliminate the one who makes me the most crazy.

I got back to California on May 4, 2007. Our rehearsal schedule for the new tour was to begin on May 7, which it did. At the end of that rehearsal day, literally three minutes after we had finished, I got the call that Mum had died.

I had all my furniture in a 30-foot trailer, which was driven out here on a truck, and Jack (my dog) and Leo (my cat) were living with me in a one-room studio apartment in Woodland Hills. I was about to go out on a three and a half month tour, and I didn't want to buy a house until I got back from it. It was really shitty timing. The whole thing was very depressing, just all of us in this one little room.

It was a tough time, all the way around. I was feeling really alone. Even my friends didn't seem to be as close, and I was really let down that Misty hadn't called me after my Mum's death. Eventually, she did, but it was a couple of weeks after the fact. I'll never forget that, or forgive that. She insists that she called, and I don't know why she does that, because it never happened.

It was a very strange time for me. With Misty, I don't know what was happening. I don't know if I was just very lonely, and all I could remember were our good times together, but I started feeling that spark for her, again. I still had this love for her.

We had lived in our apartment in Encino together, then bought the house up in Canyon Country and lived there for four and a half years. But, then it just turned bad. She became a hard person to live with. High tempered, and argumentative, she would do things just to spite you. She'd cut off her toe to spite her foot.

The weird thing is that I went out with her on May 28 for dinner, in hopes that we could get back together. I was ready to sip the soured milk again. Maybe it was better, now.

She was seeing this metrosexual looking model type who had been over in Australia for two or three months. I was telling her things like, "Do you think this guy is ever going to love you like I do? Come on! You've been around enough to know who has the heart, who has the love, so do you want to make this happen? Let's go do what you always wanted to do."

Misty always wanted me to marry her, and I wasn't going to do that. Not just with her, but with anyone. Suddenly, I was willing to do that with her, and rekindle something that had gone so wrong just two years earlier. I was willing to do it.

She said she couldn't, that she was involved.

That was well and good. I took her home, dropped her off, and went to hang out at Howl at the Moon in Universal City. My friend Jullian promotes there. That's where Ashley walked into my life.

First, let me stipulate the ages, so you can get an understanding. When I met Traci, she was 22 and I was 38; 14 year gap. Misty was 21, and I was 41; 19 year gap. She was the kind of girl who always worked, and always contributed to the house, but I had to constantly bitch, and complain before she would do it.

This is the problem that sabotages my relationship with Ashley. I'm the sole proprietor in this thing, and I don't like it. But, I'm getting ahead of myself.

Misty2 was 34, and I was 48; another 14 year gap. Now, I've got Ashley. I'm 48 at the time, and she's 22; 26 year gap. I'm just lucky, I guess...or maybe not. You decide.

With Ashley, we hit it off so hard, and so quick. We were on the phone constantly. I fell in love with her almost overnight. She was way too young, and I knew it, but she seemed like a pretty sharp cookie, and we had so much in common, that I was willing to overlook that and pass up my better judgment.

However, my relationship guards were standing watch at their posts. I can tell you this much, it's a horrible thing to be a man who is quick to love and be loved, yet be a bit guarded against that thing that makes him most happy. Where's the line? Do you open up again, and risk being hurt one more time, or do you keep it all at arms length?

There's no good answer to that, I'm sure. In the end, you make your decisions and live with them. In my case, I'd rather lose love than not love at all. Your life is better for the experiences you put it through...and I've got a great life.

Ashley didn't have very many world experiences, though. She'd never been intimate with a guy, never lived with one. Those were things that I just couldn't believe. This was my angel, man.

So, yeah… I loved… and lost… again.

She started coming out on the road with me. Ashley and I had a connection for one another. She's very funny and talented. We loved being around each other so much that it's like were the only ones there, even when were standing around loads of people.

Ashley was born in Torrance, California, actually at the same hospital that Michael and Marcus were born in. Then her parents moved up north to Paso Robles, California. I went up there a few times with her. It's a nice, funky, small town atmosphere. Her parents are pretty good people and we got along.

She and I had so much in common, even with our considerable age gap. Most of the time, I didn't think about it till she did some of the stuff that twenty-two year old people tend to do.

At that age, they think they know it all, almost without exception. I did it; you did it; It's all part of that fucked up transition from being a kid to being an adult.

Ashley wanted to be an actress. Unfortunately, she had no clue how to get there, and had nothing on the ball for it. Yet, she would talk about "when I'm this famous actress"?

There's reality, and there's fantasy. If you plan right, the two will intersect, and you get both, but it isn't easy. You have to fight for it, and fight hard. Ashley had the fantasy part down, and I want her to realize those dreams, but I couldn't help her with it. I don't know anything about that business.

Ashley has many of the same problems that other really young women have.

She has "Princess Syndrome." I'll explain.

So many girls spend their entire life being told that they are "little princesses." They're catered and coddled to the point that they grow up feeling that the world owes them something. They feel they are a princess, and should be treated accordingly. It's a horrible injustice that parents, particularly fathers, do to their daughters.

They wind up living in a fantasy world, and when they begin to discover that their world doesn't really exist outside childhood, they get lost and don't know what to do.

That's Ashley. I love her more than I can explain, but the "Princess Syndrome" continually sabotaged the relationship. She's smart. She's got a lot going on upstairs. Unfortunately, there's no life experience to back it up. It's like learning to drive a car. You can know all the road rules, and everything about how a car works, but until you've actually done it, you don't know shit.

Meanwhile, I get stuck trying to get Cinderella's fucking shoe back on her foot! That is, unless she's acting like an adult. She's never been an adult, mind you, so she doesn't have a point of reference. She's had some jobs. She worked at Disneyland for three years, playing Snow White, and there's been a few others sprinkled around since. Mostly, she likes to surf, boogie board, your basic California girl, and I couldn't help but be entranced by her! I proposed to her very fast.

I gave her a big ring while I was out on the road in 2007. She moved in with me, and while she worked, she never contributed anything to the household. This is our biggest source of friction. I'm not a Sugar Daddy. Never have been, and never will be. Refuse to be.

It was a struggle with her. When she was sweet, she was sweet and fine, and I loved her. However, she had a propensity to argue. Argue, hell; she was downright combative, and over anything at all. If I talk about the shape of a bottle, she will disagree with me. If I say the sky is blue, she will call it cobalt or something.

I liken it to a kid with their parents when they are trying to buck the system. It's not to be insulting to her, but it's what she has to work with as far as life experience. She's got the princess mentality, and the natural sarcasms of someone who is still a child at heart.

So, in March of 2008, she moved out for about three weeks. When she moved back home, it was simply because we missed each other horribly. However, she continued to pay rent at the place she was at, despite the fact that she didn't live there. Instead of contributing to the household she was a part of, she ignored it.

All I want was someone who would pitch in; someone who will help out. I'm not asking for someone to cover the whole thing. I'm not even asking for someone who covers half. I just want someone who behaves like they are part of my life, and not owed a piece of it.

We went through the summer like this, and by the start of fall, it was coming to a head. She was working at an aerospace engineering company as an administrative assistant. She wasn't making great money, certainly not by Southern California costs of living, but she was making some, yet still refused to contribute.

I pushed her about it, and in November of 2008, she moved out again. I found myself in a familiar place. I was going out, meeting some cool girls and having a good time, but I still had this love for her that I couldn't get past. I had to give it one more go. I had to at least try to get past our issues enough that we could make this work, because I knew the love was there.

We've spent the last year or so in this same routine. Move in, move out, fight, make up, break up, get back together. Round and round and round and round… sounds like a song I know!

The final breaking point came just recently. Ratt had booked a gig with Queensryche, Tesla and Skid Row on a pleasure cruise. It was good times to be had. Unfortunately, it was here that I learned what an actress Ashley really is.

We got into an argument that stemmed from her talking about our private issues to anyone and everyone. I had told her repeatedly, "Stop dragging our private shit out for everyone to see." She wouldn't listen, though. Every time I turned around, she would be talking it out with complete strangers or casual acquaintances.

I'd had several friends warn me that she was trying to set me up for something. Naturally, I didn't want to believe it, but looking back….

When we would argue, it was always the same; regardless the issue. I'm the kind of guy who needs some space when I get upset. I just want a little time to myself to get my thoughts together and be rational. Ashley simply would never allow me to do that. She wouldn't leave me alone. She would stay in my face, constantly. Yelling. Screaming. Saying the worst, most foul and inappropriate things to me or about me. Almost as if she was baiting me to hit her.

If I ever put my hands on her during these moments, whether it was to take her shoulders and lead her out of the room, or to take her hand to calm her down, it wouldn't matter. She would immediately start yelling, "Don't you touch me! That's assault! Don't you fucking touch me!"

Assault? Really? You mean, I'm going to have to call the cops to get you out of my fucking bedroom? Really?

Needless to say, the warning signals were there.

On the cruise, I hear through Robbie Crane's wife that Ashley is at it again; talking about our private moments. It pisses me off, so the argument with Ashley begins. It's three o'clock in the morning, and while I'm ready to end the fight, she won't let it go. I'm ready for bed, and she keeps going on and on and on and on...

...and I put my hand over her mouth.

In hindsight, I can see where this move might backfire on me, but it seemed harmless enough. I wasn't being physical or abusive, I simply covered her mouth so I could have a little peace. She bit me. HARD. Hard enough that my finger was swollen and blood-blistered.

She immediately jumps out of the bed, crying out for me not to hit her. Keep in mind that we are on a cruise ship. Robbie and his wife are in the room on one side of us. Stephen is in the room on the other. It's clear that her "act" is intended for the band to hear what was going on. Finally, she jumps up and runs across the hall to the security office, crying "domestic abuse."

The security officer comes in and checks it all out in his security officer sort of way. Ashley had told him that I "punched her in the face." It's clear that she's full of shit, and nothing happened, especially anything where SHE was hurt or abused, nevermind the wound on my finger where she went all "Hanibal Lecter" on me. So, the whole thing became a non-event.

It was a non-event to everyone except me. She had done all of this bullshit drama at my place of work. This is the place where I have a public image to maintain, and an expected code of conduct from my band mates, and she's making out like I'm some sort of gorilla out to beat her down.

God, what a depressing time. It's times like that when you can wind up doing some kooky things. Which, of course, I did.

We had an empty wine bottle in the cabin on ship, and you know how the old movies always had the marooned castaway throw a bottle with a note in it out to sea, in the vain hopes of being rescued? Yeah, I did that. I was marooned in a relationship that I desperately wanted to work out, yet if anyone ever needed rescuing, it was me!

I wrote a note, tucked it down in the bottle, and threw it into the ocean from the observation deck of the cruise liner. It was symbolic, of course, and I simply forgot about it.

Funny thing – about three weeks after the cruise, I get an email. Seems the bottle had found it's way to the shores of Florida, and a little girl from Canada had picked it up and given it to her parents. They were all vacationing there from Quebec, and were blown away by this unexpected, random thing that their daughter had found.

They didn't know who I was, but the note said I was Bobby Blotzer, drummer for Ratt, and I was playing a show on the cruise liner… blah, blah, blah.

When they got home, they looked me up online and checked out the band, then contacted me to say they had my wine bottle! It was fun. I responded, and we had a good laugh about it. Now, they have a story they can tell for years to come about how they got a message in a bottle from a bummed out, love struck rock star!

Yeah. Relationships make you do some strange shit. The worst part is not realizing it's over until it's way too late.

When we got home from the trip, I was done. She was staying in my guest bedroom at that point, and I just couldn't deal with her anymore. It was time for her to go. It was Christmas '09, and we had plans made from before the holidays; parties and what-not. So, I decided to fight through the drama until the New Year, but the decision had made itself. I didn't need to help it along. Come January, we were done.

On December 17, I went out with some friends to have appetizers and cocktails at a local restaurant we all like. Ashley was at the house, and we had passed each other as I was leaving. Feeling a little guilty, I called her and asked if she wanted to join us, which she did.

The night goes on, and we get back to the house around 10:30. She heads straight to bed, but I've got house stuff to do. I was checking the patio heaters I'd bought for the Christmas party we were throwing for the coming weekend, drinking a little Merlot, and checking the household out in general.

I was listening to some music, low and slow, while I was doing all of this. She starts texting me about how loud it is, and that she can't sleep. It was the Beatles. It was barely on. How she could even hear it, when I could barely make it out was beyond me. The texts continued, getting progressively meaner. Finally, she comes out in full banshee mode. It's on.

Before it's over, with the yelling, screaming, cursing and bullshit that she normally brings to the fight, she added a few new wrinkles to the mix. After slamming doors (which had just been remodeled from damaged she had previously caused), she comes back out of her room and continues the fight.

Over the next several minutes, it gets heated, verbally. I wind up calling her a cunt (which women absolutely hate!) It's at that time that I realize why she stormed back into her room. In her hands, she is concealing a video camera and is recording our argument from the upstairs landing.

I took the camera away from her. Keep in mind, this is the only time I've gotten physical with her in any way, and it wasn't a punch, slap, bite, gouge, or any other physical trauma that occurred. I accidentally caught her hair in my hand while going for the camera. Did I pull it? Not on purpose, but probably. Ashley's hair goes down past her waist. She pulls it when she sits down. So, yeah, it's a good chance that it got pulled in the scuffle for the camera.

Once I had the camera (which I desperately wanted to smash on the tile, but didn't), she immediately goes to the phone and calls the police, crying "domestic violence."

I was done. I left, and went to a hotel for the night. She was absolutely out of control.

The next day, I go down to the police station. I figure that if I'm getting accused of God-knows-what, I'm going to at least make my statement. I'm soon to discover, though, that the story she told the cops the night before is significantly different from the truth.

She tells the cops that I hit her and yanked her by the hair, going all Cro-Magnon on her!

The cop behind the desk looks over the computer files, and then excuses himself to check another computer. Keep in mind, that because of the OJ Simpson murders,

California now has laws where the DA's office can file charges whether a victim wishes them to, or not. It's a felony charge. It's prison time.

They arrest me for domestic assault. Ashley never presses charges. In fact, the cops who took her statement referred to her as a drama queen. There wasn't a mark on her, and she didn't look like anything had happened. She just wanted the attention, I guess. However, that didn't matter. The DA was the person to decided how this proceeded, not Ashley, or me.

$50,000 bail, and I'm back on the street sweating this trumped up charge that my immature fiancé brought on me.

I get back to the house, and tell her to bounce. Get your shit and get out. This relationship simply isn't going to happen. It was a hollow feeling for me, especially since she already had most of her shit packed up to go.

In the end, nothing was ever filed by the officers, the DA or the courts. In their eyes, it was a non-case. Ashley was actually kind of bummed out about that. I sent her a text about it, talking about her out-right lies to the police.

She sent back the following: "Lies, oh wow. You need help, or serious punishment. I won't miss you anymore. Enjoy your pity party. You're guilty and soulless."

Ten minutes before that, she was sending me texts with Beatle lyrics in them about missing one another and shit like that. Crazy shit.

In the end, had I not tried to do the stand-up thing by going to the police, I probably wouldn't have been arrested or anything. It would have just went away. But, it didn't.

Not by a long shot.

I suppose it's my own base nature that puts me into these situations. From a certain point of view, one may think that I'm too co-dependent, or that I have no direction in my love life. That isn't true.

I am a man who looks for, and expects to find, the best in people. When I meet a woman, it's an opportunity for me to find a completion to my life; my missing piece, if you will. While it may seem naïve on my part, I can assure you that it's not. Life is too short to not take a chance on love.

And, I can tell you that I've loved all the women in my life, for better or worse.

Ashley became the worst of the worse.

I was talking about all of this with Misty. Ex-M-1. We've stayed in touch and remained friends, so it was a friend kind of thing to do.

She could tell that something was wrong with me, and pressed for the story. I told her that it was in confidence, and she swore it would never leave her mouth. Unfortunately, so personal issues got in the way, and she was pushed out of the Christmas party that Ashley and I (now just me) had planned. I had to ask her not to come. It pissed her off, and hell hath no fury, right?

She blabs the story to some of these motor-mouth musician types here in LA. They are big gossip hounds. Robbie Crane calls me and tells me about it. This guy had called him and asked "What's up, I heard Blotzer punched his girl in the face?"

The next thing I know, it's all over the internet. Metal Sludge even ran a Photoshopped picture of Ashley and I where her face had been made up to be all bruised and shit. It was obviously messed with, and those guys did it for comedic factor, but fuck me!

It's worldwide. Blabbermouth. All over the radio. Everywhere. My friends and family all know that I didn't do anything, and that there wasn't even a report filed, but the fans don't know that. They form their own opinion, and it's usually fed by what's in print or online.

What a fucking drag. I was spiraling down over this stuff, and Ashley seemed to take great glee in it.

I truly loved this woman, so it was hard for me to really admit that it was over. It took a lot to make me admit that, because I still wanted to see the good in her. I still wanted to see the love. But, even my closest friends were stepping up and pointing out the obvious.

When the police charges were dropped, Ashley was angry, and her gloves came off. I can't believe the decisions she made in the days following the decision by the D.A. to not charge me.

She did everything she could to make me admit that I had abused her in some sort of way. She would leverage me against other people we knew, and she talked

CONSTANTLY to anyone who showed even a vague interest. One thing about Ashley – she loved to hear herself talk. She would talk, talk, talk, talk, and almost everything was a defamation of me, and trash talk me to everyone; yet when it came time to gain attention as the fiancée of a famous rockstar, she would be right there on my arm, all smiles and profiles.

But, I simply would not admit to something I did not do. I NEVER harmed Ashley. The police knew it. The courts knew it. Our friends and family knew it. Everyone seemed to know it except Ashley. I don't know if she had lied to herself so much she believed it, or if she was trying to manipulate the situation to her favor, setting up a lawsuit, or palimony suit, or some bullshit like that.

She filed a restraining order against me, doing it in as public and high profile a way as she could, again trying to make me out as a monster. I'd had enough. After going to jail over this woman, then having my name drug around in the mud by the tabloids, AND our friends being forced into it as well, it was time to put a stop to the whole charade.

Two days before she filed the thing, she was at my house trying to reconcile. Two days AFTER she filed the thing, she's still texting my phone three or four dozen times a day, trying to reconcile. It was a total mind game for this kid. Finally, on the day before Valentine's Day, she sends me a text saying, "I can't be happy with you in my life." And, that was it. Mind you, this was well AFTER she had already filed the restraining order. I was done with it. Completely burned.

On the 16th of February, her brother Rex drops by the house, unannounced. I'd tried earlier in the week to talk to him; to make sure he and the family wasn't buying the bullshit his sister was selling about my smacking her around. That was important to me, because while her family is pretty kooky, they are good people.

So, here's Rex. He telling me that he's on my side and that he understands, because she used to pull this kind of shit with him all the time when they were kids, getting him in tons of trouble with their parents and playing it off with her melodramatic style.

Everything seems good with the two of us. He's on my side in the thing, even offering to be a character witness against his sister when the court convenes for the restraining order hearing.

Then it happens.

As he's leaving, he slips a piece of paper on my table, and walk away from it. I'm like, "Bro, you left this." He looks at me a little sheepishly and goes, "No, man. That's yours."

It's a court summons. He served me on behalf of Ashley.

Didn't really know how to take that. He explained it away by saying he wanted it to come from him, instead of her sending the sheriff's department to my house again. Maybe he's being straight up with me, but it sure seemed convenient. Regardless, at that point, I only had four days to respond to the summons, so I was scrambling.

I had my witnesses together in short order, and they all made prepared statements on my behalf.

Jon Jensen, my good friend, and Ashley's employer told the courts in his statement that, "Without making any comments regarding Ashley's performance at work, in her personal life I have found her to be a very immature and manipulative person. My history of interactions with her also leads me to believe that her main interest in Bobby has been to further her ambitions to be an actress by leveraging his name, influence, access, and contacts. I have shared a lot of personal time with the two, both individually and jointly, and I have never seen Bobby physically harm or threaten her, or anyone else for that matter."

His statement was a long one, but he wraps up with, "My observation has been that when Ashley gets what she wants, she's good to him. When she doesn't get what she wants, she extends every effort to slander his name and reputation, and to make him miserable through her verbal harassment and mean-spirited and sometimes threatening text messages. ... I believe this Restraining Order is another attempt at revenge for his refusal to accept her back into his life. Subsequent to both his arrest, and most recently serving him with the Temporary Restraining Order, Ashley has enthusiastically shared with random employees in my Company, how she's punished Bobby. She is enjoying this thoroughly as if it's the best thing that ever happened to her. I know with certainty that a restraining order against Bobby is not necessary, it's not within his character and he has moved on."

Another friend of ours, Michael Smith, said this to the courts, "I think Ms. Saint'Onge realized the end of the relationship was imminent and out of spite/anger intentionally attempted to provoked Mr. Blotzer into a confrontation with the premeditation of making claims that would damage his reputation and career. Upon seeing that the DA didn't agree with her accusations nor any evidence to support such claims she has now gone to another step in defaming Mr. Blotzer's name and reputation by asking for a "restraining order"against him. I feel it is clear that Mr. Blotzer would be more than happy to NEVER contact Ms. Saint'Onge again but a "restraining order" against Mr. Blotzer is not deserved nor warranted."

Finally, my good friend Jenna Stulak O'Connor had this to say, "Though all couples argue/fight as that is normal, I have never seen Bobby get physically abusive with any of them, including Ashley. I have to be honest and state that I have never been able to bond with Ashley as I think she is very odd and immature. I have been out with them on several occasions where she seems to try to provoke an argument if he does not agree with her odd perspective on situations. I could give many examples of her odd and immature behavior, including her calling him stupid in front of a group of his friends / people on several occasions, roller her eyes at him, etc... Coming from a girl who still wants Disney sheets on her bed..."

Ashley was permitted to cross examine my witnesses, and they held up fine. I cross examined hers, and they did not. After all was said and done, the judge verbally berated Ashley on a number of issues, and found in my favor.

No restraining order. More importantly, no Ashley. I don't hate her; not at all. But, the love is gone. I don't regret it, either. Ashley and I were good for a while. I can't speak for her, but my love was genuine, and for a while, a felt hers was as well. I just think it was tainted with her own selfish motivations, and her intense desire to be "The Princess." I hope she finds the help she needs, and grows up.

Grows up without me, thank you very much.

At this point, I'm seeing someone new. She's beautiful, and an amazing woman. She's got her own money, her own life, and doesn't "need" me to justify herself. She can do that on her own very well. Will it go well? Is she the one? Who knows? But, I intend to find out, because when love is good, it makes up for those times when it isn't. Makes up for them, and justifies them all at once.

I can't wait to find those answers because my life is better for the experiences, remember?

I will admit, with all of the relationships I've had since Jeni, they all have the same bitches and gripes about me. I sometimes have tendencies that get on their nerves. I'll get a little loaded. I'll listen to my music until four in the morning…loudly. I don't drink hard liquor anymore, because I become a bit of a weirdo. I'm not violent, or anything like that, but I'll get kooky. No doubt. So, I stick to Coors Light, wine, and a few Jager-Bombs. No harm, no foul.

What I've learned, though, is that the Princess Syndrome holds solid with the majority of women in this world. They feel that men owe them a living. We don't. At least I don't, obviously, especially with the women I've been with. Misty and Ashley were the worst at that. Jeni and Misty2 always contributed, so it wasn't much of a problem.

I'm trying to be less controlling in my relationships, because that's been a problem that's come back to bite me in the ass a few times. For instance, I'll give them my opinion on what they are wearing, but I've learned not to volunteer the information.

There's something about looking at a woman and saying, "You're not going to wear that, are you?," that is guaranteed to ruin your night. It's not what they want to hear. Creates major waves.

The same week as the Ashley arrest bullshit, we had scheduled a party at the house for a bunch of our friends. Of course, Ashley didn't attend, which led to the avalanche of questions that concerned friends will tend to do upon hearing of a failed relationship.

I was having a hard time with that party. I just didn't want to be there, and was really down.

When the phone rang, I figured it was nothing big and could probably let it go to the answering machine. Instead, I picked up, and my little brother Michael was on the other end.

My step-father, Pete, was dead.

It wasn't an unexpected thing. I'd known for sometime that it was coming, and had even told Michael to be prepared for it. Pete was a heavy smoker and had been on oxygen for a while. He went out much the same way my Mum did two and a half years earlier.

I didn't know how to feel about it. It was weird, in that Pete and I were never really close, and he certainly didn't look over his shoulder very long when he took Michael and left Carol and I to live next door to the whacked-out Mexican.

But, still...he was the only father I could remember. Now he's gone. It's the closing of an era in my life. My parents are gone.

I didn't make it to the funeral.

My goal in this point in my life is to take what I have left, maximize it and have something worthy to leave for my sons. Hopefully, it's something substantial. Hopefully, this latest run with RATT will last longer than the first one, and we all retire with smiles on our faces, because when it's done, it's done.

I want my boys to take the fruits of my life and use them for their own successes. With any luck, my boys will be smart with what I leave them. They'll be smarter than I was with all the money I've made.

Money is fun to spend, and everyone knows that. But I'd advise anyone who owns their own business, or has a lot of money, stick some of that shit back for retirement, because it comes up on you a lot quicker than you expect.

I want to say a special thanks to everyone out there that has always come out and supported RATT and our music. We can't thank you enough for supporting us and our art. We'll keep doing this as long as you keep supporting us. I'll keep doing this as long as we can keep our shit together in RATT, which is NOT EASY, let me tell you. It's a love/hate relationship. I love the guys, but sometimes I really hate them too. Thankfully, I love them more than the hate stuff. Hopefully that sentiment is returned. Hopefully.

I'm looking forward to another 15 years with RATT.

Hopefully, we're all smart enough to stick with this, and do the right things for our families, and ourselves. None of us would be nearly as successful without RATT as we are with it. None of us would be bigger than RATT on our own.

I hope we don't fuck it up for everybody, because we've tried other things on an individual basis. Stephen has toured solo. Warren and I have worked other projects. It doesn't work out as well. A lot of bands go through this. Aerosmith went through it. It's just the way things are.

That's how the universe works for bands.

On June 25th, I woke up and felt really bummed. I have felt this way before, but this time something was really bumming me out, and I didn't know what it was. I told Ashley that every time I feel this way, something weird is going to happen or has already happen; true story. I had decided to help Ashley get a car, because the one she had always had problems and I was always the one fixing it. Her parents weren't able or willing to help, so I was the lucky winner to replace the junker.

We went out looking for a car. We stopped at the mall, and while she was spending a gift card in Victoria Secret, I sat in a chair still feeling the strange sensation that something wasn't right when my phone rang.

"Hello?"

"Hey dad!"

"Hey! What's up?"

"Did you hear about Michael Jackson having a heart attack?"

"WHAAAAAT? NO! When?"

"It just hit the news."

I said, "Well I doubt there's anything to it. He's just doing something for press to hype his new shows in the UK." This was at 1:00 PM.

We arrived at Railway Motors, a used car lot in Valencia Ca. at 2:00 PM. I asked them to turn on the TV and told them what I heard from my son. I had been listening to the radio on the way there and there were unconfirmed reports of his death. I was telling the salesman Larry there.

He was like, "NO SHIT?,"

"Yes turn it on." And we sat there for the next two hours in disbelief, shock and sadness. I was up the whole next week glued to anything and everything Michael.

I had a strong bond to Michael. We were the same age. He was 2 months older than me. I got turned on the Jackson 5 in summer of 1970, and loved every great hit they put out. I stayed with Michael and the Jackson 5 through their careers and all the way through June 25th like it was a brother who's career I watched and supported.

Every party I've ever had, we ended up playing Michael Jackson music. On my boat when we're at the lake, come nightfall, the girls are up dancing to Michael Jackson's greatest hits. I promise to never let that end.

I really think he was a very special human being and a gift to the likes that we'll never see again. What do we have now to replace? Nelly? Jay Fking Z? Whom I can't stand. No one.

We'll never see the top three best ever replaced, Michael Jackson, Elvis Presley, and the Beatles.

Thank god I was here to have seen them while they were alive, to listen to their music on the radio and have them become a part of my core existence. As of this writing, I'm still having problems accepting this death.

RATT headlining Nokia Time Square, 2009.

Father and Son (Michael), tour 2009

Me and Jon Jensen skiing in Lake Tahoe, 2010.

38

THE YEARS OF THE RATT: PLUNDERING THE HIGH SEAS!

The Chinese Zodiac runs on a twelve-year cycle, and is based on various animals.

1984 was the year of the rat. It was also the year "Out of the Cellar" broke, and RATT conquered the 80s metal scene.

The cycle spun for another twelve years, and in 1996, we were once again in the year of the rat. That was the year RATT reunited and toured again, pulling us all out of the quagmire that was Nineties music.

Another dozen trips around the sun, and we were back, with all the usual acts of piracy. We blasted through a fantastic European tour. It was the year of the RATT!

Kinda...

I had high hopes for 2008. I wanted it to be a blast off year for the band. We were working again, there were talks of a new record deal, and I was ready for it to be a platinum experience, similar to 1984, know what I mean?

Of course, the best laid plans of RATTs and men often go awry, or something like that.

As usual, Stephen, Warren and I were at odds, and the wedge just kept getting deeper and deeper between us. We were all on different pages. Now, not to toot the proverbial horn, but I'm the most reasonable of the three of us when it comes to business. Face it, I have the most riding on this, but, our myriad of problems was crushing us, to tell the truth.

There was no real structure to the tour, just fly-out dates. There were a couple of runs through the House of Blues that were sold out; Anaheim, Hollywood, San Diego and Vegas (baby). Those were great shows. So nice, we did 'em twice! But still, no real rhyme or reason to what we were doing. It's shit like that which grates on me like nothing else.

The situation necessitated a new Operating Agreement between the three of us. Logic says, if the three original members can't co-exist, neither will the band. We knew it when we first got back together, and that's when we started working on the thing; way back in March of '07.

By the time we signed the agreement, it was still March ... fucking March of 2009! That's how long it took to get this thing worked out and signed. It was brutal. Absolutely brutal. Among the many items in this agreement was a "Code of Conduct" that each of us had to agree to abide by. We just couldn't get our collective shit together and be in agreement, and the future of all things "RATT" COUNTED on it!

For instance, the new record deal.

There was a record deal on the table with Road Runner Records, who handles Nickleback, Sammy Hagar, Candlebox, several others. Tom Lipsky offered us the deal in April 2008, but there was no way we could sign the offer until the Operating Agreement was worked out. Needless to say, we didn't get the record deal signed for almost a full year.

I can't believe that Road Runner held out for us that long. It's amazing, and something that NEVER happens in this business. I'm stunned we kept that deal. They threatened many times to pull the offer if we didn't get it together and get on board. Thankfully, those guys are really long suffering, and they hung out for us.

It was the little issues that became the real sticking points. There were things in the Operating Agreement that I refused to sign; likewise with Warren and Stephen. It was crazy assed stuff that would threaten my co-ownership of the RATT name. No chance I'm agreeing to that. Warren wouldn't agree to give Stephen his full shares of the company stock, despite the fact that Stephen still gets a third of every dollar the company makes. The list goes on and on. I honestly thought the band was going to break up.

There were just too many issues to solve RATT's problems overnight. John Corabi couldn't hang with the dissension between Stephen, Warren and myself anymore. It came to a head, and he bailed. So, that made things even more difficult. In the midst of all this organizational bullshit, we were out a rhythm guitarist.

So, it was hell getting it worked out, yet, here we are! Agreement signed! Deal done! New album done! New member found!

Carlos Cavazo, he of Quiet Riot fame and fortune, stepped in as RATT's new six-string God. That's a little weird, since Carlos is more of a lead guitarist than a hard assed, grinding rhythm guy, but Warren really pushed him to us.

Don't get me wrong. I absolutely love the guy, and he's been a long time friend, despite all the nonsense with Kevin DuBrow and the guys in Quiet Riot back in the day. It's just an odd adjustment. Sort of a "two roosters in the hen house" kind of thing. I know that Robbie Crane and Stephen both had reservations about it, but Stephen came around. Two-to-one vote. Hey, Carlos! Welcome to the party, bro!

The good news is that Carlos is as good a guy as you can hope to find in this business. He's got this loose, pacifist style that makes him really easy to work with, and while the chemistry of RATT has changed, his contribution to the creative aspects and sound are off the charts. The guy has mountains of talent. Moreover, he's eager to use it to further the future of RATT.

All in all, we're in a good place as a band. "Infestation" hit the shelves in April of '10. The first studio album from the band in eleven years, and the new single, "Best of Me," is setting the standard for downloads at the label. The buzz for this thing is better than anything we've had since the Round and Round album. The label is as excited as they could be, seeing the possibility of a hit album on their hands.

That's a great feeling, one that we haven't had in a very long time..

Carlos Cavazo actually penned, "Best of Me" with Stephen. As I write this, the video is scheduled to shoot in a couple of weeks. I can't wait. It's a breath of fresh air for the RATT boys. We're all writing new stuff, and getting into road shape. It's as if the glory days have never left us, we just misplaced them for a minute.

Thank God, because our rock and roll life is still out there, waiting on us. We've seen it. All we have to do is honor it.

Back in 2007, we had a huge year. Stephen was back, and the crowds really responded to it.

2008, wasn't as good, but we still did well. We just had so much baggage to deal with, and the tour with Extreme wasn't without it's dramas. It slowed everything down.

As usual, I'm still in debt. It's almost a source of amusement to me. Almost.

I still tend to spend too much; on the house (in the midst of a remodel as we speak); on entertainment; on my women; plus, this housing market in California is murdering us! There's nothing like watching the value of your home plummet 25% in nine months. It'll drain the color from your face, that's a fucking guarantee, my friend!

Stephen is still his nutty self. Warren is still the torture master. Robbie still needs Ritalin. Carlos, that pacifist gunslinger, is settling into his new role with ease.

And me? I'm just the Blotz; dubious backbone of the greatest underachievers in rock and roll... and I love my life because of it.

The new album is rock solid; some of the best stuff we've ever done. This summer, we hope to tag up with my flying fish buddy, Matthias Jabs and the Scorpions. Sounds like a lot of fun.

Here's to a 51-city run! One city for each of my illustrious years on this floating rock!

Wow. That's sobering. I'm 51. If you figure that I can avoid the big pitfalls of cancer, ticker-issues, or an out of control driver on the 405, I might have another 30 years to go! It's not a lot of time; especially when you consider I'm well over half finished with this particular journey! And, the time is going by faster. It seems like yesterday that my Mum left us, and it's been almost two years.

Before my ashes are dropped in the deep blues of Havasu, I might have a few more things to get done. Rest assured, I'll get them done colorfully! Then, in a handful of years, we'll see where RATT and I have gone, and I'll write it all down again.

Just for you. The loyal "give-a-shit" crowd!

According to the Chinese calendar, things born of the Year of the Rat are noted for their charm and attraction for the opposite sex. They work hard to achieve their goals, acquire possessions, and are likely to be perfectionists. Rat people are easily angered; their ambitions are big, and they are usually very successful.

Sounds good to me, bro!

If all goes well, we'll sit down in 2020 for a sequel to this book. We'll call it "THE YEARS OF THE RATT: PLUNDERING THE HIGH SEAS IN THE NAME OF RATT 'N' ROLL". My brothers, Stephen, Warren, Robbie, Carlos, and, yes even Juan, John and Jizzy will have taken their roles and split the booty of our conquests. All this under the watchful spirit of the Pi-RATT King, standing in all his Viking-like glory, and shredding his King V through whatever existence is next!

And, to you, our loyal give-a-shit crowd, I make the following promise. RATT N Roll will continue until music dies, and the Blotz's ashes are floating in my five favorite coves of Lake Havasu. Until that time, we will continue to raid and plunder and pillage your cities!

After all, a Pi-RATT can only do what a Pi-RATT does.

Peace Out!